Praise for *Butterflies*. . .

Jocelyn
Tough, smart, athletic, she passed up a career playing volleyball and went on to run the exclusive preschool Butterflies and Puppydog Tails. She always knew what she really wanted. But sometimes, the quest to find it was full of surprises . . .

Eve
The innocent who never forgot her humble roots—even after she married a studio head and her fortune grew . . .

Gabrielle
The polished perfectionist, who applied for admission to Butterflies before her baby was even born, she hid a troubling secret . . . that . . . . . . to shatter

The party girl, ... the depths—and drove a . . . . . ble husband, Landon . . .

Amanda
The Hollywood insider whose brittle shell and cynical wit hid an insecure heart—and whose lusty marriage to producer George Foster hid a deep emotional hunger . . .

They'd all made mistakes. But they wanted something better for their kids. And they had to compete like they'd never competed before to earn their beloved children a coveted spot at the most exclusive preschool in Santa Monica . . .

Butterflies . . .

Butterflies...

Martha Goldhirsh

JOVE BOOKS, NEW YORK

BUTTERFLIES . . .

A Jove Book / published by arrangement with
the author

PRINTING HISTORY
Jove edition / September 1999

The Penguin Putnam Inc. World Wide Web site address is
http://www.penguinputnam.com

ISBN: 0-515-12563-6

A JOVE BOOK®
Jove Books are published by The Berkley Publishing Group,
a division of Penguin Putnam Inc.,
375 Hudson Street, New York, New York 10014.
JOVE and the "J" design
are trademarks belonging to Penguin Putnam Inc.

PRINTED IN THE UNITED STATES OF AMERICA

10   9   8   7   6   5   4   3   2   1

In Hollywood, the best show in town isn't on the screen. It's at the preschool.

One

Eve Carmelina's eighteenth birthday changed everything. Up until that day, her life had been silently mapped out. There was an understanding that she—like her family, her neighbors, and her friends—would work hard, marry, and have children; who would themselves continue the chain of hard work, marriage, and children.

Eve knew that there was nothing wrong with this kind of honest living. Not a thing. But, without saying it, she knew that she wanted more. She felt a difference inside herself, and she wanted things in her life to reflect that difference. She wanted her life to match her secret feelings.

Different was an understatement for what she was to get.

Eve's birthday party was out on her family's front lawn. If you could call it that. There was no grass. Just brown dirt. Eve couldn't remember there ever being anything green out front. Not a tree or a flower. Just layers on layers of tamped-down dust with a few pathetic, dying patches of decrepit weeds. Even they were brown.

She drew in the dirt, using a stick for a pencil. She made primitive sketches of places she wanted to visit. Hawaii. The Empire State Building. The moon. Houses she dreamed of living in one day, always with a yard that actually had grass.

"What the hell is that?"

Eve looked up. It was her father, Hank, standing over her. He was studying her drawing. Squinting. Trying to understand.

"It's Los Angeles, Daddy."

Her father took another swig off his beer can, and moved a little to the left, as if by moving, he could see what she saw, there in the dirt. Hank wore old blue jeans and a white short-sleeved shirt with the words "Carmelina Rest Stop" inked in on the breast pocket. His name was embroidered below the family business logo. Hank. The shirt was dirty; the underarms, permanently yellowed from a lifetime of sweating in the same place; and the embroidered name was frayed. Eve's mother had sewn "Hank" on a dozen of those shirts. Slowly, carefully, she'd sewn.

Hank peered down at his eldest daughter. He moved his big black work boots so he wouldn't scuff her drawings in the dust.

"Don't look like Los Angeles," said Hank. " 'Course I only seen pictures. Maybe it's somewhere else."

"Nope," said Eve. "It's Los Angeles."

"Why're you always drawin'?"

He was drunk again. He never asked her questions about herself when he was sober. Sober, he was simple. Drunk, he was inquisitive.

"I'm goin' there," said Eve. "Tonight. That's where I'm gonna be."

"Well, send me a postcard," he chuckled, and walked away. "Damn, that child's crazy," said Hank, not meaning for Eve to hear. But she did.

"I'm not a child!" she yelled after him. "I'm eighteen!"

Hank turned back to his spirited eldest daughter. The big sister to the five other Carmelina children. Spit and fire in that one, he thought. There was no talking to her when she got an idea in her head. She was a good girl, but she wasn't like her mother. No, sir. That's what made her difficult. She wanted things. She wanted them hard. Hank hated that about his girl. He hated that she wanted things he couldn't give her. He swallowed half his beer in one gulp and turned away from her.

Eve left her stick drawings and went to sit on the front stoop of her house, where she watched the Vegas sun set. She was mad at her father for not believing that she was leaving. She was mad at her family for not being different. She couldn't be mad at her mother, though. Not Mama. Poor Mama. Eve imagined her mother giving birth to her eighteen years ago. She must've been all big, uncomfortable, and hot in that Las Vegas August. Hot as hell, but bright as heaven.

What a relief it must have been for Mama to get to the air-conditioned hospital. Eve would miss her mother, when she left. But she wouldn't miss her enough to change plans and stay put. And Eve knew that in some private place in her mother's heart, she, too, wanted Eve to leave. Because she loved her.

Mama might have left, herself, long ago, if she hadn't met Hank, and gotten pregnant with Eve. Leaving just wasn't a choice Eve's mother could make. Not now, not ever.

Eve had waited for this day, August 12, her eighteenth birthday, so she could leave her home for good. She'd known she couldn't leave before then. But now she was legal. An adult. Nothing stood in her way except herself. No excuses, no obstacles. The open road was ahead of her. Even if it did look like one big, empty desert.

She looked around, wondering if she'd ever have another birthday here again. All the Carmelina children's birthday parties had taken place in the same spot, year after year. In the front yard. Cake and juice for the children and cocktails for the parents. In the daytime for the young ones. Later as they got older.

Eve remembered the taste of wax under the rims of little, flowered Dixie cups and the thick, sweet smell of the Hawaiian Punch inside. How when it spilled, it stained the ground, anchoring the dirt to the earth, until the wind blew the water dry, and the dust blew the red blotch away. Things disappeared in the desert. Eve didn't want to be one of them.

She remembered the disappointment as all her special birthdays had become everyone else's typical drunken evening. The children had all been sent home, but no one had gone to check on them. The grown-ups, and the teenagers who passed for legal, drank the yeasty-smelling sodas in cans. The beers after beers after beers. Cigarettes. The sweet smell of an occasional joint wafted out from behind the house, away from disapproving elders, who knew, but didn't do anything about it.

The smoky, moldy breath of Eve's parents as they gathered her up and kissed her eyes, having suddenly realized she was still awake, wandering around the near-dark, dusty yard, among them. The secret smile they shared when they were inebriated. Holding her tight, meeting each other's eyes over her little body. Our big girl—never the baby. There were always babies, but Eve was always the big one. Even when the others grew past her in height. Eve was still the first. A special gift. They'd kissed her eyes again.

Then, just as quickly, they forgot her, when someone said something that made everyone laugh. Loud and sloppy. Until someone, usually someone overweight, would break into a coughing fit and there would be banging on that person's back and some real concern, hushed whispers about paramedics, and then quiet talk about who had the last heart attack that they could all remember. *Bypass* was a word Eve remembered hearing. She used to think they were talking about the freeway, not someone's heart. Bypass. The *s* part of the word sounded like a snake, slurred by drunken parents, in the night, in the yard.

A bypass. . . .

That would bring the noise down. Until all you could hear were cigarettes being sucked on, and pop tops off beer cans tinkling, like some odd scrappy orchestra, as they were dropped into empty tins.

When the noise came down to that quiet hush, Eve knew her birthday was over. No talk. Someone snoring, slumped over, in a lawn chair. Just the sounds of motions, functions not meant to communicate. The sounds that came with just being.

The house at 22657 Prairie Star was run-down, and it never quite got fixed. Not properly. It was not the kind of run-down that a few cans of fresh paint could take care of. This house had eroded. From desert weather. From neglect, and then from acceptance.

"Let's just paint the porch, Daddy," Eve had said. "I'll do it myself."

"Whazza point?" Hank answered. His breath sprayed spit and beer. "I work all day pumpin' gas. My back's sore. I don' wanna be workin' my whole goddamn life, goddamnit. The house works. Leave it alone."

Sunset. Finally. Eve silently marked her last night in Vegas. Hot and moving out of sight, the sun always promised a cool evening, the only relief from living in an open-air oven. Time to wash off the grime and the dust that was forever getting on and under everything. Cars, homes, bodies. Shower fresh was short-lived. Feeling clean was fleeting. Sweat and dust were omnipotent.

Eve went inside to finish packing her things. Her sisters and brothers were like background noise outside. Like a jackhammer, drilling up the street a couple of blocks over. Hard not to be aware of it at first. Then easy to forget. Until it stops. Sweet silence.

They were all too busy getting ready for the party to notice Eve walk through the house and go into the bedroom she shared with her two sisters. Tracey, fourteen, was in charge of invites. Liz was in charge of getting the neighbors to buy the beer. Liz was sixteen, and the neighbor boys would do anything she wanted. Chuck, who was fifteen, was in charge of trash, and Steve, seventeen, was supposed to get the present. They'd collected twenty dollars among them, to buy something nice for Eve, but somehow, the money got spent. On beer. Or gas, being that the neighbor boys who had to go buy the beer charged for the drive. Or something.

"What are you doing in *here*?" Liz asked Eve, as she appeared in the bedroom doorway. Three single beds. Sears flowered sheets, once red and gold, now faded to pink and pale yellow. "It's your birthday!"

Liz pulled her big sister out of the bedroom and onto the front lawn. It was full of people. Eve surveyed the crowd. They were mostly the same people who'd been to Eve's birthday parties her whole life. Some neighbors, a few forgettable high school friends, her brothers and sisters, and her father. Most of them were pretty quickly drunk.

Eve's mother, Betty, had to work at the gas station that night, so she'd said her happy birthdays to Eve before she'd left at six. She'd be back after she closed up the station at eleven. Eleven-thirty at the latest.

"Save some cake. If you can. If not . . ." her mother had said. But she didn't say what.

"I might be gone by then, Ma," said Eve.

"I know," said Betty. She was late for work and didn't want to think about Eve leaving. "I know, I know. . . ." She anxiously checked her pockets.

"What are you lookin' for?" said Eve.

"Jimminy Jesus," said Betty, grasping the necklace that hung around her thin, wrinkled neck. "Here it is. I thought I'd pocketed it. My mind's slippin'." She took the necklace off her own neck and held it out to Eve.

"Saint Christopher," she said.

Eve stared at the gold necklace with the charm of the patron saint of travelers. It was gold-plated. Over the years the gold had worn away. Mostly the necklace was brown now. Cheap jewelry.

"But this is yours, Ma," said Eve. She knew her mother loved that necklace.

"I didn't have a chance to buy you somethin'," said Betty, looking at her watch. "I wanted to, but. . . . Take it. For your trip. He'll watch over you. And if he doesn't, at least you got yourself some jewelry, huh?"

She tried to make a joke, but the truth was, she was fighting back tears. Eve tried to smile at the joke, but she couldn't. She had never been away from her mother before.

"Thanks," said Eve, and she put the necklace on.

"I'm late, hon," said Betty, and pecked her eldest daughter on the cheek. "You drive safe, now."

Eve had told them she was going to Los Angeles to live. But

they'd all laughed. Not at her, exactly. Just laughed. Up at the sky. It was kind of a strange reaction—nobody said, Don't go. Nobody slipped her any extra pocket money or said, Call if it doesn't work out. Nobody said, You're always welcome back. They just laughed. And reached for the chips. But the bag was empty so someone went to the store.

Eve was all alone in this. She didn't know a soul in Los Angeles, and she didn't have much of a plan except to get out of Vegas. Everyone she knew who stayed put ended up working in the casinos, or at their family business—a gas station, in her case. The Carmelina Rest Stop.

She'd already spent every weekend during high school pumping gas for mall money. Her hands always smelled like gasoline, no matter how much soap and hand cream she used. She couldn't wait to get rid of that smell. Whenever she felt scared about leaving, she thought how awful it would be ten years down the road if she stayed. And then twenty and then thirty and then forever.

Eve didn't make a formal goodbye. There were no lingering hugs, no phony farewell speeches to neatly wrap things up. When the clock struck midnight, she blew out the candles on her cake. Someone already had a knife, and started cutting slices.

Someone else—one of the boys—suddenly grabbed a hunk of icing off the cake with his hands. Then flung it. In seconds, a food fight had begun. Eve ducked out of the way of a glop of flying homemade icing. It was harder than the store-bought kind, and it hurt when it hit, which excited the boys in the group.

She backed away from the food fight, the empty keg, the party, and watched her present become her past. Her bags were already jam-packed in the trunk of the ten-year-old Camry she'd bought with pumping gas money. She backed into the car, stumbling, bumping the door handle with the back of her thighs.

This was it. She felt a light wave of sadness, as if someone had died, only everyone she really knew was there. She held back a sob. She didn't want anyone to see her cry. Not at her party.

Eve turned, got in her car, and drove away. Nobody acknowledged her leaving. They didn't notice.

It didn't hurt her feelings. She had expected it to be this way. It made leaving easier. But the next time she left somewhere, she hoped to be showered with kisses, hugs, and tears. She hoped that someone would try to talk her into staying.

The next time she left someplace, she would be somebody special, not just the oldest of the Carmelina children. Her leaving would make an impression. Next time.

Eve headed her car for the 10 West freeway, wiped her tears away, and slipped out of Vegas.

Once she hit the highway, the radio kept her awake. Eve had planned to pull over to the side of the road, lock the car, and sleep, when she needed to, but she never got tired. In fact, Eve had never been more awake in her life.

She had picked Los Angeles because it was the closest place that was the most different from where she'd been. She knew this because of what she read in magazines and from what she saw on television. Los Angeles was very different, and different was what she wanted.

Eve drove all night and into the day, right through California, straight to the ocean. The eight-lane freeway finally ended and turned into the Pacific Coast Highway. Eve drove north, with the ocean on her left. The sight of all that water and beach, as such a casual part of everyday life here, was exhilarating. The sun looked different here. Bouncing off the water, it was reflective, instead of direct and oppressive, the way it was in Vegas. Eve squinted even though she was wearing sunglasses. Her sense of purpose heightened. She was here!

Eve pulled over on Sunset Boulevard and parked her car. She was getting cramped from sitting for so long, and she was itching to walk on the beach. She got out and stretched. Her legs were stiff and so was her neck. Her white shirt was sweaty and creased. Her bones felt like they'd been molded to the back of the car seat. She whipped off her old sneakers and walked barefoot, straight over the gravel parking lot and onto the sand. She didn't stop walking until she was at the ocean's edge—and then in it—and her toes were buried in wet sand. She cuffed her blue jeans and stood, clutching her sneakers and staring out, barefaced, clear-eyed. The ocean was the biggest thing she'd ever seen, except for the desert. Only this was the exact opposite of everything she had known up to this moment. The desert had made her feel hot, dusty, and weak, but the ocean felt cool and clean. She could give herself a new life here. Reinvent herself. Be creative and let her imagination run wild. She could do anything here. She had nothing to lose.

"I'm here," she thought to herself, then said it aloud. "I'm here." She spoke quietly, but her words were distinct. "I'm here." She said it louder. Consciousness came, and she looked around again.

Suddenly, she realized that the lifelong familiar smell of gasoline, from the family pumps, was gone. All she could smell was the sea salt. She reached for the Saint Christopher necklace that her mother had given her, but her neck was bare. She panicked and felt with both hands, her neck, her clothes, anywhere the necklace could have fallen and gotten stuck. She went back and searched her Camry, behind the seats, on the floor. But the necklace was gone.

Two

Jocelyn Stone parked her brand-new maroon Jaguar convertible on a numbered side street. She stepped out of the car and rose to her full height. One inch short of six feet tall. She wiggled her toes inside her green J. P. Todds. A warm Santa Ana breeze blew her dyed and streaked blonde hair around. She tried not to lick her lips. They were dry and puffy. Chapped. She made a mental note to buy more lip moisturizer next time she was at Fred Segal's. She went through tubes of it when the Santa Anas blew. Jocelyn hated this weather. It was seventy-five degrees at eight-thirty in the morning in September. Earthquake weather.

She smoothed the seat belt wrinkles from her size six, color-coordinated, Oxnard discount mall clothes. Only the discerning eye could tell that she wasn't wearing a thousand-dollar ensemble. She'd had her housekeeper iron her clothes the day before, then she'd touched them up herself that morning after her six a.m. Pilates workout. Her body was sore from the exercise. If it were up to her, she'd let herself go just a little. But being around so many hyperperfect bodies, she felt self-conscious. Heidi, her new personal trainer and the mother of one of her students, wanted Jocelyn to be her calling card. If Heidi could get Jocelyn as a client, then every mother in Hollywood would notice.

Heidi wanted Jocelyn to try Pilates and spinning. Jocelyn tried them, but she didn't get it. Sit-ups, jogging, and real bicycling on an actual bike that went somewhere when you pedaled were fine, but she didn't like fads.

Jocelyn double-checked the parking restriction signs on the street and beeped her car, locking it with the remote control on her keychain. The keychain had twenty-three keys. All but two were for the preschool.

"Jocelyn!"

Jocelyn privately rolled her blue eyes. Fans. Already. It wasn't even nine a.m. yet. She turned to see, a few yards away, a woman who had a yoga mat rolled up under one arm and was sipping a giant Jamba Juice. The woman's two children were in a double stroller, which their chunky, Latina nanny was pushing. The bottom of the stroller was loaded up with Noah's bagels and containers of sun-dried tomato cream cheese.

"New car?" called the mother, whose name Jocelyn couldn't remember. She was wearing a strappy yoga leotard with nothing underneath and nothing left to the imagination. Her nipples were sticking out, and she was carefree. She acted like she was fully dressed instead of near naked.

Jocelyn gave a polite but noncommittal half wave, half nod, and started walking. She didn't want to stop and chat. If she stopped to chat with this one, in five minutes she'd be mobbed by every parent who happened to be out on Montana.

Jocelyn was, without a doubt, the queen of Montana Avenue. With her regal, long-legged gait, she ruled this upscale, deceptively low-key area's commercial district from Seventh Street to Seventeenth. Not because she was rich or famous, ran a studio, or owned real estate. Or because she was married to someone important. None of those things were true.

Jocelyn had never married. She wanted to, but never found anyone she felt was right. Now she was forty. She still had an amazing body, without a snip of plastic surgery. She got the attention of men wherever she went. But once they got to know her, they were scared off.

Her social life depressed her, and she tried not to think about it. But when it got her down, she played sports.

As a college student at UC Santa Barbara, Jocelyn had been a volleyball star, with offers to play professionally when she graduated. Jocelyn treated volleyball with the same intensity as she did her major—child development and education—but she always saw the game as a hobby. She knew her real purpose in life.

Children. It was never a choice for her. It was something she knew she had to do, and it came easily.

She never knew why, exactly—it was just an instinct. Jocelyn didn't question her instincts, she followed them. And this was no exception.

When she graduated college, her parents told her she had been adopted. Over brunch at Citronelle, an elegant French restaurant in Santa Barbara. They gave her a Seiko watch, and the news. Jocelyn was shocked, and then calm. She'd had a good life growing up with her adoptive parents in Laguna Hills. Nothing to complain about. But with the news of her own adoption, her commitment to caring for children became stronger.

She immediately went to New York University for her master's degree and, during that time, she got practicum experience teaching all over the country. She caught on to everything fast. The same way she had played volleyball. The thing she learned most from teaching children around the country was that they were all the same in so many ways. The children, the parents, the dilemmas, and the delights. All that said, she missed California. The volleyball courts other places were indoors—hard and cold and with glazed, wooden floors that screeched under sneakers. The weather around the country was erratic. And there was no beach in America like a California beach.

Her relationship with her parents had changed. With graduation, moving to New York, and "the news," all having come pretty much at once, she felt an invisible cord with them had been cut. It just happened.

New York was cold and windy for much of the year. Jocelyn jogged and played racquetball, but she missed surfing, volleyball on the sand, and seeing men in bathing suits daily. She wasn't intellectual, she was practical. She didn't care about the things people debated at cocktail parties here. She just wanted to work with kids. Not talk about it.

As soon as she graduated, Jocelyn caught the first plane back to Los Angeles, where blondes outnumbered brunettes four to one in the domestic terminals.

Settled in a new two-bedroom West L.A. apartment with a balcony overlooking the courtyard pool, Jocelyn relaxed and refocused. She took a job as a preschool teacher at All Hallows Church. There she met the professional friends and backers with whom she would get the support to eventually start her own preschool.

Everything fell into place. Her job, her family, her career. All that was left was her personal life.

Men loved Jocelyn. Maybe because she never took dating seriously. She just wanted to have fun and relax after working like a fiend. She liked male company and she liked sex, but not as much as she loved her work. For the next ten years, Jocelyn became a hot dating ticket in Los Angeles. She was a potential trophy wife. The men she knew wanted women with a career, whom they could flaunt. Like an Armani suit or 700 series BMW.

Jocelyn became a coveted date.

But the way she saw it, she just had too many calls and too many social commitments. She had to find a way to weed out the men. So she devised The List. It started after a party at her home for the four female teachers on her staff. They had just ended another successful school year, and were feeling giddy and loose. Two pitchers of margaritas offset only by a platter of nachos made all of them silly. When they left, Jocelyn sat down with pen and paper and made The List:

1. looks—must have some
2. career—must have one
3. intelligence—must have lots
4. past "baggage"—not so much
5. open-mindedness—a must
6. loves children—a must
7. respects my career—a must
8. wants a family—definitely
9. doesn't believe in divorce
10. doesn't believe in abortion
11. sex—follows his instincts in bed

There were subcategories, too.

Jocelyn showed her friends The List. They loved it. Pretty soon, lists were "the thing" in town, and everyone knew that Jocelyn had started The List.

Her popularity surged, but the men she knew began to feel judged. They knew about her list. They also knew simple economic principles, which they applied to dating. She was in demand, and they were in abundance. They knew that cheapened their value. The men began to fear being held up to The List. They didn't like the idea that they were being discussed and compared.

Out of fear, they stopped calling Jocelyn. In dribs and drabs, and then altogether.

Jocelyn hit thirty-five. What was considered her "spunk" at twenty and then "verve" at thirty, quickly became "ball-busting" as forty approached.

Rejected suitors, bitter that she hadn't picked them, began to spread the word that there was no pleasing her. Men said she was hard. At first she laughed it off as ridiculous. But after a while, it saddened her to see other women, women she thought had less to offer than she had, getting not just dates, but marriage proposals, families, homes—the things she wanted, and thought she was supposed to have. She couldn't understand how something so important to her was passing her by.

Jocelyn hit the therapist's couch with a big thud. Half a case of tissues later, she decided she didn't want to change.

"Are you crazy?" the therapist asked her.

"Excuse me?"

Jocelyn didn't like sarcasm.

"You have the world by the tail. Everything is going your way. I don't know why you choose to see the problems."

That was the last time Jocelyn paid for advice. She went back to her old way of dealing with problems—she worked out. She ran, she went to the gym, she did everything to keep her mind off the disappointment of her social life.

Then she opened her own preschool. She'd gotten backers, found a perfect spot in Santa Monica, and named the school Butterflies and Puppydog Tails. It was a huge hit.

Jocelyn fast developed a reputation for running a top-notch school. She knew exactly what to do for everyone's best interest—"her children's" and "her parents'." Dating fell way into the background. She had her hands full and she was happy with her success.

She established Butterflies and Puppydog Tails Preschool on an understated, inconspicuous piece of property on an upscale Santa Monica street.

Jocelyn liked it low-key. There was no reason for a flashy facade, as far as she was concerned. Besides, she couldn't handle any more applicants.

Everyone who was anyone wanted their children to go to Butterflies and Puppydog Tails. The problem was that the preschool was only set up for thirty children every year, and siblings of alumni got priority. That meant lots of people didn't get in. The waiting list was massive. The rejection letters were mailed in bulk.

Jocelyn had underestimated the power of rejection in a town of overachievers. An admissions rejection didn't mean, Find another school. Not to this community. It meant, Find a way in. There must be something fabulous here. And the reality, that there actually was, gave the preschool tremendous heat.

Jocelyn had had opaque, hunter green canvas woven into the school's wrought-iron gate to create a simple facade that blocked the view. Nobody could see in. She created a private sanctuary where her students spent their toddler years. Purple and magenta bougainvillea grew over the top of the gate, and was meticulously clipped weekly. It became impossible to see in.

An unexpected reaction came from the tabloid paparazzi, who decided that there must be pictures to be had if Jocelyn had put up a wall. They tried almost daily to snap shots of famous folks' kids in the sandbox. Jocelyn considered their presence annoying, but something she had to live with, like the rest of Hollywood.

But there were rules inside her school. The children could not wear fancy clothes that couldn't get dirty. She knew this cramped the style of mothers who lived to dress their children like china dolls, but Jocelyn wanted all the kids to feel comfortable when they played.

They couldn't be late in the morning, they couldn't bring junk food in their lunch boxes, and they couldn't be picked up late after school ended—and that was just for starters.

The school was nestled between Baby Stuff, home of the five-hundred-dollar children's step stool and other equally precious items, and Child's View, another children's clothing store with thirty-five-dollar T-shirts for kids. Jocelyn had chosen this spot years before the neighborhood had become upscale. She thought the outrageous prices were ridiculous, and the mothers that shopped around here even sillier for doing so, but that quickly changed when she realized most of them were shopping for gifts for her.

At first the gifts embarrassed her. They were gifts she could never afford for herself. Not on the salary she allowed herself. But as her school became more successful, the gifts were things she could afford but would never waste her hard-earned money on. She graciously thanked everyone with handwritten notes on green stationery that was engraved with her initials in black. JS.

Jocelyn Stone. Everyone loved her because she was so good at what she did. They were grateful and pleased.

Hollywood parents loved her "back to basics" preschool. They commuted daily from up to an hour away, just to give their children the best. They tried hard to instill "normal values," and surround their kids with "regular folks" by sending them to Butterflies and Puppydog Tails. But the biggest giveaway that there was nothing normal here, was front and center, curbside.

The cars.

Illegally double-parked. All up and down the stretch of street in front of the school. Some with motors running. Some with chauffeurs at the wheel. Shiny new BMWs and Mercedeses; Range Rovers with juice boxes littering the back seats; crisp new Volvo station wagons with two and sometimes three car seats strapped into the back; Hummers and vintage convertibles with famous actor parents at the wheel (the chauffeurs were not asked to drive these pet cars). An array of buslike utility vehicles with four-wheel drive—even though the most rugged terrain they would navigate was the four stories of covered parking at the West Side Pavilion. An occasional dark limousine showed up and there was often a cherry red Corniche with, ironically, smoked-glass windows. These were all cars of the parents who were picking up and dropping off their toddlers.

The Corniche had become the subject of gossip among the parents waiting for their children. None of them could imagine driving it, let alone owning it. That car, they all clucked, was such an obvious cry for attention. It was so "look at me."

The driver was a gorgeous Swedish au pair who didn't care a whit about the others' clear disapproval of her employer's vehicle. Walking past, she'd wave to them with the hand that was carrying her iced decaf, skinny Frappuccino. In her other arm, she carried a six-month-old, her other charge, settled on her hip. Poor things in their leased Porsches, she thought. Can't even afford a decent back seat. She was the most fortunate domestic in town.

Needless to say, there was not a single used Toyota or beat-up family wagon in sight. Even the regular nannies drove their employer families' Mercedes station wagons. Only the teachers' cars were "normal." Meaning they were five and ten years old. Often bought used, not new. And not automatically traded in every three years for something different. The teachers, however, with all their normalcy, were encouraged to park several blocks away.

Despite the $40,000 and up sticker price procession outside the preschool, Santa Monica still gave the illusion of normal, mid-western values. Life appeared understated.

Absent were the tight-fitting luncheon suits and well-practiced, made-up faces of Beverly Hills ladies. Never on Montana. Locals merely threw on a sports coat to wear with their jeans for lunch at the glass-walled Cafe Montana or at Louise's Trattoria. And the shoes were always flats. Never heels. You could even spot Birkenstocks, especially near the blocks where there were yoga studios.

"I hate my fucking mantra," explained one devotee to her yoga instructor, as they bought organic, free-range egg salad on wheat-free, dairy-free bread and vegan potato salad at Wild Oats across from the yoga studio. He didn't raise an eyebrow or alter his measured breath.

"Then, let's make an appointment to have it adjusted," he said, his deep, low voice soothing and even. "There's no reason for you to have a mantra you hate. Let's get you comfortable."

He flashed a beatific smile, no doubt channeled from some spirit on another plane.

Behind the healthy, bare faces and big, covered drinks were the most famous (and soon to be famous) stars, strolling freely. Usually with some writer or producer tagging just half a step behind, anxiously pitching them something "extremely viable." On Montana nothing was more common than a double stroller, a yoga mat, and a feature film script in hand.

The shopping on Montana was choice. Fifty adorably chic boutiques offered casual and couture; several stores offered antique and contemporary furniture, like Room with a View, where you could score an old-fashioned wicker crib for $2,000, or Imagine, where an adorable set of bunk beds would put you back $3,000. There were also half a dozen charming florists, patisseries, and restaurants. Not only could moms drop off their children at school, but they could also pick up a few treasures on the way home.

There was a gourmet organic market with twenty-six different varieties of vitamin C, twelve different echinaceas, twenty different acidophiluses, sixteen different kinds of melatonin, and eight Saint-John's-wort combos among the shelves and shelves and *shelves* of vitamins, elixirs, and herbs. All quietly promising a better life to those who buy and swallow. There was a ravioli store, which sold by the pound fresh lobster ravioli, wild mushroom ravioli, or, when it was in season, pumpkin ravioli. There were three power yoga centers, a spinning studio, and six coffee shops in ten blocks: two Starbucks, Seattle's Best, Diedrich's, Coffee Bean and Tea Leaf, and Pasqua.

At Pasqua, a bodyguard for celebrities could be seen many afternoons nursing a latte grande for hours. Waiting for something to do. He smiled often and threw out friendly pickup lines to the myriad braless, pantyless, "nothing comes between me and my Danskin" yoga soldiers in their spaghetti-strap leotard tops with bare midriffs, who stopped for sugar-free, fat-free, wheat-free bread. His lines usually revolved around the quality of the weather; sometimes he'd wonder out loud if an earthquake was coming because of all the ants in his condo. There had been a three-point-one in Bakersfield. No kidding?! Really? One woman held her fresh, warm baguette under a sweaty armpit, shifting, squeezing the bread and inhaling its aroma suggestively, as she and the bodyguard joked about faults and the Richter scale.

Then there were the juice bars. The din from their row of whirring blenders made it impossible for conversation at lunchtime. People ordered Pacific Passion, Orange Zinger, Hawaiian Lust, and Beta Carotenes—big, thick drinks that required a strong suck on a straw or else a spoon. Then there were the added boosts. Spirulina, ginseng energy, vita vitamins, immunity powder, digestive tract spurts. Those truly committed to the juice lifestyle downed plastic shot glasses filled with freshly extracted wheatgrass juice.

One store even left complementary organic doggie biscuits in bowls, out on the sidewalk, for the neighborhood dogs.

There were also organic vegetables and antibiotic-free, hormone-free beef for sale at a little store nestled alongside an old-fashioned sweets shop with shelves of candy necklaces, jaw breakers, and fresh-scooped Italian ice served in paper cups.

"Santa Monica is God's country," a local realtor confided to her client over her sugar-free, organically grown lemonade. She was on her way to show properties to this thirty-year-old TV writer who had created a new hit series. He had a million five to burn, and wanted in. The realtor planned to get him into a three-bedroom for one-point-seven. She knew more about his residual package than he did. She also knew that it was a seller's market. Everybody wanted in here.

"The dirt under a teardown here goes for a million dollars," she said, hungrily eyeing a glass case of gingerbread men cookies.

"I mean, it's crazy. It's insane, I know it! But for me, let's face it, it's great."

The nannies and housekeepers loved it, too. This neighborhood was the best gig in town. Other neighborhoods, like Beverly Hills, Brentwood, and Bel Air often had more traditional stars as residents, and they paid better salaries. Up to a thousand dollars a week. But those jobs required traveling and working on the family's vacations, often several weeks or months a year. A few of those homes even had video cameras placed around the house so they could monitor the nanny's interaction with their children. Some even required their help to sign legal waivers, legally binding the maids and nannies and drivers to a contract that prohibited them from selling their stories of life on "the inside."

North of Montana, however, uniformed maids were nonexistent. These were liberal families. They wanted their help to wear whatever they wanted to. That way, the employers could pretend that they had an "equal" relationship. The help smiled, returned their employers' occasional embraces, and overheard more than a few conversations like this: "We just adore Sanchez, I don't know what we'd do without her. Mammacita's been with us for six years, except for the one year she disappeared. I don't know. She just didn't show up, but other than that, she's like family. I mean, she came back, and she's been with us ever since. We are so lucky."

There was "in-house" crime—crime that was never reported to the police because it wasn't considered "real" crime. "Real" crime was reported on the television news. "Real" crime happened to other people in other neighborhoods. Here, when the entire box of laundry detergent "disappeared," or a blouse got "lost," or a gold bangle just "never turned up"—everyone felt lucky. Lucky that it was just a bracelet, and not the gems. What's one blouse lost, but a reason to go shopping for a new one. And at least they're taking cleaning supplies, whoever "they" are. They probably need it. So what if sheets got ripped off from a linen closet? Or even a car—that's right, a car. What is insurance for, anyway? Stereo systems, so what? As long as nobody was harmed.

The children were safe. That was the important thing. That was all that mattered.

The elaborate alarm systems were never tripped. The in-house robbers knew the codes—were even given the codes, and their own set of house keys. That's how trusted they were. Their em-

ployers never accused or pointed a finger. Even when a family's
stolen Jeep Grand Cherokee was found in Pacoima, in a neighborhood where their housekeeper's family lived. After all, they
had insurance. They had so much. But if they ever lost Lupe for
any reason, they wouldn't know what to do. After all, she was
practically family.

Realtors knew that values here were skewed, but the buyers
didn't care. They liked the other people here. Double-income,
double-graduate-school-educated parents parked their assets here
to raise families. It wasn't like up in Malibu, where you weren't
sure who was doing what behind those private gates on the rustic,
isolated seaside properties. Only weeks ago the Malibu police had
had to call in the state bomb squad because a sixteen-year-old
was building explosives in his bedroom, unbeknownst to his parents. And then there were the handful of playboy celebrities who
beat up their girlfriends with frightening regularity.

North of Montana was different. People moved here to be with
other people like themselves, who shared the same values. They
worked together, shopped together, drank lattes together, attended
their children's birthday parties together. It was impossible to
walk a block on Montana and not pass half a dozen strollers at
any given time.

North-of-Montanans liked the closely populated feel of the
neighborhood, knowing their neighbors, and being able to walk
from their homes to restaurants for dinner at night. It was the
closest thing to the best of New York City in all of L.A., which
was why so many of the transplanted East Coast families moved
to this neighborhood.

Jocelyn never dreamed her preschool would ever turn into a
Hollywood establishment. Like the Brown Derby had once been,
decades ago. Like Musso and Frank's, more recently. Like the
Grill and the Ivy were now. Cocktails and eating out no longer
topped the list of things to do. Families were in, and preschool
was big.

Butterflies and Puppydog Tails was to the Hollywood crowd
what the Algonquin roundtable had been to New York's literati.
The biggest directors, actors, and producers all gathered outside
the gate, in the afternoons waiting for school to end. Waiting to
pick up their precious children.

And while they waited they talked. Deals were made outside
the preschool gate. Fathers who'd had no interest in their children's lives suddenly couldn't wait until their kids were old

enough for preschool. Careers could surge because of what happened outside that school.

The industry loved Jocelyn. They liked her combo: she was blonde and beautiful, and she caught on to everything quickly. They liked her ability to scan a room and read it in a second. It was a trait her students' parents usually found in their lawyers, bankers, realtors, and studio executives—but rarely when it came to anyone who cared for their children. And they loved that she was in a peripheral field. She didn't want a deal. She didn't want to be in a movie. She didn't want anything from them. She just wanted to take great care of their children's educational development. Jocelyn and Hollywood were a match made in heaven.

It had happened so fast. A couple of famous actors and producers had sworn by her school. When they saw her show up at industry parties . . . that was it. Within a week, word was out. Not only did people want to get their children into her school, they were afraid to not have them in her school. Frenzy built. Before long, the entire town wanted entrance for their kids to Butterflies and Puppydog Tails.

The preschool application process was entirely up to Jocelyn. She was the entrance committee of one; she alone made the big decision on who got in. She did all the parent interviews. She read all the applications, and she made all the reference calls. Hollywood shut down the week Jocelyn mailed out her acceptances for the coming school year. Of course, the inside circle already knew if they were in or out, but the others waited outside their homes for the mailmen. On the edges of their palm tree–laden estates.

Admissions was serious business. Jocelyn didn't turn her nose up at any unsolicited bribes, gifts, or offers of unmitigated volunteerism. Not any more, at least. She now saw the big picture and knew the value of a good donation. Jocelyn liked rich people because they provided opportunities. One happy multimillionaire could mean full scholarships for children who didn't have rich parents, raises for the teachers, more education for both Jocelyn and her staff, and special music, art, and science projects for her students.

But she never lost sight of the school itself. She watched during "circle time" to see which children needed any special attention. Spotting speech development problems, aiding with separation anxiety or divorce trauma, and helping parents set boundaries to remedy in-class discipline problems were just a few of the many specialties in her repertoire.

She wasn't afraid to take to task parents who showered their toddlers with lavish gifts like pool tables, child-sized electric cars, and massive video game libraries. She didn't like spoiled kids, and she didn't like parents who spoiled. If the parents wanted to spoil themselves and each other, she was all for it. To spoil a child was another thing. That Jocelyn had rules and stuck to them garnered respect.

If the parents wouldn't cooperate with her, she asked them to leave the school. Regardless of their Oscars, Emmys, or bank accounts. She wasn't interested in money or fame. Just children.

Which is how there came to be more rich and famous people's children per square inch of sandbox at Butterflies and Puppydog Tails than at any other preschool.

It was also how Jocelyn Stone inadvertently got Hollywood by the balls. She had a tighter grip than any director, studio exec, or movie star. Jocelyn was the only one who could immediately get studio presidents out of meetings and on the phone. Except for their wives, Jocelyn was the one person who could pull major motion picture stars off hundred-and-fifty-million-dollar movie sets.

It wasn't fair. It wasn't good. It wasn't bad. It was reality. Jocelyn's reality.

She had carefully built Butterflies and Puppydog Tails over the years, and she knew she had to be cautious about who she let in, and who she kept in. It was all she had. It was who she was. And it was fabulous.

Three

Gabrielle Gardener strolled Montana, sipping a Pacific Passion with an immunity boost of echinacea and goldenseal. Her long, shiny black pigtails flopped against her back. She had carefully braided her hair like a magazine picture she had admired. Gabrielle was five months pregnant and hadn't moved to maternity clothes yet. She was wearing an old Sonia

Rykiel she had gotten in Paris. It was feminine and spoke volumes about her taste. Expensive, sophisticated, studied.

Gabrielle was on her way to the preschool. She'd heard all over town about Butterflies and Puppydog Tails. And she was determined to get a spot for her unborn child.

Suddenly, Gabrielle heard a crash. Right in front of the preschool, a blue Ford Explorer rammed into the side of a parked black Mercedes. Jocelyn rushed out of the gate at Butterflies and Puppydog Tails. She'd heard the crash. She sized up the situation immediately.

She recognized the family in the smashed black Mercedes as one of hers. She ran to help them. Abruptly, the driver of the Ford Explorer jumped out of his car, and so did the driver of a red Honda Civic in front of the Mercedes. The Civic had blocked the Mercedes while the Explorer had rammed it on the side. It was a trap.

The drivers charged the Mercedes. They were both scruffy, overweight men with cameras. Long, powerful lenses aimed into the Mercedes and snapped pictures of the people inside. Fast and furious. The clicking of the cameras and the blinding lights of the flashbulbs were like war. The sound of artillery, the explosion of light.

The photographers threw their bodies across the front of the Mercedes so they could shoot inside. They were mercenary.

The family inside the car covered their faces with their hands and their clothes, shielding themselves from having their pictures taken. The father, a famous action film star, grabbed a child-sized *Star Wars* knapsack from the floor, and held it up to shield his image from the paparazzi. The knapsack was lumpy. Inside were his son's walkie-talkies, which the boy had packed for sharing at circle time.

"Get out of here!" Jocelyn yelled at the photographers as they swarmed the Mercedes, trapping the passengers inside. She tried to pull and tug at them, but it did no good. "I told you to stay away from here. This is a school. These are children and families!"

Gabrielle watched carefully. She had heard about Jocelyn. The sun-streaked jock who had gracefully made her way into child education and now ran the most powerful institution in Hollywood. The preschool. Gabrielle didn't quite know what to expect, but she noticed Jocelyn's confidence and command. She seemed brave, and yet, not brash. Gabrielle liked this about Jocelyn.

The paparazzi pushed Jocelyn out of the way, hard, trampling her in the process. They yelled at the famous passengers, calling them by name, baiting them to look up for a photo. Jocelyn quickly got up and ran back to the car, determined.

The father in the car lunged for the smashed-in door handle and tried to get out, but the door wouldn't open. The Explorer that had crashed into his door had jammed it, so he couldn't get out. He was trapped in the car.

"Calm down," said the wife. "They're just doing their job."

"Look what they did to your car!" said the action star. "Is that their job?"

"It's just a car," she said. She could tell her husband was holding on to his temper by a thread. "Don't let them see us fighting."

"Watch out!" said Jocelyn as she pushed past the paparazzi with all her might and helped the famous-in-her-own-right wife of the movie star out of the car. The two children in the back seat looked scared. They turned to their mother, but she was focused on her husband.

"He just had heart surgery," their mother pleaded to the photographers. "Please, leave him alone. He isn't supposed to get worked up."

"I'm fine," said the big film star, tensely. Then through gritted teeth, he said to his wife, "I want to beat the shit out of them."

"Don't," she hissed back. "All we need is another stupid lawsuit."

"Get out of the way before I call the police," yelled Jocelyn, outside of the car, to the photographers. "I've told you before, stay away from my school!"

"Just get the kids out," the action star barked at his wife. "I don't want their pictures showing up in the tabloids."

At that moment, Jocelyn quickly opened the back door where the two red-headed children were buckled into their car seats. Their father had red hair himself, but dyed it dark because nobody would cast him as an action hero with red hair. He wondered, with two red-haired kids, how long it would take for the tabloids to get that story on the front page.

"Come on, kids." Jocelyn helped the children out of the car. They were shaken by the commotion, and reluctant to get out into the fray, but they gratefully clutched Jocelyn's familiar hands. "Come on." She led them safely through the mess. "Let's go inside."

"Cover their faces!" their mother yelled to Jocelyn, who wrapped her arms around the children's faces. The wild photographers tried to pry her arms away, but years of volleyball had developed her arm muscles. She kept the children's faces shielded while she hurried them to the gate. She wanted to kick the photographers in the balls, but she knew they'd sue her.

"Don't shoot the kids!" their mother yelled at the photographers. "Please!"

Jocelyn whisked them inside the preschool. The gate slammed shut behind them. Safe.

The noise of children playing in the school drowned out the commotion on the street. Jocelyn saw the kids relax a little. She helped them with their lunch boxes and sweatshirts, and got them set up with their friends in the sandbox, and on the swings. She was relieved to see the children seemed okay. She hoped the parents were making out all right.

"Come on, honey," said the wife, offering her hand to her husband. "Climb over the stick shift. Get out on my side. Can you do it?"

"Yes, I can do it," he said, frustrated. He was a big man, and the car, even though it was top of the line, luxury, was not built for adults climbing around inside it. "I just don't want them getting a picture of my ass in the windshield."

Sirens blared in the distance, coming closer.

The wife got out of the car herself and addressed the photographers, who kept clicking. "You won, fellas. You got your pictures. Now, can you please move your car so my husband can get out?"

"Sure thing," they said with sudden politeness. "Hey, how's he feeling? Since the surgery?"

A few seconds ago they were like animals. Now that they had the shots they wanted, they had found their manners.

"Fine," she said. "He's just swell."

"Good to hear it. Take care." And they packed up and quickly moved their car.

She hated them. Ever since her husband had had to have heart surgery, there'd been a $150,000 bounty for the first post-surgery picture of him. The tabloid readers probably wanted to see if he was going to die or not. Everybody loved it when a celebrity suffered.

Gabrielle, who had been standing there, watching, mesmerized by the whole incident, took some deep breaths. Her heart pounded.

"You okay?"

The pet store owner had come outside to watch the commotion and was concerned about Gabrielle in her delicate condition.

"You want some water?" He nodded at her pregnant belly. "Sure gets hot fast."

"No," said Gabrielle. "Thank you. I'm fine. That's very kind of you."

"Always something going on at that school," said the pet store owner. "Kids are cute, though. You sure you don't want some water? It's no trouble."

"No, thank you," said Gabrielle, and she walked toward the preschool. At the iron gate she took a deep breath, and then forged ahead, past the gate, into the yard, and finally, into the building.

It was free play. Jocelyn watched, making sure the children she had just rescued were really okay. She followed them with her eyes as they ran off to play on the elaborate wooden jungle gym structure with its flags and canopies in bright colors.

"Hello. I'm Gabrielle Gardener."

Jocelyn turned to see Gabrielle standing there, smiling up at her. Jocelyn didn't like strangers in her school. She didn't allow it, actually, not without an appointment. She figured that Gabrielle must have snuck in during the commotion just now.

This time Gabrielle extended her hand to shake. Jocelyn took it. She wasn't sure if Gabrielle was applying for a teacher's job, or a parent applying for a student's spot. The pigtails were confusing, but when the wind blew her dress, Gabrielle's belly gave her away. Definitely a parent.

"I just came by to submit this application." Gabrielle held out a manila envelope. Crisp, clean, perfectly typed on the dotted lines.

Jocelyn relaxed. Another one who wanted admission. At least she wasn't dangerous.

"Please don't tell me this is an application for that one," said Jocelyn, nodding at Gabrielle's pregnant belly.

Gabrielle blushed. "I'd be lying," she whispered.

Jocelyn smiled and rolled her eyes. This happened time and again lately.

"You were the most impressive volleyball draw in the state," said Gabrielle. "You were a formidable player. I saw pictures of you in the newspaper. You're quite an accomplished sports-woman.''

"That was a long time ago," said Jocelyn. She figured Gabrielle for twenty-five years old. Maybe younger.

"You know, they have a security program at The Center, in Hollywood," said Gabrielle, her tone sobering. "I saw what happened outside."

Jocelyn knew what she was talking about. The Center for Creative Children was another preschool on the other side of town.

"I've been putting it off," said Jocelyn. "It just seems so . . ."

"So 'Hollywood'?" Gabrielle laughed.

"When I used to think of security, I thought of fire alarms, and those burly security guards with uniforms," said Jocelyn.

"How retro," Gabrielle joked.

"I can't believe that security now means keeping the paparazzi away. From my school! It's unreal. What's happened?"

"You're in the big leagues," Gabrielle sighed. "Blazing the trail."

"I'm just a preschool director," said Jocelyn. Sometimes she still couldn't believe it. Preschool director. It had been her dream for so long, and now it was her life.

"You're not *a* preschool director," said Gabrielle. "You're *the* preschool director."

"Maybe I should just give in and go all the way," said Jocelyn. She knew that Gabrielle was right. She was just too humble to say it out loud. "I obviously need more help than I have. I wish I could say that the scene outside was an isolated incident."

"Whatever you decide will be exactly right," said Gabrielle. "But I know someone who does security for the Center. I could get him if you want. He's a friend of my husband."

"Herbie Johannssen," said Jocelyn. Her mind raced. Herbie was the premier security guy in town. He kept many a celebrity wedding and funeral paparazzi-free. He was also Swedish, blond, and adorable.

"You already know him," said Gabrielle.

"I dated him," said Jocelyn. "He's very good."

Gabrielle raised an eyebrow. "Oh . . ."

"At his job!" said Jocelyn. "I meant, he knows what he's talking about. *And* he was a good date, too." Jocelyn grinned lustily.

"That's good to know," said Gabrielle. She wasn't comfortable with dishing. Not like that. Gabrielle was a little bit of a prude. Proper. Ladylike.

"I should get back to work," said Jocelyn, nodding to the children.

"Wait." Gabrielle panicked. She was still holding the application. Jocelyn hadn't taken it from her. She had to get Jocelyn to take it. That had been her purpose in coming here.

Jocelyn walked to the gate, and stood there waiting for Gabrielle to follow her. She had one hand on the gate, ready to escort Gabrielle out.

"I'm sorry," said Jocelyn, when she saw Gabrielle wasn't moving. "I have a policy: I don't accept applications for unborn children. You're not the first."

"But you took Elise Finch's," said Gabrielle.

Hmmm. Jocelyn thought that had been a well-guarded secret. Obviously not. It was true, she had taken Elise Finch's application for her unborn child. But only because Elise was friends with the Clintons and Barbra Streisand and that whole Hollywood–Washington, D.C. crowd. Jocelyn wanted very much to work with Hillary Clinton on her children's campaigns.

"Would you just keep it—in consideration?" Gabrielle asked, waddling over, and sticking the application out to hand to Jocelyn. Jocelyn didn't take it. "The baby's probably going to be premature. It could be born any day now. I just don't know what I'll do if we don't get into your school. I know we'd be great supporters if we did."

Gabrielle was a pro. Polite laughter. The veneer of fast friends. Jocelyn had seen it all before. The politician in maternity clothes.

"I wish I had more time to chat, but I've got to go," Jocelyn said. She opened the gate for Gabrielle, and stuck out her hand to shake. Gabrielle put the application in Jocelyn's outstretched hand, instead of shaking.

"Thank you," said Gabrielle, and quickly waddled off.

Before Jocelyn could even attempt to hand the application back to Gabrielle, a lone photographer called out to her.

"Jocelyn! Over here. Look!"

Boom. He snapped a few shots. The flashbulbs blinded Jocelyn. When the spots went away, Gabrielle was gone, and so was the photographer.

Four

Eve spotted a restaurant on the beach, not too far from where she stood in the sand. Gladstone's. She realized she was hungry. It was early. Not quite seven in the morning, but there were a few cars in the restaurant parking lot. Maybe it was open.

She left her car parked on the Pacific Coast Highway, and walked toward the restaurant. It was a weather-beaten, dark wood building with porches and open decks. There were tables and chairs everywhere. Even outside.

Sawdust was sprinkled all over the restaurant floor and seagulls as big as large cats dive-bombed the deck, looking for scraps of dropped food. Eve grabbed a handful of peanuts from an open barrel by the door and started cracking the nuts open.

"One?"

A waiter wearing a Gladstone's T-shirt and holding a menu smiled at her. Welcoming. He was big and young and muscular and blond and tan. Just like she imagined all Los Angeles men would be.

"Just coffee," said Eve.

"Would you like to sit out on the deck or inside?"

Tears welled up in Eve's eyes. Suddenly, she felt like she was going to heave or cry or faint. Everything she'd been suppressing about this trip—that it would be easy, a breeze, just a move—had been all wrong. This was going to be huge. Catastrophic. She was all alone, and she'd lost her mother's Saint Christopher necklace. She was slipping over the edge.

Eve suddenly lost it. She burst into giant sobs and collapsed onto the waiter. He didn't act at all surprised. He put his arms around her while she soaked his shirt with tears. Eve couldn't help but feel how solid and strong his chest and arms were. He could probably lift her with one hand. Like a dumbbell. She pulled herself together and backed away.

"I'm sorry." She couldn't look him in the eye. This was humiliating.

"It's okay," he said, nonchalantly.

Eve reluctantly looked up at him. He smiled. Calmly, serenely, as if this kind of episode happened every day.

"No, really," she said, sniffing and wiping her nose on her sleeve. "It's not okay. You're the first person I've met in Los Angeles, and I'm acting like a moron."

"Oh," he said with the first hint of surprise. "I figured you just came from yoga."

"Excuse me?" Eve wiped her eyes on her other sleeve.

"It opens you up. Exposes your chi to the world. Makes me cry every time. Especially after ashtanga. It's really potent. Intense," he tried to explain.

Eve looked blank. She had no idea what he was talking about, and she was certain she should.

"Come on," he said, taking her hand and leading her out to the deck.

"But—but—"

"Sit here." He acted so at ease with her. Like he was an old friend or something. "I'll bring you some juice."

"But I just want coffee," said Eve, sitting.

"You need juice," he said and left.

She wanted coffee. Oh well. She deserved whatever she got. He was probably going out to call the police. Or the mental institution. She took a deep breath and tried to relax. She thought about how she had just fallen apart in the arms of a total stranger, and she wanted to die.

Eve looked around. He had seated her at a small weather-beaten wood table overlooking the ocean. She had an incredible view of the waves breaking on the beach.

"Here."

Eve looked up. The waiter was back and he placed a huge glass of thick, pinkish orange juice in front of her. It seemed a lavish presentation, for juice.

"Thank you, but—"

"I'm Corey," he said. "If you need anything . . ."

"Coffee," she said quickly, wrinkling her nose, trying not to insult him. ". . . Corey," she added.

"You don't need coffee," he said. "This is a power smoothie, and I threw in some bee pollen—no charge. You'll feel wonderful." He winked and left.

Eve watched him go. Weird. She tasted the drink. It was thick, like an entire meal. The straw it came with took too much work.

What she really needed was a spoon, but she didn't have one, so she sipped. It was rich and delicious and as she settled into her chair with her drink and the ocean in view, she felt healthy. And tired.

"Of course I slept with him."

Eve looked over as another waiter seated a famous model, a woman Eve recognized instantly. The model was with another woman and a man in a suit holding a cell phone to his ear. They sat two tables away.

"I mean, he won an Oscar," said the model. "What was I supposed to do? Not sleep with him?"

"Yeah, but the Oscar was for screenwriting," said the other woman. "It's not really an *Oscar* Oscar."

"First of all, I saw it, and it was real, and secondly, he's directing now."

"Low budget?" said the model with disdain.

"He's deeply talented," said the other woman. "Which is the real reason that I slept with him."

Eve couldn't believe it. This was the same woman she'd seen on television and on the cover of *TV Guide*.

She was so excited. A movie star, already!

"So?" the man asked, dialing another number. The cell phone didn't leave his ear.

"He was terrible. I mean, as a writer, he was great; the second he started directing, though, his dick didn't work. He laid on top of me with his full body weight, and then nothing. And to top it off, he only had one testicle!"

Eve tried not to listen, but it was impossible. The model was talking in regular restaurant volume, the wind was carrying her voice, and there was no one else there except for Eve.

"Cancer?"

"He wishes it was cancer! His mother snipped it off because it never descended. It might have gotten twisted or something. I don't remember, exactly."

The man in the suit cringed and made a terrible sound. "I'd rather have cancer," the man said.

Eve wanted to plug up her ears, but she couldn't help herself. The conversation was disgusting and at the same time, riveting.

"He *must* have been abused."

"His films are so angry."

"So violent."

"He does have a thing with women."

"He hates them!" said the model. "I think he has systemic yeast." She sipped her water. "Oh, God, I hope this isn't from the tap," she said, and held her glass up to the light to examine the water.

"Why do you think he hates women?" asked the man.

"All that violence," said the model. "Everyone knows that if you get too much yeast in your system you start acting out. Just look at his films! I mean, the yeast is practically up there on the screen!"

Eve took a huge sip of her drink and got brain freeze. Her head ached. She heard the man in the suit making more phone calls on his cell phone. Work calls. Eve's work ethic loomed. She remembered that this was a weekday and began to feel guilty that she wasn't working, too. Now that she was here, she had some more ground to cover. She needed a job and an apartment. And she needed to find out what "systemic yeast" meant. And to remember to stay away from men who had it.

She got up and walked to her car, looking for Corey to say goodbye and to thank him for the juice, but he wasn't around.

"Excuse me, miss," the model was calling to Eve. "Yes, you."

Eve turned sixteen shades of red at once. She'd never spoken to a famous person before.

"Come here."

Eve obeyed. She quickly considered asking the model for an autograph, but then changed her mind. She was afraid that in her present state of mind, she might lose control and start crying on the model the way she had on Corey. That would be too awful.

"Take this away. Thank you."

The model handed Eve three drinking glasses. Eve didn't have time to think. She had to make sure the glasses didn't fall onto the floor and break.

"Thanks, thanks," said the man with the cell phone, and they all went back to their conversation and forgot Eve, who backed off, carrying the three empty glasses.

She looked around for somewhere to put them. Then, without knowing why, she walked to her car, still carrying the glasses. She got into the car, turned it around, and headed for the valley. With the glasses jiggling next to her on the passenger seat.

Five

Nancy Jane Helena had never uttered a mean word in her life. Not to anyone's face, not behind their back, not even in her dreams. She was just not a mean person. She'd been around meanies all her life, but she'd never become one. Nancy credited her disposition to her good upbringing and her faith in God. She wore a delicate gold cross around her neck. She never took the cross off. Not even when she was having sex with someone she'd just met.

Nancy wasn't a slut. She just liked to have a good time. And why not? She was a good student all through high school. A good daughter her entire life. She had always turned the other cheek. The worst thing she'd ever done was stay out past her curfew, but she always lied and came up with a good excuse, and her parents always believed her. Her family loved her. They never thought that Nancy would give them any trouble. Not their Nancy Jane.

Nancy's parents, Connie and Buck, were normal, upper-middle-class Connecticut folks. Her mother was a satisfied homemaker and her father sold insurance and got plastered on weekends. He loved to drink beer in his tool shed. Sometimes with a friend, sometimes with his son, Baker, who was a year older than Nancy. Baker and his dad would go through six-pack after six-pack before dinner, and sometimes while they were drinking, they'd even use some of the tools in the shed to repair some household project. A squeaky porch swing or a broken sheet of lattice in the gazebo.

By the time Nancy turned twenty-one and graduated from Connecticut College, she'd earned a reputation as a definitive, hardcore party girl, albeit a nice one. She went wherever the best party was being thrown. By plane, train, automobile—whatever. Senior year, she scheduled all her classes on Tuesdays and Thursdays, so she could travel for parties the rest of the week, always showing up just in time for Tuesday eight a.m. classes. Her folks laughed about their Nancy Jane. She always called them Sundays after church—something she never forgot to do—and this alleviated their worries. How bad could it be if she always went to church?

"Nancy Jane just loves a good party," giggled Connie over cocktails with the girls. "That daughter of mine'll go anywhere to get to the best bash. I'm not sure which one of us she takes after more." That cracked them up. Connie and Buck liked a good laugh almost as much as they liked a good cocktail.

"Aren't you worried?" asked a neighbor who was nursing a greyhound with extra grapefruit juice. It was a Sunday afternoon at Connie's, and the women were marinating T-bone steaks and thick chicken breasts in their own kitchens for their respective grills that night. But now, it was their "girls' cocktail hour."

"Nancy Jane is a good student," said Connie. "I mean, she gets B's . . . mostly. She's a good girl."

"Nancy Jane is sweet as pie," said one of the other neighbors.

When Nancy's big brother, Baker, graduated and became an investment banker, no one was more excited than Nancy. She knew he would be invited to parties with the "grown-ups" he would meet in the real world. She was right. Baker took Nancy to parties and introduced her around. He was beginning to suspect he liked boys better than girls, and bringing his sister took the pressure off his getting a date to show the world he was straight.

Nancy was a big hit at the parties. But not because of her looks. The truth was that Nancy Jane wasn't pretty. She wasn't ugly. She was just what you'd call handsome. She had a pleasant face, brown hair, flawless skin, and she was thin. Enviably thin.

That part was not natural. The thin part. Nancy got reed thin from doing coke. The grown-up parties Baker took her to were given by and for other successful businessmen, and the "treats" were excessive. There were often a lot of expensive drugs, as well as good champagne.

Baker brought Nancy to these parties, but once there he lost track of her pretty quickly. They would catch up the next morning when Nancy pounded on Baker's door to drag him to church. Often, she was hung over, unshowered, and looking like hell, but she always went, and always insisted that her brother go. It was at church that Baker met Juan Montero, a Puerto Rican documentary filmmaker who had a place in Chelsea, and they hit it off immediately.

Baker began to drop Nancy at the parties, and then take off to secretly spend the nights with Juan. Juan knew a lot of independent filmmakers, who didn't do the party circuit that Baker and Nancy moved in. Baker began hanging out with Juan and his film friends, an entirely different circle. They shunned the Hollywood scene, spoke contemptuously of formulaic high-budget movies, and debated auteur theory into the wee hours of the morning. Baker loved this and he also loved Juan. The two quickly became a couple.

Nancy promised not to tell her parents about Juan as long as Baker kept taking her to the parties. The deal was a no-brainer for Baker. He got the invitations and dropped Nancy off, alone, with cab money to get herself home. Only, since he wasn't babysitting his sister any more, he didn't notice that she was going hog-wild.

By the time Nancy turned twenty-four, she had up and moved to Los Angeles. She liked the weather, there were always great parties going on, and, mostly, she liked that the older men she met were interested in marrying younger women like her. In New York, lack of commitment was in the air, just like oxygen. No matter what age the men were. Nancy dreamed of having a house with a white picket fence, a couple of kids, and a husband. Her chances in Los Angeles were much better.

She got Baker to help her land a job as a temp at Smith Barney. He used his bicoastal connections, and then visited his little sister whenever he could. But Nancy didn't care about the job per se. She had no interest in a career. The thing she liked most about her work was the hours. Six to two. The office opened with the New York Stock Exchange and closed with the New York Stock Exchange. With this job, Nancy could be home by three, nap, reshower and dress, and be out of the house for dinner parties, then after-dinner parties, then after-hours parties. Nancy did a rotten job as a temp, but everyone at Smith Barney liked her still. She was well-bred, smart enough, very, very nice, and had a sense of humor and an easy temperament. Nothing phased her.

Not even all the drugs she was consuming. Nancy was doing so many drugs, and eating so little food, that she dropped down to one hundred pounds, which, at five foot eight, made her look emaciated. As her body whithered away, Nancy just kept shopping for smaller, tighter clothes. In fact, it wasn't her body that made Nancy realize she had a problem. It was her credit card bills. She had bought four entirely different sized wardrobes in less than a year because her body weight continued to dwindle and her clothes just didn't fit.

Finally, her friends came to her apartment and staged an intervention to confront her with her drug problem. Nancy was touched by her friends' intervention, but, honestly, she couldn't place all of their faces. A lot of them she had met at parties where she had been loaded and sensory-deprived. No matter. She still knew that the intervention had taken a lot of time, thought, and planning, and she was grateful.

To show her gratitude, Nancy went straight to drug rehab. She put up zero resistance. After all, it wasn't like she felt she needed to be anywhere else, and the idea of meeting a new group of people at rehab wasn't unappealing. Besides, the whole thing made her feel just a little bit like Holly Golightly.

When Nancy finished rehab, she sent thank-you notes on engraved Crane's stationery to all the thoughtful people who had thrown her first intervention. All the ones whose names she could remember. She also held a progressive, potluck dinner to show her thanks. Everyone who had cared about her was in her prayers. She lit candles for them all at church.

Through it all Nancy remained positive. Not to glamorize the drug addiction, but Nancy liked to put things in a positive light. Out of all bad came good, she liked to think. And so it was with the drugs. In fact, it was through all the lines of coke that Nancy met Landon Greene.

Landon was a rich, Jewish, record producer and manager, who, at twice her age, had never married and was straight. Nancy didn't care about his money. She didn't care about his age. He was unspectacular looking. Would blend into any crowd. Except that he always hung out with young people, so he did stick out because he was fifty-two.

Nancy just cared that Landon had potential. He was tall and had dark gray hair that he wore short. His dark glasses were often in place. He hunched over, as if he were hiding something in his belly.

Landon wasn't bad looking. He was just insecure about his appearance. Nancy flattered him to make him feel better about himself. Charity begins at home, she told herself, and this was an easy thing for her to do. Take on Landon as a project. He needed her, she thought.

After a while, Nancy actually began to find Landon very, very attractive. She liked the power he commanded. She liked that he led adventures. He flew her all over with him. He threw parties. He picked up huge dinner party tabs at restaurants, and set the schedule for the rest of the night. He knew what to do.

What she didn't know was that Landon had a profound disgust for himself. It was the force that fueled his insatiable need to beat everyone at business. If he could earn respect and awe, then it didn't matter what anybody said about him. He didn't realize that nobody had said anything really derogatory about him in decades. To him, the humiliation of his youth was just below the surface. The teasing he'd endured as a child and gawky teenager was indelibly stored in his mind as brutality. He would never forget it.

The boys and girls at Beverly Hills Elementary had mocked him incessantly. Or so he thought. He didn't realize that everyone had endured the same mocking. Kids and teenagers could be cruel, and Landon was sensitive. Extra sensitive. And myopic. A tough combination. He heard only what people said to him. Not what they said about each other.

Convinced he was ugly, as a teenager he had gone in for a consultation with a plastic surgeon. The surgeon had made some crack about hoping his parents had a lot of insurance because this job was going to be a doozy. It was a joke, albeit a callous one. Landon hated the surgeon and never went back after the initial office visit.

He became surly with his parents, blaming them and their genes for his looks, his lack of grace, his lack of talents. Not knowing how to handle his pain, he cursed them, broke things. They were at a loss.

"It's your fault I'm ugly and stupid," he would say to them. They didn't know whether to deny that he was unattractive or to be defensive. They knew how smart he was, and they knew there was no winning this argument. In fact, there was no winning any argument with Landon. He was aggressive and bright, and whatever side he took, he drove home with a point of steel.

"It's your fucked-up genes," he'd rant. "I went through all the family albums, and there isn't a decent-looking relative between the two of you. I wish you two hadn't decided to reproduce . . ."

Therapists suggested self-esteem exercises, but Landon saw right through them.

"Cut the bullshit," he'd say to his parents, his many shrinks, his relatives who were in on the plan to help him. "I know I shouldn't be depressed. You should. *I'm* not the one with the ugly son. You are!"

When Landon told his parents he wanted to go on a European high school exchange program, they were relieved. Not only would this get him out of their hair, it might actually help him, they thought. So, Landon went to Paris to do his senior year in high school there.

In Paris, nobody bothered him about his looks, and if they did, he couldn't understand their French well enough to make out the details. He made friends there, and lost his virginity with a Parisian prostitute. He had gone with his two French friends to see this prostitute in Pigalle. She told his friends she charged fifty francs apiece. Landon waited in a living room for the fifteen minutes his friend was in the bedroom with her. When the friend came out, the second friend went in. Landon clutched his fifty francs in his hand. His palm and fingers were sweating. He was gripped with fear at what was about to happen.

"What happened?" he asked his friend.

"She stuck it in," said his friend.

"And then?"

"And then, you know."

The second friend was out after only five minutes. Red-faced, he said he needed to go get a coffee. Landon clutched his money and walked into the bedroom, where the prostitute sat on the bed, waiting for him. She wore a black lace nightgown. Her face seemed to change with the dim light and the smoke. The room was small and smelled of cigarettes and perfume.

Landon started to undress.

"Just the pants," she said, in French.

Landon stopped undressing. He noticed she was looking at him intently. He rebuttoned his shirt and, instead, took off his pants.

"Shoes, too," she said.

Landon took off his shoes and socks.

"One hundred twenty francs," she said, crossing her arms over her chest, challenging him.

At that moment, Landon had an epiphany.

"Do you want to pay or are we finished already?" the prostitute asked, holding out her hand for the cash.

He picked up the blue jeans he had dropped on the floor and pulled out all his money from the pocket.

"Two hundred francs," he said, handing her the extra money.

She looked confused, but not pleasantly so.

"What do you want me to do?" she said. "Do you actually think you can do it twice?"

Her insult was refreshing to him. At least she was being up-front. He was sick to death of people lying to him. Pretending he was something he wasn't. Normal and attractive.

"I want . . ." he said slowly, and with all the command he could muster—more than he had ever mustered up in his entire life, "I want to be very, very good." He said this slowly and pronouncedly. "Do you understand?"

She looked at him, then at his money, and smiled.

"Sure," she said. "Come on."

She patted the bed next to her and pulled her nightgown over her head, revealing her entire body—the first naked female body Landon had ever seen in real life. In seconds he was ready to go. The transaction itself was an enormous turn-on for him. He had taken control of a situation with his brain and his wallet.

The whole sex act took less than ten minutes, but the prostitute told him he was a magnificent lover, and when it was done, she kissed his hand, tenderly.

Landon learned a lesson he'd always remember. There were certain women, who, when paid enough, would do anything. And they were not stupid women. They were not unattractive women. They were people just like him—only women. He made an oath to surround himself with them.

Buoyed with new confidence, he made a decision that if and when he went back to the United States, it would be to beat everyone. To beat everyone so badly they would never laugh at him, or speak unkindly of him again. And if they did, he would destroy them. He had a new confidence.

Driven by the memory of the French prostitute, Landon returned and decided not to go to college. Fuck 'em, he thought. Fuck 'em all. He started a business with five thousand dollars he borrowed from the Beverly Hills bank where his father had gotten his mortgage. And the rest was history.

Now Landon Greene was worth close to a billion dollars. He became a record producer and music manager, and had scores of friends. Mariah Carey and Puff Daddy sent him gifts monthly. He had a stable of rap star wannabes, fighting to get close to him, and he was trying desperately to put together an all-black Spice Girls group. That was his latest project.

"Find me Boyz II Men, only women!" he yelled at his lawyers.

They looked at each other uncomfortably.

"We can't do that, Lanny," they said. "It's not our job to do that."

"You work for me, don't you?"

"We're your lawyers, Lanny. That's all."

"Then fuck you, you're fired," said Lanny. "Myrna! Get me some men!"

The lawyers panicked, and didn't move. They whispered among themselves.

Myrna, Lanny's assistant, teetered in on five-inch high heels. Everything from there on up jiggled violently, as she fought to maintain balance and hurry into her boss's office.

"Lanny, we're not 'men.' We're your lawyers. It's not our job to find you new groups."

"It's not your job? Then why am I paying you so much? I'm paying you a fucking fortune, isn't that right? If all you're gonna do for me is advise me of my legal rights, I don't need you. You're not cost-effective."

They couldn't argue with that. Lanny could get new lawyers in a heartbeat. He was constantly negotiating new contracts, which meant he generated tons of work—and tons of income— for his lawyers. And they were well paid. Very well paid.

"We'll get on it," one of them said. The others grimaced. They hated Landon's tyranny, and yet, it was also inspiring. He was always working, always looking to improve. His bad temper was something his employees all had to endure. It was democratic. Nobody got more or less. Everybody took some shit from him.

"Good," said Landon. "Find me a bunch of black girls who can sing and dance—and who don't have kids. No mothers! I want dumb broads who can tell a joke for a sound bite. I want their brains to last only as long as a rock video. I don't want political agendas. I don't want aspirations to compose. I want black fucking Spice Girls. Tits, asses, voices, and ambition."

Everyone filed out.

Landon was left with Myrna.

"Mr. Greene?"

He turned to look at her. She was an eyeful. He got an idea.

"Do you know anyone black who looks like you—you don't have any black cousins, do you?"

"No, sir," she said. "I don't think so. Should I get some?"

"Not funny," said Landon. He hated jokes. "Call your family and find out if there's anyone who intermarried and bred," he said.

" 'Intermarried and bred'?" she repeated. "This isn't animal husbandry." He made it sound like a science experiment. But for him, business was business and very little was personal.

"I'll give you a million bucks if you have any black cousins," he said, making it very clear. "And girls—not boys," he added quickly. "Get me girls. And get my A&R people out of their comas. Tell them to get their fat, lazy asses in here *now!*"

"Get me, find me, get me, find me," Myrna sang to herself, mocking her boss. She didn't mind the abuse. She knew Lanny was drop-dead serious about the million dollars for a black cousin. She went to call her mother.

Nancy didn't know about Landon's past when she met him at a party. And then again at another party. She liked that Landon was on top of the heap wherever he went. That was the main thing she noticed about him first.

For his part, Landon noticed Nancy's uplifting spirit from across a crowded screening room at the premiere of a rock video one of his clients had just made. Her smile was bright. She was happy and unharmed. She was daring, looking for fun, without being challenging or ball-busting. Everything was a kick to her. There were no ulterior motives. She shined.

When she met Landon, she wasn't intimidated by his age, his money, or his lifestyle. She was just up for a party, confident that she'd have a good time. Landon quickly grew fond of her. When he found out about her regular church visits, despite any debauchery she engaged in during the week, he was smitten. This was a woman of contradictions, and he loved that.

She always looked good and always conducted herself like an ambassador. She had no enemies. She was naughty enough— taking some drugs, having some sex—yet she still managed to be the sweetest person he'd ever met, with the most positive outlook. And without being stupid.

When Nancy checked in at the drug rehab in Rancho Mirage to dry out, Landon was genuinely concerned. He liked her and didn't want anything bad to happen to her. He called her every day and sent flowers once a week. When Nancy got out, he threw her a huge party at a suite at the Four Seasons. At the party, Landon offered her coke, and was grandly impressed when she declined. He was even more impressed when, after the guests left, she had sex with him sober. That had never happened to him. The usual way Landon got sex was to pay, or to get a girl so wasted she couldn't see straight. But Nancy didn't care about that. She saw through his looks. She didn't need or want drugs. She just wanted to be with him.

Landon thought of himself as an old, rich, Jewish guy. He liked the idea that Nancy was a variation on the shiksa goddess. Okay, so maybe shiksa goddess was a stretch. Nancy wasn't quite goddess—the big, blonde type that infiltrated Los Angeles daily. She didn't have big breasts or a *Playboy* centerfold wet-and-ready look, like the others who hung around him. She wasn't a nymphette. But she was quietly strong and she was kind. She was loyal and not looking to move on if someone richer came to town. Landon saw Nancy as a good investment, and he decided he wanted sole ownership.

He proposed marriage with a five-karat diamond surrounded by six different semiprecious stones, and an ironclad prenuptial agreement. He got down on one knee, showed her the prenup and then the ring, after which he popped the question.

"Will you marry me?"

He waited for her answer. They were in the back seat of his limousine, in the middle of a horrific traffic jam on the 405 South. They were heading for the airport. Landon was taking Nancy to Vegas for the weekend. He wanted to gamble.

"Yes," said Nancy, and laughed.

"What's so funny about this?" he asked.

"You didn't demand," said Nancy. "You asked."

"Am I demanding?"

"Are you kidding?" She giggled. " 'Get me, find me' is your middle name."

"Oh." He considered this.

"But the answer to your request is yes," she said.

They kissed. Then Nancy put on the ring. It was huge. And beautiful. And original. It sparkled brightly as she signed the prenup on all the lines where the lawyers had made *x* marks for her.

"I've been thinking about the entertainment industry," said Landon as he pocketed the agreement.

"This ring is amazing," said Nancy. And it was.

"I'm going to buy a talent agency," he said, staring out the window as they passed a billboard advertising a Turner Pictures movie. "I'm sick of musicians. I want to deal with actors. Would you like to go to the Oscars?"

"Landon," said Nancy, seriously. "I have to warn you of something."

That got his attention. She'd signed the agreement, taken the ring, and was disclosing something—now?!

"I want the whole thing," she said solemnly.

"What whole thing?" He wondered if he should have been more wary. He had wanted this to be romantic and idiotically dripping with innocence and sweetness. Like her.

"The whole nine yards," said Nancy. "I want a white picket fence. I want children, pets . . ."

Landon smiled and relaxed. He'd been right. She was sugar through and through. "Okay, you got it, babe."

"Good," she said and snuggled into Landon, thinking to herself that if there was a little pocket change left over for her own island in the Caribbean and a private jet—that would be swell, too.

Six

Landon and Nancy got married fast and luxuriously. The wedding invitations were sent overnight mail, as the wedding was only seven days away. Nancy and Landon rented practically the entire tiny Caribbean island of Mustique for the wedding. Mustique was an English island, and Landon had produced albums for several of the British rock stars and musicians who owned homes there. They helped out when it came time to rent houses and the one restaurant for the reception kitchen.

The tiny airport runway, barely as long as most Beverly Hills driveways, was busier than it had been in years. The airport was not equipped for anything bigger than a twenty-seat plane. There was no control tower, just an island native, who waved planes in with his bare hands. There were no runway lights, either, so the planes couldn't land after sunset. There was also the island's wild goat problem. The goats tended to graze wherever they pleased, sometimes on the runway.

Celebrities were rampant at the wedding. Prince Andrew and Sarah Ferguson made appearances, and stayed in two of the many

Royal Family–owned homes on the island. Friends from Landon's business ventures and family, mostly from Nancy's side, were housed in rental homes on the beach and in the hills. The houses were mostly designed by Sir Collin Tenet, a former set designer who'd once owned the island and had great influence on its meager but lovely architecture.

Nancy's parents, Connie and Buck, arrived drunk from airplane cocktails. They stayed pretty much soused the entire time they were on the island, and thought Landon was quite a guy to pay for their daughter's wedding. The gesture almost got them to like Jews. Which was a topic they never brought up with their daughter—her marrying a Jewish man the same age as her own father. It was just a nonissue. If anyone brought it up, they laughed it off. Isn't it a hoot? Our Nancy Jane and a Jew? Who's practically Buck's age?!? It's a scream, that's what it is!

Sort of the same way they laughed off Baker's friend Juan, who accompanied Baker to the wedding. Connie kept referring to Baker and his new roommate, Juan, as "such good pals." Buck slapped Juan on the back a lot, and made sports references whenever he could. That Juan understood the sports stuff kept Buck satisfied. He didn't want to know anything more. Which was fine for all of them. No confrontations, no problems. Another round of drinks.

The whole thing happened too fast for Nancy. The wedding, the guests, the many new friends, the gifts, the honeymoon on Mustique, and the cell phones that never stopped ringing for Landon. She had to make him promise not to carry or answer one during the ceremony. Landon was starting his own agency, after realizing that to buy one would be less cost-effective. Instead, he was pillaging the existing agencies, stealing agents—and their biggest clients—for himself. It was very exciting for him, and all of Hollywood was abuzz over the new agency, which Landon was calling TGA—The Greene Agency. *Variety* and the *Hollywood Reporter* put the news on the front page with screaming headlines.

The wedding reception was alive with good wishes—for both the marriage and the business deal. Nancy accepted congratulations on both. She knew that being Landon's wife would entail this kind of thing. But after the guests had gone, she tried to get Landon's mind back on her and her alone. It didn't work. They island-hopped to Bimini and St. Kitts, then to Cap Juluca on Anguilla. Landon was enthralled. Nancy thought it was because of the wedding.

"I wish your parents could have made it," said Nancy, as she and Landon cuddled on the deck of the yacht they'd rented for the week.

"You do?" Landon asked, amused. "Why's that?"

"Because they're your parents," said Nancy. "It was your wedding. Your first and only wedding."

"Frankly," Landon said, "I'm glad they didn't come."

"How can you be so cold?" Nancy asked.

"Because they refused to come," said Landon.

Nancy sat up and looked at him.

"What do you mean?" she asked him. "I thought you said they were too sick to make the trip."

"Come on, Nance," said Landon. "They live in Miami. How difficult would it have been?"

"But you said—"

"I lied," said Landon. He saw Nancy look at him, confused and wounded.

"Is it because I'm not Jewish?" she asked.

"No!" He laughed, a tad too loudly. "Not at all."

"It is, isn't it?" said Nancy. "It's because I'm not Jewish."

He looked at her. She knew.

"I didn't want to hurt you," he explained, and got up to pace the deck.

"What are you talking about?" Nancy asked, her voice sounding small and young.

"I did invite them," he said.

"But—you said . . ."

"You were right. They wouldn't come because you're not Jewish," he said. "You're smart."

Nancy just made a noise. It was hurt and shock and disbelief. It came out like a poof. Like a little cloud escaping from her.

"Fuck 'em," said Landon. "They don't control me. Nobody controls me. I do what I want, when I want."

"Just because I'm not Jewish?" she asked, wide-eyed. She couldn't imagine . . . but then again, she didn't have to imagine.

He looked at her across the deck. His eyes were stormy.

"Do they want me to convert?" she offered. "Because I don't care. I will."

"Do you know my real name was Greenberg?"

"No," said Nancy. "Did they change it?"

"Yeah," said Landon with contempt. "You know why?"

"No," she said softly.

"Because they hate themselves. They didn't really want to be Greenbergs. They wanted to be Greenes. Because Greene is ambiguous. Greenberg isn't. Greenberg is what it is."

"I'll do whatever they want," said Nancy.

Landon turned on her angrily. "You'll do what I want—not what they want," he bellowed. "You belong to me. You're mine. Not theirs."

"I'm sorry," she said, and poured herself a drink. She needed to get drunk. Whenever something upset her, a little drink helped. Even with rehab behind her. She had more on her plate than any drug counselor could imagine. "I didn't mean to upset you."

"You didn't," he said, and tried to calm himself down. "You're perfect just the way you are."

She felt a little better. Landon walked over to her, and sat next to her.

"You're perfect," he said again, and kissed her sweetly. But the mood had changed.

When the trip finally, and abruptly, ended, Nancy and Landon went back to Los Angeles, and moved in together in his Wilshire Corridor condo. Landon lived in the penthouse of a twenty-eight-story building he owned on Wilshire. He'd had the three-story apartment decorated by a team of decorators one of his friends had used. There were no rough edges, no room for improvement. The condo was "done." Finished. Nancy was like the missing Barbie doll in Ken's Dream Palace. There was nothing for her to do. The cleaning, the cooking, the arrangements for parties or dinners—there was staff on hand to take care of everything. All Nancy had to do was be ready for the next adventure.

Seven

With Nancy behind him, Landon grew even stronger. He was ruthless and restless at business. He became even more of a master through his insatiable hunger for more and more.

He oversaw huge deals at TGA and quickly got to know all the studio executives and movie stars—the currency in this new part of his life. He bought the Peninsula Hotel so that he would have a place to hold court, and quickly became more widely known than ever.

Landon was enormously pleased with himself. His ego grew in direct proportion to his net worth. "Talent" stood in a long line to be represented by TGA, and then to get Landon's attention. He knew how to change careers and, therefore, lives. He could make a starlet into a star in seconds. But to his huge ego came not just the true talent, but also the wannabes. Women, loose and tight, flocked to him like never before.

Nancy was shocked at the blatant disregard women had for her marriage. She saw it with her own two eyes—cheap slutty trash would take his wedding-banded hand and shove it up their dresses. Landon thought it was all a joke and told Nancy not to take any of it seriously. He didn't, and she shouldn't either. But she did. Everybody around them—their "friends"—just laughed at the ridiculous situations Nancy and Landon were in—girls throwing themselves at Landon right in front of Nancy. They took their cues from Landon, though. When he laughed, they laughed. When Nancy frowned, and looked ready to cry, they looked to Landon to tacitly tell them what to do. He laughed, so they laughed, too. Nancy turned away and held her tears in. Until later, when she was alone.

It was hard for most people to feel sorry for Nancy. They saw her as an office temp who married a rich guy old enough to be her father. They saw her as wealthy through her marriage to Landon. If he wanted to misbehave, she was expected to look the other way. But she couldn't. She loved him. So she watched, and then she anesthetized herself.

"I'm sick of all the sluts," Nancy said to Landon as she threw her purse down on the sofa. It was 3:30 a.m., and they'd just come in from a party after a party after a party after a party. She was way past exhausted.

Landon headed for the liquor cabinet. He grabbed a bottle of tequila and slugged from it.

"Don't start with the vestal virgin act," he said, letting some tequila drip down his chin and onto his shirt.

"I'm not *acting*," she said, her voice rising. "I don't like it, that's all."

"You used to be fun," he said. "You used to be young."

"What?!"

Landon just walked away. He hated Nancy's dismay at the situation they were finding themselves in. The reason he had fallen for her was that she was always up for the latest—always on the edge. Since they'd gotten married he'd been uncomfortably aware of how she clung to him. He didn't know why she couldn't be a good wife and support his happiness like everyone else did. And just back off.

Nancy walked upstairs toward their bedroom, alone. She asked herself the same question: Why couldn't she let it go and just be happy? What was wrong with her? But she couldn't come up with an answer that let her rest. She didn't like what was happening. In fact, she hated it.

"And you could lay off the drinks yourself," she yelled down the stairs.

"Fuck you," he said, reappearing from a patio. "I'm not the one with the problem."

"It's not just the drugs, Landon," she said, softening a little. "It's the women. You don't act like a husband."

"This ain't the suburbs, babe," he yelled at her. "Welcome to Oz."

"Just tell them to back off. That's all I'm asking. I know it's not your fault. I just don't like it."

"Grow up," said Landon. "They don't mean anything to me."

"Well, they do to me," she said quietly and continued up the stairs to the bedroom, then shut the door. Landon didn't follow her.

"Get over it," he yelled, not caring if she heard him or not. She did. Through the bedroom door.

She stood there, hearing his words, *Get over it,* echo over and over in her head. She didn't want to go to bed angry. She didn't want Landon to go out. If he went out, she knew he wouldn't be in until the next night. She was going to solve the problem. There was at least one solution to every problem.

Nancy went into her two-room walk-in closet and put on her most alluring satin negligee, then she went to the kitchen and poured herself a glass of champagne. She quickly got a little bit drunk. She took the bottle and an extra glass down to Landon, who was smoking a joint in the living room. He was surprised to see her tipsy, with alcohol in hand.

"Well, well." He smiled evilly. This was different. "Well, well, well. What do we have here?"

"An apology." Nancy swallowed. Who cared if she didn't really mean it? The important thing was not to get in a fight with her husband.

Landon nodded, assessing the situation. Nancy stood there, feeling stupid, not sure if he was going to be nice to her or start yelling again.

"Want some?" Landon offered his joint to her.

"Sure." Nancy giggled. "Why not? What else could I do that's wrong?" she joked and walked toward him. She tripped over the ottoman, drunk.

Landon just laughed, and let Nancy get up without helping her. She made her way over to him. He offered no hand to help. She started to kiss and paw at him. He let her, watching her work at him, amused, until she had him fully aroused. Then he lowered her onto the sofa, pushing her silk negligee up, above her waist.

"I'm not using birth control," she whispered into Landon's ear right before he entered her.

"I'm too old to be a father." He laughed. "And you're a drunk."

"I want a baby."

Landon laughed harder now. "*You're* going to be a mother?"

"Sure." She smiled. "Why not? Don't you want a little, fuzzy baby?"

"Not especially," said Landon, pumping her with more fervor.

"We can move out of this penthouse," she said, paying more attention to her decorating plans than the sex they were having. "We can get a big house with a yard."

Landon didn't say anything.

"We can get a dog," she said. "You like dogs, don't you?"

Landon didn't answer. He couldn't. He was getting ready to finish.

"I told you when you proposed to me. I told you I wanted children and a house. It was part of the deal."

The deal. He would've smiled if he could've.

"Whatever you want," he said as he climaxed.

Nancy left Landon passed out on the sofa. She went to the bathroom and threw away her birth control. She felt better. This could be her project. This one would be all hers.

Eight

Eve opened the *Los Angeles Times* Classifieds section. She sat on the floor of her Studio City apartment. It was empty. She couldn't afford furniture. The former tenant had left a mattress. Eve adopted it as her bed. The apartment had one bedroom, a tiny bathroom, and the second room was living room and kitchen all rolled into one. Its windows faced a driveway and a ten-car garage structure that was for the cars of the tenants in her building. Eve's Camry sat in its appointed space in the structure. The apartment was noisy and it was hot, but it was hers. Now all she needed was a job.

She knew she'd get something. Especially when she opened the newspaper and saw pages and pages of help-wanted ads. Eve liked work, and whatever she chose as a job would redefine her life. Hell, anything at this point would redefine her life. She was happy.

She scanned the columns, looking for her new profession. Electrician, dentist, engineer. Not realistic. Insurance sales. Not what she had in mind. Counselor. Camp? Cosmetic P/T, Avon. Nah. She needed full-time—F/T Driver. She'd had enough driving. Lamps Plus. Maybe. Her heart beat faster. She felt that by picking one of these ads, she would send her life hurtling in one of thousands of different directions. Fate at her fingertips, and no idea where to call first. Finally, like more than half of unemployed Los Angeles, Eve decided on "REST—Gourmet Italian Rest." A waitressing job.

Eve called and was told to come in for an interview. Pins and needles excitement. She drove to the restaurant on Ventura Boulevard in Burbank. It was called Gianni's, and it looked fine. Nothing fancy. Nothing she couldn't handle. She opened the door. It was heavier than it looked, and she suddenly had to support the door with her body to get it open. As it closed behind her, Eve had trouble adjusting her eyes to the darkness.

"Thank God, you're legal!"

That was all she heard. Everything was black. She squinted and walked in the direction of the man's voice.

"I'm Gianni." He got up, his chair scratching the floor, and walked closer to her. She began to see whole figures. Gianni had big, black, bushy eyebrows, a stubbly chin. He had a strong handshake, thick fingers, fleshy palm, hairy forearm that brushed her hand. And he smelled good. Not like aftershave, but like Italian food. Fresh-baked bread.

Gianni went back to where he had been sitting at a table by the kitchen. There were red-and-white-checked tablecloths. Dark wood chairs. A bar with old-fashioned bar chairs. Dark wood walls and red lanterns that gave the place the feeling of a cave. Nothing like Gladstone's, the first place she'd been.

Noise was coming from the kitchen. Yelling in Mexican. Yelling in Italian. Pans banging. Something sizzling on a griddle. Gianni was eating his lunch alone in the restaurant. He didn't invite Eve to sit down.

"You have a social security card?" he asked with his mouth full of food.

"Yes," she said, surprised at this question. She stood, playing with her shoulder bag strap.

"Driver's license? Clean record? No accidents? Insurance?"

"Yes," said Eve. "I just drove all the way from Las Vegas. Not a dent."

"Good," he said, and sat down to eat the salad on the table in front of him. It was oily and full of sliced meat. Gianni was only a little older than Eve, but he was different. Mature. In charge. "Sometimes I need you to make deliveries."

That hadn't been what Eve had expected, but she didn't get a chance to object.

"I'll need a map," she said, hesitantly.

"Good. When can you start?"

"Right away," said Eve. This was happening so fast.

"Good," he said. "Come in tonight. Five o'clock. I'll have Lisa train you. She's my sister."

"Thank you," said Eve.

"You have a phone, right?" Gianni asked. Salad dressing dripped from his stubbly chin. He wiped it with a paper napkin.

"Yes," said Eve. "Just got it."

"Good," said Gianni. "Leave me your number, and come tonight. Wear black pants and a white T-shirt. You have that?"

"I'll get it," said Eve.

"Go to the Gap," said Gianni. "It's cheaper. I'll start you at $7.50 an hour. Plus tips."

Eve nodded. She was trying to figure out in her head how many hours she would have to work to pay her rent and have some money left over for other things, when Gianni got up and took his plate into the kitchen.

"Go home," he said. "You'll need the rest. You have salt?"

"Salt?"

"Salt. Kosher salt. Fat salt. Get some. You put it in the bathtub. Turn on the water—very hot. After work, you soak your feet. Keeps away the calluses. You got kosher salt?"

"I don't have calluses," said Eve.

"You will," said Gianni. "After tonight, you will."

Eve had not been expecting this kind of advice.

"Go!" he said, as he himself got up and took his dishes into the kitchen. "And take one of those applications by the door. Fill it out, bring it back at five."

Eve obeyed. She walked back outside. The midmorning sun glared. White bright. But nowhere near as hot and oppressive as the desert in Vegas. This was a fabulous hot. This was hopeful and bright. She had a life. A job, an apartment. . . . She went to the Gap, whistling all the way. When she paid for her clothes, the clerk hesitated before handing her her change.

"Do you need a job?" the man asked. He was wearing the same clothes that were sold in the store.

"Me?" Eve was shocked to hear this. She didn't expect to be offered two jobs in one day.

"You'd be perfect," he said. "You have the look and a great attitude. And I really need someone on the floor."

"I just got a job," she said proudly.

"All the good ones get taken," he sighed as he handed her the change.

"Thanks," said Eve. "Thanks a lot." She walked across the floor, then turned, happier than anyone could possibly be, and waved hard to the guy. "Goodbye! I'll be back!"

It was a very good day. Los Angeles was better than she'd expected. She was happy and excited.

Eve barely had time to drive home, try to call her parents in Vegas, realize the phone still wasn't connected, go out and find a corner pay phone, call GTE, wait on hold, hang up, call again, get disconnected, call again, tell the operator the problem, go home and realize it was time to leave for work, wash up, get dressed, and turn right around to start her first day.

"Hey, new girl," Lisa greeted her that night. Tall and dark like her brother, with a long ponytail down the length of her back, Lisa was also direct and in charge. "I'm Lisa. What's your name?"

"It's Eve," said Eve, as Lisa pulled her into the kitchen by the arm.

"You're right on time," said Lisa. "That's good."

Lisa looked Eve up and down. "And you got the uniform right. Two things." She handed Eve an ordering pad and an apron. "Lotta flakes in this town. It's a sad day when being on time and getting dressed puts you ahead of the game."

With Lisa's help over the next few days, Eve got the hang of the basics of waitressing pretty quickly. But the pace was something she hadn't been prepared for. The restaurant filled up like a flood twice a day, at lunchtime and for three hours at dinner. The chef kept his head down and his hands moving, making pizzas, pastas, and sauces. Eve made salads for a while. That was easy. The waiting on tables part was tough. Until they got their wine and their beer, the patrons—mostly studio executives, Lisa told Eve, and a good thing, as they charged everything to the studios—were impatient. They wanted everything specially ordered.

"No eggplant."

"Hold the salami."

"More ice."

"No ice."

"What year is the merlot?"

"I think this fork is dirty."

Gianni and Lisa ran the restaurant that had once belonged to their now elderly parents. They were kind, and they worked hard. They were also thrilled to have Eve. She was quiet, didn't complain, and caught on quickly.

"I can't believe you didn't go to college," said Lisa, sipping a glass of wine during a lull one afternoon between the lunch and dinner rush.

"I never thought about it," said Eve.

Lisa looked darkly at her over the rim of her glass.

"You're like Alice," said Lisa.

"Did she work here?" said Eve.

"Alice in Wonderland," said Lisa. "You ever read that book?"

"Not really," Eve admitted. "But I think I know the story."

"Lotta people who read it say it's about drugs," said Lisa. "But I think it's about this town."

"I like it here," said Eve, smiling broadly. She looked around at the kitchen, the whole restaurant, at Lisa, her new friend. "I like it a lot."

In time Eve began to notice the regulars. The suits were the studio executives. The talent were the actors, flamboyantly dressed. They usually had detailed grooming. Bright colored glasses. High heels. And the more successful they were, the less flamboyantly they dressed. TV actors were flashier than movie stars. The writers looked unemployed, depressed, and wore blue jeans and unkempt hair. The producers wore jackets and carried cell phones, which they liked to use a lot.

But there was one table—the worst table in the restaurant, back by the kitchen door. It was dark, noisy, and the regular table of one man who kept Eve on edge. He wore blue jeans, T-shirt, suede bomber jacket. And when he took the jacket off, Eve could see that he worked out.

He always ordered the same thing. Linguini with clams. Linguini with clams. Linguini with clams. He varied the water. Always bottled, but sometimes sparkling, sometimes flat. Never touched the bread. Never had dessert. And never left when he finished. He always lingered. Until almost everyone else had gone. She kept looking at him, and he kept looking at her. Every time he came in.

He didn't chat or make small talk with the waiters. He just ate and then read. Newspapers, books. Sometimes he read handwritten notes. Sometimes typed notes. Sometimes he jotted things down. But he always sat in the same place, at the table in the back.

"Who's that?" Eve asked Lisa. "He comes in every day at lunch."

"Mr. Evanston," said Lisa. "He's a regular."

Eve was surprised that Lisa referred to him so formally.

"Hey, you have a boyfriend?" Lisa asked.

"No," said Eve. "Do you?"

"Yeah," said Lisa. "I met him *out* of the restaurant."

"Oh," said Eve. Lisa's meaning was not lost on Eve. "I get it."

Lisa fidgeted. "The men who come in here," she said, "they're customers first."

"Fine," said Eve, nodding. "Of course."

"Mr. Evanston's a good customer. We're a small restaurant. We can't afford to lose good customers. You understand, new girl?"

Eve turned bright red.

"Just don't date the customers," said Lisa. "They don't want waitresses anyway. They're all married to rich girls who went to college. You don't want to lose your job over one of these guys."

"No! I don't want to lose my job," said Eve. "Lisa—I would never—I didn't mean to—I was just curious."

"Yeah," said Lisa, lighting up a cigarette. "That's how it starts. Curious."

"I love my job here," said Eve. "I love you and Gianni. I understand the rules, and don't worry. I won't date any of the customers."

"Hey, new girl, why don't you come out with me and my boyfriend. We'll set you up. Blind date. It'll be fun."

"No, thanks," said Eve. "I don't think so."

"I promise to fix you up with someone cute."

"No," said Eve. "I'm fine. But I do have one question."

"Yeah? What's that?"

"When do I stop being 'new girl' and start being Eve?"

Lisa smiled. They were gonna be just fine.

After six months of working eight- and ten-hour shifts, sleeping alone in her hot, muggy Studio City apartment, and hitting the beach on weekends with a book she never read, Eve began to think about men. Not boys. Men.

She'd had a boyfriend in high school, and had dated a few guys before and after him, but this was different. She felt lonely. She started to let herself dream of having a boyfriend to complete the picture. Sometimes she even let herself fantasize about having a husband and a family. The kind of family she saw in magazine articles where everyone smiled and lived in homes with swimming pools that were built into the ground—not the above-ground, plastic ones her neighbors in Vegas had.

Dating for sport wasn't in the picture. She'd seen her brothers do it. They'd go wherever they thought they could get sex the fastest, and they'd stay as long as they had the sex, or until something better came along. No, she wasn't interested in that kind of thing.

The months continued to pass and Eve spent her nineteenth

birthday soaking her feet in saltwater in her tub. She called her family on the phone.

"Hi, Mama."

"I wanted to call you first," said Betty.

"Next year," said Eve.

"Happy birthday," said Betty. "Happy birthday, baby."

"Thanks," said Eve. She swished her feet around.

"What time is it there?" Betty asked.

"It's one hour earlier."

"Oh," said Betty, confused. "One hour earlier?"

"It's seven o'clock," said Eve. She was tired and frustrated.

"Well, it's eight o'clock here," said Betty, amazed.

"I know, Mama," said Eve. "One hour later where you are."

"You sure it's seven where you are?"

"I have to go," said Eve. She needed to get off the phone, or she would snap. She had called her mother hoping to get some satisfaction. But the call didn't do it. And that it didn't, made her mad.

"You have big plans tonight?" her mother asked.

"Soak my feet and wash my hair," said Eve. "And call you up."

"You know," said Betty, "you can always come home."

"Thanks," said Eve. It wasn't what she had wanted to hear. At all.

"What time is it now?" asked Betty. " 'Cause it's eight-eleven here."

Eve hung up and cried. Alone in her bathroom, barefoot and nineteen.

The phone rang. It was Lisa.

"Eve, Carlos is sick. Can you come in and take his shift?" Lisa asked.

Eve sighed. Working on her birthday.

"Sure," said Eve. Why not? What else was she going to do? She went in, worked the shift, and, dead tired, fought back tears.

"Tough day?"

Eve was leaning against the back wall of the restaurant. She wasn't sure who had spoken. It was Mr. Evanston. The man at the table for one was talking to her. First time. She sniffed back her tears.

"It's my birthday," said Eve.

"Well, happy birthday," he said.

"Thanks," said Eve. She wanted to stay and talk, but remembered her warning from Lisa. She walked back to the kitchen.

"Buy you a birthday drink?"

She turned and took a good look at him. The sparkle in his eye. He held up a glass of water, inviting her to join him. He had a head full of hair so thick, it looked like a gray mop. At this moment, it was hanging over one eye. He looked like a contented puppy dog.

"Thanks," she said. "But I couldn't. Not while I'm working."

She said the last sentence without her thinking. Once out, she realized it sounded like a bit of an invitation. A way to continue their conversation elsewhere. Later. After-hours. She immediately blushed.

"I understand," he said, and drank the water himself. Then turned back to his table. His food. His book. His life. Without her.

She stared at him wistfully. Her blush disappeared. Just like the conversation. She walked back to the kitchen and spent the rest of the evening working, with what felt like a sliver of a splinter in her heart. As if now, something was in there, and she couldn't get it out. She was mad at herself. She'd left Las Vegas, and for what? To be a waitress? With no future? Big step up, new girl, she thought to herself. She'd had enough guts to pack up and leave the state where she was born. Why couldn't she get herself out of this rut? She'd gone from one rut to the next. She tortured herself with thoughts of "what if." What if she'd joined Mr. Evanston for a drink? What if she'd sat down at his table? What if she'd continued the conversation instead of cutting it off?

After that night, Eve couldn't work without looking to see if Mr. Evanston had come in. If he was at his table. If she could catch his eye. She began to really take notice of him.

He never harassed the waiters like so many other customers did when their orders didn't come exactly the way they wanted. And there was something about him. It wasn't his walk, his clothes, his looks. It was something beneath the surface.

He had an edge. Eve could see it just beneath the surface. A little flame of angst inside him that stayed on, like a pilot light in a stove. Eve recognized it because she had the same light. The light that fueled her move west; the same light that got her to muster all her courage to talk to him again.

He looked surprised when she spoke an entire sentence, complete with subject and verb, instead of just a noncommittal "Hi."

"Do you want some more clams?" Eve asked. "Linguini?"

He had stood to leave. He looked down at his empty plate. He'd eaten every bit of food there. He smiled at her, amused that she would think he wanted seconds.

"Or juice?" she said. "Do you ever go out—I mean, out of here, and get juice?"

He squinted at her, trying to figure out this angel in an apron.

Eve squirmed uncomfortably. This was the first time in her life she had ever attempted to ask a man out. She knew this wasn't how it was supposed to go. Not this badly. He was giving her nothing. No visible response.

"You know," she said, as if he didn't understand. "Juice . . . from fruit. . . ."

She was dying. Why couldn't he answer her? Why wouldn't he stop staring at her? Why couldn't she behave normally? He finally turned his back to her and walked away. She felt like she'd been shot. Put out of her misery, and left alone to die.

"Forget it," she said. She should never have done this. It was against the rules. She would probably be fired. "Never mind."

She took her pad and tray and headed to the waiter station near the bar to find some work, so no one would see how red her face was with humiliation. She was looking down, wiping a thick wineglass for spots when she heard a voice behind her.

"I don't drink juice."

She whipped around. He was standing there. She'd only ever seen him walk in, take his table, and walk out. Never had she been so close to him. He was practically whispering. Eve felt the breath from his words on her face.

"Oh." She had to look up to see his face. He was so tall. Standing very, very close to her. Giving more thought to juice than juice warranted.

Eve was instantly reduced to adolescence. She could almost feel the braces growing onto her teeth, poking the soft part of her mouth. Gouging her flesh. Making her crave the little white plastic box of wormlike wax. Relief to be applied to the prickly steel braces that kept her teeth where they were supposed to be, not where they wanted to be. The sweat on the back of her neck, and under her armpits. Twelve-year-old armpits with the faintest, thinnest hairs beginning to grow. Hints of womanhood. Hints of adult life. Hairs slashed away with a used plastic razor, stolen from Mom's shower, stolen from Dad's shaving supply shelf. Fine twelve-year-old skin shorn with a dull razor. Red streaks, chafed by sweat borne of anxiety about a boy being so close he might touch or smell you. Armpits caked with Secret deodorant that wasn't working like the ads promised. Because of this: the mere vision of the empty Coke bottle someone glibly produced. The bottle that meant way more than someone having quenched a thirst. That bottle meant a game of spin the bottle. Kissing someone for the first time. In public. Under scrutiny. Emotions battling—wanting to be kissed, but not like this!

Stop it!

Eve shook herself, mentally, from her tangle of past emotions. This was different. At least she and this man, Mr. Evanston, were having a conversation. He had come back and answered her.

"Hey, Eve!"

Eve whipped her head around. It was Lisa.

"We got customers."

Lisa frowned at Eve and nodded toward the door, where two men with *Variety* and the *Hollywood Reporter* under their arms had just walked in and were waiting to be seated.

"Customers," Eve said to Mr. Evanston, and she left him. Eve went to seat the men. When she had done that, she turned to look, but he was gone. Like a former apparition. Eve looked everywhere in the restaurant, with one clumsy pirouette of her body. He was not there.

For the first time since she got to Los Angeles, Eve felt depressed. Like she'd lost something.

Bad thoughts came like a flash flood. What did she think she could do here? What did she really think? She wasn't being honest with herself. The truth was she wanted more than just a job and her own apartment. She was chasing a dream coming out here. Like Cinderella, hoping she could marry a prince and become part of royal society and escape the gas stations and the arid, barren desert she came from. But why should any prince notice her? Whether she was pumping gas or answering phones, it was all the same. She was just a girl with nothing special to offer. She worked hard. Big deal.

She finished her shift, said her goodbyes, accepted without a word Lisa's glare for having engaged a good customer in conversation, and went out to the parking lot.

A black cloud was hanging over Eve, when she heard someone say, "How do you feel about red meat?"

Eve looked up. He was there. At a pay phone. One hand on the receiver. He held up one finger for her to wait while he finished the call. Then he hung up and, carrying his cell phone in one hand, came out of the pay phone and over to her.

"Why do you use the pay phone if you have one of those?" she asked, pointing at his cell phone.

He looked surprised to realize he actually had a cell phone in his hand.

"Oh," he said, considering the tiny phone. "Well, it doesn't get great reception. And I like the booths."

"Phone booths?"

"Yeah," he said, looking back at the booth wistfully. "I like the privacy. It's like a hug—a phone booth. It's warm. Close."

Eve blushed.

"So, red meat. . . ." He left his words hanging there.

"You mean, like, hamburgers?" This time she was calm and he was the one who looked skittish.

"I was actually thinking more of meat loaf," he said. "What do you think about meat loaf?"

"Sure," she said, thinking that she'd maybe made a mistake approaching this guy in the first place. He was cute, but he was weird. What did all this talk about beef mean, anyway?

"I know this place in Venice that makes great meat loaf and mashed potatoes," he said, staring at her. "It's not new, but it's, you know . . ."

Eve wished he'd finish his thought. He was obviously trying to ask her out, and this was getting painful for her. She wanted him to put her out of her misery.

"Consistent."

She nodded.

"You know," he went on, looking uncomfortable, "I'm older than nineteen." He seemed to be apologizing for his age.

She giggled.

"Quite a bit older."

"I know," she said.

"My name's Fuller, and I've never been married," he said, looking out at her from under big brows, tucking his chin into his neck, slowly, giving her the chance to reject him.

"Me either," she said.

He bit his lip, trying to find a way to say what he needed to say to convey what he wanted her to understand.

"A lot of people—women—consider that a black mark," he said. "Like there's something wrong with you."

Eve nodded.

"I'm forty," he said.

"I thought we were just talking about meat loaf," said Eve. She scrunched up her forehead. She didn't understand at all. . . . It was like he was disclosing deep, dark secrets, but, to her, they didn't seem so terrible.

His face lightened. Brightened. He loved this girl—right away. A lot.

"You're right," he said, laughing. "We were. Just meat loaf. So, would you like to have dinner with me?" He squinted, as if to brace himself for her rejection.

Eve flushed from head to toe. At last. A real date. Her first one in Los Angeles. The Spin the Bottle memory faded fast, replaced by this new one.

"Yes, I would."

"Great," said Fuller, letting out a huge breath. "I'll pick you up tonight?"

"Tonight?" Eve seemed surprised.

"You're not busy, are you?" Fuller asked, suddenly nervous again. "On such short notice?"

Eve wasn't sure if he was feeling like maybe he'd gotten the booby prize or not. After all, a popular girl would be busy already.

"Well, actually, I am," Eve lied.

"Oh. . . ."

"But I'll cancel." Eve smiled.

"Okay," said Fuller. "Then, seven?"

"Seven is perfect."

Nine

Eve wasn't sure what to wear for an evening that featured meat loaf and mashed potatoes. At an old, consistent restaurant, no less. Hell, it was probably a diner or a coffee shop. A hamburger joint. A hole in the wall. She probably shouldn't even be worrying about what to wear, but she wanted this to be the kind of date where one worried about appearance. Damn.

She hated herself for thinking this way. For convoluting things. For wanting them to be something, then feeling badly for wanting it, then compensating, then agonizing. She laughed at herself, and calmed down.

Just stop thinking, she thought.

Fuller was just some guy. The first in a string of dates she would eventually have in Los Angeles. She would have to kiss a tankful of toads before she found a prince. She was only nineteen, and Fuller was toad number one. There would be a toad two, toad three, and toad four, no doubt. Just get through this night, she told herself. Eat the meat loaf, kiss him on the lips, and pretend to have a boyfriend that just came back into town if he asks for a second date.

The doorbell rang. Eve panicked. None of her calming thoughts worked. She opened the door.

Fuller stood there. In blue jeans, a white shirt, and a sport coat. Eve thought he looked great. She had hoped he would be wearing a tie and a suit. But why would he wear a tie to go to a coffee shop? He's just a guy, she thought to herself. And you, new girl, are just a gal.

"Do you want to come in?" she asked.

Fuller peeked in and looked around from the doorway. Eve's apartment was a standard-issue 1950s boxy one-bedroom, decorated with throwaways and cheap stuff. He'd seen this kind of place a million times, and he had no interest in seeing it again. It depressed him.

"Nope," he said. "Not really."

"It's not much . . ." she apologized. "I mean, I just got into town and . . ." What could she say? This was the most she could afford. It was the best she could do. "The truth is, I put down a deposit on this place in the Colony, up in Malibu, you know? Where all the stars live?"

"I've heard of it," said Fuller, knowing she was just playing with him. "It's a real dive."

"Oh, not my place," Eve joked. "It's real big. Right on the beach."

"Beachfront property?" He smirked. "Insurance must've been a bitch."

"It was," she said. "I'm moving in next week, after they paint the place. This was all that was available.''

"Real estate is brutal. Now, come on, let's go," he said, taking the steps down, three at a time.

Eve stood there. She wondered if she didn't follow him, if he'd just keep on going without her.

"You coming?" she heard his voice call from the bottom of the stairwell. He was waiting for her.

"Yup," she said, and shut the door and followed him out. When she got to the bottom of the stairs, she stopped. What a picture. There was Fuller, looking tall and sleek, holding open the door to a black Porsche convertible for her. She had to stop and pinch herself.

"Nice car," said Eve. "I never noticed it in the parking lot at Gianni's."

"I don't drive this one during the day," he said. "It gives the wrong impression."

"You're parked illegally." He was in a red zone.

"Then, let's go before I get a ticket."

"This is my first date in Los Angeles," she said as she buckled her seat belt.

"I wish you hadn't said that."

"Why not?" she asked.

"That's a lot of pressure to put on a guy."

"Don't worry." She laughed. "I don't expect much from you."

"Oh, great," he said with a laugh. "Thanks a lot. Then I guess I'm all set."

The freeways were jam-packed. It took almost an hour to get to Venice. As they got off the freeway and drove the surface streets, Eve began to get worried. The neighborhoods were looking bad. Scary. Graffiti. A gang on the corner. Why was he taking her to such a bad neighborhood?

They pulled up to what looked like an industrial building and left the car with the valet parker. Half a block away, Eve could see the beach. And the homeless, the vagrants, and the artists who were walking on the wild side at night on the boardwalk in Venice.

"Hope you're hungry," said Fuller. He'd been quiet on the ride over. He held the restaurant door open for her. It was a giant door with the number 72 on it.

"Where are we?" asked Eve.

"Seventy-two Market Street," he said, with one hand on her

back, guiding Eve inside. "I don't like the trendy, new places."

The restaurant was filled with people, all casually dressed and intent on their conversations. Eve noticed lots of wire-framed and big, chunky black-framed glasses on the people. This place was nothing like Gianni's and nothing like the Vegas she'd known.

The front room was cavernous and minimal. Three metal sculptures hung from the ceiling. Fuller and Eve walked into the back room. Three giant abstract paintings hung on each of three walls. The fourth wall was opaque glass. You could see the bodies moving behind it, but couldn't make out the details. A pianist played a grand piano at the front of the room. This was nothing like the coffee shop Eve had envisioned for their date.

All of a sudden, Eve realized that she had been completely wrong about Fuller. He wasn't the coffee shop type at all. He was totally different.

They sat down and ordered. The linen tablecloth felt wonderful under her hands. Eve didn't ever remember eating on a table with a clean, white cloth. Formica under her hands was familiar. But not linen. And nothing like this. She felt like Cinderella—all these glasses. Water, wine, and a third glass that she couldn't quite figure out. Candlelight, bread with a pool of golden olive oil instead of pats of butter. Crudités with an avocado garlic dip instead of the only other dip she'd ever had—the one made with onion soup mix. Fuller was right.

"I told you," he said. "I told you it's the best."

"Are you always right?" she asked him.

"I have pretty good instincts," he said. "How about you?"

"I don't know," she said, smiling. "I haven't really made a lot of mistakes, but I haven't really done much yet."

Fuller squinted at her, quietly examining again.

"What?" she said, feeling self-conscious and naked. "What?"

"I have a feeling," he said slowly, "that all that is about to change."

Eve found herself falling in love with Fuller as he studied the wine list, choosing the best wine to suit their meal. To suit their evening. She loved his expertise and his quiet confidence. She watched him flip page after page of wines. He was familiar with this sort of thing. Wine lists. Fast cars. First dates.

Fuller was taking care of everything with such ease. She was drunk with happiness and excitement before she'd even touched a drop of the wine he chose.

"What is it, exactly, that you do?" she asked.

"I write, and I direct."

Eve took a quick breath.

"Shit," she said. Then she quickly covered her mouth. She hadn't meant to curse, but it had just come out.

"What?" he asked, concerned. "Don't tell me you don't date industry people. I should have told you up front. I just figured you knew—I mean, I did a little acting in some movies, I thought you might have recognized me." He laughed to himself. "What an ass I am."

"What's 'industry'?"

Fuller looked hard at Eve. She wasn't joking. "Oh boy," he said. "You really don't know what 'industry' means?"

Eve shook her head.

"Entertainment."

Eve nodded, waiting for more. She didn't understand.

"I'm not like the others," he said. "Well, all right, maybe I am. But I don't think so—not really. I don't know."

Fuller started talking and kept on going. He talked about his life in a way he hadn't done in a long, long time. He wasn't sure why he was doing it at that moment, but he couldn't stop. He was on automatic pilot. He told her how he was feeling burned out. He'd written and directed some minor hits and minor flops, and he felt like inside he was a fireball who was living a mediocre life. And he didn't want to be.

"It's like I'm driving, and I just can't shift into the right gear," he said. "And I love driving, but I can't do it right, and it's frustrating the hell out of me."

"I know exactly what you mean," she said. "Well, not exactly, but I feel the same way."

"You do?"

He knew he'd been right about her. He knew his instincts were on target. This girl—this young woman. She was the one for him. He held back the delirious happiness he felt. He'd been on hundreds of dates in his life, and this was different. There was an ease and an understanding between them that he'd never felt on any other date.

Eve became much more relaxed. Fuller was interesting and funny, and he talked to her as if they were equals. Just two people. They had very different life experiences, but it didn't matter. They had the same feelings.

"When was the last time you were in the right gear?" she asked. "I mean, driving, life, you know. . . ."

This time Fuller stopped cold. He looked surprised. First at the question, and then at her.

"What?" she said. "What did I say? Is there food on my shirt?" She was afraid she'd said or done the wrong thing.

"No, no, it's a good question," he said.

"Oh." Eve was a little relieved.

"It's a really good question."

"Well, when *was* the last time you were in the right gear?" she asked again, loosening up a little more. "When was the last time you can remember things feeling right?"

"You know," he said, thinking deeply. "I don't know." He shook his head in disbelief. "I can't remember."

"I don't think I've ever been in the right gear," said Eve. "It's not like anything's ever been terrible. You know . . . nobody molested me. Nobody died in my arms when I was, like, six or anything."

Fuller laughed. She had perspective and a sense of where she was in the world.

"You know what I mean?" she asked. "Those are truly terrible things. And none of those happened to me. So, I don't want to be complaining, but still . . . I feel like there's more that I want, and I don't have it. I don't even know if I can say what it is."

"I know exactly what you mean," he said. "But I have a feeling that deep down, you do know."

"I just always had this feeling of not being where I was supposed to be," Eve went on. "That's why I came here. The drive across the desert was the closest I felt to doing the right thing at the right time."

"Did you leave a boyfriend?" he asked.

"No," she said. "I'm just nineteen."

"Please don't make me feel old," he teased.

"How could I leave someone at nineteen?" she asked, and again, he marveled at her sense of who she was. Her sense of herself. "I mean, how could I *really* leave someone?"

Fuller stared into her eyes. Looking at something she didn't think she saw when she looked in the mirror.

"You're so mature," he said. "And you're also so . . ."

"Young?"

"No," he said.

"Inexperienced?"

"Not really."

"Unsophisticated?"

"I'll be the writer," he said.

She laughed.

"I can't think of the word," he said. "But it's different. That's what you are."

Eve smiled to herself as she remembered that less than an hour ago she had considered ditching Fuller with the excuse that an old boyfriend had come back to town. Now she was having such a wonderful time.

"Did you leave someone?" she asked him. "A girlfriend?"

Fuller didn't answer. He picked up his fork and started eating. Pensively. Uh-oh.

"Someone serious?" Eve asked.

Fuller swigged his wine, finishing the glass in one gulp. A waiter was watching and rushed over to refill his glass. When the waiter left, Fuller took another swig.

"Amanda Marinetta," he said.

Eve almost died. She knew that name. Amanda Marinetta was an actress! A movie star! Eve had seen Amanda Marinetta in *People* magazine. She'd seen her in movies. She'd seen her on television.

As Fuller talked about his relationship with Amanda, all Eve could think about was that Fuller knew this woman, he'd lived with her! Dated her—just the way he was beginning to date Eve. Maybe he'd even taken her to this same restaurant in the same car, ordered the same food—slept with her! Eve's heart raced. If Fuller had been so intimate with Amanda, what would he expect of her? She took a long drink of water. Her hands shook.

"We were playing house," Fuller said. "I mean, I loved her, but I wasn't in love with her. I didn't respect her. Not enough."

"You didn't respect her, but you lived with her?"

"I didn't respect her . . ." Fuller stopped.

"Finish," Eve commanded.

"I didn't respect her enough to marry her and have a family."

Eve held out her glass for more wine. At first attentive, Fuller had lost himself in the conversation.

"I guess that's something I want."

This was becoming all too much for Eve. Just a year ago she was pumping gas in torn jeans and a dirty T-shirt. And here she was having dinner in a fancy restaurant with a director who almost married a movie star. What was she doing? Whose life was she living? She had no business here. She began to feel faint.

"I'll be right back," Eve said, and stood. Fuller had been in

the middle of a sentence, but it didn't matter. Eve was overwhelmed. She left the table and started to head for the bathroom.
She had to get away, splash some water on her face, and get out
of this lie. Because that's what it was. She bumped into a chair—
the person in the chair turned to look at her.

"I'm sorry," said Eve. She walked across the room, more
quickly. She was sure everyone was looking at her. She started
to feel sweat on her forehead and under her armpits.

A big, bald man with a handlebar mustache, and wearing the
largest tuxedo Eve had ever seen, walked in front of her, narrowly
missing a personal collision. He put his hand on her back as he
passed, to guide her out of harm's way. Eve stopped. Just stood
there in the middle of the restaurant. She watched the bald, tux-
edoed man walk to the shiny grand piano in the front of the
restaurant. He sat down and began to play. Debussy. Eve was
hypnotized. The music, the restaurant talk, the clinking glasses,
the kitchen noise in the far background. The pianist looked over
at her and winked. The wink snapped her out of her daze. Eve
felt the blood return to her body. She looked around.

Fuller was watching her from across the room. His gaze was
attentive, with a slightly concerned look she was beginning to
recognize as solely his. Eve took a deep breath and forged ahead,
toward the bathroom. She opened the door to go in, but fell forward because someone from inside the bathroom opened it at the
same time, to come out. It was a man.

"Oh, excuse me," she said. "I thought this was the ladies'
room. I'm so sorry."

"It is," said the man. "Men's, too. What's the big difference
once you're in there?"

She double-checked the back of the door, but it just said POW-
DER ROOM. She walked inside the bathroom for one, locked the
door, and tried the doorknob just in case. She didn't want any
unexpected visitors. She was having just about all the excitement
she could handle for one evening without being barged in on.

The bathroom decor was cold, damp cement with exposed,
shiny silver plumbing. She splashed water on her face and looked
in the mirror. Yup, still Eve Carmelina. The girl she knew. She
wouldn't let herself down. She was going to be fine. She left the
bathroom, walked back to Fuller, and sat back down.

"I'm telling you too much," he said. "I'm sorry. I'm so used
to actresses—you know, I didn't even ask—are you?"

"What?"

"An actress?"

"No," said Eve. "No! I'm a waitress. You know that."

"See," Fuller said, smiling delightedly. "I knew it. I knew you were different. I'm not used to this, either."

"Me, either," she said.

"You'll have to forgive me. I don't usually spill my guts like this. At least not until the second date."

They smiled together.

"I want to hear more."

"You sure?"

"Yes."

Eve listened as Fuller continued. She didn't touch the rest of her meat loaf. She was fascinated and completely attracted to Fuller. If an earthquake took place during their dinner, Eve wouldn't have noticed. She couldn't take her eyes off him.

They drove home in his Porsche without speaking. The convertible top was down and the sounds enveloped them. The passing car radios blaring in and fading out, the ocean roaring along the coast, a coyote howling in the canyons. The movement, the sounds, the wind in her face and hair all hypnotized her. Eve hardly remembered the ride. It seemed like all of a sudden they were at her doorstep, and it felt as if they'd taken a long journey together.

Fuller took her hand, and looked down at her fingers. Long, thin fingers. Nails unpolished and short, round, and natural. He studied her hands for a while. Eve felt the heat from his hands holding hers. They were large, smooth underneath and a little hairy on top.

All of a sudden they were both giddy.

"What?" Eve laughed. "What's so funny?"

"I feel better," he said, his laughter subsiding. He looked into her eyes, still holding her hands in his.

"I probably won't need to see you for at least another two weeks, I feel so great," Fuller told her, laughing. "But how about tomorrow? What are you doing tomorrow?"

"Tomorrow?!" Eve almost yelped. She was pleased that he wanted to see her so soon.

"Don't tell me you have to work."

"I have to work."

"I told you not to tell me that," he said.

"I don't lie." Eve smiled, then added, "Not well, anyway."

"I know," he said and put her hands against his heart and held them there. Eve could hardly breathe. "Thank you for a wonderful evening."

"Aren't I supposed to say that?"

"Only if you want," he said.

"Everything was perfect. Except . . ."

"What?"

"Nothing," she said. But he wouldn't let up.

"Is this where you tell me you've been tested and you're positive?" he asked.

Now it was her turn to be shocked. "Tested?"

"For herpes? Some venereal thing? You're married?" he asked. "What is it?"

"Oh, please," she said. "God, should I ask you those things? I didn't even think about them."

"If you want, you can," he said, "but you'll be satisfied with all the answers."

"Okay, well, good."

"Wait, don't tell me—you have a string of convicted felonies in your past?"

"No!" she yelled. "I'm not like that."

"You have kids in there—quintuplets. Are they in the closet or under the bed?"

"Will you please stop," she pleaded, laughing.

"Then, what?" he asked.

"I was just a little worried that I only like you because you're a director who drives a Porsche and looks great in jeans."

Fuller studied her. "Really?" he asked, amazed.

There was a moment, while he looked at the ground and scratched his chin, that Eve thought maybe this was the end of this.

"You think I look good in jeans?"

Eve laughed. "Great," she said. "I said great."

"So that's it?" he asked. "That's the thing you needed to tell me?"

"I just—I couldn't live with myself if that were the reason," she said. "I mean, and if it were the reason, then eventually we'd wind up breaking up, because that's not really a reason to stay together, and if we're going to end up breaking up, we might as well do that now—don't forget, I'm nineteen. I could be shallow without knowing it."

He burst out laughing.

"Oh, come on," said Fuller. "I am completely positive you

are not shallow, and, rest assured, I'm not that successful. I couldn't sell that bag of bones Porsche if I tried—the engine's a wreck—and if you were really that shallow, you would've known my last three pictures and their grosses. Even at nineteen."

"What's 'their grosses' mean?" asked Eve.

"Nothing interesting," he said.

"I might want to find out," said Eve. "I may want to be shallow one day."

"You don't have a chance in hell," he said. "Not one chance in a million."

He leaned over and kissed her lips, chastely, taking her by surprise.

Eve was enchanted and disappointed. She wanted to at least get one good kiss in. A movie kiss. Feel his body against hers through their clothes. She saw him grin. He could tell she was disappointed, and he was glad.

"I know you're dying to get me into bed," he said, taking her aback, but not altogether in a bad way.

"I am not!" she said indignantly.

"It's okay," he said. "I know this whole thing is about sex, for you. But forget it. If you really care about me, you'll have to wait."

He stepped away, still watching her, a smile on his face. Teasing, coy. "Good night."

"What about tomorrow?" she asked.

"I'll be here at seven. Can you cook?" he asked.

"Uh, yeah . . . sure." She hadn't been expecting that.

"Good. I'll bring the wine," he said, and turned his back to her and left.

"Red," she said, getting the last word in. "I hope you like hamburgers."

"With cheese," he said, as he turned on the engine.

Eve went inside. Then peeked back out. Fuller was watching to make sure she was in okay. She waved. He nodded and drove away. His car's engine roared.

Now *that*, Eve thought, was a perfect night.

Ten

The first time Gabrielle laid eyes on Joey Gardener he was at a party; he was playing the piano and singing old standards. "Until There Was You." "I'm in the Mood for Love." His voice wasn't half bad, and neither was his playing. But what was outstanding were his looks. He could have been a Calvin Klein underwear model. Tall, sandy-haired, green-eyed, muscular, and handsome.

Gabrielle quickly learned that Joey was a success story waiting to happen. He was young and had a job as an assistant to a blockbuster producer on the lot at Disney, but the buzz in the industry was that he wasn't going to be someone's assistant on Dopey Drive for long. He was on the fast track. He knew lots of people and was well liked.

Joey had started the surfing club in Malibu. Originally, with David Geffen, who considered him a protégé. Then lots of other studio executives, agents, and actors would show up to surf with them. They began to have an unofficial surf-before-work club. They scoffed at anyone who went to a respectable gym. L.A. Sports Club was for those who couldn't hack the elements. Surfing was way cooler. Everybody knew it.

The group changed clothes in the deserted Malibu parking lot after their six a.m. surf, talking about their wipe-outs and their best rides. They showered when they got to their offices. The secretaries would shake their heads in disbelief when the saltwater-soaked bunch came to work after riding the waves. But they respected this group. It was clear.

And Joey was on his way up. No question about it. He was going to be a major deal-maker.

When Joey finished playing, at the party, he got out a guitar and strummed while someone else sang. He was just looking around when he spotted Gabrielle in the crowd. She stood out like a comet.

Joey was instantly smitten. Gabrielle was gorgeous, perfect. He later found out that anything she undertook, she finished as if she'd been in a race. She was blue-ribbon in a town that was Wimbledon, the Steeplechase, and any Olympic Village all rolled into one, at least as far as the competition for great women was concerned. Gabrielle was like a young Jacqueline Onassis. Slight, thin, but perfectly sculpted, her natural body was any model's ideal. She spoke French fluently and had traveled extensively.

A recent UCLA graduate with no plans to work, Gabrielle was always good-natured, impeccably dressed, and drove a brand-new car that was clean as a whistle. She kept busy without appearing ambitious. Ironically, to appear that unambitious was a full-time job for her.

Gabrielle enchanted Joey with stories about her family that she tempered so much, she seemed to have sprung right from a Norman Rockwell painting. She told him of family trips to Europe, Australia, and Thailand, and she laughed at how her father spoiled her by buying her a car, paying the rent on her apartment, and financing entire new wardrobes each season. Gabrielle was like a doll you put in a glass case, and gazed at, admiring its perfection.

They quickly became a serious couple. Joey was always tender with her. She was the kind of woman real men married, he thought. He knew that with her, he would be a better man. There were no obstacles to their courtship. It was flawless, and both Joey and Gabrielle knew their lives were set.

Gabrielle's parents were divorced. Her father, Arthur Cliffwood, had remarried twice, the second time to one of his former clients. He was an architect with a temper and good looks. He had built about a dozen homes in Los Angeles that were so distinctive, they were called Cliffwoods. Modern, with sharp edges and jutting angles, Cliffwoods were works of art. Hard to maintain. Impractical for families with young children, but always stunning.

His new wife, Christie, was twenty-eight. She was recently divorced from a famous producer, who had dumped her for an older sexpot movie star. Christie's marriage to Arthur was her second marriage, his third. Arthur worshipped Christie. She was young, beautiful, rich (her ex-husband had given her a handsome settlement), and glamorous by association—her former marriage to Hollywood royalty.

Gabrielle was profoundly jealous. Her unmitigated life quest to gain her father's approval was refueled by this marriage. Christie set the proverbial bar, and she set it high. Gabrielle had much to aim for—in her mind. But she never got there. Ever.

Gabrielle's mother lived in Barcelona, and Gabrielle hadn't seen her since the divorce ten years ago. She sent her an invitation to her and Joey's wedding at the Bel Air Hotel, but her mother never responded.

Gabrielle didn't show any sign of upset. Her wedding was perfect, and she laughed off things like her mother's absence. Nothing bothered her. Though Gabrielle wasn't Jewish, they had a rabbi conduct the services because it was important to Joey.

At the reception Joey played the piano and sang love songs to Gabrielle. She beamed at him from the other end of the piano, where she'd positioned herself to allow the photographer a perfectly angled shot.

When the wedding ended and the guests had left, Joey found Gabrielle on the floor of their honeymoon suite, huddled in a heap, sobbing. As soon as Gabrielle saw Joey, she quickly dried her tears and tried to hide them from him, but it was too late. He had seen her weeping.

"What happened?" Joey asked, taking her hand.

"Nothing, darling," lied Gabrielle, pulling her hand away to mop up her makeup. She stood, and as she did, pieces of cut-up plastic credit cards fell to the floor from her lap.

Joey picked them up. They were Gabrielle's platinum American Express Card, Diner's Club, and several gold Visas and MasterCards. He looked at them. They were Gabrielle's, with her name printed on them. Only they were cut in pieces. He looked at her, but she offered no explanation; she merely took them from him, neatly sealed them in a hotel stationery envelope, and threw the envelope in the wastecan.

"Honey, something happened," Joey pressed. He knew Gabrielle would never harm her precious credit cards. "Why did you cut up your credit cards?"

"I didn't," she said.

He marveled at how she now looked like she had never cried at all. Her face was serene and calm. Not at all puffy and red. She possessed tremendous self-control.

"My father said that now you can pay my bills," Gabrielle smiled weakly.

"But, who cut up your cards?"

"It doesn't matter," she said coolly and went into the bathroom. "I'm going to change my clothes. Excuse me," she added, politely, and shut the door.

They had never fought, and Joey didn't want to now, but he

wanted answers. He went to the bathroom door and knocked, gently. She didn't answer.

"He cut up your credit cards?" Joey said into the silence. "Your father?"

There was the gentle rush sound of Gabrielle's wedding gown and slips brushing against the tile, as she took them off.

"On your wedding day?"

Joey was shocked. He couldn't understand this. Granted, he didn't know the Cliffwoods intimately. Their meetings had been casual and in crowds. But still. He'd never considered such a thing happening, and if he had, he certainly wouldn't have expected it to unfold this way.

Eleven

Gabrielle embraced marriage. To her, marriage was not just love, but a way to distance herself from the past she refused to speak of to anyone. Including her husband. Marriage made her feel like an entirely different person, and that was joyful for her.

She began to dress differently. Less like an eager recent college student and more like a young heiress. She gave up backpacks for handbags. She gave away every pair of trendy shoes she'd bought at the mall and replaced them with classic driving shoes and variations on pumps. Jackie O could've taken lessons. Gabrielle studied the lives of young royals, and went to great lengths to copy their dress, their homes, and their traditions.

Joey was stunned by the bills. He wanted his wife to stop shopping quite so much, but ever since he'd found her sobbing on their wedding night, he'd tiptoed around her. He had been surprised at her crying, but more surprised at her behavior after that. She acted like it had never happened. Her denial made him wonder who Gabrielle really was.

He didn't want to upset her again. Especially since they'd decided to try to have a baby. When they didn't conceive right away, Gabrielle felt anxious, but Joey was sure if they relaxed, everything would be fine. Relaxing for Gabrielle meant shopping.

So, even though Joey began to feel financially strapped, he only mentioned her spending very gently, and then when she didn't stop, he just scrambled at work, looking for more projects and more opportunities. After all, she was going to be the mother of his children one day soon. He wanted to treat her right.

Gabrielle rewarded Joey's good behavior, which was how she saw it, with sexual favors, and Joey decided that this was just the way a marriage worked. Give and take. He resigned himself, and they were both as happy as they could imagine being.

On their first anniversary, Joey confided his secret dreams to Gabrielle. He told her that he wanted to try to make a career as a musician.

Gabrielle laughed, and then looked into his eyes to see if he were joking. He wasn't.

"You can't be serious," she said.

"Why not?" Joey asked playfully. "Maybe I could even front a band."

"I suppose it could be a hobby," she said, seriously. "I could fix a music room for you. I've seen some beautiful antique music stands at the swap meets."

"No, hon," said Joey gently. "I don't want a hobby. I want a career. As a musician."

"But, darling . . ." she sputtered, not sure what to say next. "But what about your job?"

"I'll quit," he said. "I'll get another job doing something else if I don't get music work right away."

"Why would you get another job?" she asked. "The one you have is so promising."

"It's been my dream," Joey explained. "My whole life. I just fell into this movie stuff. It isn't really me."

"Why didn't you tell me before?" she asked, her face turning steely.

"I wanted to be sure," he said. "I mean, I thought you'd like it. Some musicians really make it. We can go on tour if I have a band. If you want to stay here, I'll get studio work. Do gigs on the weekends."

"Gigs!" she said with disgust.

Joey could tell he was in trouble. Her face said everything that her words didn't. She was furious and frightened and trying to keep her manners in check.

"We'll be okay," said Joey. "If it doesn't work out, I can always come back to this."

"At the bottom, maybe," she said. "You've invested a lot. You've come a long way. You can't just come back to where you are now."

"It doesn't matter."

"Maybe not to you," said Gabrielle. "But I've worked hard to get here."

"Don't you have dreams?" Joey snapped. He hadn't wanted to get defensive, but it had happened. This was officially a fight.

"Yes, darling," she said. "This is my dream! All of this! How can you tell me you want to run off to be a musician, and dash my dreams?"

"I'm sorry, babe," said Joey. He wasn't giving up, but he knew that if he was going to do this, he needed his wife's support, because it would mean big changes for both of them. He would wait a little longer before bringing it up again.

Gabrielle took his silence in the days to come as something else. She thought he had finally come to his senses and realized how foolish a career change would be. Especially one as volatile as music. She thought everything was back on track, when really he was just regrouping. He would not give up on this. He could see himself as a musician. A musician married to Gabrielle. He wanted it all.

Gabrielle was out shopping when the doorbell rang. Joey was reading scripts with one eye, watching sports with the other, and yakking on the phone to one of his pals. He was wearing only boxer shorts, and he considered not answering the door, but when the hard, sober knocking began, he changed his mind.

Joey opened the door and saw two uniformed men. He didn't recognize the uniforms as Westec security guards. He didn't recognize them as local police officers.

"Federal marshals," said the officer. Joey eyed their weapons. "Are you the son of Arthur Cliffwood?"

"Son-in-law," said Joey. "Is everything all right? Is Mr. Cliffwood okay?"

One of the officers stepped back a few feet, as a courtesy, and radioed on his walkie-talkie.

"We have contact with relatives," said the officer into the radio. "Investigation is under way."

"We need to come in and talk to you," said the other officer.

Joey opened the door and let them in, then listened in shock as the marshal explained that Gabrielle's father had gone bankrupt, and had legally listed his children as responsible parties for his debts. At one point in time the children, Gabrielle and her brother, had signed an agreement to act as such a responsible party. Gabrielle's brother was a student, deep in debt himself. Gabrielle was now married to Joey, who was a responsible party.

Arthur Cliffwood's creditors needed payment—demanded payment—immediately. Cliffwood had left the country, with his wife, and, as far as anyone could tell, Joey and Gabrielle were on the hook.

Joey couldn't believe this was happening. While the marshals broke the news to him about Mr. Cliffwood's checkered past, a federally marked truck backed into their driveway and movers began taking away Joey and Gabrielle's possessions. Wedding china, silver, stereo equipment—anything that was worth real money. They left one sofa, the bed, and the books.

One marshal waited with Joey for Gabrielle to come home. He wanted Gabrielle's diamond engagement ring and diamond-studded wedding band. When she walked in the door, her face turned white. Joey ran to her, immediately more concerned for her health and well-being than anything else.

She let Joey lead her to the sofa that was left, and she sat, stiffly, and looked around. She didn't need to hear the marshal's explanations. She knew. She surrendered all her jewelry and then they were left alone. Just Joey and Gabrielle. The house was theirs for thirty days, after which it would belong to the bank, who would auction it off to pay the government.

Gabrielle was in a functional coma. She sat and stared, while Joey left message after message for Mr. Cliffwood, but he never picked up or called back.

"I'm sorry, darling," whispered Gabrielle, as if in a trance. "I can't believe this is happening again."

"Again?" Joey asked. He had been in crisis mode, but this quickly jogged him out of it. "Gabby, why didn't you tell me?"

Gabrielle didn't answer. She was surprised he was so calm, and not losing his temper. She stared straight ahead and didn't blink. Joey was worried about her. She did not look well.

"Should we call the doctor?"

"They took everything," she said in a monotone. "They even took my wedding band!"

"It's okay," he said and held her. "It's just stuff. We still have each other. I love you, and that's all that matters. I'll make enough money to buy you new stuff. Bigger stuff. Better stuff."

She looked up at him, still trancelike.

"As a musician?"

"No," said Joey, somberly. He would never let her down again. Not like her father had. He would take care of her. "I won't become a musician. I'll get us out of this."

"I'm pregnant," she said, her face still and quiet.

"You're kidding," Joey whispered.

She shook her head.

This wasn't the way either of them had wanted this moment to happen, but it was here. Joey took her hand and squeezed it.

"A baby . . ." he said, trying to grasp the miracle when everything around them was so chaotic.

"This can't happen again," Gabrielle said so quietly and determinedly it gave Joey goose bumps.

"It won't," said Joey. "I promise."

"And nobody can know about this," said Gabrielle. She was mortally embarrassed. This was the worst thing that could happen. "I don't want anyone to know that my family is bankrupt," she said. "It's demoralizing."

"It doesn't really matter," said Joey, but he was shocked himself. His words were coming out automatically. "We're going to have a baby. Nothing else matters."

"This is not the way I want people to think of me," said Gabrielle, not thinking of the baby. She was regaining her self. There was nothing she had to do in terms of the baby. Just drink milk and take prenatal vitamins. But the rest of her life—that needed control. Serious damage control. "Nobody is to know about this," she commanded, her voice steely and determined. "Nobody."

"Nobody knows," whispered Joey. "Nobody will ever know."

Twelve

Fuller wanted to marry Eve. They'd dated for a year, and enough was enough. He was way past ready. He was anxious. He'd known since before their first date that he wanted to marry her. He'd known when he'd seen her waitressing the first time. There was just something about her—he couldn't put his finger on it. It was more an instinct than anything else. He'd wanted to propose to her after their first date, but he knew that he couldn't. It wouldn't have worked. So he held back on the subject for a year. All the while, growing more and more anxious to make her his wife. He wanted to move on with her. Finally, he couldn't wait another second.

In a town full of actresses, both professional and wannabes, Fuller knew how highly unusual it was to meet a pretty young woman who had no interest in the movie business. Eve didn't want to write, direct, act, or produce; she'd never seen *Variety*, didn't even know what "the trades" were, and hadn't slept with anyone since her high school boyfriend. A virgin, by Hollywood standards.

She was beautiful and sexy. Fuller knew it, but it was nice to hear his friends tell him she was hot. And fresh. Untouched. Innocent, even, in a way. She hadn't become a fashion victim, hadn't colored her hair, hadn't had her nails done or exercised as part of a group.

When Eve wasn't working or hanging out with Fuller, she rode an old rusty bike. On her bike, she explored different neighborhoods, or rode along the bike path by the ocean. She also took long walks by herself, and all the while she daydreamed. Her daydreams were pretty old-fashioned. She wanted a husband, kids, a house with a yard and a tire hanging from a tree to swing on, and a station wagon.

Fuller was completely smitten. "A real woman"—that's how he described her. Not one of the mutant females he knew so many of, who wanted to have a career and pop out a kid, then take on a new project or job and pop out another kid, only because time was running out and they might miss an opportunity. Those women scared him. He'd dated enough to last a lifetime. He didn't know how to be with them. Had he been younger, he would have chased after them, but at his age, he knew what he wanted, and what he wanted was Eve.

There was a warrior buried inside her quiet, feminine exterior. That contrast and combination was what drew Fuller to Eve. He felt that, in her, he had met his soul mate. He wished he'd met her sooner.

Their regular dates turned into a spillover of their lives. Overnights at her place, overnights at his place. Her clothes in his apartment, his clothes in hers. Buying big-ticket items together.

Purchasing a good mattress for her apartment. A new sofa for his. He couldn't imagine buying something without her input. Not because he was insecure or needy, he just valued her opinion. Eve had no hidden agenda. She wanted what was best for Fuller. Simple.

He was just so happy whenever he was with her. Not that he needed to be with her every second of the day, but he did need his "fix." A phone call, hearing her voice on his answering machine, getting a silly postcard she'd found and sent him. He needed to know she was there for him. The rest was a formality.

As for Eve, she couldn't help feeling like she was in the eye of a tornado. All around her things were spinning, and she was in the center where it was calm. If she stopped to think about what had happened—the new city, new job, new boyfriend, with whom she was certain she was madly, deeply in love and wanted to marry—she would faint. So she didn't. But she couldn't help every now and then remembering that her boyfriend was a Hollywood film director. She had to scream in the car and pinch herself hard to get back to reality. Whose life was she living, anyway? It's my life. It's just my life, she would repeat to herself, until the words seemed to make sense. Fuller was just a guy. A wonderful, fabulous guy, whose scent she could smell even though she was on her way to work and he was miles away, in his apartment, writing a new script he wanted to direct.

Sex was sublime and effortless. Fuller was glad that Eve found classic, traditional sex satisfying. He hated sex with women who wanted to try anything new, whether it was pleasurable or not. Fad sex. It was just a subcategory of conquest sex. The type that people had just in order to talk about it later.

For Fuller, sex with Eve was natural and wonderful. No pressure, no limits. They were on the same wavelength about everything.

On their one-year anniversary of dating, Fuller took Eve to the beach. It was an overcast morning. They walked around the sand and rocks at Big Rock in Malibu. The tide was low and Eve found fun in the tidepools that formed by the rocks. Anemones waved in the water, their hairy tentacles looking exotic. Sea lions sunbathed only ten feet away on a barnacle-covered rock that was as tall as a house.

"I want you to marry me," said Fuller, finally letting out the words he'd thought to himself so many times. That they hung in the air instead of choking him in his throat was a relief.

Eve was so surprised, she wasn't sure she had heard him correctly.

But when Fuller took a ring from the pocket of his denim shirt, Eve knew she had heard right. She stared at the ring and tried not to gasp. It was a band of small diamonds all around. She had never seen so many diamonds in one place—not in real life.

"I want you to be my wife because I love you more than I've ever loved anyone," he said.

Eve looked into his eyes. They were twinkling as though they were full of electricity. His mop of gray hair blew in the sea breeze.

"You want to marry me?"

It wasn't a question she needed answered so much as a thought she needed to hear out loud. To try and convince herself that this landmark in her life was truly happening.

"I want to have a family with you, and I want to grow old with you. You're who I want to spend the rest of this life with. And if there are any other lives after this one, I want to spend those with you, too. I want you for infinity."

Eve wept silently. "You mean eternity," she said.

"I mean everything," he said. "Whatever is the most, I want it with you." Fuller's eyes were dry and clear. He had never been so sure of anything in his life. This wasn't exciting—it was like walking a path he'd walked before. Focused and sure.

"Yes," said Eve. "I'll marry you."

She took the ring and slid it on her finger. It fit perfectly, and it made her feel different. Like she'd crossed some line.

Fuller kissed her long and lightly, and then he held her in his arms and looked out to the farthest point on the horizon. Eve looked at the minuscule stitches on Fuller's shirt.

"So," said Fuller, still holding her enveloped in his arms. "Do I get to meet your family?"

Eve jolted back to a reality she had lost sight of, her family. Back in Vegas. Running the gas station. She felt guilty and a wave swept over her. She had all but forgotten them since she'd moved out here, and she'd never been happier. She'd talked to them several times, but she'd never said much about Fuller. She didn't know why. But now, Fuller would meet them, and she wasn't sure she was ready for that.

"Sure," she said. "At the wedding."

Thirteen

"I'm sending your plane tickets overnight mail," Eve said into the phone.

"What?" her mother said, loudly. It wasn't that she couldn't hear. She didn't understand.

"Plane tickets, Ma. For the wedding."

"But—I already bought tickets. Bus tickets."

"You can't take the bus."

"Why not?"

"Because it takes too long. It's hot. It's cramped."

"It's the bus," Betty said with a laugh. "It'll get us there."

"So will the plane. Faster."

"Oh, come on. You can't afford plane tickets. Not for all of us." Her mother laughed. "Honestly, Eve."

Eve didn't know how to explain. "I can, Ma. I want to. Fuller wants to pay for them. We both do."

"Oh, no," said her mother. "You're not wasting your money on that. You're going to be newlyweds, you and that Fuller fella. You need to start savin' up."

"Mother, I'm sending the tickets. They're bought. You just show up at the airport. Can you do that?"

"I can," said her mother, exasperated, "but I think it's foolish. I think it's wasteful—"

"Good," said Eve, hearing only the agreement and trying to ignore the rest. "I'll pick you up at the gate and bring you to my apartment. It'll be a little cramped, but you can have some privacy that way."

"I suppose you and your fiancé will be staying together."

"Yeah," said Eve.

"Well, that's okay by me," said Betty. "I'll roll up some sleeping bags for the kids—unless you got some there."

"No," said Eve. "I don't."

"Well, don't you worry," said Betty cheerfully. She was glad to feel useful for something in this wedding. Even if it was just sleeping bags. They were necessary, and she could provide. "Don't think another minute about sleeping bags. I'll bring enough for everyone."

The week before Christmas everyone was in a cheery mood. The baggage checker at Southwest Airlines listened to Betty explain that her daughter's wedding was the reason they had all the sleeping bags that put them over the limit for unpaid luggage. So, because it was the holiday, and because Betty was flushed with excitement that made her cheeks look just like Santa's wife, the baggage checker let the sleeping bags go as carry-on pieces. The Carmelinas shoved them under their plane seats and flew to L.A.

Even though it was seventy-five degrees in Vegas and sixty-five in Los Angeles, people talked about the seasonal weather as if it were a drastic change from the rest of the year. Eve's mother had bought a set of wineglasses with Eve's and Fuller's initials engraved in them. She'd gone to the mall, specially for them. She guarded the silver-wrapped box carefully all through the trip, holding them on her lap when she could. She wanted Eve and her new husband to enjoy the glasses unbroken.

"Ma! Dad!"

"Eve!"

Their airport reunion was sweet. Hugs and kisses, then everyone looked everyone over carefully, and remembered.

"She's so thin," said Betty to Hank, who didn't really notice or care. "You're so thin," Betty said to Eve.

"Wow." Tracey and Liz both grabbed Eve's hand to gape at her ring. "It's beautiful."

Eve tried to pull her hand away, but they wouldn't let her. Even Steve and Chuck were impressed with the diamond band.

"Come on," said Eve, pulling her hand back. "We have to go." But Betty and Hank were looking now. They were remembering their own engagement. The diamond chip on Betty's ring was very different from Eve's.

"It's real nice," said Betty.

Eve relaxed a little.

"Thanks," she said. "Now, let's go! Traffic is going to be wild. You've never seen traffic until you've driven the L.A. freeways at rush hour."

During the whole drive to her apartment, Eve pointed out this and that. Landmarks that were famous, some that were just personal. She drove them past Gianni's, where she still worked and where she'd met Fuller.

Betty could see her other children listening with the ears of the converted. She could see them coveting Eve's life. She wondered how long before they would follow. If they would. She had never expected her daughter to move away. Down the street, around the corner, but never this far. She fought back tears.

Eve's apartment worked perfectly for the Carmelinas. There was room for all four sleeping bags. Eve apologized for not having more time, but with the wedding tomorrow, there was so much to do.

"What about dinner?" asked Hank. "Isn't there a rehearsal dinner?"

"No," said Eve. "No rehearsal. It's going to be pretty informal."

"Well, I think we should meet this fella first," said Hank, pulling at his belt. "I want to know who's marrying into my family."

"You'll love him, Dad," said Eve. "He's wonderful."

"We'll see him at the wedding," Betty said to Hank. She took his hand, and he noticed. It was not something she did normally. Betty was feeling emotional. "It'll be fine. Let's not give Eve anything to worry about. This is her wedding, and we're all here."

The next day, Eve sent a limousine to pick them up an hour before the wedding.

"This can't be for us!" Betty exclaimed as she found a place by her feet for the wedding present. The wrapping paper was now looking like it had been shuttled a long way, but Betty took special care. "She said she was sending a car. This ain't a car. It's a limousine. Not much on gas mileage, I imagine." The brooch with the Christmas elves she wore on her dress was digging into her skin. She adjusted it.

"Who the hell gives a crap," said Hank, giving Betty's ass a squeeze as he got in behind her. "We're not paying for it."

Betty squealed when Hank pinched her.

"This is what all the movie stars ride in," said Tracey, as Steve helped himself to the bar. "I've seen this on television."

"Then what the hell is Eve doin' with a limousine?" Chuck asked.

That one stumped them.

"Far as I know she ain't no movie star," said Hank. "Far as I know."

The limousine drove them north on the Pacific Coast Highway

into Malibu and dropped them off by the front door of Geoffrey's Restaurant, where other limos were doing the same with other guests.

"This ain't no church," said Hank, getting out and eyeballing the place. Eve's father was wearing a tuxedo he'd rented at the Sears Roebuck in Vegas. He'd folded it up and packed it in his suitcase for the trip to L.A. Even though the tuxedo had been squashed into a suitcase for ten hours, it was miraculously unwrinkled. Of course, it was one hundred percent polyester.

"It might be one'a those crazy Southern California churches," said Betty, looking the place over skeptically. Betty wore a bright dress with sparkles, not sequins, glued on the front in the shape of a starfish. Her shoes were bright pink. She'd dyed them to match the pink in her dress. They were the exact same shade.

"I think it's beautiful," said Tracey. "I love it here."

Betty eyed her daughter with a knowing look.

"I don't see no steeple," said Hank, looking around for something familiar.

"Please come in," said one of the restaurant staff. He was friendly and paid no notice to the Carmelinas' unusual style. All the staff were friendly and cool, chiseled and ready for anything. They loved waiting on famous people, and were rarely disappointed. This restaurant was a magnet for famous diners.

"Merry Christmas," said Hank to the staff member.

The staff member smiled as if he hadn't heard. "Have some champagne, and take a seat," he said, enunciating with special clarity. All the speech classes he'd taken were evident. "The wedding will start shortly."

"Don't look like no deacon to me," said Hank.

"I think he's a waiter," said Betty.

"Wha' the hell are waiters doing in this church?" said Hank. He was getting confused, and then angry at himself that he was confused.

"It's a restaurant, Daddy," said Liz. She was embarrassed.

"I can see that with my own two eyes," said Hank. "I don't know why we're in a restaurant when I came all this way to see my daughter married. We should be in a church's where we should be."

Hank, Betty, and Eve's brothers and sisters walked through the restaurant as if they were walking on Mars. They took champagne from a table where fifty flutes were being filled with Cristal.

"Fancy," said Betty. She drank the champagne as if it were Gatorade. "Got a kick to it."

"You think they got any eggnog?" Hank asked.

"It's a weddin'," said Betty, admonishing her husband.

"It's still Christmas," said Hank.

"I think her husband's shit-kickin' rich," said Tracey. "This is really fancy. I think."

"I agree with Tracey," said Chuck.

They wandered through the bright restaurant where twenty guests were standing, drinking champagne. A man in a suit walked into the middle of the crowd.

"Welcome," he said. All talking ceased. "Welcome to the wedding of Eve Marie Carmelina and Fuller Matthew Evanston."

A string quartet began to play. Fuller, wearing a beautiful blue suit, walked down the aisle.

"What the hell kind of wedding is this?" said Hank. "Where's the chairs? Why're we standing?"

"That's him," said Betty, nudging Hank.

"He looks like one of those, how do you call 'em? One of those Jews," Hank said to Betty, just a little too loudly.

Betty squinted and looked hard at Fuller.

"My word, will you look at that beak? I believe he is a Jew."

"She's marryin' a Jew?" Hank squawked, as quietly as he could. Which wasn't that quietly.

"I told you we shoulda met him first," said Betty. "I knew she'd up and do something crazy like this."

"Do you think we should object?" said Hank.

"No," said Betty. "It's all right. . . . I think."

Eve walked down the aisle, alone. She looked serene. She wore a beautiful white dress that was simple and long. She let Fuller's gaze guide her down the aisle. As long as she focused on his eyes, and nowhere else, she felt okay.

"Where's her veil?"

"What kinda dress is that?"

"I think it's beautiful," said Tracey.

"Why aren't we walking her down the aisle?" said Liz. "Why isn't Daddy?"

"Maybe it's a Jewish thing," said Hank. "Maybe that's why there's no eggnog."

"Maybe it's 'cause we wouldn't know the aisle in a place like this, if it came up and bit us on the ass," said Steve.

"Shut up," said Liz. "Just shut up." She spoke loudly enough to draw stares from other guests. She turned red and shut up, herself.

Eve took her place next to Fuller. He took her hand, and she dug her nails into his flesh. He looked straight into her eyes. She was nervous. More than she'd ever been. With his other hand, Fuller unpried Eve's fingernails from his fleshly palm and smoothed each finger until her hand was relaxed. Eve closed her eyes and tried to listen to the marriage ceremony—her marriage ceremony—but before she knew it Fuller was kissing her. That was it. They were married. Eve had blanked out through the whole thing.

If Fuller hadn't held Eve's hand throughout the reception, she might have walked straight off the cliff that the restaurant was built onto. She was in a waking dream state. The delicious half sleep that never came often enough. The only thing that brought her out of it was when her mother grabbed her in both arms and squeezed her so tight Eve had to gasp for breath.

"Let go," Eve wheezed. "Mom . . ."

Betty let her daughter go, and held her out at arms' length to look at her.

"You almost crushed the air out of me," said Eve, laughing and catching her breath.

"You're awful thin," Betty said again. "You always been this thin? I never noticed. Of course, I never seen you in a dress like this."

"You're so beautiful," said Tracey.

Eve hugged Tracey.

"And thin," said Liz, critically. "Too thin."

"I'm not thin," said Eve. "I'm just right. And if I am thin it's because I'm too happy to eat these days."

"I've never been too happy to eat," said Betty. "Happy's always made me eat a little more."

"Your husband's rich," said Tracey.

Eve was embarrassed, but before she could say anything, Betty pulled Eve's ear to her mouth so she could whisper to her daughter, "Why didn't you tell us he's a Jew?" It wasn't much of a whisper; everyone around them heard. "I woulda gotten him one of those menorah things," she said, pronouncing the word *menorah* with special care.

"Mom . . ." Eve was even more embarrassed, until Fuller grabbed Betty and gave her a giant bear hug.

"What shall I call you?" he asked Betty, breaking any tension. Betty looked up into Fuller's big brown eyes, and she melted a little.

"Well, ain't you somethin'," said Betty.

"Call her Betty, son," said Hank, and shook Fuller's hand, gripping it hard. He liked Fuller. "And call me Hank."

"Nice to meet you, Betty, Hank," said Fuller. "I'm glad you could make it."

"Never met a Jew," said Hank, sizing Fuller up.

"Dad!" Eve was going to die.

"Not that I know of," said Hank. "I suppose one or two may have slipped by me. They don't always tell you their personals."

"Actually, I'm half Jewish," said Fuller.

"What do you know?" said Betty, reaching for another glass of champagne from a passing waiter carrying a tray of filled flutes. "He's like a fraction."

"My mother was Jewish, and my father was Greek," Fuller said. "They passed on years ago, but if they were here, they would love your daughter."

Betty smiled, enchanted. She liked him. Even if he was different than what she was used to.

"That's where you get that nose from, I imagine," Hank said.

Eve wanted to just die. Some of the guests were beginning to titter and nod toward Hank and Betty.

"Have you tried the sea bass?" Fuller said, politely changing the subject and pointing to the buffet. "It's Eve's favorite in all of Los Angeles."

"Sea bass?" said Hank. He'd never heard of it.

"We came here on our one-month anniversary—of dating," said Fuller. "And I knew if we ever married—if your daughter ever agreed to have me—this was where I wanted to do it. Right here in this restaurant. I proposed to her on the beach, did she tell you that?"

The entire Carmelina family had passed judgment on Fuller by that point, and it was all good. They could tell he loved Eve, and he treated her well and with respect. Really couldn't ask for more, they told themselves. They couldn't have been happier. He was just as nice as nice could be.

Eve saw her family falling for Fuller, and she relaxed. Everything would be all right. She gazed up at her new husband and in that moment none of her past mattered. Not her mother, not her father, not the gas station or any of her past. This was a new life for her.

"Fuller!"

Eve stepped back as a beautiful woman suddenly walked between her and Fuller.

"Amanda!"

Fuller dropped Eve's hand and hugged the woman. He seemed reluctant to let go of Amanda. She had blue eyes and shiny black hair cut in a bob that was messy and "just fucked" looking. She was buxom and fleshy in a sexy, healthy way. Eve watched curiously. She'd never seen Fuller embrace another woman before. Not like this. And not someone so beautiful. The two finally let each other go, and both turned to Eve.

"Eve, this is Amanda."

Eve remembered. Fuller's ex-girlfriend. The one he'd lived with. The movie star. Her stomach dropped. Amanda was beautiful. She had a tiny nose that was in a constant state of flare and her eyes were so light blue they were almost silvery. She looked like a young cousin of Elizabeth Taylor.

"I'm so happy for you," said Amanda. She kissed Eve on the cheek. "I really am."

Eve was doubly uncomfortable because her parents were standing right there.

"Amanda, this is Eve's family," said Fuller.

"Mom, go try the caviar toast," said Eve, pushing her mother toward the buffet. Betty looked confused.

"The fish!" Eve said, shoving her mother. "Go that way!"

Betty and Hank and the rest of the clan hunkered over to the buffet, where everything looked strange to them.

Amanda smiled with understanding. She knew exactly what was happening. "Are you going on a honeymoon?" Amanda asked, changing the subject quickly to make Eve feel more comfortable.

Eve didn't answer. She was completely stunned by Amanda's beauty. Stunning and voluptuous, Amanda's fleshiness was the exact opposite of Eve's naturally reed-thin body. Eve felt like a boy next to Amanda.

"Maui," Fuller said.

"Maui is beautiful," said Amanda. "Are you taking her to Hana?"

Eve felt herself becoming jealous. She wondered if Amanda and Fuller had ever been there together. If she was sloppy seconds. She didn't like being the third wheel in the conversation, even if she was the belle of the ball.

"No," said Fuller. "We rented a private house."

"As it should be," Amanda said, nodding. She looked at them both with a depth that Eve didn't quite understand.

"Excuse me. I see someone I have to talk to," Fuller said as he walked away.

Eve couldn't believe Fuller just left her there. With his ex-girlfriend! It was the worst thing he'd ever done to her. Eve stood there nervously.

"This is a beautiful wedding," Amanda purred. Her voice was so soothing. "I wish I could have a wedding like this, but George wants to elope."

"Oh," said Eve, feeling better already. "George? Is that your boyfriend?" Eve asked.

"Yeah. We're getting married soon," Amanda whispered. "But don't tell anyone."

Eve glanced down at Amanda's stomach, thinking Amanda must be pregnant. That was the only reason Eve could think of for not wanting people to know you were marrying your boyfriend. Happened all the time back where she came from in Vegas. But Amanda's stomach was flat as a board.

"You know how the tabloids are," Amanda explained.

"The tabloids?"

"I'm marrying George Foster," said Amanda, suddenly looking at Eve with new interest. Amanda realized Eve had no idea that she was with George. "God, I'm sorry. I'm so self-centered, I thought everyone knew."

"I don't know who that is." Eve shrugged apologetically.

Amanda cocked her head and stared at Eve curiously. Then she nodded.

"Good," said Amanda.

"Oh, God!" Eve yelped. Several people turned to see if she was all right.

"What?" said Amanda with alarm, looking Eve over for some sign of blood. "What is it?"

"He's *that* George Foster—the producer—I'm sorry. I guess I forgot. I should have known." Eve couldn't believe it. George Foster was the biggest action producer she had ever heard of. All his movies starred Sylvester Stallone or Arnold Schwarzenegger. He was positively famous.

"It's okay." Amanda laughed. "There's no reason you should know him."

"Wow," said Eve. "Okay. I know him now."

"Anyway . . . that's why we're eloping. Otherwise I'd love to have a wedding just like this."

Eve looked at Amanda, wide-eyed, as if Amanda had just told her she were marrying the president of the United States.

"That's really something," said Eve. "He's famous. Not that you're not. I mean, you are, too."

"I'm crazy in love," sighed Amanda. Eve smiled, warming up. This, she could relate to. "I guess you know about that," Amanda purred. Eve wondered how she was able to do that. Make her voice sound like a contented cat's.

"Hmm," said Eve. She liked Amanda, but there was something about her. Amanda knew too much. She was fluent in a language that Eve was just learning to speak.

"Those your parents?" Amanda nodded toward Betty and Hank.

"They came in from Las Vegas," said Eve, embarrassed. Her folks looked almost like hillbillies compared to the other guests, who were mostly Fuller's friends with some people Eve knew and liked from Gianni's sprinkled in.

"They remind me of my folks," said Amanda. "But they're back in Texas. Seems like a lifetime away."

Eve stared at Amanda. Never in a million years had she thought she would like Fuller's ex-girlfriend, but she did.

"My father's from Texas originally," said Eve.

They were silent a few moments, almost shuffling in their fabulously high heels.

"Why did you and Fuller split up?" asked Eve.

It came out of nowhere, but Amanda didn't laugh or make Eve feel uncomfortable for asking. In a way, they were both relieved that the question was out on the table.

"I don't know," said Amanda. "Lot of things, but I think it boiled down to he didn't love me enough."

"But you loved him enough," said Eve, surprised at her boldness. She just wanted to get things straight.

"It was a long time ago," said Amanda.

Eve took a glass of champagne from a waiter passing with a tray.

"Why don't we have dinner when you get back from Maui? The four of us?"

Eve lost her breath. Dinner with George Foster?

"Okay," said Eve, trying to sound unflustered. "I'll call you. I guess Fuller still has your number."

"Actually," said Amanda, getting a pen and scrap of paper from her Chinese silk purse and scratching her phone number out, "he doesn't. I moved in with George last month. Officially."

"Congratulations," said Eve.

"It's a step," said Amanda, and she handed the phone number to Eve. "Here's the number. Call when you get back."

"Isn't George Foster married?" asked Eve, and she felt awful the minute she said it, because it was something she'd read in the tabloids.

"Oh, that's not really a marriage," said Amanda.

Eve didn't understand, but she knew enough to know that there was something going on that she would have to get translated later.

This reminded her of something from her first day in Los Angeles. "Do you—" She stopped and quickly covered her mouth.

"What?" asked Amanda.

"Nothing." Eve laughed.

"No, what?" Amanda pressed.

"Do you know what 'systemic yeast' means?"

Amanda stared at Eve and made a crazy face.

"What?"

"Systemic yeast," said Eve.

"No," said Amanda, "but it doesn't sound good."

"Sounds terrible, doesn't it?" Eve laughed.

"Uh-huh," Amanda laughed back, and walked away.

Eve stared down at the phone number Amanda had just handed her. It was just a bunch of digits, but if she dialed those digits, she'd reach the Foster house—and not just by accident. The seven digits connected her to a completely different world. One she'd only dreamed about up to now.

Fourteen

Nancy thought that all marriages became routine. She thought it was just part of the nature of the beast. So, when it happened to her marriage, she didn't worry. Not at first. There were only so many ways to make eating, sex, and partying exciting. This seemed like a natural step in the life of a marriage, but after a few months, one or the other of them lost the energy to keep working at it. It was hard for her to remember which one.

Eventually the routine became a glaring problem. Nancy didn't mind it so much, except that Landon hated it. Loathed it, even. Routine made him feel old. Boring. Unsuccessful. He'd spent his entire life devoted to the new and exciting. He was hooked on change. The only way he was happy was if he had something new to look forward to, and since he now knew everything about Nancy—had conquered her, in a way—he found her predictable.

They still jetted off at a moment's notice to Cannes, Telluride, or Toronto to attend some special film or comedy festival or even to take a vacation—but the phone became like a third person in their marriage. Landon was addicted to it. He was always running for it. Knowing it would probably contain a call with his next thrill.

Landon didn't start out disliking Nancy. She was the same sweet person as always. He just disliked the predictability, which was what made him feel like she was a burden to him. She became connected to his feeling bad. So, he just stayed away from her and spent more and more time at work.

Nancy felt rejected, and the harder she tried to get him back, the worse things got.

She wanted a baby, and Landon didn't exude enthusiasm over the idea. He didn't nix it either. But the sex got weird. Once he knew that they were doing it to make a baby, he couldn't do it. He just couldn't. And this made him not want to do it at all. At least, not with Nancy.

Nancy never met a problem she couldn't solve. She found herself drawn to situations and people she felt she could fix, or help.

So she decided on a great solution: She would meet Landon in a suite at the Peninsula during his lunch hour. She arrived wearing a coat with pretty much nothing underneath except some racy lingerie. A garter belt and stockings with a matching bra. She felt fabulous and sexy, and pretended not to mind that Landon fantasized about someone else. It was a lunchtime fuck.

Landon had begun to have such encounters with women other than his wife. They didn't feel like sex to him. More like sport. He still considered Nancy his wife and his main commitment. He would never consider marrying one of the sluts he did between one and three on weekdays, when he wasn't "doing lunch" with the components of some deal—which is how he thought of the people in the industry. As components, not people.

Nancy thought that her hotel trysts with her husband were a success. She opened house accounts at Trashy Lingerie and Frederick's of Hollywood, and had an entire closet built for the perverse wardrobe she acquired just for lunch at the Peninsula. She hated the quality of the merchandise, but there was nowhere else to go for the disgusting little outfits she needed to help Landon perform his conjugal duties and make her a mother.

At home, they rarely had sex. Landon smelled Nancy's natural insecurity. It was that poisonous whiff—stronger and more lasting than any perfume sold in a store—that was the beginning of the end for their marriage.

Their hotel interludes became more and more peculiar. They tacitly agreed to act as if they were outright strangers. Landon's favorite was to pretend Nancy was a hooker, and Nancy obediently played the part. But secretly, she was picturing her own fantasy: that Landon was a loving husband. Their sex life only existed in the seven-hundred-dollars-a-day suite that they used for a few hours at a time. There they conceived their baby.

As Nancy grew bigger, she stopped visiting her husband in the hotel, and Landon traveled more and more without her. He made movies that won Oscars, he created television shows that raised the ceiling on the prices of stars. Two million dollars an episode. Two point three. Two point four. He was on fire.

Nancy suspected Landon was having affairs, but she never dared ask him directly. She knew the answer would devastate her, and, in her delicate condition, she preferred to stay calm. So, she prayed for the best. She managed her life realistically. Instead of demanding or accusing, she asked Landon to be more affectionate to her. To appease her, he wrote her love letters. In between fucking "MAWs"—models, actresses, whatevers.

Nancy didn't know the details of his bad behavior, but she had her suspicions. Whenever an upsetting thought came into her head, she tried to distract herself. To take her mind off things, she took up a new hobby: smoking. Even though she was pregnant, Nancy began smoking cigarettes. She knew it was bad for her health, and for her baby's, but she rationalized that the stress it alleviated would be even worse than smoking. In a twisted way, Nancy figured that, given the circumstances, smoking was a good thing. Even pregnant. She prayed for her baby, nonetheless.

But the novelty of the cigarettes wore off shortly, and she found she needed something else to take her mind off her disintegrating marriage. So Nancy read old love letters—the ones Landon had written her ages ago. She smoked and clutched the letters until they were smudged and crumpled. Like a child clutching a blanket, a poor substitute for the real thing, Nancy held those letters tight. But she couldn't fool herself for long.

Landon came home high and drunk one evening when Nancy was nine months pregnant and told her he was leaving.

"For a business trip?" she asked, her voice cracking. She knew what he meant. She just couldn't bear to say it.

"Yeah, whatever," he said, leering. *Whatever* hung in the air after he had finished speaking.

Nancy couldn't scream or cry. She felt her throat close up.

"What about the baby?" she managed to get out.

"Nothing for me to do," said Landon.

Nancy had never been hit in her life, but Landon's words felt like a slam across the face. She felt awful. Guilty and ashamed.

"I'm going to lose the weight," she said defensively. She was sure that must be the reason he was leaving.

"I hope so." He said it offhandedly, but it confirmed her worst fears. It was the weight.

"I'm nine months pregnant," she shrugged, sheepishly explaining, but she felt wildly self-conscious. "I'm almost done with this."

Landon put one hand on the doorknob to go. Nancy went to him, and kissed him on the cheek, and whispered in his ear: "I will, Landon. I'll lose the weight. Will you stay if I lose it?"

She hated herself for wanting him, especially when he was being so awful. But something about the pregnancy made her feel more vulnerable than ever. She didn't want to be left. Not now. Not like this.

Landon walked away, to the waiting car and driver. He disappeared into the car. Nancy watched the giant black car pull out of their driveway. It was the worst image of her life, and it was imprinted in her head forever.

"Would you like some tea?"

Nancy turned to see who was speaking. It was one of the women she had hired to help with the house, but whose name she could no longer remember.

"I can make you some tea. With those lemon cookies you like."

"No cookies," Nancy said, quickly. Nothing fattening would cross her lips. Ever again.

"Right away," said the woman, and left.

Nancy turned back to look out the window. The driveway was empty and still.

Nancy walked to the library and shut the door, but she couldn't cry. It seemed the appropriate thing to do, but no tears came. She was too stunned. She sat in the huge peach sofa with green and mauve pillows made of silk and looked out at the rose garden. She felt the coolness of the material against her skin, but she couldn't feel her heart. She just sat, dry-eyed. Empty.

Nancy had heard rumors of Landon's new girlfriend, but she'd chosen to write them off as dirty, untrue gossip. She heard the girl was a new, hot model, just twenty-one or maybe not even that old. Thin, long blonde hair, big tits, knockout body. The works. She waited to hear that Landon was getting this girl a part in a television show or a movie—she knew he liked to "sample" the talent before he moved it on, but when this girl became just a girl in his life, Nancy knew that it was different. This time, he had a girlfriend. Not just a fuck. This one had an invisible sash, like Miss America: Landon's girlfriend.

Nancy wanted her husband back. She couldn't wait to lose the weight she'd gained during her pregnancy. She dreamed about being thin and wearing a bikini and walking the beach in Mustique where she and Landon had been so in love at their wedding and on the honeymoon. She was determined; she would lose the weight, and then some, and Landon would forget he had ever looked at another woman. He would look at his beautiful, thin wife, and his wonderful new baby—his gorgeous family—and he would feel whole.

She just knew it.

He was being awful, but she knew he loved her, deep down.

She was not going to abandon her family. Not even when her husband was behaving like this. She couldn't. She would work her ass off, quite literally. She would win him back and have the family she always wanted. The whole nine. She would have everything.

Fifteen

March Greene was born, but neither of her parents were really there. Her father, Landon, was out of the country, and her mother, Nancy, had requested to be knocked out. It was not popular to be completely anesthetized, but Nancy didn't want to remember the birth. She just wanted the baby out, and wanted things to go back to the way they were as quickly as possible. If she could have selectively wiped out her memory for the past year, she would have.

Nancy's new assistant, Digby, called and left a message for Landon in Cannes to get him the news. He was elated. A daughter! He flew home immediately, returning the call from the plane, then limoed over to Cedar Sinai Hospital. Dressed in jeans, a T-shirt, and a black leather blazer, Landon looked more like a criminal than a new father. He hadn't bothered to shave or comb his hair, and the security guards all jumped when they saw him walk through the front door. Hands on their weapons, they watched carefully as he passed through the metal detector without setting it off. As he got on the elevator up to the maternity floor, he didn't see the guards shaking their heads in disapproval.

Nancy, on the other hand, had put on makeup. She was wearing a new negligee, trying to look sexy instead of matronly, as she lay propped up in her hospital bed. Waiting. Hoping that the baby would be the glue for her marriage. If Landon saw her and the baby she was practically presenting to him as a gift, he'd want to come back to her. She had butterflies in her stomach, despite labor and all the drugs she'd been given for the delivery.

Landon stopped by the nursery first. He looked in the picture window from the hallway to see the new babies. There were nine. He spotted March right away. The small, red face, the shock of black hair, the dark eyes. There was a second of timelessness for Landon as he stood there, in which he forgot who he was. Major Hollywood mogul? Womanizer? Husband? Son? For that rare second, while he stared at his baby daughter, he was just there. Just a guy.

Nancy had slipped an orderly a hundred dollars to keep tabs on when Landon arrived on the maternity floor, and where he was, and when he was coming to her room. So, when Landon found room 311, Nancy was sitting, poised, reading a book, made up, dressed beautifully, and prepared for his entrance.

"She's beautiful," said Landon. For a split second Nancy thought Landon had meant her, and she was disappointed when she realized he was talking about their daughter. "Good show."

"She looks just like you," said Nancy.

"Really?" Landon was pleased, but he demurred. "I think she looks like you." Landon took a long look at Nancy, and something he saw made him want to stay in the doorway, and not come any closer. She didn't look like the Nancy he knew. The fun-loving kid, always up for a party, so in love with him, ready and willing for anything he wanted. She didn't look like the kind-hearted woman he had married and then grown to dislike. She looked like a mother. Somebody's mother. He felt their ties disconnecting even more. Slowly and surely.

"Did you see her suck on her thumb?" Nancy asked. She was afraid to talk about anything else but the baby. The baby was the only thing between them that was pure and good. "It's so cute when she does that."

"Yeah." Landon grinned. Nancy loved seeing him like this. "She's great."

"I really think she looks a lot like you," she repeated, but too eagerly, and too nervously. Landon smelled the insecurity. The effort to please him.

"She has your coloring." Landon meant it as a compliment. Nancy's fingers flew to her face.

"Too pale?"

"No," said Landon, feeling slightly sickened at her self-doubt. He hated it. It made him feel like not talking anymore. He clammed right up.

"How was Cannes?" she asked, already feeling dread. How could she have been so stupid to let the conversation go there? "Any good films? Did you win anything?"

"I wasn't in Cannes. I've been in Hawaii," said Landon. Nancy looked surprised.

"Digby said you were in France. I thought he called you there."

"I set up an office there. They found me. On the Big Island."

"R and R?" she asked, trying to laugh.

"C'mon," Landon replied, laughing. Nancy loved to see him laugh. "Me? R and R? No. Actually, I'm thinking of buying a company."

"Pineapples?" mused Nancy.

"Sugar," he said.

"What about the movies?"

"I'm getting bored with movies."

"So you must have a house there," Nancy surmised. "Did you buy a house?" For us? She didn't dare ask the unspoken question. She was too afraid of the answer.

"Four," said Landon. This kind of news didn't surprise Nancy. Landon owned and sold things—people, properties, shows—so often that she gave up trying to keep track.

"I'm getting out of here this afternoon," said Nancy. "I sent the cook up to Malibu Seafood to pick up swordfish steaks." They were Landon's favorite.

"I can't stay," he said.

Her whole body slumped. This was what she had expected, deep down, and also dreaded. That he would leave her again. She wished she could be knocked out, just like she had been when she gave birth. She didn't want to know or remember any of this.

"Why not?" Pointed, challenging, it was the part of herself she felt was the least attractive, but she was losing her vanity.

"I'll call you," he said, coming to her bed to say goodbye. He wouldn't be trapped. Not by a woman. Not by a man. And surely not by a conversation.

"I was thinking of having one of those Jewish things. A baby naming."

Landon didn't answer.

She tried to be brave. "Will you be there? Do you want to invite your parents?"

"No," he said.

Nancy fought back tears, but it was no use. They came anyway.

"Did you even tell your parents that they're grandparents? Did you even tell them you have a daughter?"

Landon saw her tears and was paralyzed. He knew he was

hurting her, and, at the same time, he hated her vulnerability.

"Do you need anything?" he asked.

She shook her head, and bit her lip to stop the crying.

"I'll call you tonight," he said and kissed her on the lips. Fast.

"I know about her," Nancy said as Landon was walking out the door. He stopped in the doorway and turned to her. She stared at him full on, her tears ruining her makeup, her eyes square on his. "I know you have a girlfriend."

Landon shrugged. It wasn't defiance. It was, So now what? He stood there, preparing for whatever she was going to say next.

"Is she thin?"

Landon nodded, amazed that this was what Nancy chose to ask.

"Are you in love with her?" Nancy asked.

Again, Landon shrugged. "We have fun," he said.

Nancy nodded and looked away from him, down at her hands, white and swollen with water weight.

"You don't demand anything from me anymore," she said, sadly. It was the truth. "You don't sing your song, 'find me, get me,' anymore."

"I'm going back to Hawaii," he said. He didn't like maudlin moments. There was no point. Besides, she was just stating the facts. Facts that he already knew.

"I love you," she said, but Landon just started to leave.

"I gave you a child," she yelled after him, angry.

Landon stopped, and stepped back into the room. He responded to her anger. "You should have asked me if I wanted one, first," he said.

Nancy was stunned. She couldn't imagine anyone saying or feeling the things Landon did.

The cell phone in his pocket rang. Landon answered it, and as he did, he left. Nancy could hear him talking jovially on the phone as he walked away, down the hall to the elevator. His voice faded the farther away he got.

"You're by the pool?" Landon said into his cell phone. Nancy strained to hear. "Are you naked?" Landon said with lust in his voice. And then the person on the other end of the phone said something that made him laugh a deep, dirty laugh. One that the nurses in the maternity ward didn't usually hear while on duty.

"You sonofabitch!" she yelled after him, not knowing if he heard her or not. She threw the book she had been pretending to read against the wall. It fell, shut.

She called Digby.

"I need something," she sobbed to him.

Digby bit his lip. He had only been working for Nancy one week, but he liked her, and he knew she was going through hell. She'd given him free rein of her home, her things—he knew other personal assistants who had taken advantage of these situations, but not him. He was completely devoted.

"Say the word and it's yours," said Digby. He was two years out of Princeton and had an intense desire to be a Hollywood entrepreneur. He was going about it in a most unconventional way. While most of his friends with similar desires got prestigious jobs in the mailroom at CAA or William Morris, he signed up with a fancy temp agency, and when Nancy called for help, he was hired after one meeting with her. She liked his well-groomed, clean-cut, East Coast look, his pedigree, and his swift willingness to sign a confidentiality agreement Landon's lawyers had drawn up. The agreement was Landon's requirement for all help that Nancy hired. She could hire as many people to help her as she wanted. As long as they signed the contract, which strictly prohibited them from talking, writing, or giving any information to tabloids, neighbors, or anyone that had anything to do with anything that went on during their employment.

"Patty's Pizza, chopped salad? Teuscher's chocolates? Fred Segal shoes? Just tell me, I'll get it."

"I want . . ." Nancy started to cry. "I want you to tell me what to do."

Digby was unprepared for this, but he thought fast.

"Do you want company?" he asked matter-of-factly.

"I don't know." She sighed.

"I'll be there in twenty minutes," said Digby. He was already in the car with the key in the ignition.

Nancy got as depressed as she'd ever been. This was a mighty bad bout. She let the tears go, and sobbed. Let it all out. She felt exhausted. More exhausted than after delivering her baby. She was at the bottom of a black hole, and there was only one way out. Up the slippery sides. Nancy finished sobbing, wiped her makeup off, and decided what to do next.

Sixteen

Eve's honeymoon was glorious. There were no events. No "things they did." It was one long blur. Champagne and tuna tartare, and dancing naked around the hotel suite—on the beds, in the window, and in full view of anyone walking past.

At one point, Eve started to sing, "Ain't no mountain high enough, Ain't no valley low enough . . ." Naked, out the door and into the hallway—Fuller ran after her with a big hotel towel, trying to cover her up, as she cavorted past guests, waiters, and bellboys. But he found her act hysterical, and pretty soon they were both laughing so hard they couldn't speak. Fuller tackled her, and they convulsed with laughter. It was the best time they'd ever had.

They felt like they'd won some secret, fabulous prize of a lifetime.

The rest of the honeymoon was the ocean, the pool, the mountains, the volcanoes, the vegetation, the restaurants—and it all blurred. Skin and suntan lotion and champagne and the sweet smell of leis. The smell of Fuller and herself, mingled into a musky perfume. She'd never forget the smells. The feel of the gritty sand everywhere, and the clean hotel sheets, as she fell, literally, into bed. Happy.

Eve got pregnant on her honeymoon. She found out when they returned home. Eve was calm and deeply pleased. She wanted a baby and a family. She was also aware that this meant things were changing. Again. Fuller was beside himself with excitement. Eve took extreme pleasure in his reaction. She started to weep.

"What?" he asked. "Is this hormones?"

"No." She laughed. "It's you."

"What?" he asked. "You're afraid our son's going to look like me? Act like me?"

"No!" She laughed more. "Fuller—I'm just not used to the father being so happy."

"Are you kidding?" he practically yelled. "I'm a procreator. This is what I'm alive for."

She had never heard anyone say what she felt so many thought. It was a moment she knew she would always remember.

"I'm caveman. I'm Adam. I'm the first man on earth!" He jumped up on the sofa and beat his chest, looking to the sky.

Eve laughed and laughed. And so did he.

"I'm your husband, baby," he said as he jumped down and took her in his arms. "I'm your man."

It was the most comforting moment of her life.

Fuller and Eve got dressed up and giddily went to celebrate with a luxurious dinner at Michael's. For a girl whose idea of dinner out used to be the drive-through window at McDonald's, Eve was getting used to Fuller's wining and dining. She had sampled all of the most wonderful restaurants in Los Angeles. She'd even started reading cookbooks and cooking magazines and was trying to make some of Fuller's favorites at home. She was thrilled to find the recipe for 72 Market Street's meat loaf, and the look of surprise and delight on Fuller's face when he tasted it was worth a million bucks.

Fuller insisted that Eve quit work. The suggestion seemed silly to her.

"Why?" she asked, wide-eyed.

"Because you need to rest," he said.

Eve didn't understand.

"Why?" she asked again.

They both laughed.

"Because," he said. "Just . . . because." It wasn't something he had analyzed. He just felt it was right.

"Fuller," she said gently, "women work. This isn't that big a deal. I'm just having a baby. I can still function."

She remembered watching her pregnant mother lumber to the gas pumps to fill up a customer's tank, even when she was in her ninth month. Eve felt like she was spending her pregnancy in luxury compared to her mother's life. She chose baby furniture. A glider. Looked through huge books of baby announcements to choose the one she wanted for her baby. She loved the pampered feeling. Like she was the queen. But she felt guilty, too. Like, maybe she didn't deserve this. It wasn't the way she'd grown up. She'd only seen this kind of thing on television. In magazines that were glossy and airbrushed.

"You function perfectly," he said. "You're amazing. I just thought you'd want to have some time . . ."

"To do what?"

"I don't know," he said. He was getting flustered.

"Fuller, I feel useless. Like I'm sitting around hatching this big thing—I mean, I know it's our precious baby, but I want to be doing something. I want to help."

"I love you," he said.

"Me, too." But she felt uneasy.

"I wanted to give you this time," he said. "I guess that's what I was trying to do. I wasn't implying you were incapable or anything. I know that this is the last time we'll be just the two of us. After this . . ."

They both giggled again, but Eve felt tears come to her eyes.

"I'm a little scared," she whispered. Embarrassed to admit it.

Fuller shifted uneasily in his seat. He was scared, too. "I know. But we have the best doctors—we know everything about epidurals."

"Not that," said Eve. "Not labor. I mean, after. I'm not sure who I'm supposed to be. How I'm supposed to be. My mother just worked and worked and worked and worked and that was okay."

"You don't have to do that," said Fuller, then quickly added, "—if you don't want."

"I've worked my whole life, one way or another," she said. "I'm not looking for a free ride."

"Of course not!"

"This is all new," she said, and more tears fell. But they fell over her smile, and Fuller took her hand.

"For me, too," he said.

The process of "having" the baby seemed natural to Eve. She didn't buy a single book about mothering. But Fuller's friends forced them on her as gifts. She finally had a stack up to her knees of "self-help" mothering books. She leafed through them, but they didn't seem helpful. Just redundant. This was stuff any woman already knew.

The gifts came almost as soon as anyone found out, to congratulate Eve and Fuller on their expected baby. Nobody sent anything simply wrapped. Everything was delivered in baskets. Even a book couldn't come wrapped flat. It had to be stuffed in a basket, wrapped up in cellophane, and then tied with a fabulous ribbon. It was all a big production.

To Eve, the books and all the gifts that came even before the baby was born seemed silly. Like making a mountain out of a molehill. But she liked the excitement of the doorbell ringing, and finding the delivery man, or the UPS guy, standing behind some big, cellophane-and-ribbon-wrapped basket of goodies. It was like Christmas for nine months, and then some.

Eve had moved into Fuller's two-bedroom Studio City apartment after they'd gotten married, and now that she had quit her waitressing job it wasn't just a place where she "crashed" after work. Fuller's apartment had everything they needed to live comfortably, but it had always seemed to Eve to be mostly functional and never cozy. Now she had a real chance to make her feminine presence apparent in the apartment. She bought flowers and plants, sewed throw pillows from floral prints, and framed photos that Fuller had tacked to a bulletin board. She cleaned the apartment, organized drawers and bookshelves, painted walls, stenciled borders, replaced handles and pulls, and put up window treatments. The apartment was transformed into a real home. After a month, there was nothing left to do. Eve was bored. She found herself searching for more ways to keep busy.

"You don't have many friends," Fuller said to her one morning as they were finishing up breakfast. He noticed that Eve was out of activities. "In fact, you don't have any."

"You're my friend," said Eve, pouring more pancake batter onto the griddle.

"No more pancakes. I'm stuffed."

"But I made all this batter," she said. There were two gallon jugs full and waiting on the counter. Fuller just stared at her work.

"Stop cooking, honey," said Fuller. "And stop cleaning. This place is clean enough to eat off the floor, and we have enough food in the freezer to have ten Thanksgiving dinners tonight."

Eve sighed. She knew that Fuller was right. But she didn't quite know how to go about making friends. She and Fuller didn't know their neighbors, and, besides, most of them worked. Eve didn't have old college buddies because she'd never gone in the first place.

"Why don't you give Amanda a call?" he suggested.

"Amanda? I can't call Amanda Marinetta."

"Why not? You two might get along."

"Oh, come on! We're so different," said Eve. "I mean, we live in completely different worlds. It would never work."

"Okay," said Fuller. "Forget it. It was just an idea."

"You mean, like invite her for lunch or something?" Eve said, trying to find room in the refrigerator for the batter. There was none.

"Or don't," he said. "It's no big deal."

"I can't just call up Amanda Marinetta," Eve said. "She's, like, a celebrity, and I'm just a girl from the sticks. I don't know anything, and she knows about facials."

Fuller laughed.

"Well, it's true," said Eve, embarrassed that Fuller was laughing at her. "I'm a simple person. She's sophisticated."

"You know," said Fuller, "all this time I thought you didn't want to call her because she and I used to date. I thought you were insecure about that."

"Insecure about you?" she teased him. "Are you kidding? I have you right where I want you."

"Good," he said, kissing her neck. "And for the record, just in case you want to know—you're better in bed."

Eve didn't get mad. She was glad to know. It was a question she'd always wondered, but was afraid to ask. Afraid to seem petty, and afraid of the answer.

"I am?" she said. "Because I don't think about sex. I mean, I just do it. Should I think about it?"

"Why are you getting like this?" said Fuller. "Relax. You are the greatest."

"I just don't know people who have been in movies," Eve said, feeling uncomfortable. "I'm not sure I'd know what to do."

"Well, you're going to have to get used to it," said Fuller. "This is Hollywood. That's what people come here to do—be in movies. It's not a crime, you know—and they're just people. They're not all freaks."

"I know," said Eve. She stopped doing the dishes. "I guess I just feel like, What on earth would she want to be with me for?"

"Will you stop that?" said Fuller, losing patience. "She'd want to be with you for the same reason I want to be with you. You're wonderful."

Eve loved Fuller. This was one of the many reasons why.

Eve left a message on Amanda's answering machine, but after two weeks, Amanda still hadn't called her back. Eve didn't say it, but she was sure that she had been right. Amanda had no interest in a peon like Eve. An oaf. A waif. She made up words to describe herself—all of them denigrating. They were too different, she and Amanda. She was a bumpkin, and Amanda was glamour personified.

So Eve tried to forget her tacit rejection by Amanda, and she went on with her dull routine—growing bigger, cleaning, cooking—until one day the phone rang.

"Eve? It's Amanda," said the voice on the other end of the phone. "I'm sorry it took me so long, we were in Telluride forever, but listen, do you want to have Starbucks or something? I'm pretty free now that I'm back."

Just like that. They made a date for later in the week, and Eve showed up at the Starbucks on Montana with a half-eaten Ben and Jerry's ice cream bar in her hand. She looked around, but didn't see Amanda anywhere.

"We could have met for ice cream," said a voice behind big sunglasses. "We didn't have to pick coffee."

Eve turned toward the voice and saw it was Amanda behind the giant dark glasses. Eve almost didn't recognize her. Gone were the beautiful white pantsuit with pearls and the French tip–manicured fingernails from the wedding. Amanda had transformed. She was wearing Birkenstock sandals, a tight tie-dyed T-shirt, a bandanna around her head, and big, khaki shorts. Gone was the bob—her hair was now long black curls cascading out from under the bandanna. She looked like a hippie, only she was way too gorgeous. Five foot ten and there was no hiding that figure. Amanda gave Eve a hug.

"Oh, I'll still eat here, too," said Eve. "I was just starving, and there was this sign—outside Wild Oats where I parked—and they have these new ice cream bars. You want some?" Eve offered a bite to Amanda, who accepted. She took a nibble and made a face.

"Ugh," she said. "That's deadly fattening. Give me some more." She took the whole bar from Eve and bit off a giant bite, accidentally smearing ice cream all over her face. Eve had to laugh. She'd never politely offered to share and had someone take her up on it with such enthusiasm.

"I didn't recognize you," said Eve. "I like your hair. It's different."

"Oh, this? I change it a lot," said Amanda. "George likes it. He's a little freaky that way. Doesn't like to sleep with the same girl twice, if you know what I mean." Amanda laughed.

Eve joined in politely, but uncertainly. She didn't know what Amanda meant—or she wasn't sure she wanted to.

"I don't mind," said Amanda. "It's fun. Like dress-up. This is a weave," she said, pulling her now long hair. "I want to hear how you are," said Amanda, "but I have to talk first or I'm going to burst."

"Next," said the woman behind the coffee bar.

Eve quickly realized they were next in line. "I'll have an iced blended decaf mocha with fat-free milk and no whipped cream," she said to the woman behind the counter.

"Two," said Amanda, "and one chocolate coffee cake."

"Two," added Eve, and they giggled together. Right away Eve had a feeling that maybe they were going to be good friends after all. Despite the differences between them, and their worlds.

"Look," whispered Amanda. She held up her hand so that Eve could see that on the fourth finger of her left hand Amanda was wearing a huge diamond engagement ring and a gold wedding band. Amanda wore the diamond turned in, so it was on the palm side and no one could see it.

Eve looked at Amanda for explanation.

"We eloped!" Amanda whispered.

Eve started to shriek with glee and Amanda started to shriek. Until the two of them were jumping up and down, giggling, laughing, hugging, and making a spectacle of themselves.

"Next!"

"Excuse me," a man pushed in front of them to order. Amanda grabbed their food, slapped down some money, and led Eve to a table in the back.

"That's why I didn't call for so long," said Amanda. "We went to Colorado—George has this ranch—and we've been fucking our brains out ever since. Hey, the guy who married us—he wore a goddamn Stetson."

Eve swallowed. She wasn't used to cursing, but Amanda clearly was. The cusswords just slid off her tongue.

"I can't believe that we've been able to hide it from the press for so long," Amanda whispered. "George's going to have his PR firm issue a press release this week, so we're holing up in the house for a while until it all blows over. You wouldn't believe the fucking paparazzi. They're ruthless."

"What about his wife?" Eve asked. "I mean—his ex-wife?"

"They're done," said Amanda. "I mean, they've been done for a long time. But it's over. She's out of the picture."

Eve thought how hard that sounded. Out of the picture. Like mafia talk.

"So . . ." Eve swallowed hard. "You were seeing him while he was . . ."

"I can't help myself," said Amanda. "I just fell in love, and, yeah, I fell in love with a married man, but look how it all worked out!"

Eve tried to smile, but there was something inside that felt weird. Insecure.

"I know what you're thinking," said Amanda. "You're just married and this isn't going to happen to you."

"I wasn't thinking that," lied Eve.

"Look," said Amanda. "It's my life, not yours, so don't worry. I can't imagine you'd do half the things I've done." Amanda took a long drink. "Which is probably why Fuller loves you."

Eve was wild with wonder.

"He's very loyal," Amanda said with a faraway look in her eyes. "Fuller."

"Oh, I know," said Eve.

"I'm not saying that because we used to be a couple. I'm saying that because of the way he looks at you. The way he acts around you—the way he talks about you."

"He talks about me?"

"Are you kidding?" Amanda made a gagging motion with her finger in her throat. "He's completely in love. It's disgusting, really. He worships you."

Eve felt great. She laughed. She felt full of love. For Fuller, for her baby, for Amanda—even for herself. She didn't feel like an oaf or a waif or a bumpkin. She felt like a woman.

"Me, I'm a wreck. I mean, in your relationship, it's like Fuller loves you more than you love him."

"That's not true!" Eve protested, then thought again. "Is it?"

"Well, that's how it looks," said Amanda. "In mine it's the opposite. I just took one look at George, and he took one look at me, and that was it. I knew I would always love him more than he loved me. Not that he doesn't love me. It's just the way it is. Things are never equal. You know? It's just life. I hate that, but I have to live. I have to have fun. You know? I have to get fucked at least three times a week or I'm a complete and total wreck!"

Eve's eyes grew. She'd never—ever—heard anyone talk the way Amanda did. Not even the slutty girls in high school were this open. They were ashamed of their sexuality, hiding behind raccoon black-lined eyes, hair that hung over their faces. They showed off their bodies in halters and bare midriffs, daisy dukes that exposed their bare buttocks, but their eyes—they always hid those. Amanda was different.

"George is good for me that way. I mean, we had to be careful in the beginning. George just had to deal with his wife. But now that he has—I'm married to him! We can fuck legally!"

Eve couldn't imagine. Even though they were having coffee together, just the two of them, Eve felt like they were on different planets. Amanda sensed this, and reached out and touched Eve's arm.

"What?"

"I don't mean to be rude," said Eve, swallowing. "It's just that . . . don't you feel sorry for his wife? I mean his first wife?"

"Please," said Amanda. "George took care of her. Believe me. Besides, I should be thanking her—I'd send a gift basket to her if I didn't think it would piss her off. Really—I owe her big time."

"How so?"

"If it wasn't for her neglect, he never would have looked at me twice."

"You don't really think . . . that that's why you're together, do you? Because of neglect?"

"I don't know," said Amanda. "I don't care, either. I mean, I care that he did the right thing in the end—she's *very* well taken care of. If she wasn't, I'd probably only have one orgasm instead of a string—out of guilt."

Eve didn't know whether to laugh or not, but Amanda was serious.

"But now that she's set—I have to take care of us."

Eve looked sad and confused. All she could think about was how she would deal if Fuller met someone else while they were still together. Amanda saw Eve's sad face.

"Look, she got, like, forty million dollars, okay?" Amanda said, lowering her voice. "So wipe those puppy-dog eyes off your face. I mean, look, I didn't end their marriage. I just showed up. We fell in love. Besides, I hear she's already living with someone swell."

"Forty million dollars?"

Eve wondered how high forty million ones would be, stacked up. She had no concept of that kind of money.

"This isn't about you, baby," said Amanda, caressing Eve's face. "Can you imagine Fuller leaving you for anyone? No. He wouldn't. Because he loves you. If George loved his wife, then he wouldn't have fallen in love with me. And if she loved him, she wouldn't be fucking some architect as we speak."

"How do you get to have forty million dollars?" Eve asked. She remembered that if someone filled their tank at the gas station it totaled twenty to forty dollars at the most. Depending on the size of the gas tank.

"Hey, forget it," said Amanda. "I don't want to talk about money and have this turn into one of *those* kinds of conversations."

Eve had no idea what that meant.

"Tell me about you. How *are* you?" Amanda asked, really meaning it.

Eve wasn't used to that. "How are you," in Los Angeles, Eve found, was usually a formality to get to the real question. Which was usually the asker wanting something. But Amanda really wanted to know how Eve was. For real.

"Well, I'm pregnant," Eve squeaked.

"No!" Amanda yelled, and pounded the table dramatically. Everyone in Starbucks stared over at them. "No!"

"Four months," said Eve, nodding. "I'm exhausted."

"I don't believe it!" Amanda bellowed. "That's amazing!" Amanda got up and hugged and kissed Eve. Eve was taken aback with Amanda's effusiveness. She was also embarrassed because Amanda was making a little bit of a scene.

"Can you tell?" Eve giggled, offering her stomach for appraisal. Amanda glanced over and shook her head no.

"Only by your very un-Hollywood appetite," Amanda laughed, looking her over. "I guess the honeymoon went well."

"Yeah," said Eve, blushing. "Hawaii was beautiful."

Amanda just smiled at Eve, like she was deciding whether or not to say something. "Well, good for you," she finally said. "I want a baby so badly. I'm not like you. I'm old."

"No, you're not," said Eve. She guessed Amanda was twenty-nine.

"I'm thirty-five," said Amanda.

"Really?" said Eve, shocked. Amanda looked much younger than her age.

"Hey, I can count my eggs on one hand."

"Women have babies at thirty-five all the time," said Eve.

"Yeah, well, that's not my only consideration," said Amanda. "Not everyone's meant to be a mother."

Eve marveled at Amanda's wisdom. One minute she had her mouth in the gutter, the next, she was a sage.

"It's a hard thing to decide," said Amanda. "To really know. Besides, babies need two parents—I think. I'm not sure George is ready. I'm not sure he'll ever be ready. Some people should just support children in other ways. Y'know?"

Eve thought she was going to cry. This was the best coffee date she'd ever had.

"Anyway, the other thing is that George's a little gun-shy, but maybe he'll come around. Especially after he hears about you."

"About me?" Eve froze up at the mention of her and George in the same sentence. George was a colossally big deal, and Eve was less than a little speck. "You're going to tell George about me?"

"'Course," Amanda said, trying to put her at ease. "Why wouldn't I? We're going to be friends. I can just tell."

"Okay," said Eve. She felt like she was being swept along on a tidal wave. Amanda was very persuasive.

"Good." Amanda smiled happily and went back to wolfing down the chocolate coffee cake. "You know what I'm going to do for you—I'm going to take you to meet Jocelyn." Amanda was so pleased with the idea. She grinned proudly.

"Who's Jocelyn?"

"Don't tell me you don't know who Jocelyn is."

"I don't," said Eve, wincing.

"Well, I suppose there's no reason for you to know her up to now. You're not in the kid world, yet."

"Who is she?"

"Jocelyn is only the most important person in this town—if you have children," said Amanda.

"Is she a baby doctor?" asked Eve.

"No!"

"An obstetrician?"

"No!" Amanda laughed. "I can't believe I'm having this conversation—it's fucking great! You're a fucking piece of work—no wonder Fuller is insane about you. You're like a virgin."

Eve blushed hot red.

"Relax," said Amanda. "It's a compliment. I love that you don't know her."

"Really? Because I'm not feeling so great about it," said Eve.

"She runs the preschool," Amanda told her in a hushed tone.

"There's only one?" asked Eve.

"Only one that's any good," said Amanda.

"In all of Los Angeles?"

"Only one that counts."

"Really?" Eve was intrigued.

"Trust me," said Amanda. And Eve did.

Seventeen

Eve and Amanda walked down the street together, sipping coffee in takeout cups. As they approached the block of Montana where the preschool was located, Amanda steered Eve across the street, away from the school. A swarm of double-parked cars was beginning to assemble outside the iron gate.

"There it is," said Amanda. She touched her face to make sure her dark glasses were in place. "Butterflies and Puppydog Tails. It's an amazing school."

"Then why are we crossing away from it?" asked Eve.

"There are always photographers lurking around."

"Why?" asked Eve.

"To get pictures of celebrities taking their children to school."

"Oh." Eve tried to grasp all the details of this life. There seemed to be new ones added every minute.

"The photographers are awful, but not nearly as scary as some of the mothers," said Amanda ominously. "But they're the same mothers who show up every time there's something worthwhile. That's the thing about them. They're like human mercury in a thermometer. The more of them there are, the more sure you can be that something is hot."

Eve nodded, trying to learn. She was confused. "But you said this was the best school."

"It is a great school. It's the best preschool in town. But that means that everyone wants to go. You should apply."

"When the baby's born," said Eve.

"Are you kidding? People apply there before they even get pregnant—and the ones who can't get pregnant, they call the fertility doctor, then speed-dial the preschool right after. It's insanely competitive. You should call them. Tell Jocelyn you know me and George. It's the only way you'll get in.''

''To preschool?'' Eve balked. She hadn't even decided whether to do pastels or primary colors for the baby's room.

''Trust me,'' said Amanda. ''Do it for your baby. You don't want to be left out in the cold. Everyone's enrolling their unborn children. You'll be on a huge waiting list. Even this early.''

''I don't know,'' said Eve. ''I mean, I never went to preschool. What is it, anyway?''

''It's coloring and snack time and sandbox,'' said Amanda. ''But—just read the paper,'' she sputtered. ''There are creeps out there, passing themselves off as child care. I mean, turn on the six o'clock news. It's all you have to do.''

''That doesn't happen to people I know,'' said Eve. ''I mean, it happens, but to other people.''

''Eve,'' Amanda said seriously. ''This is the big city, honey. We've gotten death threats at our house. Me. The girl you just shared a piece of cake with. Someone wants to kill me.''

Eve wanted to say, But that's because you're famous. You and your husband have to hide from the tabloids. She and Fuller were just . . . regular people. Sort of.

''Death threats?'' Eve asked. ''People want to kill you?''

''Yeah, and not just the people who know us,'' Amanda joked. ''But, seriously, everybody who's had a movie open in this town gets them. Some are fakes and some aren't.''

''Wow.''

Amanda put her arm around Eve's waist, and they walked together.

''I'm just saying you have to be careful, that's all.''

''How do you know so much about children and preschool if you don't have kids?'' asked Eve.

Amanda was taken with Eve's directness. Most people didn't ask her that question. They just assumed that when someone Amanda's age didn't have children, it was because she couldn't. They felt ashamed for her, and kept quiet because they were afraid to broach a subject they thought would upset her. It was all their own insecurity that kept that question quiet. Which was fine with Amanda. She liked keeping most people at a distance. It was easier all around. She was careful about who she let into her life.

''I just know.'' She smiled. Eve accepted Amanda's answer; it was enough for her. "I didn't know anything about Hollywood when I came here, and I know it sounds weird, but there are rules."

"Rules?" said Eve. This sounded ridiculous to her.

"Nobody tells them to you. I'm breaking the rules by telling. So don't give me away," Amanda whispered playfully. But she wasn't kidding.

"Darwin would've gotten the biggest erection from this town." Eve didn't understand.

"You don't have to play by the rules," Amanda assured her. "You just have to know them. That they exist."

"I don't know if I want to be in this game." Eve laughed, but she was serious.

"You already are, hon," said Amanda. "You're married to Fuller, and he's part of Hollywood. You're going to want to be at Butterflies and Puppydog Tails. It's not just safe, it's excellent."

"I might just take care of my baby myself," said Eve. "You know, stay home, be a housewife."

"Great," said Amanda, smiling at what she considered Eve's naïveté. "I think that is wonderful. But just in case . . ."

They walked in silence for a while, then Amanda spoke again.

"If you apply and you get in, you don't have to go. You can make that decision later. I'm just trying to make sure your ass is covered. That's all. Do whatever you want. I'm done talking about this."

"Why are you being so nice to me?" asked Eve.

"God, you're looking for a motive already," Amanda said, laughing. "How long did you say you've been here?"

"Well, thank you," said Eve. It seemed so simple.

"I'm glad we're friends," said Amanda.

"Me, too," said Eve, and swung her arm around Amanda's waist. The two of them walked away that way. Like girls. Carefree and innocent.

Eighteen

"I'm home!" Amanda yelled, throwing her keys in the basket on a shelf by the front door. She was in a good mood. Being with Eve had been refreshing.

"Honey, I'm in here! Come on in!"

Amanda recognized George's professional voice immediately. She knew that he was in the company of someone he wanted to impress. With her.

"Only if you're naked," she yelled back, knowing she had an audience. Polite, and some lusty laughter from the other room.

She checked herself out in the 1920s piecrust mirror on the wall, and decided to brush her hair a little first.

George was entertaining two television actors—one a major recording star, as well. They were all laughing, drinking lemonade and eating pretzels from a crystal dish, when Amanda bounced in. Her energy immediately enervated the room.

"Hi!" she said, immediately recognizing the television stars. "Is this a four-way, honey?"

More laughter. Amanda was the star.

"Not today," said George, feeling her butt. She was his trophy wife, sex symbol, whore. With a brain bigger and better than any of theirs. And he knew it, and he knew that she knew it. The understandings between Amanda and George were endless, complex, and yet they worked.

"Amanda, meet Leslie and Bo."

"I'm a huge fan of both of yours," she said, rehearsed. This was the line she'd learned to use years ago.

"Thanks," said Bo, bobbing up and down. Too afraid to look her over, dying for her to leave the room so he could give her the up-down with his eyes.

"I'm a fan of yours, too," said Leslie. "I've seen your work. It's very good."

George raised his eyebrows to Amanda, and tucked in his chin. He was clearly making a deal with these two. Working with

George would catapult them into "overnight" success stories.
Amanda had seen this happen before.

"Thanks," said Amanda, and went over to give George a
smooch. She stuck her tongue in his mouth, and George pulled
her away. Reluctantly. Pleased.

"Whoa, honey. We've got company," said George, bragging
and scolding. The whole dynamic worked.

"I can't keep my hands off him," Amanda explained to the
guests as she caressed George's ass. Her lipstick was gone, wiped
off from the kiss. "We're newlyweds."

"Congratulations," said Leslie. "I heard."

Bo just bobbed.

"So, I'd better go before I do something else to embarrass
him," said Amanda. "It was nice meeting you all."

She left the room, her performance finished. She knew that
George liked to be the envy of his peers. So she did a little acting
here and there. No harm done. In the background, she could hear
them talking about how great she was, and George steering the
conversation back to business. The movie he wanted to make.

Amanda went to the kitchen, whistling, and opened the silver
doors of one of the two subzero refrigerators. She began opening
Tupperware containers and eating food with her fingers. She
kicked her shoes off. They landed in the middle of the floor. The
cook came by and scowled at her.

"Sorry," said Amanda to the cook, and put the food down
while she got a fork. Then she continued eating from the containers, but this time with the proper utensil.

"Would you like me to fix you a plate, Mrs. Foster?" the cook
asked, with no sign of the steep condescension the entire staff
knew she felt toward Amanda.

"No, thanks," said Amanda. "Your food is so fabulous, I can't
wait for a plate. I have to eat it like this."

The cook, who was fat and fifty, was named Karen Raif. She
disliked Amanda. She felt that Amanda had broken up Mr. Foster's last marriage, and the cook liked Mr. Foster's last wife. The
last wife knew the difference between a béarnaise and a hollan-
daise sauce. The last wife appreciated a roue. She could tell
grilled radicchio from wilted endives and shallots from green onions. The last wife made the cook's work enjoyable. This one was
trouble.

This one had a reputation already. She ran around naked, not
caring who saw her. She made love with Mr. Foster in any room

at any time she liked. She drank wine straight from the bottle, not even caring what year it was, and she requested what the cook liked to call "White trash food." Jell-O molds with "surprises" inside. Marshmallows, candies, coconut flakes. The cook cringed just thinking about it. She longed for the last wife. She wished someone would request a roasted corn chowder or a crab-meat soufflé.

"Did anyone call for me?" Amanda asked, her mouth full of potato salad.

"I'm sorry," said Karen, meaning, she couldn't understand Amanda with her rude manners. "Come again?"

"My phone?" said Amanda, finishing her food, and stuffing her mouth again. "Did anyone call?"

"I wouldn't know," said Karen innocuously. "I don't answer your phone, ma'am."

Amanda smiled at Karen. Her best fake smile. When Karen waddled out, in her white standard uniform and crepe-soled shoes, Amanda cursed her.

"Bitch," she said under her breath.

"Tramp," said Karen, under her breath, as she made her way to the lavish servants' quarters. Three apartments with full baths, and separate entrances, where the staff slept in case the Fosters needed them after hours.

"I'm jazzed!" said George, coming into the kitchen.

"For your atom-bomb-in-space film?" Amanda asked.

"They want to do it," said George, pacing in circles, his hands moving at double time in smaller circles. He did this when he was excited. "I've got my director by the balls, I've got my actors in my pocket, and the studio is going to lie down and beg to make my picture."

"Are you sure the studio will okay those actors?"

George looked at her as if she were an idiot and not his wife.

"I mean, they're just TV actors," she said.

"It's my picture," said George. "The studio can fuck itself. If they won't okay Leslie and Bo, I'll go somewhere else. Fuck 'em."

"Yeah, fuck 'em," said Amanda. She loved this boytalk. All the cussing and swearing. It was fun. "Fuck 'em, fuck 'em, fuck 'em."

"We're going to start preproduction in two weeks," said George, circling the stainless-steel cutting table where the cook prepped Mr. Foster's healthy foods.

"Fuck 'em, fuck 'em, fuck 'em, fuck 'em," said Amanda, switching to cole slaw. "Let's fire Cook. She's mean."

"Nah," said George, shaking his head. "She's the best cook we've had." By "we," he didn't mean he and Amanda. He meant he and his former wife and he and Amanda. All lumped together. George and whatever woman he was married to or fucking. Amanda decided to drop the subject. It wasn't worth a battle. She had to choose carefully with George. Besides, he was right. Karen was a good cook.

"I want to start shooting in fourteen weeks," said George.

"Is there a part for me?" she squeaked.

"A huge part," said George. "The most important part."

"Really?" She got excited and put down the food. "Should I lose weight for it? What's the part?"

"My wife."

She smiled. She knew that this was more important than any acting job. Hell, why not be honest. Her career was going to be as a Hollywood wife, and a mom if she was lucky. She understood her position. She understood what she'd given up, and what she got. She wasn't angry, bitter, or scheming. She was fine with it.

"Fuck 'em," she said, and took off her shirt, presenting herself to her husband. "I'm the fucking wife. Fuck 'em, fuck 'em, fuck 'em."

"Have you always been like this?" George asked, as they started making love in front of the open subzero.

"No," she said. "It's because of you."

"I've never met a woman who wanted so much sex," he said, happily.

"Maybe we should call a doctor," she said, teasing.

"To join us?"

She stopped and looked at him. He'd never mentioned anything like this, even in jest.

"I don't want anybody else," she said. "I don't do three ways. I don't share."

George looked at her, his interest piqued. She knew that look. Torpedo focus.

"You've never . . ."

"Once," she lied.

"With . . . ?"

Amanda didn't answer.

"Do I not want to know this?" he asked.

"Know what?" she said, guiltily.

"Is this where you tell me you made it with one of my best friends? One of my leading men? Women?"

"It's not important," said Amanda. "My past is my past. I did stupid things—I've told you this. You know, actresses . . . I was getting experience for my career."

"Anything for a part," said George.

"It was a long, long time ago," she said. "And I don't want a third person in our bed."

"Okay," he said. "Done."

He started to kiss her again, but this time she needed more coaxing, and when Cook walked in, George was slowly eating spaghetti carbonara off of his new bride's naked belly.

Amanda opened her eyes, sensing someone's presence, and saw Cook standing in the doorway, half her body peeking in, watching George and Amanda make love on the kitchen floor in front of the open fridge. Amanda closed her eyes again, letting Cook know that she didn't give a flying fuck who saw her in her own house. With her own husband. Cook left, silently swearing never to make that pasta dish in this house again. She let the door slam. George started, but Amanda just laughed.

Nineteen

"I met someone nice," said Amanda, when they'd finished. George lay facedown on the kitchen floor, breathing heavily. Amanda picked through the refrigerator for sustenance. She found some cold wild-mushroom tortellini and started munching.

"I never noticed this floor before," said George. "It's so . . . matte. Can you have a decorator do something to it? Give it some texture? Like that kitchen in that Woody Allen movie with 'Radio' in the title."

"Sure," said Amanda. "But don't you want to know who I met?"

"Sure," George said, half interested. He couldn't believe his good fortune in this wife. It was his fourth one, and, frankly, after the first marriage ended, he'd lost faith in the institution, but not the habit. He figured he'd have a string of wives. Just like the cars he bought, which he loved so much. Even after they failed him time and time again. Finally, though, he just couldn't drive them and get the same joy anymore. But this one. Amanda, she was something. An original.

"Fuller's new wife. Eve."

"Fuller got married? Your old loser boyfriend?"

"Yeah. You wouldn't go to the wedding because you were jealous, remember?" she said, zinging him. "I had to go alone?"

"I hate weddings," he said, and stood up naked, looking around. "Where the hell is Cook?"

"Does Cook have a name?" Amanda asked.

"Probably," said George as he walked around the big kitchen. He still had part of an erection jutting out from his body. "I'm fucking starving."

"I thought I'd invite them to dinner one night. If that's okay," said Amanda, handing George a Tupperware container from inside the fridge.

"Whatever you want," he said, opening the container. "Do I have to be there?"

"Yes," she said. "The only people we ever have dinner with are actors or directors you're going to work with on your next project."

"What the hell is this?" he said, looking at the contents of the Tupperware.

"Risotto," said Amanda, peering inside. She tasted it. "With scallops."

George handed the risotto to her, and went to the refrigerator himself. Amanda heaped fingerfuls of it into her mouth. She made a mess.

"So, is this his first marriage? Fuller?"

"Yup," said Amanda. The two of them stood there, naked, picking through the fridge. "Frankly, I'm surprised he did it at all. Just never seemed like the marrying type."

"Poor guy. First marriages are hell," said George. "Sure. Invite him. Invite her—what's her name again?"

"Eve."

"What's she do?"

"Nothing," said Amanda. "She's nobody."

"Great," said George. "I love nobodies."

"You do not," Amanda teased him. "You only say that in interviews."

"Well . . ." George considered this. "They do waste a lot of time."

"Define 'waste of time,' " said Amanda, reaching for George's erection. She started working on him, and he dropped the teriyaki chicken chunks he'd been eating. They splattered all over the floor.

"With you," he said, watching her go at him, hungrily, "there's no such thing."

Twenty

Gabrielle was busy. She didn't like to see herself as a victim, even though life dealt her problem after problem. She tried only to see the joy and the work ahead of her. When she was alone, she thought of herself in biblical terms. Her problems were "her work." She found happiness in being busy. Doing good. Making things better. Like Joey.

Gabrielle just knew she'd made the right decision when she chose him to be her husband. He was joy in her life. Love, dedication, responsibility. Everything that embodied marriage in her mind.

She was convinced Joey would take care of her. He would see her through this challenge her father had left them. This enormous debt. But she knew that she couldn't sit by idly. She was not lazy or useless. She had to help. She had to play her part. She had work to do.

Gabrielle was committed to seeing that Joey was successful. She began to groom him for greater things, starting with his clothes, then his car, then his mannerisms and vocabulary.

Joey hated his transformation. He felt like a picture his wife was producing. She had her hand in every aspect of his life, and she was unbelievably focused. Joey felt forced, pushed, trapped, and uncomfortable. But he never told Gabrielle. He couldn't. She was like a steamroller.

First she'd found this rental house that they couldn't afford at all. Then she got the realtor to drop the price to what they could barely afford. Then she furnished it on credit cards he had no idea how she'd obtained, since their credit record was ruined, or so he'd thought. She created an illusion of success to the outside world. Joey wondered how much she bought into it herself.

At parties and premieres Joey always headed straight for the drinks. A couple of beers to loosen up, and he was much better. Without the beers, Joey didn't like who he was anymore. He never played the piano at parties or at home. Never replaced the one the federal marshals had taken. Never sang. Not even when he was alone. It was as if his voice were gone. His tongue cut out.

While Gabrielle worked to find joy in life, Joey began to lose his.

When she was barely nine months pregnant, Gabrielle scored Joey a lunch date with Peter Shelton, the president of Allstar Studios. He didn't have time on his books until one month later, but it didn't matter. Joey was in the door.

Gabrielle had gone about this coup methodically and carefully. First she had met Shelton's wife, Missy, by scoping out the best shopping on the Westside. It was only a matter of time before she happened to run into Missy. When she did, Gabrielle was charming. At first it was polite hellos—"You look familiar— were you at the *Titanic* screening?" When they kept bumping into each other, their brief chats turned into talks, and, eventually, Missy was sure she had just met a new, undiscovered social gem. A "friend."

They began to speak every other day on the telephone and saw each other once a week. They made lunch dates, arranged teas, and dreamed about the baby play dates they would spend together with their children. They discussed the places they'd go to- gether—Cartoonland and Bright Kids, the two most popular in- door playgrounds on the Westside.

When Gabrielle was sure that Missy liked her well enough, she zeroed in for the kill: She brought up Joey.

The rest was pure Gabrielle.

"What do you mean, I'm having lunch with Peter Shelton?" Joey asked his wife.

"Cocktail, Mr. Joey?"

Joey jumped off the couch, shocked to see a strange woman offering him mineral water with a lime on a tray.

"What the fuck?"

"Joey, this is Consuela," said Gabrielle. She took the drink off the tray and placed it in front of Joey. "Thank you, Consuela," said Gabrielle. Consuela smiled at Gabrielle, and left.

Joey watched Consuela leave, and tried to figure out what she was doing there. "Where did she come from?" he asked Gabrielle when Consuela was out of earshot.

"She's our new maid, darling."

"We have a maid?" Joey asked.

"I just hired her," said Gabrielle. "She's exquisite. She used to work for Michael Eisner."

"Why do we have Michael Eisner's maid?" said Joey. This was too much. "How did we get Michael Eisner's maid?"

"Well, I wasn't going to hire a stranger," said Gabrielle.

"But we don't know Michael Eisner," said Joey.

"Everybody knows Michael Eisner," said Gabrielle. She sipped Joey's drink. "I spoke to him myself yesterday."

"You talked to Michael Eisner?!" said Joey, alarmed. "About what? You didn't, like, hit his car or something, did you?"

"No!" Gabrielle said, as if Joey were dense. "I inquired about Consuela. She listed him as a reference, so it was perfectly legitimate for me to call."

"Who listed Michael Eisner as a reference?"

"Our maid did, darling. Consuela. I had to check her references."

Joey took the drink from Gabrielle's hand and sipped it himself, then winced.

"What the hell is this? Mineral water?" Joey almost spit it out. "Miss," Joey yelled, "can I get a vodka on the rocks, please?"

"She's not a waitress, Joey," Gabrielle said, giggling. "You don't have to call her 'Miss,' you can call her by her name. Consuela."

Consuela came back in and took the mineral water from Joey. He watched her walk out. Consuela was broad and short. Sturdy looking.

"You probably hired her just so you could talk to Michael Eisner," said Joey.

"He was just lovely," she said.

"Yeah?" said Joey, sarcastically. "So, are we all having supper? Us and the Eisners? Skiing together in Aspen this winter?"

Gabrielle didn't know he was kidding. To her this was serious business.

"Not so fast," she said. "These things are delicate."

Consuela brought Joey his drink. He thanked her, uncomfortable in her presence.

"I feel like I'm supposed to tip her," said Joey, watching Consuela leave.

"You don't need to tip her. You already pay her a good salary," said Gabrielle.

"How much?" asked Joey.

"Four fifty."

"A week?"

"Cash," said Gabrielle. "Nobody will know."

"Know what? That we pay her four fifty a week cash? Do you know what that would be if we took out taxes? That's like seven hundred a week! We can't afford that."

Consuela came back in and handed Joey a coaster, then disappeared.

"Besides, how do we know she won't steal from us?" Joey whispered.

"Because we pay her so well." Gabrielle laughed. "She'd be crazy to lose this job."

"She's walking around our house, and we don't know who she is!" said Joey, getting nervous.

"Joey," said Gabrielle, "she's been checked out. Believe me. I hired her from a nanny agent. She's been fingerprinted, investigated, vaccinated—she's not going to steal from us."

Joey drank his vodka quickly. "You make it sound like she's a pedigreed dog," he said.

"If you're feeling liberal guilt, don't," said Gabrielle. "We were checked out, investigated, and had to give references, too. It was all mutual. Nobody is getting taken advantage of here."

Joey wasn't so sure. "What about when the Feds came and took your jewelry to pay your father's debts? Didn't that show up while we were getting checked out?"

"Oh, Joe," she said. "People here understand that kind of thing." She put her hands on his shoulders and started massaging out the tension that had quickly knotted up his muscles there.

"Forget about Consuela," said Gabrielle. "This lunch with Peter Shelton—that's something to think about. Now, that's where you should focus your energy, darling."

Joey drained his drink. He wanted another. Right away.

"It could lead to a job, Joe."

"I can get my own lunches, thank you," said Joey.

"I know," said Gabrielle. "I know you can. I probably

shouldn't have said anything to Missy, but I just started bragging about how great you are, and the next thing I knew, she was staring at me with that predatory look."

"What predatory look?" Joey asked.

"You know, darling—that look," said Gabrielle. "That look a person gets when they have to have something. That's how she was looking at me. She wanted you. For her husband."

"Mrs. Gardener, excuse me," said Consuela, appearing in the doorway. "Do you want me to serve your dinner in the dining room or out on the patio?"

"The patio, thank you," answered Gabrielle.

Joey was amazed. Gabrielle was so at ease with Consuela— and Missy and Peter Shelton, and Michael Eisner. She was so at ease with change.

Twenty-one

Gabrielle had her baby later that night. She woke Joey, gently, after midnight. She had already packed her bag and prepared his meals for the next several days. She held out a cup of cappuccino. He looked at it, then at her. Like she was nuts.

"Why are you giving me coffee?"

"Because you haven't slept much, honey," said Gabrielle. "I need you to get up."

Joey looked at the clock. Twelve-eighteen—a.m.

"Why?" he asked, squinting at her. She was dressed. With makeup on.

"I'm in labor," she said.

Joey was amazed. At her control of every situation. Even childbirth. They drove to the hospital, stopping for red lights. Joey had always imagined careening through them, Gabrielle screaming and writhing in pain in the back seat. But real life couldn't have been further from that fantasy. Gabrielle perspired, and focused inward. She was quiet. But no one would have ever known she was in labor.

Their first child was a son, Zachary.

The birth was uneventful. Gabrielle didn't want Joey in the

labor room, and that was okay with Joey. He knew that fathers were expected to be there, in the "front row," but he didn't want to be there. Not really. The fact that Gabrielle didn't want him there either was just fine. He had planned to spend the night in the hospital on one of the cots in the new mothers' room, which they'd seen during the hospital tour. But Gabrielle didn't want him there. She wanted him to be home. Comfortable.

Gabrielle took to mothering like it was a new sport—one not unlike lacrosse or field hockey. She took over from the hospital nurses without a glitch. She had devoured every book on childbirth—before the big event, during, and after. She felt well versed and confident. Once back home, Gabrielle was constantly in motion. Joey was in awe. Occasionally she complained that she was tired, but then she got through it, and, before long, they all got used to the fact that they were three. Gabrielle, Joey, and Zach.

After the baby, Gabrielle saw Joey less, as she became more of a manager than a partner. She managed the home, Joey's career, Zachary's life, and her own. She was always organizing and working. She always had the baby at her breast or in her arms.

Gabrielle and Missy Shelton went back to their "good friend" schedule as soon as Gabrielle had lost her pregnancy weight. Which happened quickly. Between nursing, jogging, and working out daily, Gabrielle was fit again in a short time. She didn't look like a new mother. She looked like a model.

She already talked about having another baby. She did everything like it was so easy. She couldn't wait to move on to the next thing.

Twenty-two

Gabrielle laid out Joey's clothes on the bed. She chose an Armani suit and an unusually quiet, brown Versace tie. She stared at the outfit, then changed the gray shirt for a beige one. This was the same way she laid out Zachary's clothes every morning. Gabrielle held up a pair of Oliver Peoples tortoiseshell eyeglasses.

"I don't need glasses," said Joey as he came into the bedroom, freshly showered. "I can see fine."

"These make you look very smart," said Gabrielle. She stood back and assessed her creation. "They make you look like an untapped genius. Erudite. Anyway, they're just glass. Not prescription. Faux glasses!"

Joey examined them, and then put them on.

"They feel weird," he said, but he looked in the mirror and was shocked at how great he looked. Gabrielle was right. The glasses were a perfect touch.

"Peter Shelton wears glasses," said Joey, suddenly wondering something. "Do you think they're fakes, too? Do you think really he can see perfectly?"

"You'd better go, darling," said Gabrielle, checking the time while she quickly dressed her husband. Joey took a good look at himself in the mirror. Then Gabrielle took his hand and led him to the door, where Consuela stood with Zachary in her arms. Gabrielle handed Joey the car keys and a fresh personal bottle of water. She kissed him and watched him get into his car, as if he were going off to war, and then the women stood and waved him off, as he backed out of the driveway.

"Good luck," said Gabrielle.

"Good luck, Mr. Joey," called Consuela.

Lunch at The Grill was easy. Couple of grilled fish, couple of mineral waters, lots of talk about kids, wives, families, and, finally, projects. It felt more like lunch with a friend than lunch with someone who could change his life.

Before Joey even got back home again that afternoon, Gabrielle already knew the outcome of the lunch. She had called Missy, who had called Peter in the car. Peter told Missy that he was impressed with Joey's education and that he liked Joey's lack of ambition. The thing Peter Shelton hated most was some dippy, twentysomething, flavor-of-the-month, Ivy League hotshot, who was determined to get his job. Joey was nothing like that. He was a solid family man. Loyal. Shelton hired Joey as a creative exec at Allstar Studios, and felt pleased with his decision. He knew that he could count on Joey.

Missy called Gabrielle back to relay the information. She told her how much Peter loved Joey, but not the reason why, of course. Lunch had been a huge success. Joey was in.

Gabrielle screeched with joy, then called everyone in town to tell them the good news. She was hoarse by the time night rolled around. She consumed most of a bottle of Cristal and very little of the food Consuela had cooked them. She rewarded Joey in bed, and he was pleased that he'd made his wife so happy.

Gabrielle was still ecstatic the next day, and planned a fabulous party for Joey to celebrate his new job. She carefully cultivated a mild buzz around town. She didn't want to appear too excited, because then everyone would think Joey was grateful and pathetic instead of deserving and easily lucky. She walked a thin line to pull this off, and she did it well. People were calling people to find out how to get invited.

At the party, Joey recognized half of the guests. The other half he didn't know at all. They were people Gabrielle thought Joey should meet. For work. She had invited them to get to know him. Joey felt the same way he'd felt at his Bar Mitzvah. Embarrassed, unsteady, the star of a show he had been forced into yet knew he had to do because his family wanted it. He shook hands, tried to be polite, and counted the minutes until the whole thing was over and everyone went home.

Gabrielle had a ball. The party went even better than she had expected. Everyone had been trying to get to know Joey. And Joey kept resisting. He appeared to the guests to be modest and humble. Gabrielle knew this was a perfect demeanor for him. Especially for this party.

She knew that with her behind him, Joey couldn't help but move up. She was right.

Twenty-three

After a whirlwind three months Joey was promoted from creative exec to vice-president. He was the hottest executive in Hollywood. He was speeding up the ladder and everyone noticed.

Three months after that, the hoopla of congratulations began to wind down. The heat began to recede. Joey struggled to get through the weirdness and the guilt that nobody spoke about, but that everyone knew came hand in hand with undeserved success.

Joey found that there was nowhere left to hide. Everyone at

the studio was becoming quickly aware of what he did and didn't do—of his talents, or, in Joey's case, lack of talent, lack of passion, lack of genuine interest in making big-studio movies.

After a year in his job, rumblings began that Joey might be fired. Not just in the halls and by the proverbial water coolers, but out on the street. Word had even permeated the Hollywood wives' and mothers' circles. Women speculated over cell phones while waiting in the carpool lanes, watching their five-year-olds practice soccer, or after yoga classes, at Starbucks and Robek's Juice, or DiDio's frozen ice shop. Gabrielle, of course, found out, and became enraged. She didn't deny anything, she just went straight to Joey.

She knew exactly how to handle him. Swallow the anger. First things first. In their order, in their place.

Gabrielle prepared a wonderful homecooked dinner, and after they'd dined, she took Joey on a stroll around the rolling hills and flowered gardens in the backyard of their newest home, this one purchased. They were in over their heads in the two-million-dollar mini estate in Brentwood. But the bank who gave them their mortgage owed Allstar favors. Allstar had sent Fidelity Union at least two dozen major motion picture clients for mortgages, some as high as six million dollars. Allstar was a good customer of the bank. So, when the Gardeners mentioned that Joey was a vice-president at Allstar, the bank gave them their mortgage right away. If Allstar bet on Joey Gardener, then they would, too.

Joey, Gabrielle, and little Zachary moved into their beautiful new home and, once again, Gabrielle refurnished and redecorated. She had had the grounds specially landscaped with a koi pond, fountains, and stone benches placed around the property. Almost everything was falling into place so nicely. Zachary was almost two. Gabrielle was pregnant with their second child, and their home was wonderful. Now, if she could just make sure that Joey was on course.

Gabrielle walked Joey, on that special night, to the big swing that she had had hung between two old eucalyptus trees only just that week. She had choreographed the stroll before he came home. She'd decided the family swing would be a perfect place to cut to the chase.

"I love being married to a studio executive," Gabrielle whispered, snuggling close to Joey. They were sitting together on the swing and rocking, gently. He hiccuped, and moved his head away, trying not to breathe on her. He was already plastered, having drunk far too much wine at dinner. He knew his breath was potent from the liquor. He had consumed almost three entire rolls of mints to hide the smell.

It was still light outside, but the sun was low enough in the sky to put a chill in the air. Joey pulled Gabrielle in close to him. He loved when she was happy. "I'm so proud of you," she said, planting a kiss on his cheek. "I'm so glad I married a real player and not just one of those generic Hollywood *wannabes.*"

She spat out the last word with contempt, but Joey was too drunk to cringe. Inebriated, he pondered instead. Alcohol was wonderful at times like these. He fully appreciated and was grateful for its effects.

"I think we need to move faster on the preschool issue," Gabrielle said, going over her mental checklist. "We're still on the waiting list, and I will just be mortified if Zachary doesn't get in by September—and I don't want him just in, I want him in the morning group."

"What do you mean?" asked Joey, confused.

"The afternoon group is just civilians," Gabrielle said with contempt. "Nobodies. I want morning. That's where all the important children are. Can you call Peter Shelton? See what he can do?"

"Call the president of the studio to get my kid into preschool?"

"He's not the president of a studio, Joey. He's your friend."

"He's my boss."

"That's how it all works, darling." She smiled sweetly. "We're friends with our business colleagues."

Joey never felt comfortable with the way people threw that word around in L.A. *Friend.* It didn't mean the same thing it meant in other parts of the country. It was more subjective here. Friends were people who could help each other. When they couldn't help each other, they were no longer friends. "Used to be" was the answer you gave when someone asked if you were still friends with an out-of-favor powerhouse. Used to be. Haven't seen them in a while. Wonder what they're up to. Not really meaning it, just spitting out the lines like a doll with a string in its back, programmed to say certain things when the string got yanked.

"And what about Tom Hanks?" Gabrielle asked, knocking Joey out of his reverie. She was on a roll. "Can he put in a word for us?"

"Tom Hanks?" Joey balked. "Why would Tom Hanks do something for me? I don't even know Tom Hanks."

He hadn't meant to argue with her. He always lost. Especially lately. He knew that any argument would be futile. Whatever she didn't have, Gabrielle would find a way to get. She would just arrange a dinner date with Tom Hanks and Rita Wilson. She would get them to meet whomever they needed to meet.

"Everybody wants to meet you, honey," said Gabrielle. "You're very important. You can develop a movie. You have that power. It's intoxicating. I wish you knew that."

"I'm not going to fabricate a meeting and a friendship with Tom Hanks just so he can get my kid into some preschool."

"Then fabricate a meeting to do a project together."

"Do you hear what you're saying?" he asked her.

"It's not *just* preschool, Joey," she stressed. "I want Zachary in with the right sort of people. Surely you do too."

"They're not even people," said Joey, trying to make sense of this. "They're three-year-olds."

"There are going to be play dates and parties—this could be another big career opportunity for you," Gabrielle instructed him. "You will meet a lot of the right people if Zachary is in the morning group."

"*I'll* meet the right people in preschool?" Joey asked, rhetorically.

"Yes," said Gabrielle.

"*I'll* meet people in preschool." Joey started to giggle. "What about Meg Ryan and Dennis Quaid? Can't they get us in?"

"How is my child's preschool going to be a career opportunity for me?"

"It's an opportunity for everyone involved," said Gabrielle. "Everyone wins."

"It's not a game," said Joey. But in that instant, he began to think that maybe he was wrong.

"Why are we arguing?" Gabrielle asked. "Zachary is almost three years old, and I want to send him to this school. I've made up my mind. So just help me."

"Okay, okay. I'll talk to Peter."

"*And* Tom Hanks. And Will Smith."

"Fine," said Joey. "I'll find a way."

"I wish we could get the Fosters to give us a recommendation," Gabrielle said, biting her nails.

"Do you know them, too?" Joey asked, amazed.

"Not even close," said Gabrielle. "Maybe I can meet someone who knows her. Maybe you could talk to him."

"I don't know George Foster."

"Make a movie with him then. Those violent, action films always do well. Maybe then you could invite them over."

"Sure," said Joey and kissed Gabrielle's head. Her jet black hair was flat and shiny and parted on one side. She was perfect, like a doll. He was in awe of her. Even when she was like this. "Whatever'll make you happy."

"Thank you," she purred. "We just have to get into that preschool. Jocelyn Stone, the one who runs the school, she's very discriminating."

"The pretty one?" Joey asked.

"Mmm, former athlete," said Gabrielle.

"Oh, yeah," said Joey, remembering some of the guys talking about her. "Volleyball. . . ." He adjusted his crotch. "Long legs, right? Blonde?"

"I sent flowers, I baked cookies, I donated library books to her school, I bought plane tickets at her school's silent auction fundraiser last spring, and I'm still not in."

"What do you think of the name Murray?" Joey put his hand on her stomach, feeling for a movement from the tiny five-month-old fetus inside her.

"Murray?"

"Only if it's a boy."

"Murray?!" She laughed.

"For my father?"

"Murray Gardener?!"

"For my father," he repeated, hurt. "It was his name."

"It's just that it's so . . . Jewish."

Joey looked at her like she was nuts.

"You need some new clothes," said Gabrielle, quickly changing the subject. She sat up straight, so she could look at Joey more clearly.

"I don't need clothes," he said, yawning.

"You need an entirely different look. I don't know why it didn't occur to me before."

"It's not my clothes that are the problem," said Joey sharply.

Gabrielle's skin prickled. Every hair stood up on her arms.

"It's me," he said, softly. "It's my life."

She tried to stay calm.

"I can get you some books at the Bodhi Tree if you want," she offered. Her annoyance was clear. "Is that what this is about? A mid-life issue? Because I thought we took care of the music problem."

He smiled bitterly. The music "problem." He wondered if she considered him the husband problem—or maybe just the husband "issue."

"No," he said, "it's not that. I just get bored at work. I'm not that interested in movies. I mean, it's like I pulled the brass ring, and it wasn't that hard, and I don't even want the grand prize."

"Well, I do," she said, smiling. "Anyway, we have to. We're over our heads in debt."

"I know," said Joey. He had to look away. Looking at her was too painful. They had reached an impasse.

Gabrielle didn't like this. She sat up and pulled away from his snuggle.

"I've heard some rumors," she said. "I hate gossip, but it's impossible not to hear it."

Joey yawned and shrugged. There was a lot he loved about his life here. The perfect house in Brentwood. A horseshoe-shaped ranch house with five bedrooms, a pool, a little waterfall that gurgled. Gabrielle had decorated the whole place herself in about two seconds flat. It had cost a fortune, but the credit cards held up, thank God.

"What's going on?" she asked. "Because I want to help."

"Nothing's going on," Joey lied. "I don't know anything about these 'rumors' you're talking about."

"Joey, I see you. You blather on the telephone at work. You take extraordinarily long lunches and long weekends, without worrying about what's going on at the office. It's almost like you'll do anything to keep from going in to the studio."

"I can't help it," he blurted out, and sat forward in the swing, making it lurch. Gabrielle held on tight so she wouldn't fall off. "I don't love business," he said. "I don't give a shit about 'creative meetings' that aren't creative. You can't schedule in 'creativity' for an hour before lunch. It's just not a job I'm naturally suited for."

"That's exactly what everyone's saying," she said. Joey was constantly amazed by his wife. She not only über-ran the house, she knew everything that everyone said. She was like a one-woman CIA. She knew it all. "And frankly, we can't afford bad word of mouth when I'm campaigning for a spot in the morning group.''

Joey looked at her like they were speaking two different languages.

"Look, I'll get you into the goddamn preschool," he said, raising his voice. "I'll get you morning or afternoon or midnight—whatever you want—but you should know . . . that what everyone's saying, as you put it—well, they're right.''

"What are they right about?" she asked ominously. Tacitly daring him to tell her the truth.

"That I dread it," he snapped. "I dread it all. I loathe the writers and their meetings—I zone out. I glaze over. I'm the first to admit it. They're sitting there, pitching their brains out, trying to explain a character or a plot to me, and I'm somewhere else. And don't think I don't know that they make jokes about me. All the writers and directors in town think I'm an idiot, but they don't dare say it to my face. Because I'm the man. I'm the suit."

"All men hate their jobs, darling," said Gabrielle. "It's the way it is."

Joey stared at her, sadly.

"This is it. This is life. I want to help you. If you don't like this job, we can strategize together. We can parlay this job into another one that's even better. You have leverage as long as you're at Allstar. If you're fired, you don't."

"I hate my job, and I suck at it!" There, he'd said it.

"If you get fired, you can say goodbye to me and the children."

Joey's stomach dropped.

Gabrielle got up off the swing and walked purposefully away, into the house.

"Wait a minute," Joey called after her. She ignored him, and shut the door. Hard and tight. Joey got up and went after her, but she was too fast for him. He heard the bedroom door slam shut. He stopped still.

There was no longer any choice. He could not lose his family. Which meant he had to hang on to his job. Which meant Joey had to do something to make himself indispensable to Allstar Studios. And fast.

Twenty-four

As soon as the epidural wore off, Nancy got on the phone.

"I need to speak to Radu," she said authoritatively.

"This is he," said Radu, the locally famous trainer to all the swimsuit models. His Eastern European accent was thick.

"Radu, this is Nancy Greene. I need your help. Right away."

"Of course, Mrs. Greene," said Radu. He had heard of her, her husband, their empire, and he was excited to be speaking to her in person.

"How soon can we start?" she asked.

"Well, I can make some room for you this afternoon," said Radu, wondering how he was going to move other clients to accommodate Mrs. Greene. He knew that she was the key to a whole new clientele, a whole new level of success. He was looking to expand, and this could be the call that would do it for him.

"I don't know," said Nancy, looking down at her inert body, under the covers. "I've got this epidural thing, and I can't quite feel my legs yet."

"What?" Radu didn't understand.

"I had a baby today."

"Today?" Radu loved this. She was crazy and she was determined. The perfect combination for him.

"I need to get into shape," she said, confidentially. "I want to be in the best shape of my life."

"Why don't we make an appointment for next week," said Radu. "Any time before then . . . is just too soon."

"Next week?" Nancy squeaked. "Radu, you don't understand."

"Why don't I come by and we have a consultation," said Radu. He didn't want to lose her as a client.

"Perfect," she said. "I'm at Cedars-Sinai Hospital. Room 311, in the maternity ward."

"You're still in the hospital?" he said.

"How's two this afternoon?" she asked. "So far, I don't have any other appointments."

"I'll be there," said Radu, in amazement. If she was truly this disciplined, he was going to have a wonderful time with his new client.

"Good," said Nancy. They both hung up. She sighed. Okay. Things were moving, now. She didn't care what the cost was, she needed a trainer at her beck and call. She was no longer pregnant, and she was going to do something about all the weight that was still on her body. Now.

"Flowers!"

Nancy looked up from her bed. A hospital attendant was wheeling into her room two carts filled with huge, expensive floral arrangements, metallic silver and pink balloon bouquets with "It's a Girl" printed on them, and stuffed animal gift baskets. The attendant started to unload the gifts.

"Stop!" Nancy said to the attendant. "I don't want these."

The attendant was surprised.

"Just give me the gift cards."

He pulled the gift cards off and handed them to her.

"Now, I want you to donate all these flowers somewhere—are there any mothers in the hospital who might appreciate these?"

The attendant didn't understand. He looked at the flowers. He thought that anyone would appreciate them. They were beautiful arrangements.

"Never mind. Just make sure they go to other mothers," said Nancy. "Poor ones, if you can find any."

The attendant started to back out, slowly and clumsily, wheeling the carts into the hallway.

"If you hurry, you can deliver them while they're still fresh." She tried to smile. "Those gardenias fade to brown in a second."

The attendant knocked one pot of flowers over, as the cart collided with the doorjamb. Nancy could tell he didn't understand a thing she wanted.

"You know what? Just leave them there," she said. "I'll call the hospital administrator to make sure they get delivered to the right people."

"Yes, ma'am." The attendant took the flowers out, but banged into another cart that was coming in. More flowers and gift baskets. The first attendant gave Nancy's instructions to the second attendant, and he, in turn, gave them to a third, who was down the hall with yet another cart of flowers. It was like a parade.

Nancy looked at the cards. Bruce, Demi, Warren and Annette, Iman and David, Arnold and Maria, Brad, Gwyneth and Winona, Leo, Madonna and Oprah, Rosie and Parker and Belle—celebrity business partners—as well as a slew of relatives and lawyers and accountants she'd met only a few times, but with whom Landon did regular daily business.

"Are you nursing, Mom?"

Nancy looked up at the black nurse grinning at her from the doorway. The nurse held baby March in her arms. She was crying, red-faced.

"Baby's hungry, Mom."

Nancy looked down at her breasts. They were big. Bigger than they'd ever been.

"Will these stay like this?" she asked the nurse. The woman started laughing. She was jolly, and she thought she'd heard it all.

"No, hon," she said. "They go back down. It's temporary."

"Huh," said Nancy. She examined her near-exploding chest. "Too bad." Now she knew what to do next. Get breasts. She'd buy some new ones. Just like these, but full of saline instead of milk. The kind that would never go down.

"Mom? Are you nursing or not?"

"Sorry." Nancy laughed. "No. I'm not nursing. Can you give her a bottle?"

The nurse smiled and made a U-turn back to the nursery to get some formula for March.

As soon as they'd left, Nancy felt a pang. A yearning. An anxiety.

"Wait!" she yelled.

She realized what it was. She needed her baby with her. It was a physical longing.

The nurse returned, carrying March. The baby was still balling.

"Will you let me give her the formula?" Nancy asked. The nurse smiled.

" 'Course I will," she said. "I was just waiting for you to ask me."

The nurse handed the baby to Nancy, then left to get the formula. Nancy looked down at the tiny bundle swaddled neatly in hospital blankets. Her little face was red and angry. Nancy studied her, and brought her up to her face.

"I love you," she whispered. The baby didn't stop crying, but her eyes turned to try to focus on her mother. As if she recognized Nancy's voice.

"Don't cry, honey," she cooed, and settled her. She fit so nicely just under Nancy's arm. Nancy felt immediately better. The nurse returned with a bottle.

"Want me to show you how to do it?" the nurse asked.

"I think I know," she said, and took the bottle, and put the nipple to March's lips. The baby struggled for a few seconds, and then took the bottle. Nancy fed her daughter. She stopped crying. Nancy started. Silently.

"There you go," said the nurse, and left.

Nancy looked down at March. She was content, sucking on the bottle, nestled in her mother's arms. Nancy smiled at her, peacefully. It was the first time she'd felt content since she'd gotten married. Maybe there was one person in her world she could satisfy. March.

Twenty-five

At home, Nancy fell quickly into a routine. She worked out like a fiend. Radu was a constant presence in her home. He got her started on a high-energy diet, and was impressed with her enthusiasm. Nancy embraced her workouts with fervor he'd never seen.

When Radu wasn't coaching her, she got massages three times a week, dyed her hair blonde, had her teeth bleached white, got her lips shot up with silicone, had cheekbones "implanted," and, of course, she shopped. Church fell by the wayside, along with her husband. They were both absent from her life. Nancy had lost something, and she had gained something else at the same time. Determination.

Sometimes, wiping out all the work she'd done in rehab, she took drugs and alcohol to try to remember what it was like to be happy. But the drugs never helped for very long, if at all. She couldn't get the right mixture. There was no gray area. She was either too sober—and too lucid, her mind clicking away—or else she was completely passed out with no memory of how, exactly, she got there. The other bad thing about the drugs and alcohol was that they made her workouts less effective. So she quit. Just like that. Except for the amphetamines. Those helped her get more done during the day.

Losing weight and making herself a better body was her goal. To the outside world, it had become her obsession.

Shopping was one of Nancy's passions and punishments. She was fanatical about it, hunting down beautiful things with a fervor. She often found herself sweating as she plowed through Fred Segal, her eyes darting from boutique to boutique, not missing anything. Whenever she saw something she liked she quickly asked the person wearing it where she'd bought it. How much was not a question for Nancy. That didn't matter.

She didn't like shopping with friends because they always wanted to gossip, giggle, and stop for a cold drink when their energy sagged. Nancy's energy never sagged when she shopped. Shopping was sobering and intense for her. Serious business. She didn't quite use her husband's terms—"Get me this! Find me that!"—but those were the directions she gave in more pleasant phrases. "Could you? Would you? When can I have it?" Digby was always kept busy getting and finding for Nancy, his boss. He didn't mind. He liked the work.

The only problem was, there was one thing Nancy couldn't buy—her old body.

In the dressing rooms, she silently berated herself. Having baby March had wrecked her figure. There was fat where there had been none before. Her waist was gone, replaced by a column of flesh rolls, puckering around her belly button where the extra pregnancy skin had once rounded over her daughter. The young, fresh clothes didn't fit right. Nancy asked for a size ten, but the salesgirl told her that this probably wasn't the store for her.

Nancy whirled around and fixed her big lavender eyes, newly tinted by contact lenses, on the grad who was just doing the retail thing for the summer before she zipped off to USC.

"What do you mean?" Nancy asked, holding the too-small size-eight dress out for the girl to take away.

"We don't carry size tens here in Santa Monica," the girl responded through gum-chomping jaws.

"I'm not really a size ten," Nancy croaked. "I just need one in this dress. It runs small."

"Well"—the girl looked at the dress and bit her lip—"I could try to special order it for you, but I don't know . . ."

"Why do you have to special order it?" said Nancy, tears welling up in her eyes. "Why don't you carry size tens in this dress?"

"We don't carry size tens in anything," said the girl, examining Nancy's eyes. She'd never seen eyes that shade of lavender.

"Why not?" said Nancy, feeling very vulnerable.

"We don't cater to those sizes," said the girl.

Those sizes. Nancy felt like she'd been hit with gunshot.

"Why don't you try the department stores," said the girl. "They have big sizes."

"But I'm not a big size," Nancy said, then immediately wished she hadn't. She was embarrassed that she was caught in this moment. By a stranger.

She went back into the dressing room and disrobed. Stared into the mirror at her body. She was wearing a floral print Natori bra and panties that cost $150, but they couldn't hide the fact that Nancy was no longer a *real* Fred Segal customer. She was someone who wore "those" sizes.

"I've been dieting and working out eight hours a day," said Nancy, turning to examine her body.

"You look good," said the girl, glimpsing Nancy's body in the dressing room and nodding encouragingly. Nancy realized she'd left the curtain open. "For a mom," the girl added.

Nancy cringed for a fraction of a second before she lost it. Tears rolled down her face, and she started to cry.

"Are you okay?" asked the girl.

Nancy let an audible sob go. The girl didn't know what to do. She looked for Digby, but Nancy had sent him off to buy her makeup in another part of the store. The girl shut the dressing room curtain. A naked body was one thing, but emotional outbursts were something that would attract attention.

"God, do you have your period or something? Do you want some Midol?" she asked through the curtain.

Nancy shook her head. "No," she said. "I haven't gotten my period back yet."

"Maybe you're pregnant," said the girl. "That's why you're so puffy."

"I can't be pregnant," sobbed Nancy. "I haven't had sex since the baby."

The girl looked around for help. This type of situation hadn't been part of her two-week retail training course. There were no managers or other salespeople in sight. The girl wished Nancy would stop crying.

"I went without sex for a while once," said the girl. "My face really broke out."

Nancy stopped crying. She looked up at the curtain, as though to glare at the girl on the other side. Who *was* this person?

"Sex really, really helps your complexion," the girl said.

Nancy took a giant deep breath and got it together. She pulled on her clothes. She looked at the blue gingham sleeveless dress in a size eight. It was the enemy.

"Hold this for me," said Nancy, coming out of the dressing room and flinging the dress, hanger and all, at the girl.

"But it's not your size," said the girl, confused.

Nancy was already dressing. "It will be," she said.

"We only hold things for five business days," said the girl, getting uppity. She looked Nancy over, thinking there was no way Nancy was going to a size eight in five days.

"That's all I need," said Nancy, smiling sweetly at the girl, thinking, Poor stupid thing, you just won't get it. Nancy left the dressing room, marched out of Fred Segal, and fired up the cell phone. There is always a way to get what you want, she said to herself. Then she even laughed, thinking this could be her personal mantra.

"And get it for me in every color it comes in." There. She felt better. "Get me" made her feel much better.

Twenty-six

Dr. Jacobson didn't argue with Nancy. He listened carefully and pointed out the pros and cons of the kind of plastic surgery she was proposing. Nancy listened to his responses with equal care. Then she told him with conviction that she wanted it done, and she wanted it done yesterday. She was not willing to wait, she'd already worked her hardest, and she was still not satisfied with the results. And if Dr. Jacobson wouldn't fit her in, she would find someone who would. Dr. Jacobson liked Nancy. He recognized her convictions in himself. He was happy to make room for her. And he knew that someone like Nancy would be a great repeat client.

Nancy ordered the works done. She had the maximum safe amount of fat sucked out of her body. She gave herself new breasts, choosing a pair that she thought were sophisticated and appropriate for her frame. She wanted the overall result to flow. Just like a good house with architectural integrity. No stand-up Barbie breasts for her. Nancy wanted to look like her new body was a gift from God, not Dr. Jacobson.

She stayed in the hospital overnight, not telling anyone where she was, except March's nanny. Then she checked herself in to the Bel Air Hotel, not coming out of her room once in the five days she was there. She had the room service left outside her door. When she'd hear the footsteps fade away, she'd open her room door a crack, first making sure her big sunglasses were in place and her white, fuzzy Bel Air robe was wrapped around her body. Then she'd quickly yank inside the tray of food or the stack of magazines she'd ordered. She didn't want to be seen. At all.

When Digby drove Nancy home, she went straight to March, carefully picking her up and cuddling her, even though the doctor had told her to go easy around her new breasts for at least a week or so. Then, when she saw March was fine, she put her down and made a beeline for the answering machine to see if Landon had called. He hadn't. She picked up the phone and called him herself, dialing his office number with shaking fingers. They said he was in Hawaii, and gave her the number. She dialed again.

"Landon, it's me," she said, surprised he picked up the phone himself. He usually traveled with his assistant, or hired one wherever he went. She tried to banish the thoughts of him having wild sex with young women in the daylight—women who made him forget his work, something she'd never been able to do. Why else would he be in the house and not the office?

"Nancy," he said, sounding glad to hear from her.

"You should see March." She smiled. "She's precious."

"I'd like to," said Landon, but he didn't offer anything else.

"Listen, why don't you come home?"

There was no response, and she wanted this so badly.

"Just for a weekend," she said, even though it was painful to compromise that way. Her stomach grumbled with anxiety. She so wanted him for more than a weekend, but she didn't want to push. Let him come home and get a load of her new body. He would never want to leave again if she had her way.

"I've been thinking about it," said Landon.

Nancy's heart leapt. "You have?"

"I don't know. . . ." he said. "The family . . . I've been thinking about family."

Yes. Nancy's heart soared. The family! That was what would hold them together. She knew it.

"I think it's going to be big," he said. "Family. Fifties values. Sex has ruined everything. AIDS, then all these babies everybody wants, there's no choice. Family is going to be a hero. I told Myrna to find me a family band—like the Partridge Family, or get me the Osmonds. Black Osmonds. Or Latina Partridges."

"You're doing music again?" she asked.

"Yeah, movies bored me."

"Well, come home when you can," she said, waning some, but still exuding confidence. "We'll be waiting for you."

"I want to move back in for a while," Landon said with emphasis on the *while.* Nancy was euphoric. "It's getting, I don't know, boring. Besides, I'd like to give it a try—family. Have somebody get my home office ready."

"Good," said Nancy. "I will. Just come."

The truth was that Landon's girlfriend had gotten boring long ago, and he had felt no commitment to her. After all, it wasn't like she was his wife. He had started sleeping with other women. All young, leggy, and aggressive. All variations on Nancy. But there were so many of them that they began to blur. He mixed up their names—sometimes he couldn't even tell them apart at all. And in the end, he didn't care.

France, Hawaii, Telluride, Aspen, and Sundance had become big drags. They weren't the playgrounds Landon thought they would be when he first started doing entertainment. He'd made his mark, and now he was bored again. Restless. He was looking for the next big score.

Landon's valet packed his bags, and had them waiting in his stretch limo to take him to the airport, where he boarded his private jet, and got very drunk for his flight back to Los Angeles. From the plane he made four calls. One was to Nancy, telling her to expect him for dinner. Two were to the two girls whose names he could remember, telling them he was leaving on business and thanking them for a good time. The last call was to his lawyer to make sure the girls were out of his properties by the end of the week.

Twenty-seven

Nancy was thrilled! Landon was coming home! It had been almost a year since he'd been home for good. He'd come and gone, but it never felt like he lived there—which was his intent. This was different. He was coming back to her. To the home they'd built together. She was overwhelmed with emotion and pumped full of adrenaline. She ran around the house making and executing plans. She was wild with organization and then momentary reorganization. Even Digby had trouble keeping up.

Nancy made sure Landon's favorite foods were prepared. She had Digby drive all the way up the Pacific Coast Highway to Malibu Seafood, twice, for fresh swordfish and shrimp. She had Matsuhitsu on call with platters of fabulous sushi. She had extra-lovely fresh-cut flowers in the house from the Empty Vase and Suzanne LeMay. She had Digby oversee getting Landon's favorite clothes, which he had left here in the closet for so long, cleaned and pressed. The Wine Merchant was delivering a case of champagne, restocking the Greenes' wine cellar, and making sure Landon had a box of cigars in the den ready for his arrival.

March's nannies were instructed to have her wardrobe spotless. If March made a mess, she was to be immediately redressed. And March herself made cards and pictures and strings of beads for her father. It was going to be a grand welcome.

Then Nancy went to work with her Filofax, her Rolodex, and Digby on two lines while she was on another. Nancy called their friends and invited them to dinner parties that week and the next. She made reservations at all of Landon's favorite restaurants and several new, hot ones. Then she went to work on herself.

Nancy had the masseur placed on call for the week. He was to be entirely at her disposal, and she wanted him carrying a beeper twenty-four, seven. She'd pay for him to cancel his other clients. She wanted the facialist, manicurist, and an aromatherapist to come to the house, and the feng shui master was given a set of keys and free rein with the property to make last-minute adjustments, so that the home would be peaceful and harmonious for Landon's return.

Next Nancy rang up Fred Segal and had some new clothes sent over—size six—''just send whatever is great.'' Those were her directions. Get me, find me.

When all that was done, when she'd gone over her lists with Digby, her lists with the nannies, and her own lists herself, when there was nothing else she or Digby or anyone could think of, she went into her room, shut the door, and climbed fully clothed into the empty bathtub. She sat there, very still, in the porcelain tub. The cold, hard walls felt like the only thing around her that was real. She didn't know what she would do if this didn't work. Up until that moment, she hadn't let herself think of that possibility. But as she did, she took one big, shaking inhale, and let everything out in racking sobs. She cried from a place deep, deep inside that was her center. Because, somehow, Nancy had lost her way. And she knew it. She needed to be back on track, and she didn't know how to get there.

Twenty-eight

Nancy's plan was to act like nothing had happened. She didn't want to make Landon feel guilty. She didn't want him to feel bad about himself or anything. She didn't want to give him a reason to leave again. She wanted him to stay. She wanted him to love her and be the missing piece of the family she was creating. She wanted him to feel strong and attractive and powerful.

''Please, please, please, please, please,'' Nancy whispered in quiet prayer to herself when she heard Landon come home. She then rushed to greet her husband with a warm and loving embrace.

''Hi!'' she sang as she hugged him hard.

''Hey,'' Landon said, hugging her back, then holding her out to look at. He didn't like it—any of it. The lavish greeting made him balk. He knew he'd treated her worse than shit. She should be pissed off beyond repair. Hell, if it'd been he who'd been treated that way, he'd be getting revenge. Twisting, evilly, until the victim cried out for respite.

But Nancy wasn't like that. She was still a sweet person down to her core. It was like she was hardwired with sweetness. But that didn't help things. All Landon knew was that this behavior of hers, this welcome-home charade, wasn't normal. No wife welcomed back home a man who'd left her when she was nine months pregnant. He should be punished, not lauded. It wasn't right, and it made his skin crawl.

Nancy sensed that something was amiss, but she wasn't sure exactly what, so she went for the high road.

"March! Somebody find me March."

A nanny, old and heavyset (Nancy's choice when hiring—she didn't want any temptations for her husband), carried March into the room and presented her to Nancy, who handed her to Landon. Landon lightened when he saw his daughter, fat and pink, beautifully dressed in a soft white cotton baby gown, her tiny bare feet kicking out from underneath. His disdain for Nancy disappeared, for the moment, because of March. Even though March was still a baby, Landon could see that his daughter was feisty and smart. He also had a feeling that the girl was going to be a giant pain in the ass someday. Just like him. It made him smile.

Nancy saw Landon enjoy March, and she rejoiced. Any little inkling that Landon was happy made her think they could work it out. That things would be all right. That this would just be a "bump" in their marriage. Something they could get over.

At dinner, Nancy told Landon of their social plans for the week. Landon listened to the amazing job Nancy had done with everything in such a short time. It's really all he could do—listen—because Nancy didn't stop talking. Not even for a second. It wasn't nerves. It was instinct. She was sure that if she let in even a moment of silence something awful would happen to fill that gap. So, she gabbed on and on relentlessly.

Landon was awed by how she had turned their house into a palace. Her staff wasn't made up of the typical domestics he'd seen in his friends' homes. Nancy's staff worked quickly, with respect and professionalism. As if this were the White House or Buckingham Palace. He knew good work firsthand, and he admired that part of her. A lot. They drank two bottles of wine while Nancy rambled on, and by the time a different old and heavyset nanny, this one the night nanny, put March to bed, they were drunk.

Nancy suggested they go into the living room, where she'd had a roaring fire built. Landon grabbed a third bottle of wine and offered Nancy a swig. She didn't want any more, but accepted anyway. There was something intimate in sharing wine that way—and intimacy was what Nancy wanted.

"It's good to have you back," she said, sinking into the sofa.

"Yeah, well, thanks," said Landon. "It's good to be here."

In Nancy's best dreams, Landon came home, professed his love for her, offered a colossal apology, and vowed to make everything work. In reality, she was hoping for some (any, really) sketchy derivation of any single part of that dream.

"You look different," said Landon, giving her a scrutinizing once-over.

"I've been working out," she said, feeling embarrassed.

"I know what it is!" Landon exclaimed. "You got new tits!"

He was genuinely surprised. It wasn't exactly what Nancy had been hoping for in the way of an endearment, but she quickly jumped on the optimism in his voice.

"Do you like them?" She sat up so he could get a good look at her.

"Let's have a closer look," he said, amused.

Nancy giggled like a girl and lifted her shirt. Her white lace bra held the new, perfect breasts in place like a frame on a piece of fine art. Landon was pleased and surprised.

Nancy's heart beat faster. This was exactly the right direction.

"Yeah," said Landon, calculating the cost of his wife's new anatomy. "Take the bra off."

She didn't want to—not like this. Nancy had choreographed an entire night of lovemaking in her mind, lovemaking that started with her in a beautifully sexy outfit made of black satin. Oh, hell. She unhooked her bra and sat there, bare breasts on display. Landon reached out and touched them. She waited for his approval, knowing that they were fabulous breasts, knowing that he had to like them.

"They're great," he said, getting quickly aroused. He pinched her nipples, hard. It hurt, but she didn't care. She wanted him—in her life. She moved toward him and kissed him, softly, lightly, on the lips, the neck, the chest. Landon grabbed her face in his hands and pulled it up to meet his face, where he pried her mouth open with his tongue. She opened to meet his mouth. He pulled away. And looked at her, questioning.

"What's wrong?" she asked. This wasn't like him.

"Something's different." He looked at her face.

"My lips." She smiled. Landon looked at her lips, confused. Suddenly, he noticed that they were different. Bigger. Fuller. "Do you like them?" she teased.

"Yeah . . . yeah." He wasn't sure.

She smiled self-consciously. He squinted. Feeling the mood slipping away, she moved closer to reach the zipper on his blue jeans. She started to unzip his pants. He let her, looking her over, wondering what else was different. Without his fully realizing, she had gotten him in her mouth and he was hard and ready to come. She stopped and turned to him. He looked at her, as if for the first time since he'd come home that day.

"Let's make love," she whispered.

Landon didn't answer. He lunged at her, forcing her pants down, and her panties down to her ankles. Bottomless, Nancy lay down on her back on the overstuffed, green velvet sofa and spread her legs, inviting him in. Landon intently rolled her over, so her back was to him, then he spread her legs, grabbed her breasts from behind, and fucked her up the ass.

Twenty-nine

*I*t took six months for Landon to become completely disgusted all over again. He had thought family life would be a kick, but it wasn't. He had friends—some professionally single—who bragged about it, and made it sound like a conquest or a religious experience. They puffed cigars, made and lost millions, bought cars during lunch, and always made glowing mention of their kids and wives. It sounded like a good gig, but living it was different.

The baby demanded a great deal of attention. Landon was pleased to have a child, which automatically gave him entry to a certain quadrant of society, but after their initial introduction, he had little interest in March as anything more than another acquisition. He loved his daughter the best he could. But he got antsy in the house. Fast.

Nancy looked great, and Landon was amused and pleased with

her new body. For an entire ten minutes. At first, making love with Nancy was like being with another woman. But then he'd snap back to reality, either because she'd whisper some term of endearment that was too sweet for the bullshit he'd put her through or she'd suggest something because she thought it would please him. He hated when she was too nice. But no matter how much abuse Landon heaped on her, Nancy continued to stay hopeful.

When she noticed Landon's irritation with home life, Nancy panicked. She sent Digby out for Wolfgang Puck crabcakes and salmon cream cheese pizza. She ordered the latest hot psychic medium, James Van Praagh, to come and entertain with communications from dead relatives. She got tickets to everything, planned weekends in Palm Springs and at the Ritz Carlton in Laguna Nigel and at the Four Seasons in Carlsbad. But nothing worked. Digby was pretty much working round the clock, and even he noticed that no matter what Nancy did, bought, or changed, Landon walked around the house in a funk.

Everyone in the house came to be petrified of Landon. They practically took off running as soon as they saw him. Nancy had a second servants' kitchen and a break room installed just for the help, and had given strict directions: no one was to bother Landon. The less he saw of them, the better. Under any and all circumstances. If there was a question, a problem, they should go directly to Digby.

Nancy herself concentrated as much as she could on Landon, but it was difficult to be a vixen and run a household with a new baby at the same time. She told Landon that a bigger home would be a good idea. That way the baby could have an entire wing with her nanny, and the two of them could have their privacy. Landon grunted, and Nancy called the realtors.

In less than a week, Nancy got Landon's okay to buy a mansion on Amalfi in the Palisades Riviera section, where all the streets were named for beautiful Italian areas, like Capri, Romany, and Ravoli. Nancy hired famous local decorators to create their home.

The house was elegant and regal. It also looked expensive, and as though it was meant for someone much older than Nancy, who was, after all, only thirty. She thought it looked like something someone Landon's age would like. The irony was that Landon didn't care about things. Just feelings. Especially feelings of power. But that wasn't apparent. And if Nancy knew it, somewhere, deep down, she didn't know how to deal with it.

She was a whirlwind, working with the decorators. She finished the house and hired more staff. Three housekeepers; two nannies, each on a twelve-hour shift; a driver; a menagerie of pool men, fish pond guys, gardeners, personal assistants, and regular delivery men. When that was done, and Landon still looked unhappy, she bought dogs. Three of them. Greyhounds. Then she hired trainers and groomers, and then she bought a Persian lap cat for March. There was nothing she had left undone. Everything, in fact, was overdone.

Except for one last detail.

The preschool. March was two and it was almost time.

Thirty

Nancy was late for the admissions deadline at Butterflies and Puppydog Tails, but when she showed up for her interview, wearing a pink Chanel suit she'd had sent from a trunk show in New York, and started pouring on her charm, Jocelyn knew she had a live wire in her office.

"I don't have a single spot in morning or afternoon," said Jocelyn. She had a volleyball under her desk, and she rolled it around with her foot while she talked.

Nancy took Jocelyn's rejection as her cue to start groveling. No problem. No insult taken. It was all just part of the game, and Nancy was a player.

She quietly took her black leather checkbook from her Kate Spade bag and removed a check that she'd already written in the house before she'd left, and handed it to Jocelyn, smiling calmly.

"What's this?"

Jocelyn stared at the prewritten check. Beautiful handwriting. Measured letters. Nancy held it out. Her fingernails were French manicured. Nancy didn't answer. She just put the check on Jocelyn's desk, not giving her the option of not accepting.

"Landon and I have heard about all the wonderful things you've done here for the children, and I'd like to donate ten scholarship tuitions."

Jocelyn looked at Nancy's calm face and couldn't help herself—she didn't want to look at the check, not yet. But she couldn't help it. Her head finally swiveled on automatic pilot, and there was the check.

Sixty thousand dollars. Just like that.

Jocelyn thought she had seen it all. She'd had celebrity parents who'd donated this much, but only after a year or two at the school. As a reward. She'd gotten bribes at this stage in the game before, but the most she'd gotten was ten thousand. This was a good one. This was new.

She looked back at Nancy, realizing that Nancy, despite her young age and fancy suit, was not a babe in the woods. She had been around the block. Jocelyn was speechless.

"I'm the kind of person who likes to get involved," said Nancy. "I'm a hard worker, and a big fan of yours. So I hope you'll find a spot for our family. We'd love to be part of your team—Landon and myself."

"Well, I don't know . . ." said Jocelyn. She picked up the check and looked at it.

At that moment Nancy knew she was in. She'd learned a few things from being around Landon, and this was one of them. If they touched it, they bought it.

"This is very generous of you. I like to pay our teachers well, and our operating expenses . . ."

"I know," purred Nancy, shaking her head in understanding. She rose to leave. "The cost of living is so . . ."

"I'll see what I can do," Jocelyn said, squeezing Nancy's forearm.

"Thank you," Nancy said warmly, and stuck out her hand to shake Jocelyn's. "For everything. I hope we can have lunch. Are you busy Thursday?"

Jocelyn sputtered.

"I have school!"

They both laughed, as the rules were established. No lunch.

"No problem," said Nancy. "I understand."

"I bet you do," said Jocelyn to herself, as she watched Nancy leave.

Nancy drove herself home, instead of having a driver or Digby take her. She was feeling domestic and triumphant. Everything was going great. Everything was in place. Sort of. She picked up the car phone and dialed the number of her doctor.

"Hi," Nancy purred into the phone. "It's Nancy. I'm calling for the results of my blood test."

"Hold on," said the nurse.

Nancy turned on the radio while she was waiting.

"Nance?" Dr. Rodgers picked up the phone. "How ya doin'? How's Landon?"

"Hi, Maury," Nancy said, turning the radio off. "We're great. I was just calling about the blood test."

"Well, it's early," said Dr. Rodgers. "But your hormone levels are through the roof. And you are definitely pregnant."

Nancy's heart soared. "I am?"

"Why don't you come in next week, and we'll do an ultra-sound," he said. "Bring your husband if you'd like."

There was no way, Nancy thought, that she'd ever bring her husband to an ultrasound. It was too intimate and modern. If Landon was going to see her half naked, it would not be in a paper gown under fluorescent lights. She didn't have that kind of marriage.

"So, I'm definitely pregnant?"

"Yup," said Dr. Rodgers.

"Wonderful!" she said.

"See ya next week, hon," said Dr. Rodgers.

They both hung up. Nancy speed-dialed the house. Landon didn't pick up the phone. She drove quickly. She couldn't wait to see him and tell him the good news. They were going to have a baby!

She pulled into the circular driveway in front of her house, and, leaving the keys in the car, she ran into the house.

"Landon!"

Nothing. She ran up to the bedroom. Her heart dropped. His drawers were left open and they were empty. His stuff was gone. She flung the closet doors open. His things from the closet were gone, too.

"Goddamnit," she said furiously. She flung her purse on the bed.

Maria, one of the team of seven maids employed by the Greenes, came to the doorway and knocked, even though the door was open.

"Mr. Landon went to the airport," said Maria to Nancy.

"He told me to tell you to call him at the Hotel Bora Bora," said Digby, running up, cell phone in hand. "I paged you—"

"I didn't bring my pager," said Nancy. Her heart sank.

"Thank you, Maria," she said, barely able to conceal her tears. Maria left.

"He's dealing with the DeLaurentis family. They have this Italian olive oil company. They want to grow olives in California. He had a meeting to develop—"

"Did he say he'd be back?" asked Nancy, already knowing the answer, hoping Digby could conjure up a miracle. "Can you get him for me?"

"He just said you should call him," said Digby. "I'm sorry."

Goddamnit. He was back on the road again. Even after she'd given it her all. Just like that. With no regard for her feelings. No explanation, no note. Just a message from the maid.

"Here's his number," said Digby, handing Nancy a piece of paper with Landon's name imprinted on top and a phone number scrawled beneath it. It was not even Landon's handwriting.

"Should I dial it for you?" asked Digby.

"Sure," said Nancy. After a moment she took Digby's tiny phone and left a message for Landon on the island of Bora Bora: Call right away. Good news.

Three days later, Landon returned the call.

"Great," he said, noncommittally, when Nancy told him about the new baby.

"Aren't you happy?" she asked, hysterically. "Isn't this good news?"

"If that's what you want," he added.

Her heart sank. "Isn't it what you want?" she asked. "You know, a family? Two kids—I got March into the most fabulous preschool."

"I don't know, Nancy," he said.

Landon had never said this to her before. He was always so sure of everything. Whether he was screwing her over or he was treating her well, it was always with certainty.

"What do you mean?" she asked, scared.

"The marriage," he said. "I don't know if it's working."

"It's not," she said.

There was silence on both sides of the line. It was almost unbearable. Being honest was brutal and liberating.

"Listen, I have to go," he said. "I can't talk about this now."

"When are you coming back?"

"I'll call you. We can talk later," he said and hung up.

Nancy sat on her bed and cried. She knew he was calling his

lawyers. Seeing about a postnuptial agreement. Probably wanting to see if he could negotiate favorable terms. She knew him that well.

She didn't say a word to anyone about Landon, and no one asked. They were all so excited about the new baby, that they didn't bother to imagine that anything could be wrong.

Thirty-one

Jocelyn sat in her office, staring down at the check. She couldn't believe it. She picked up the phone and hit a speed-dial button.

"George?" said the voice at the other end of the wire.

"No, it's Jocelyn Stone. Is this Amanda?"

"Oh, Jocelyn, hi." Amanda sighed into the phone. She had been hoping it was her husband. She lay back on her bed, a giant shrine full of pillows which looked out on the rolling hills of their yard and the fantastic blue pool below.

"Listen, Amanda, I want to ask you about someone."

"Did Eve call you?" Amanda asked, scrutinizing herself in the mirror on the wall. Admiring.

"Eve? No. Who's that?"

"My friend, and I want you to pay attention to her. She's very special."

"What's her last name?"

"Evanston."

"Evanston, like your old boyfriend?"

"She's married to him. Just."

"Do we like her?" Jocelyn asked. Amanda was one of the few people Jocelyn trusted. Amanda had no reason to lie to Jocelyn. About almost anything. "We love her. She's fabulous. How're you? You working out?"

Jocelyn jotted down Eve's name on a piece of paper on her desk. She would look out for Amanda's friend.

"Not enough. I miss the beach," said Jocelyn. "Tell me what you know about Nancy Greene."

"Nothing," said Amanda. "Why?"

"She just gave me a huge scholarship donation," said Jocelyn. "She didn't have personal contacts, so she went for her checkbook. Admissions maneuver number three thousand, four hundred ninety-eight," Jocelyn joked. "I've seen a lot, but never a check like this. Not on a first visit."

"Greene, Greene . . . I don't know. Sounds like someone in the movie business to me. There's this guy—Landon Greene. Rich, old, owns a talent agency. Does some music business stuff. We don't have dinner with them."

"Then he couldn't be that important," said Jocelyn.

"I don't know," said Amanda. "Maybe he is. I don't do much dinner with anyone anymore. I'm a sex slave day and night. I don't know anything but whips, chains, and leather. Have you ever used handcuffs?"

Jocelyn hated when Amanda revealed her lust so openly. It made Jocelyn embarrassed. "I'm from Orange County. We don't talk that way."

"Oh, bullshit," Amanda teased. "I was just expecting my husband's daily phone sex call when you rang. I have to get him off at lunch when he's on the set. We do phone sex. How'd you get this number, anyway?"

"I used to date your husband, remember?"

"God, I forgot," said Amanda. "Doesn't he have a big dick?"

"I'm hanging up," said Jocelyn. "Immediately. Don't ever ask me that question."

"I'm kidding," said Amanda, not kidding about that part.

"You're disgusting, you know that, don't you?"

"Yeah," said Amanda. "I like to be disgusting. It separates me from the crowd."

"That's not what separates you from the crowd, doll," said Jocelyn. "So, what do I do? About Nancy Greene?" Jocelyn fingered the check.

"As usual, you probably already know what to do," said Amanda. "You're just calling me to gossip."

"I took the check," said Jocelyn.

"Then she's in," said Amanda. "Make another space in the sandbox. What's the problem?"

"I just don't want any trouble," said Jocelyn.

Amanda smiled. Jocelyn said that, but the truth was, she loved trouble. She found herself in the middle of it constantly.

"Well, look," said Amanda. "If you really want to know, there's only one way to find out."

"Send her an acceptance letter?" Jocelyn laughed.

"See?" said Amanda. "What the hell do you need me for?"

"Reality check," said Jocelyn.

"Yeah, right. I'm living in the middle of reality. With death threats from weirdos I don't know, and a live-in staff that thinks I'm trash and would love to see George kick me out on my ass. Y'know, I bet half my staff are paid informers for the *Enquirer*. And then I have people like you calling me for kicks—this isn't reality. Hey—how's your boyfriend?"

"I don't have one," said Jocelyn. "Know anybody?"

"I'll cook something up—you want a wealthy old prude, right? Eight inches in the bedroom, seven figures yearly, and at least six-one standing barefoot, so you can wear your heels, right?"

"I don't know why I even bother talking to you," Jocelyn said, joking.

"In or out of the business?"

"Out!" said Jocelyn, quickly. "Definitely out. Find me a nice insurance agent. Or a plumber."

"Not with those stats, I won't. But I'll keep my man radar up," said Amanda. "And in the meantime, look out for Eve, 'kay? I mean it."

"Sure, absolutely," said Jocelyn and hung up. She looked at the signature, the address, the number on the check. Then she put it in her purse and headed straight for the bank.

Thirty-two

"Who can we fix up with Jocelyn Stone?" Amanda asked at dinner. She and George were eating in the kitchen, late at night. He'd been casting all day, and Amanda had arranged for a dining rendezvous in the back kitchen instead of the dining room. George wolfed down his ultrahealthy dinner (specially designed by a nutritionist, paid for by the studio) of pasta and vegetables. He barely looked up from his plate to mumble the words:

"Ball-buster."

"She is not, honey," said Amanda.

George looked up. "Who slept with her, you or me?"

"Okay, okay," said Amanda. "But she's important."

"If she's so important then let her find her own dates."

"She has," said Amanda.

"I know," said George, his eyebrows raised.

"So, what happened?" asked Amanda, coyly. "She wouldn't swallow? She wanted food and live animals? She wouldn't submit to your videotaping the action?"

"It wasn't really a date," George backed up. "It was dinner. And she talked too much."

"Couldn't get her into bed, huh?"

"Anybody could get her into bed," said George.

"Yeah, right."

Amanda knew this wasn't true. She knew Jocelyn ran her own show at home and at school. Amanda was pretty sure that George was the one who'd been rejected. Not Jocelyn.

"I don't like to get involved in domestic things," said George. "That's your arena."

"Yeah, I know," said Amanda, a little peeved. She knew she'd made a pact with the devil by marrying George. But she loved him. It wasn't like she had a choice.

"Ask her who she wants," said George. "That's what all the guys in town do—pick their dates off the headshots from casting calls. She's got balls, let her get her dates like the guys."

Amanda remembered her start as an actress, and those nebulous calls from the agent she had at the time. Vaguely explaining a part she "could" get, but a certain actor, director, producer, or executive wasn't quite positive yet. When she would volunteer a second reading, the hemming and hawing of her agent on the line got more and more definitive. Dinner was more what the man in question had in mind. Dinner and a chance to really get to know her.

When she would demure, the offers were subtly and delicately upped. There were often monetary offers involved, with "jokes" about sexual favors, which her agent would repeat to her. Feeling her out. Seeing if she was game. She wasn't.

But she never threw an indignant fit. Instead, she would just laugh back into the phone, not giving away her disgust or repulsion for fear of getting herself blackballed by the exec, who was probably also there, blueballed, himself, at the other end of the line.

What she mostly hid was her disbelief that she was being offered five- and, several times, six-figure sums for sexual favors.

By not taking anyone up on these offers, she never found out if the casting couch was a speed zone or a dead end. What she did know was that what she got, she got on her own. And when she fell for George, he was the only person in the industry that she had ever dated or slept with—except for some other out-of-work actors in her Uta Hagen classes.

Jocelyn was the opposite of Amanda—she wanted no part of the business—which was why they were such straight-up friends. That they both had great bodies and full-blown brains, although exercised in completely different ways, gave them common experiences. In this town, anyway. Jocelyn saw the studio execs, the producers and directors, for what they were. Men with jobs. She dated them freely and slept with them if she wanted to—not because they could offer her something in exchange.

That they had nothing she wanted made them wary of her. Impotent, in a way. They stayed away and often spread rumors of her aggressiveness. Like George, they called her a ball-buster. Which couldn't have been further from the truth.

"That's the thing," said Amanda to George, who was cleaning his plate with a piece of rosemary bread. "I don't think she knows what she wants. Aside from her career."

"I know a lot of men like that," said George.

Amanda had never thought of that.

"Maybe she'd like a woman," George ventured. He looked at his wife seriously.

"Oh, forget it," said Amanda. "You are so typical sometimes."

"I've won eight Oscars," George teased her. "I'm not typical."

"Jocelyn loves men. She just devours them, that's all."

"Maybe she should produce," said George. "Now there's an idea."

Amanda gave up. This was going nowhere.

Thirty-three

Eve had a baby girl. She and Fuller named her Stella Jane. She had a huge shock of black hair and large green eyes. She was a tiny five and a half pounds, and the entire birth was quick and much easier than Eve had expected. She was born on the same day that Eve had been, so both mother and daughter had the same birthday.

Everything had been relatively easy. Eve had expected a horror show. She had heard about women demanding their epidurals and painkillers to be preapproved by their doctors—months before they even went into labor, just so they wouldn't have to wait an extra second to get their drugs. The stories spooked her. She was prepared for a siege. What she got was a simple delivery with pain, but not more than she could bear. It was all okay.

"Ma," said Eve on the telephone when she was out of the delivery room. "I had her."

"Oh, honey!" was all Eve could hear of her mother on the telephone. The rest was Betty yelling to other rooms, the yard, other yards in the neighborhood, all the while holding one hand over the receiver.

Eve could hear her father grumbling around in the other room. He didn't pick up the phone to say hello.

"He's just squeamish," said her mother. "Y'know, men."

"You're happy," said Eve, feeling exhausted. That she had called her mother made everything feel complete.

"Sure," said Betty. "You did it, baby. You got the secret now."

"The secret?"

"Now you know everythin'," said Betty. "No one can take that from you."

Eve felt disappointed. She didn't know what her mother was talking about. She didn't have any secret.

"Y'got that necklace still? The Saint Christopher's I gave you for y'r birthday? I want you to give it to my baby grandgirl. I want that to be hers from me."

"Okay, Ma," said Eve. She didn't tell her mother she'd lost it. She didn't want to disappoint her.

"Y'coming home for Christmas?" Betty asked.

"I don't know," said Eve. "I don't know, Ma."

"We can find a synagogue for your husband," said Betty. "If that's a problem."

Eve laughed. Her mother was sweet, if naïve.

They made promises to see each other. Eve said she'd fly back for a visit as soon as she was out of the hospital and settled, but she hung up feeling disappointed. For no reason she could express. She wasn't connected to her mother the way she wanted to be. She never went to visit, and the distance seemed to be growing further and further.

Eve spent the first two years of Stella's life pretty much holed up with her baby in the apartment. She nursed the baby, and suffered sleep deprivation, as every night she padded from her bed to the baby's room and back again. Nursing, changing diapers, trying to sleep, and marveling at her miracle.

Fuller wasn't around much, but that was okay with Eve. She knew that he was out producing a movie. It was a low-budget but sophisticated period piece. A romance that he knew would make mediocre box office money at best. He did it because he knew it was enough of a picture to get him another movie going, if he moved quickly. With a wife and baby at home, he felt the role of breadwinner more directly than ever before. He had a family to support. All this combined was also enough to keep him awake at night, tortured that he wasn't more successful. He felt stuck.

"Isn't there anything I can do to help?" Eve pleaded with Fuller. She hated when he was upset.

"No," he snapped at her, frustrated with himself.

Immediately, he was sorry. He knew that Eve had done a thankless job just having Stella, let alone nursing her, caring for her, cleaning, cooking, shopping, and never complaining. He knew that all the other wives he knew had housekeepers and nannies and limitless charge cards at Barney's and Neiman's. Eve never asked for anything like that. She was so excited when he bought her the red Cherokee—it was the first car she'd ever had that wasn't used. He was glad she'd be driving their baby around in a safe car.

No. She didn't deserve to be snapped at.

"I'm sorry," Fuller said.

"I hate when you're like this," Eve said.

"Maybe there *is* something you can do." Fuller looked around. "So you don't have to see me moping like this. I should have some privacy to be an ogre by myself instead of out in the open."

"You're not an ogre," she said. "Not ever."

"We need a bigger place," he said, hands on hips. He'd made a decision, and there was no turning back. "I need my own room—an office—so you don't have to suffer with me."

"Why do you have to suffer at all? Just enjoy what we have."

He knew she was right, but he couldn't help how he felt. "How can I not suffer?" he asked.

"How can you!"

"Look, maybe it's some genetic thing. Jews suffer well. I'm good at it."

"Come on, Fuller," she said.

"Why don't you find us a new house? Do you have any time?"

She didn't, but that wasn't the thing on her mind. "A house? Why not just a bigger apartment?"

"No," said Fuller, thinking on the spot. "We're a family—let's buy a real house. With a fireplace. I'd like a fireplace."

"A fireplace? It's so hot already."

"Only here in the valley. Over on the Westside, it actually snows in October," he kidded her, lightening.

"Can we build a snowman?" she asked.

"Yes. And drink hot chocolate with marshmallows."

"I've never seen snow. Do you know that?"

"Do you think you can handle the real estate agents?" he asked, seriously.

"Sure." She shrugged, having no idea why he thought she couldn't.

"Find something for around one point five," he said.

In his mind, he'd solved this problem, and was moving on to something else. "That should be good."

"One point five?" she asked, confused.

"On the Westside," he said.

"Okay," said Eve, taking a big breath, "no problem." She went back to playing with Stella. But she couldn't leave it alone. She turned to Fuller and asked, "One point five what?"

"One point five million," he explained.

"Dollars?"

"I don't know how it converts into pesos," Fuller teased, "so, yeah. Dollars would be good."

Eve was shocked. "Do we have that much money?" she asked, quietly.

"No," said Fuller dismissively. "But we have enough to finance a house for that much."

"Oh," said Eve, not completely understanding. "It just seems like a lot."

"It is," said Fuller.

She had never inquired into finances. She had no idea how much money Fuller made.

"If you really have enough money—or whatever—to buy a house that expensive, why don't you just spend a little bit of it on the house, and the rest on something else?"

"Like what?" he asked, noticing how she had suddenly called it his money, and not theirs.

"I don't know. That's so much money. Homeless people? Hungry, homeless people?"

Fuller looked at her, and his heart swelled. She was filled with innocence and such a good will. He loved her a million times more than when he'd first met her. Half a million times more than when he'd proposed.

"I'm sure I can find a house for less than that, and we could give some away."

"We'll take care of everyone else next," said Fuller. "I promise. First, us, then them."

She nodded. Even though she was a mother and a wife, at that moment she looked just like a little girl.

"Don't worry about money," said Fuller. "I'm old—I've had a head start making it—and remember: it's ours, not mine."

"I don't know how to *be* if you tell me it's mine," she said. "I don't know"—she was shaking her head—"it's scary."

"We're fine," he said. "Don't worry. At all. I'll handle all of that. You just raise our daughter like you're doing. You're doing a wonderful job," he said, dropping to the floor with Eve and Stella. "And maybe think about getting some help."

"I don't need help," said Eve, feeling self-conscious. She looked around. The house wasn't as clean as it could be, but it was hard to do everything.

"You will," said Fuller.

"I don't want anyone else here—just us."

"Yeah," he said, "but I want lots of babies," he said, hugging her and Stella. Stella grabbed his finger and chewed on it. "Lots!"

"Me too," Eve said, glowing at him. This was exactly what she had always wanted. This was it. The dream. "But is that why you're suffering? Because you think you have to make all this money to support us? Because you don't—I'm fine in an apartment. I don't need things."

"I know," said Fuller. "But let's see how we do with a big old house and a couple of servants."

"I don't want you to worry about money," she said. "I can always work. Hell, my mother worked through all of us. Still does, and she's a grandmother."

Fuller laughed at Eve's sweetness and naïveté. "I don't worry about money," he said. "I worry about getting the right script and the right director and the right cast. I worry about creative differences. Do you have any idea what creative differences are like?"

"No." She shrugged.

"They're hell," he said. "H-e-l-l."

That week Eve started looking for a new house, and was immediately deluged with phone calls and appointments from real estate agents. The project, which started out exciting for her, quickly became tedious and time-consuming. Eve was swamped. She felt like fish bait in trout season.

The phone calls and appointments were piling up quicker than she could deal with them. She tried to turn to Fuller for support and comfort, but he was as busy as she was. Busier. She didn't want to bother him, so she forged on, alone. But she could see that Fuller was still suffering. She started to realize that he'd told her to find a house so she wouldn't notice how unhappy he actually was.

She put all the realtors and house-hunting on hold. She had to help her husband first. She wanted to make him happy.

She tried everything she could think of. Food, sex, back rubs, bubble baths, sending him for nights out with the guys, bowling, movies, Parcheesi, and home-popped popcorn with root beer in cans—but nothing she could come up with alleviated Fuller's agony.

"Why do you have to do this?" she asked him, quietly, one evening.

"Because," he grumbled. "It's my life." She had never before heard an ounce of bitterness in his voice, and she didn't like it. It wasn't the Fuller she knew.

"Honey, I came from nothing. I don't need all this stuff—this life. And neither do you. I know you think you do, but you don't. I've seen people get by on way less. We've got each other, and we've got some macaroni and cheese and hot running water. We'll be fine."

"You don't know what I need," he snapped at her.

She was quiet, stung. She knew he was right, and she hated the distance that had come between them since Stella.

"I think I might," she said, quietly, but not backing down. "If you'll just—"

"Look," said Fuller, angrily. He stood up in front of her. "If I don't succeed, I can't live with myself. This has nothing to do with you. It's my personal demons. And they're real, so thank you very much, and just don't worry about me. Because you can't."

Then he stormed out of the house.

Eve started to sing to Stella, to comfort her. But the baby was fine. It was Eve who was crying.

As soon as his car pulled away from their apartment complex, Eve phoned Amanda and confided in her.

"It makes me want to cry when I see him like this," Eve whispered into the phone, not wanting to wake up Stella, who had fallen asleep on the floor next to her. "I don't want him to have to be like this."

"I know it's hard to hear this, but it's his choice," said Amanda. "He chose this business."

"Is everyone in this business moping around like my husband is right now?"

"He's creative, and he's sensitive, and he's driven." Amanda laughed gently. "He can't help it. George is the same way."

"George is?" Eve still had trouble believing George was a real person, and not some one-dimensional photo of a guy from a *People* magazine story. She and Amanda were good friends, but she'd never met George.

"Yeah," said Amanda. "And there's nothing I can do about it. I just try to give him space until he gets over it himself."

"Give him space." Eve mulled the words over. They sounded so dopey to her.

"Look, I used to be an actress. I know how it is."

"Why'd you stop?" asked Eve.

"Because," said Amanda, "George asked me to."

"Just like that?" Eve asked. "Why?"

"Sometimes, there's only room for one person with big problems in a marriage,'' said Amanda. ''The acting brought problems. Joy, for sure, but problems, too.''

''And that's okay with you? I mean, you were a star, Amanda. I used to read about you all the time.''

Amanda laughed. ''Thanks, but you're makin' me feel old.''

''Sorry.''

''Look. It's part of the bargain. I get George, and he gets a wife. I made the deal with my eyes wide open. I'm fine.''

Eve was getting tired. This was all so much to digest.

''You two will be all right. Just give him space to work it out.''

Later that night, Eve woke up from a sound sleep, unsettled. She looked at the clock. Three a.m. She listened, thinking she might have been woken by Stella, but the baby was quiet. She looked at the bed where she'd been sleeping. Fuller wasn't there. Then she remembered what had woken her. It was her dream. It had seemed so real. She had to tell Fuller.

Eve padded downstairs into the living room. Fuller was sitting in a big armchair, reading a book.

''Insomnia?'' she asked.

He looked up, surprised to see her.

''I had this crazy idea,'' he said.

''Me, too,'' said Eve. ''It woke me up.''

''You go first,'' he said, rubbing his face. It was the first time he had expressed interest in her in a while.

''I don't know. . . .'' She smiled. ''It's kind of too 'out there.' It was just a dream.''

''Tell me,'' he said.

''It was . . . well, I had this vision of you. You were wearing a suit and you were driving to an office.''

''Have you been dialing those psychic hotlines while I'm out?''

''You were president,'' she said, remembering the dream.

''Forget it,'' he said. ''I hate elections, and I'm conflicted about Democrats and Republicans.''

''Not *the* president,'' Eve said. ''President of a studio.''

''A suit?'' Fuller laughed. ''That sounds more like a nightmare than a dream.''

''Only you weren't driving one of those big black BMWs or Mercedeses. You were driving an old Jeep. It was dusty. Really dusty.''

''Like I'd just driven through the desert, maybe? Las Vegas, say?'' Fuller teased her. ''Are you sure it was me who was president, and not you?''

"Oh, come on." Eve flopped down next to him. "Maybe it wouldn't be so bad, bossing people around."

"I'm a creative guy—not an executive." He shuddered at the thought. "I'm independent."

"Okay," said Eve. "Forget it. It was just a stupid dream."

"I can't be anywhere on time, every day, day in and day out." Fuller slammed his book shut. "I hate meetings. I don't even like wearing a watch."

"I know," said Eve.

Fuller stood up and practically threw his book on the chair. "I'd have to oversee dozens of projects—I could never put my personal touch on all of them." His voice was rising, angrily.

"Honey, you'll wake Stella. Shhh."

"Jesus," he said, pacing. "Premieres, and dinners, and having to be nice to people I don't respect. I'd have to have, like, a permanent veneer. You're crazy to think I'd do that."

"Fuller, I said forget it."

"This is absolutely the worst idea I've ever heard in my entire life."

Eve was hurt, but he didn't notice. She got up and went up the stairs.

"Hey, where are you going?" he asked, surprised.

"I'm sorry you don't like my idea—I was just telling you about my dream," she said, and stomped upstairs. "I'm sorry I did it. I won't do it again. I'm just a dumb hick, Fuller. I don't know why you bother with me at all."

Eve expected Fuller to come up after her and apologize, but he didn't. He didn't come to bed at all that night, and when Eve got up the next morning, he was gone.

"He's never done this before," said Eve on the phone to Amanda, fighting back tears. "Do you think he's left me?!"

"Nah. But it sounds like you really hit his buttons," said Amanda. She was being served breakfast on the patio in her backyard. George was on another phone, nearby, trying to talk his director into casting a particular actress. The director kept insisting she wasn't fuckable. George knew that the director meant she wouldn't fuck him, that was all. But the studio wanted her, and without her, George didn't have a picture. He hated directors with visions.

Amanda tried not to listen to her husband's phone conversation, but he was loud, and she couldn't help it.

The maid set down her meal. Fruit, granola, decaf cappuccino, and fresh mango juice. A yellow bird flew over the patio. A fountain trickled. It was paradise. The separate phone conversations George and Amanda were having were in sharp contrast to their setting.

"I'm actually sick about it," said Eve. "I puked this morning when I realized he wasn't here."

"I wish I could help, but you're on uncharted ground here," said Amanda. "He never did this with me."

"He didn't?"

"Nope. But he didn't marry me, either."

"What about George?" Eve asked, tears spilling out. "Did George ever walk out on you, mad?"

"No," said Amanda, stuffing her mouth with fruit and talking through it. "Uh-uh. He just yells at me. Like I'm a bad child. The kind who did something awful and needs military school."

Eve could think of nothing worse than to be reprimanded by a famous producer. She could imagine him standing over her, berating, pointing his finger and yelling.

"It must be so awful," said Eve. "What do you do?"

"Well, I used to do nothing, but then I finally yelled back."

"You did?"

"You know what?" Amanda snickered. "He liked it."

"I should have fought back," said Eve.

"George is different," said Amanda, looking over to see if George was listening to her at all. He wasn't. He was screaming on the phone. Calling the director paranoid and sick. "He likes a good fight, and then we always make up in bed. It's kind of like creating a little storm that you know is going to lead straight to good sex."

"I feel awful," said Eve.

"Do something," said Amanda. "Don't wallow around waiting for him. He behaved badly."

"I know," said Eve, sounding glum. "I just don't know what to do."

"Did you get an interview at Butterflies and Puppydog Tails?"

"No, not yet."

"Eve!" Amanda scolded. "Do it! Stella is going to be three any second now."

"Not for a whole year," Eve defended herself.

"You won't get in if you don't go and get an interview."

An interview. The last one Eve had had was to be a waitress. This one, she wasn't sure she'd pass.

"It's so far away," said Eve, contemplating the drive all the way from Studio City to Santa Monica. "Besides, I don't know what to do about Fuller."

"You better take care of yourself and your kid," said Amanda. "Before it's too late. You don't want to gamble with your child. If you put her in Butterflies and Puppydog Tails, you know she's safe. You know she's getting taken care of—you can't lose."

"I suppose I shouldn't complain. Not with this new car and all," said Eve. "The air conditioning works all the time. Not like my old car. It's amazing. Do you know what that's like—to have air conditioning that doesn't break down? Or a new car for the first time in your life?"

Amanda laughed. She was so glad to have Eve in her life to keep her grounded.

"You once got in a car and drove from one state to the other because you thought it was the right thing to do," Amanda said. "Even with lousy air conditioning."

Eve smiled. Amanda was right.

"Will you remind me if I ever forget that?" said Eve.

"Yes," said Amanda. "So, just remember: This isn't driving from Las Vegas to Los Angeles. It's driving from Studio City to Santa Monica. For your daughter. So stop complaining."

"I love you," said Eve, elated.

"Good. I'm hanging up," said Amanda. "I'll call you tomorrow, and if you haven't applied to that preschool, that's it. I don't know what I'll do to you, but you won't like it."

"Bye," said Eve.

Eve forced herself through the rest of the day, hoping Fuller would call, but he didn't. She took care of Stella and herself, and finally phoned to arrange for an interview at the preschool. Fuller didn't answer her calls at his office, and he didn't return her calls when she paged him. His car phone didn't answer, and the day was slipping away.

After a while, Eve began to think she heard the phone ringing, but each time she picked it up, she only heard the dial tone. Day turned into night, and still no Fuller. Now Eve was scared. Her thoughts ranged from fear for his personal safety to fear for their marriage. What if he'd been murdered? What if he were having an affair? What if he committed suicide? What if he couldn't stand her anymore? What if he'd been carjacked?

Just when she was about to drive herself crazy, at a few minutes before nine, Fuller walked in the door. He was dressed up. For him, this meant a sport coat, white button-down shirt, a tie, and jeans with good shoes. This was not her normal Fuller. Something was very wrong. He looked as though he had been at a funeral.

"I'm sorry," said Eve, before he got a chance to even say hello. "Whatever I did, I'm sorry."

"What?" Fuller looked at her, surprised by her words. He was glowing.

"I was out of line," she said.

"Oh," he said, realizing she was still upset about the night before. He went to her and softened. "No, don't be sorry." He took her hand.

She was so glad he was talking to her.

"I was the one who acted a little crazy," he said.

"Okay," said Eve, putting her hands on her hips, growing furious. "Then apologize."

He laughed, taken aback by her quick turn.

"You're right," she said, crossing her arms over her chest. "You *were* wrong. So apologize."

"All right," he said, composing himself. "I apologize. I'm sorry." She didn't uncross her arms. She tapped her foot. Waiting for more. "And I won't do it again."

"And where were you?" she asked, lifting an eyebrow.

"Geez, you're tough," he said, liking this surprising side of her.

"My husband stays out all night, for all I know, all day, doesn't call to let me know he's not dead, doesn't answer my calls, doesn't answer my pages, and you think I'm *tough*?" She tapped her foot. "I think I'm pretty reasonable."

"Okay," he said, sitting down on the sofa. "I was a couple places—it doesn't matter. The thing is . . . you were right."

"Mmm-hmmm," she said through pursed lips, waiting.

"You were so right, and I was wrong."

"Fuller, where were you? Why didn't you call me?"

He sighed. "This was the most insane day of my life," he said. "I just had to do a lot of scrambling, and I guess, the bottom line is, I did it."

"Did what?" she practically shrieked. She was trying to stay calm, but he was making her mad.

"I got a couple of deals together today, and, basically, I have backing to start a small studio," he replied.

"What?!" Now Eve was the one to be surprised. She let her

arms fall to her sides. Her face changed completely. "What does that mean? I'm not from Hollywood. I don't understand you!"

"I can start out making seven pictures a year, and I can hire a small staff—three vice-presidents and a couple of creative execs, but basically, by the end of the month, I'm in business."

"Wait a minute," said Eve. "I just had a little dream. It could have been that balsamic vinegar salad dressing, for all I know. I read it does weird things. I didn't mean for you to do all this."

"You were right. That's why I got so angry. I was furious that you came up with something so simple and so perfect for me— I couldn't understand why I hadn't thought of it."

"Fuller," said Eve, sitting down. Her hands were trembling. "This doesn't just happen. You don't just go out and pull some deals together and come home for dinner suddenly a studio president—that's what you're talking about, isn't it?"

"Mythic Films," he said. "It's complicated—the backers have this company—they want that name."

"I like it," said Eve.

"And, yeah"—Fuller started to giggle and laugh—"I guess I'm president of the studio."

"*The* president?" said Eve.

"Yeah!" Fuller laughed. "Did you buy a house yet?"

Eve started to cry. Fuller went to her, and hugged her, so he could comfort her and still see her face. "What's wrong?"

"I don't know," said Eve. She stopped crying and took a deep breath.

"Hey!" Fuller suddenly remembered something. "You never asked me what my dream was."

"Huh?" Eve rubbed her eyes.

"Last night, remember, I said I had a dream, too. It woke me up, and I came down here to read."

"Oh," said Eve. "Well, what was your dream?"

"That you're pregnant," he said.

Eve held her breath, remembering. "I puked this morning," she said.

"No!" Fuller grabbed her hand.

"I thought it was because you were making me crazy."

"But, it was just a dream!" he said.

Eve just looked at him. She was thinking the same thing he was thinking.

"It never occurred to me. . . ."

"This is great!" said Fuller, gleefully.

"Get out of here," she said, pushing him away. "It can't be! Can it?"

"Yes!" he yelled.

Eve grabbed his car keys and shoved them at him.

"Go to the drugstore and get me one of those tests. I want to know for sure!"

"Okay." He smiled. "I'll be back."

"I know," said Eve. She hugged herself. Another baby . . . !

.

Thirty-four

The first day of preschool was hot. Eighty-two degrees at eight-forty in the morning. The teachers gathered in the empty classrooms, preparing for the day by smearing each other with sunscreen, and washing off the oily fingerprints they got on their drugstore sunglasses. Some wore sunhats and some wore baseball caps. They chatted about which brands of deodorant and baby powder combated the elements best. They took turns going into the bathroom, and discreetly mopping sweat from under their arms and behind their necks. Industrial paper towels blotted with cool tapwater worked fine. There was no air conditioning. It wasn't necessary for most of the year. Just a few weeks when the heat was strong. This was one of them.

Jocelyn came out of her office to join her staff.

"I hate this weather," she announced to anyone who would listen. They all leaned toward her, shuffling closer to be in her presence. She could tell that they were looking for her to lead them. Even the most seasoned of her staff still took their cues from Jocelyn. They wanted her to tell them it would be okay. Another first day of school.

"It's eerie," Jocelyn whispered. She was upbeat. "Did you notice the flies?"

Nervous laughter from her team of teachers, as they commented on the flies that had come in with the heat. She had assembled these teachers so carefully over the years. Through personal contact, reputation, and résumés that came to her in stacks—though not as many teachers applied as students. The simple fact was that the students' Hollywood families over-whelmed the teachers. They were awestruck by Hollywood life up close. A star profile in a magazine was fine, but in person, they didn't always know what to expect from the celebrities. And that made them anxious.

Butterflies and Puppydog Tails had a reputation among teachers in town. They all raved about Jocelyn—mostly about how down-to-earth she was, and what a great person she was. But they were wary of the parents of her students. Anecdotes flew. Some said Jocelyn had sold out. Some said she was hoping to "go Holly-wood," which meant marry a rich, famous actor or director. But the ones who knew her best reminded the others that Jocelyn had been a volleyball jock who loved the beach. She had chosen the property for her school because she could be near her beloved sand and sea. The Hollywood folk swarmed her. Not the other way around.

This reputation sometimes hurt Jocelyn professionally. She didn't get the best staff easily. She had to work hard and com-pensate to get the teachers to come, and then to stay.

Jocelyn offered high salaries, the highest in town. She had to. The good teachers preferred a more normal atmosphere. Other schools. Jocelyn needed a salary to dangle in front of them. She used it like a tool. It worked.

Once she got them, they stayed because they loved her. They had a career and a life with her. They became her children. Of sorts.

"I think this is the hottest first day in a decade here," said Hester, one of the lead teachers. One whose wisdom, maturity, and experience Jocelyn counted on.

Jocelyn had sent Hester and her husband on an all-expense-paid vacation to Cabo San Lucas. On the school's tab. Nobody knew that was how tuition money was spent. It was nobody's business, Jocelyn thought. This was not a democracy. It was her school. She did what she thought right. And she knew that send-ing her best teacher on vacation was a good move.

She didn't care to share or defend her strategies with parents. Let the public schools debate budgets and spending at PTA meet-ings with store-bought cookies and diluted juice in cups for re-freshments. She had her own way of doing things. Her own style. She was royalty.

The staff all looked up toward where the sun might be, and murmured some more about the heat. Jocelyn couldn't wait for the day to end, so she could drive to the ocean. She wanted a quick dip in the saltwater.

"Is it time?" one of the teachers asked.

The staff looked down at their watches. Timex and Swatch watches in bright colors. The children loved bright colors and costume jewelry.

"It's time," said Jocelyn, and stepped to the back of the yard, on the top of a little hill where she could have the best vantage point from which to observe the start of the year.

She didn't offer the teachers good luck. No luck was needed. She was prepared. Or so she thought.

Thirty-five

Eve circled her Jeep around the block of the preschool six times, and still couldn't find a parking spot. She couldn't help but notice the parade of fancy cars parked and double-parked. It would never occur to Eve to double-park or slide into a red zone. She just didn't do that kind of thing. She had never done a single illegal thing in her life. She never even drove without seat belts buckled. She always did the right thing.

On her seventh time around the block, her car phone rang. It was Fuller.

"What are you doing?" Fuller asked.

"I'm so nervous about this preschool interview," Eve said. "What if they don't like me? What if I don't get in? I've waited so long to apply they probably don't have any room for me now. Amanda was right. I should have applied years ago. I'll never get in."

"Relax," said Fuller. "*You're* not going to school today. Stella is."

She glanced at Stella sitting in her car seat in the back. She was such a good girl, quietly singing to herself. Dressed in her favorite sundress with Cinderella printed on it, and tiny Velcro sneakers with Snow White and the Seven Dwarves stitched into the white leather.

"That's *if* they let her in," said Eve quietly, so Stella wouldn't hear. "And then what if they do let her in—that means our next baby will go there too—we'll be committed."

"And so will the baby after that, and the next baby after that," Fuller joked with her. "Why are you so nervous?"

"I don't know." Eve laughed, breaking some of her tension. "I think Amanda put the fear of God in me."

"Amanda?"

"She scared me a little. Anyway, forget it. You're right about all of this," said Eve. She loved that he snapped her back to reality. "How are you?"

"I'm sitting in my big-cheese, fat-cat offices," he said. "I just gave a movie the green light. We start preproduction next week. Is this really my life?"

"Wow," said Eve, trying to enjoy Fuller's new adventure, but her stomach was tossing and turning over the preschool thing and how she couldn't find a parking spot, and now she was officially twenty minutes late for her appointment with Jocelyn. "I was just thinking the same thing—is this *my* life? I mean, we never went to preschool. We just played in the yard, and when it was too hot, we played in the house and fought to be the one who got closest to the fan."

They both laughed, and didn't say what they were thinking— thank God they had each other.

"How's your morning sickness?"

"Morning sickness is going away, actually. It's been pretty good since last month," said Eve. "But I have a funny feeling about this school that's just brought it all back."

"It's preschool, Eve," Fuller said. "There are other preschools, too—and besides, what if *you* don't like the school?"

"I never thought of that," she said. This hadn't occurred to her at all.

"Hey, I have to ask you something really, really important," he said.

"What?" said Eve, her adrenaline starting to pump.

"What's for dinner?"

"I don't know," she said. Fuller had this magically simple way of making her realize everything was okay.

"Hey!! A parking spot!" She was elated, as she slid her car into the spot. "I'll call you later."

They both hung up.

Thirty-six

The school gate swung open, and the children and their parents swarmed the schoolyard, causing a traffic jam at the entrance. Everyone yelled hello to each other. The air was filled with perfume, aftershave, and the everpresent aroma of Coppertone. Kisses and hugs mingled all the scents.

Once inside, the returning students knew the drill. They found their cubbies. Their names were already pasted on, welcoming them. They stashed their lunch boxes filled with vegetable sushi, fresh papaya, mango fruit salad, and string cheese sticks. There was also peanut butter and jelly. Then they ran for their favorite toys, some of the older, more socialized children greeting their friends on the way.

The preschool was Eden. The children didn't yet know about neurotic social inequities. They just saw the simple differences. Who had a blue shirt, and who had red. Whose skin was dark, and whose was light. They didn't attach values to colors or shapes and sizes. Not yet.

They knew that some people were homeless and some weren't, but they did not keep track of whose family had a screening room and whose family didn't. They were too concerned with what was important to them: who pushed, and who bit. Who had strawberries in their lunch box, and could their mother please get them cinnamon rice cakes just like another child had in their lunch. They shared a communal bathroom with no doors or walls between the toilets, so they saw the differences between boys and girls. They knew each other's ages, and birthdays were big deals, but mostly because of the cake. Chocolate was very popular.

Children of multimillionaires played side by side with full-scholarship students. It wasn't part of any master plan. It just happened that way.

Jocelyn was too practical to own any politics. She was self-serving. Which, ironically, was what made her fit in so well with the Hollywood elite. Without trying, Jocelyn and Hollywood had their one major character trait in common.

She just wanted things to be normal for her and the children. She didn't like parents spoiling or mistreating their kids. It made her job hard. When families were erratic, nobody knew when the rug would be pulled out from under them, and the children felt the invisible anxiety. They brought it to the schoolyard.

Jocelyn just wanted to teach basic values and make the children feel secure. She wanted to give them self-confidence, from which they could launch themselves when they were ready. She knew the world beyond her school was wild.

Nancy walked into the schoolyard with her daughter, March, and their entourage: March's nanny; their driver, Bill, a young screenwriter hoping to make connections through his employer; and Digby, who was talking on the cell phone, arranging Nancy's massage, haircut, and manicure/pedicure for her. They were a parade.

Their limousine was double-parked. Nancy didn't care if she got a ticket. She expected one. She held nothing against the meter maid assigned to the neighborhood. In a way, Nancy felt like she was giving the meter maid something to do. Nancy imagined that just looking for expired meter flags must be dreadfully desperate work. Finding one and writing a ticket must give the meter maid a sense of completion. A sense of accomplishment.

She couldn't have been more wrong.

The meter maid was nearly suicidal. She loathed her job because it put her in a no-win situation. She was mostly hated by many of the parents, because she only brought bad news. Parking tickets. As annoying and painful as paper cuts. She was immediately identified by her Santa Monica uniform—blue T-shirt and shorts—and her standard-issue bicycle. At worst, people sneered and yelled things at her. At best, they looked right through her.

The meter maid wrote a ticket for Nancy's car. Nancy and her staff watched her as they entered the school. They didn't care. To Nancy, a twenty-eight-dollar ticket was a small price to pay for a good parking spot on her child's first day of school. She considered it a charitable donation to the city of Santa Monica.

Disregard for the red zones ran rampant. This made the meter maid increasingly bitter each year.

A child's wail broke through the first-day chatter. Jocelyn looked over calmly. A new student didn't want his mother to leave. The mother was looking anxiously at her watch. She had a personal trainer scheduled for nine-fifteen, and she was trying to sneak out.

Jocelyn walked over and took the mother by the arm.

"Sit down," said Jocelyn, with a smile on her face and boot camp in her voice. "You stay until you're both ready to separate."

"When do you think I can go?" asked the mother.

"When you're *both* ready," Jocelyn said quietly, with meaning. She remembered her volleyball coach at UC Santa Barbara teaching her discipline. The coach's voice resonated in her head. The tone was the same as Jocelyn's now. "He'll feel it when you're relaxed and confident that he's okay here. Until then, you sit in one of these chairs," she said, pulling up a tiny child's chair. "And you let him see that you're here. But no cuddling, no caressing, no hugging. And he can't sit on your lap. He can just see that you're here. This is preschool. Not family time."

Other mothers eavesdropped. They knew Jocelyn was right. They also knew she was laying down the law.

"What's the matter?" Hester asked the child who was crying. "Did Alex take your cappuccino?"

The crying child burst into laughter through his tears. Alex came over at the mention of his name.

"Cappuccino's for grown-ups!" said the child, playfully.

"It is?" Hester fooled back. "Are you sure?"

"Children don't drink cappuccinos," said the child, no longer crying. The tears streaked his face, but there was a playful look in his eyes now. Other children quickly gathered to see what was going on.

"Lattes?" asked Hester. "Do children drink lattes?"

"No!!" squealed the little boy. The other children started to join in. "But they can eat the foam."

"Hello, Jocelyn," said Nancy. She kept her giant dark glasses on. She had cried that morning, and no amount of makeup could hide swollen eyes. She was feeling brittle and betrayed, but she kept up appearances, and leaned over to kiss Jocelyn. She needed Jocelyn to be nice to her. She needed some love. She wasn't getting it at home, and she was on the verge of a nervous breakdown. Pregnant, with a three-year-old and a husband who wanted a divorce. Nancy felt like hell.

No one in the schoolyard could tell. They only saw that Nancy had been the one new parent brave enough to approach Jocelyn. They thought she was snubbing them. It didn't occur to them that she couldn't bear to answer small talk. The other mothers hung back, passing judgment, critically.

Jocelyn smiled at Nancy and bent down to look at March. "Hello, March. How are you?"

March scowled.

"Hi, March Greene!" Annie, a teacher, called over from the sandbox.

"Why's she so fat?" March asked, looking at Annie. "She must eat the bad cholesterol."

"Which bad cholesterol?" Jocelyn asked, intrigued.

"There's good cholesterol and bad cholesterol," said March.

"Go play, hon," said Nancy. She didn't want any conflict. Not now. She would burst into tears if someone were mean to her today. Even her three-year-old.

March scowled at her mother, but knew from her mother's glare that she meant business. March trudged off on little legs to the sandbox, her hands in the pockets of her dress. The little girl had a bad attitude in every word, every gesture, every toddler innuendo.

"Shit," said March, lisping on the *sh* sound. "Goddamnit."

Jocelyn looked at Nancy, hard, one eyebrow raised. Nancy's parade of help hadn't noticed. They were used to March's language and behavior.

"I'm sorry," said Nancy. She had no energy left to discipline March or even think about disciplining her. She was exhausted.

"March Greene," Jocelyn said, ignoring Nancy.

Nancy wanted to die. She had no idea what was going to happen. Public humiliation, no doubt.

March turned and looked at Jocelyn's stern face.

"Come back here," she said. Authority exuded.

March tramped over, and kicked some sand Jocelyn's way. Jocelyn knelt down on her long legs until she was March's height, and their eyes met.

"I don't ever want to hear bad words again."

"Shit?" she asked Jocelyn, goading way further than any three-year-old should know how to do. "Do you mean shit? Or goddamnit?"

"Both," said Jocelyn. "Do you understand?"

March waited a beat before she answered. "Yeah," she snarled. "I got ya." And turned back to go to the sandbox.

Jocelyn had seen a lot, but this was new. She rose and turned to Nancy, who looked unsure.

"You have to be very firm with her," said Jocelyn, being the exact kind of firm she hoped Nancy would adopt. "She can't use that kind of language. It's going to make her life hell if you allow it, and then it's going to make yours hell."

"They're just words," said Nancy, trying to slough off the incident, smiling lightly.

"When I hear a three-year-old saying those words, especially on the first day of school, I know that it's just the tip of the iceberg. I have a feeling I may be hearing other 'words' before the end of the month."

Nancy sized up Jocelyn. She had heard about Jocelyn's straightforwardness. Now she was experiencing it firsthand. It was as if the huge monetary donation she had made didn't matter. Nancy couldn't buy favor. Not here. She got the message. Loud and clear. Jocelyn had rules.

March's nanny followed March to the sandbox and stood over her there, while the driver took a seat on the periphery with the other mothers. Digby found a corner of the yard to make his calls on the tiny cell phone.

The other mothers looked on with damning uncertainty. They were civilian mothers—people with no good connections to the entertainment industry. They didn't know about round-the-clock help and staff. They weren't sure if they should introduce themselves to the nanny and the driver, or not.

The industry moms knew. They bestowed distant smiles, then turned their backs, however gently, on the driver and the nanny. The help was relieved at not having to talk to them or feign interest.

"I thought we weren't allowed to bring housekeepers," one of the civilian moms said to Nancy. There was offense in her voice. Nancy felt a fight coming. She steeled herself, knowing she couldn't handle one without bursting into tears. She was fragile. Nancy sized up her critic quickly. The woman wore makeup and clothes with no style to speak of. Her worst offense was a mall haircut and an untoned body. Not fat, just the well-fed-without-a-personal-trainer look.

"Gloria's not my housekeeper," said Nancy, smiling while she instinctively checked and mentally noted the civilian mom's simple jewelry. "She's our nanny."

"Still," said the mother. "I thought it was just parents and children."

"I bring my nanny so I can talk to my friends," said Nancy

and walked back over to Jocelyn, something the civilian moms would never do. Nancy had sensed this immediately; she was thereby separating herself from the civilians intentionally.

The misconception was that she found the civilian moms to be inferior.

The deep, dark truth was that they scared Nancy more than she scared them.

The civilian mothers all watched Nancy make friends with Jocelyn. Jocelyn was royalty, and the civilians waited to be spoken to first before they would dare approach her.

Depression and discomfort shot through their group. You could see it in the way they began to cross their arms, cover their bodies, and lean against the back wall, looking for some kind of physical support.

"I don't think you need all this staff here," said Jocelyn to Nancy. She had immediately recognized the other mothers' discomfort. This happened every year when a supercelebrity joined the group, and the others were unsure how to treat the woman. Nancy wasn't a celebrity, but she lived like one.

"Who? The driver? The nanny?" said Nancy. "Digby? Digby's not really staff."

"You don't need to bring any of them. March is in good hands here," said Jocelyn. "If you don't think so, there are other schools which might allow that kind of thing. But I don't."

"All right," said Nancy, simply. "I won't bring them again."

"Good," said Jocelyn, feeling that she'd just put out a potential fire.

"Good morning, everyone!" Gabrielle breezed in, carrying a ribbon-woven basket of sliced homemade chocolate chip banana bread. *"Bonjour, bonjour!"* Her son, Zachary, walked ahead of her, and went straight into the play area, away from his mother.

"Hello, Zachary!" the teachers greeted him.

"I love Zachary's shoes," said Nancy.

"I got them at Pom D'Api, but if you like shoes like I do, you should really see the new line of children's shoes at Dolce and Gabbana," said Gabrielle as she presented the basket of goodies to Jocelyn.

"Wow," said Jocelyn, examining the baked goods. "These are still warm. Did you make them? Or did your housekeeper do it?"

"I did," said Gabrielle. "I love to bake. Wait until your fundraiser—I am going to make you a zillion dollars in baked goods sales. You'll see."

"Have you been to one of our fundraisers?" Jocelyn asked.

"Yes! Darling, I introduced you to my husband. Don't you remember?"

Jocelyn didn't. She also was not used to being called "darling."

"Oh, don't worry. You were deluged with parents."

Nancy listened, and realized how well Gabrielle knew the ropes. Gabrielle was also unphased by Nancy's staff and demeanor. She hoped that Gabrielle might be a friend.

"These are probably soooo fattening," Jocelyn said, examining the baked goods. Each slice looked fabulously moist and plump. "I'm going to have to hit the track after this."

Gabrielle laughed and took the baked goods inside. "I'll put them on your desk anyway," Gabrielle said over her shoulder. Jocelyn didn't have time to object. Gabrielle was almost in the school door. "You can give them to the teachers if you'd like."

"She's amazing," said Nancy after Gabrielle had gone. "She's Martha Stewart."

"Crossed with Zsa Zsa Gabor—*darling*," said Jocelyn. They both laughed. "She's new, like you. Her name's Gardener. Gabrielle Gardener."

"Joey Gardener's wife?"

"Yeah, you know him?"

"Not personally, but my husband does."

Gabrielle emerged from the school and made her way among the children and new mothers, smiling noncommittally, not allowing anyone to engage her in any real conversation. She had already set a ten-second rule for talking with civilians.

Jocelyn watched Gabrielle, silently marveling at her natural political skills. Gabrielle was perky and energetic, but guarded. Not open, but involved. Her warmth was tempered and self-serving.

This new crop of parents was yielding some very interesting treasures.

"Do you want some?" Gabrielle asked, coming over. She had a few mini muffins in her hands, which she offered to Jocelyn and Nancy.

"Gabrielle Gardener, Nancy Greene," Jocelyn introduced them.

"I can't," said Nancy, refusing the muffins. "I'm pregnant, and I don't want to gain any more weight than I have to." Nancy looked depressed.

"Is this good news?" Jocelyn asked, carefully.

"Sure," said Nancy, trying to muster up her best face. She didn't convince anyone. "Babies are always good news."

"How far along?" Jocelyn asked.

"Seven months." Her stomach was flat as a board.

"I'm pregnant, too," said Gabrielle. She stuck out her stomach. *"Avec bébé."*

"Congratulations!" said Jocelyn. Gabrielle, at least, looked thrilled with her pregnancy. "When are you due?"

"November," said Nancy. Jocelyn and Gabrielle both eyed Nancy. No way did she look like she was pregnant.

"December," said Gabrielle, rubbing her tummy proudly.

Jocelyn silently calculated her sibling admissions for three years from their due dates. Classes would be tight. A lot of people were having babies.

A commotion in the sandbox caught their attention. March was throwing plastic tools at a boy, whose mother was trying to settle things. Nancy started to run over, but Jocelyn quickly caught her by the arm and pulled her back.

"Let the teachers handle it," said Jocelyn.

Nancy watched nervously as her daughter yelled angrily at the children and teachers alike.

"It's okay," said Jocelyn, holding Nancy's arm. She could tell Nancy was losing it. "I'm going to give you a name."

Nancy knew what that meant. A psychologist.

"This woman is very good. She'll help you."

Nancy wished that were true. That someone could help her. Anyone. Jocelyn was right. March was just the tip of the iceberg. Jocelyn went inside to find the phone number for Nancy.

While Jocelyn was inside, March socked one child and bit another, who burst into tears and began to wail at car alarm decibels.

"I hate that we were tardy on the first day," said Gabrielle. She felt sorry for Nancy, and was trying to get her to relax and forget March's behavior. "We would have been on time, but Consuela didn't do the laundry, and I had to stop at Fred Segal to buy underwear for Zach."

Nancy tried to laugh, but just smiled. She was tired.

"I think Consuela's doing a passive-aggressive thing on me with the laundry. She heard that you bought your nanny a BMW station wagon, and now she's turning up her nose at the Volvo I bought for her."

Nancy wondered how Gabrielle knew about what happened in her house.

"I'll just die if she finds out that Melanie Griffith got her nanny a Porsche," Gabrielle added. "I mean, it wasn't a new one. It was her old hand-me-down Porsche. I think it's, like, a ninety-one or something. But still."

Nancy was impressed. That Gabrielle was so connected, and that she had actually succeeded in distracting Nancy long enough for the crying in the sandbox to wain. Gabrielle smiled. They would be friends.

"Are you taking March to the Disney premiere?" Nancy asked, assuming that Gabrielle knew of such things. "Because we bought an entire table, and I haven't invited anyone." Nancy half lied. She hadn't known anyone to invite. "Do you want to come?"

"I wish I had known that!" said Gabrielle, pleased at the invitation. "I just shelled out five hundred dollars to take Zach. . . . Of course I billed the studio, but still."

"Well, sit at our table anyway," Nancy insisted. "You can give your tickets to the teachers. They'd probably really appreciate it."

"That's a great idea!" exclaimed Gabrielle, imagining Jocelyn's pleasure at hearing of the way Gabrielle would be taking care of the preschool teachers by giving them these screening and premiere tickets. "Zach will be so excited to go with a new friend!"

"Let's go together," said Nancy. "I'll send the car to pick you up first."

"Great!" said Gabrielle. She loved the idea of taking her son to a screening in a limousine with a friend. Now, this was why she had worked so hard to get into Butterflies and Puppydog Tails.

In the play yard, Zachary ran for the swings, and March grabbed him with one arm, and slugged him across the chest with the other. Zachary stopped, and turned to March.

"Hit me again," Zachary quietly threatened, "and I'll stick your head in the toilet."

March backed up a step. She was used to intimidating children. Zachary had given her a good scare. He wasn't quite like the other children. He didn't cry and he wasn't scared of March. March glared at him, and Zachary turned and ran gleefully for the swings.

Thirty-seven

$\mathcal{E}$ Eve walked into the schoolyard holding Stella's hand. She wore black jeans, a clean white T-shirt, and sandals. The first people she saw were Nancy and Gabrielle, and she immediately wished she'd worn something more fashionable.

But she let her gaze quickly drift from the two mothers to the rest of the school. Everything looked great. The children played on swings, some were building sand castles and rivers in a sandbox, others rode bicycles and toy cars. There were art projects on tables and a bunny running loose. A live tortoise sitting in a corner of the yard stared up at her. It all looked wonderfully fun. She felt Stella loosening the grip on her hand.

"Who's that?" Gabrielle asked, gazing at Eve and Stella. Eve looked happy and apprehensive, but she also looked thin and rich.

"I don't know," murmured Nancy.

Eve felt buoyed by what she saw.

"Excuse me," said Eve, as she walked past Nancy and Gabrielle to go inside.

Eve relaxed as she looked around the school. The cinderblock walls were covered with children's art projects. Three groups of children were busy with normal-looking teachers. Singing, playing, listening to a story. Eve passed the communal bathroom, where the five tiny, toddler-sized toilets stood out in the open. Children freely came in, pulled down their pants or pulled up their dresses, and went to the bathroom, as if going without doors or privacy was completely natural. This type of shamelessness came only with childhood. Eve smiled. She wished she could have some of that back.

Stella walked freely, having let go of Eve's hand. Her eyes were wide as saucers as she tried to take it all in. Everything seemed interesting to Stella. The children, the toys, the animals.

"Eve?" said Jocelyn, from the doorway of her office.

Eve thought Jocelyn was strikingly beautiful and young, for the reputation she had. But her clothes put Eve at ease. Black pants, patent-leather loafers, and a black and white striped shirt. Mall clothes. No fashion show in here.

Eve smiled and offered her hand. Jocelyn shook it warmly. Eve liked her right away, but was also aware that this was still an interview. Jocelyn bent down to Stella's height.

"Would you like to play while Mommy and I talk?" she asked.

"Okay," said Stella, but didn't move.

"I have dress-up clothes," said Jocelyn. "Do you like dress-up?"

"It's my favorite," said Stella. "But I don't have a princess costume."

"You don't? Well, I think I have a princess costume, but I don't have a ballerina costume. What do you like to dress up as?"

"My mom," said Stella.

"Let's go see if we have some mom clothes," said Jocelyn, and she took Stella to the dress-up area. It was full of donated clothes, and some purchased character costumes. "What do moms wear?"

"My mom has a baby in her tummy."

"Oh," said Jocelyn, not looking up at Eve. "Then you'll be a big sister one day!"

"I know," said Stella proudly, and she walked away from Jocelyn to play. She approached some other girls and watched them, waiting for them to speak to her.

"I'm going to be in that office with Mommy, over there," Jocelyn told Stella.

Stella didn't look up. She was already engrossed in the clothes and toys and the other girls.

Eve watched and felt tears come to her eyes. Seeing Stella among all the children in a preschool was heartening. She saw the preschool girls talk to Stella, and Stella reply. Having conversation, making friends! What a big step!

"Come on," said Jocelyn.

She took Eve's hand, led her into her office, and shut the door. The walls of Jocelyn's office were pasted with notices and articles about child development that might be of interest to teachers and parents. Jocelyn motioned to a cushioned bench along the wall, the only other place to sit besides her desk chair. Eve sat and held her purse in her lap.

"So, you're friends with the Fosters." Jocelyn cut to the chase.

"Yes," Eve said. She wanted to say more, but decided not to.

"They are wonderful people," said Jocelyn, leading. She wanted to see what Eve would say.

"Yes, they are," said Eve.

"How do you know them?" Jocelyn asked.

For a split second Eve imagined telling Jocelyn how her husband used to date and live with George Foster's current wife. No. That wouldn't do. Too sordid. Even though it was the truth, Eve decided to evade.

"This can be a small town," she said.

Jocelyn nodded.

She already knew everything. That Eve's husband, Fuller, had a new job. She knew about Mythic Films. She knew Fuller's salary. She also knew that Eve grew up in the middle of nowhere and, somehow, managed to pull the brass ring and marry well— maybe even for love. But she had no intention of making Eve feel uncomfortable by calling her on these omissions. As a matter of fact, Jocelyn liked that Eve wasn't blabbing. Jocelyn had enough of that at this school.

"And you live way on the other side of it," said Jocelyn. Eve blushed. She was embarrassed to live in the Valley, which she knew wasn't stylish.

"It's very hot there," she said. "But it's nowhere near as hot as . . ." Eve started to say, It's nowhere near as hot as where I grew up; but again, she held herself back. She wasn't sure she wanted to open up and tell about her background. She wasn't sure what she should say to get into this school, so she changed her mind and simply said, ". . . Vegas."

"Do you go there a lot?" Jocelyn asked. "To Vegas?"

"Not anymore," said Eve. "It's too hot for me there."

"So, tell me about Stella. Is there anything I need to know?"

"No," said Eve. "She's very normal."

"Well, I will do my best to make a place for you," said Jocelyn.

"Thank you," said Eve. She was a little stunned at how quickly it had happened. She was also very happy about this news.

"I think you'll do well in the morning class."

"Well, actually," Eve said, "I was hoping to have afternoon."

Jocelyn looked at Eve queerly.

"I like to do my errands in the morning, and I thought—" Eve stopped because Jocelyn was shaking her head no.

"You won't fit in," said Jocelyn.

"Excuse me?"

"It's not that you won't fit in," said Jocelyn, diplomatically. "It's just that the others might not feel comfortable around you."

Eve was confused.

"Let me be frank," Jocelyn said, and dropped her voice to a stage whisper. "I like to keep my industry families together."

"Excuse me?" Eve said again.

"Entertainment," said Jocelyn, wondering how on earth someone as unassuming as Eve had wound up in Amanda Foster's life, and now on her doorstep. "It's not an official policy. It's just that I've found over the years that it works better. Let me take care of you because you're a friend of the Fosters," said Jocelyn, returning her voice to normal. "I'll make a spot for you in the morning, and if you're not happy I'll move you into the afternoon."

"That sounds fair," said Eve, but she was still mystified.

Thirty-eight

"Nancy," said Jocelyn as she emerged from her office. She approached Nancy and Gabrielle, who were huddling together happily. Nancy looked a little more relieved than when she had first come in, having found Gabrielle in the schoolyard. They already looked inseparable.

Eve came out behind Jocelyn, with Stella, who didn't want to leave. She was having too much fun.

"Here. Give her a call," said Jocelyn as she handed Nancy a business card.

Nancy looked at the card. It was a family therapist.

"Thanks," said Nancy. She pocketed the card, a little embarrassed, and smiled at Jocelyn, gratefully.

"Goodbye," said Eve, as she passed the group on her way out.

"Wait! Eve, I want you to meet some parents," said Jocelyn. Her sixth sense told her that Eve would fit in somehow, with these two. "Eve Evanston, Gabrielle Gardener, Nancy Greene."

Eve said her polite hellos all around. Nancy and Gabrielle were very interested in anyone that Jocelyn endorsed this way, with a personal introduction. They all stood for a beat, not sure who should say what next.

"Jocelyn," said Gabrielle, clearing her throat, as for some announcement. "I want to invite you for dinner to our home."

Nancy watched carefully. The nerve, the gall, the confidence that Gabrielle must have had to cross such a line so quickly. Even Jocelyn was startled.

"Stella!" Eve called out after her daughter, as she bolted for the swings.

"It's okay," said Jocelyn. "As a matter of fact, this will be Stella's class. She'll be in with March and Zachary. Why don't you stay? She can meet her new friends."

"Oh," said Eve. This wasn't at all what she had anticipated. It was beyond her expectations. She looked over and saw Stella pushing Zachary on the swings. As it should be, Eve thought. "All right."

"Sorry," said Jocelyn to Gabrielle. "It's nice of you to offer, but I can't do it. If I go to one parent's house for dinner, I have to go to everybody's house for dinner, and I'd never get my work done—and I'd get fat! It's just a policy I have. It's not personal."

"Well, *I'll* come to your house for dinner," said Nancy. And they all laughed. Eve liked them. "I don't have any policies about dinner," added Nancy.

The tension was broken. Gabrielle was grateful for the distraction from Jocelyn's rejection.

"Actually, you should both come to my house," Nancy said, including Eve. "My cook makes a cobb salad with crabmeat that is amazing."

"Oooh!" Gabrielle exclaimed. "Fabulous idea!"

"Come for dinner," said Nancy. "It'll be fun. I mean it. Thursday night. You, too, Eve."

"Oh, I don't know if I can," said Eve. "But I'd like to."

"Come!" said Nancy. She was very curious about Eve, and this would be a perfect way to get to know her.

"Go," said Jocelyn. "You'll have fun. I wish I could."

"Well, all right," said Eve, not sure how she felt, but committing. This is the way you make friends, she thought to herself. It's been a long time. She looked over to Stella, laughing with the girls on the swings.

"Great," said Gabrielle.

"Here's my address," said Nancy, handing Gabrielle and Eve professionally printed cards from her purse. They had Nancy's name and address, and a phone number—one that went to a service, not her house. "Come at seven." Then she turned to Jocelyn. "And if you decide to break policy, here's your big chance. We won't tell."

"Can't," said Jocelyn, and she walked away, smiling. She loved when her "girls" got along. Even though they were all within ten years of age, she felt like she was older. She had the responsibility of her school. They had families. They didn't work, the way she did. That fact kept them apart, in her mind. It was what allowed her to call them her girls. It was affection, but it was also distance. And while it made her proud, and defined who she was, it made her sad, too. Sad because she couldn't go to dinner.

"This is great," said Gabrielle, and she beamed at her new friends. "Thank you, darling."

"Yes," said Eve. "Thank you."

Nancy was the happiest she'd been all day. They all were.

Thirty-nine

Joey sat at his desk in his bungalow at Allstar. He looked at the framed photos of Gabrielle, the two of them on their wedding day and as a family with Zachary. They were all over the office. In the big easy chair in front of his desk, an independent producer, Eric Jeeves, was pitching an idea for a movie. Jeeves had a long ponytail and a pierced nose. He had just produced an independent film that had won great accolades at Sundance. He was the flavor of the month. He had a new idea for another film. Joey didn't quite grasp it, but Jeeves was full of energy.

"I'm losin' you," said Jeeves. "You're somewhere else."

"I'm listening," said Joey. "I just don't see it. Not here. Maybe over at Paramount or Sony. But it's not an Allstar project."

Jeeves sighed.

"What is it with you guys?" He didn't want to tell Joey he'd already pitched it everywhere. Joey was his last chance. If he didn't sell it here, he'd have to abandon this project. "I bring you something brave, and you tuck your balls up in your polyester loincloths."

Joey squinted. He wasn't quite sure what that meant.

"I remember when studios took care of their people," Jeeves went on. He never said just one sentence at a time. It was always a tirade at a time. He was in constant pitch mode. Always selling. But Joey didn't care about that. He was thinking about what Jeeves had said. He looked at the photos of his family laid out in front of him.

"Hell, they even got them fucked," said Jeeves. "That's how committed they were to their job. To their relationships. You know the last time I got fucked by a studio? Lunch. This D-girl takes me to Pat's for tuna sushi. Y'know what? It was warm. I puked my guts out for three days and had to take an antibiotic. D-girls are useless."

"How did they do that?" Joey asked. He was focusing in on something.

"Wha'?"

"Get them fucked?" said Joey.

"What the fuck are you talking about?" said Jeeves.

"Fucking," said Joey. "It creates loyalty, doesn't it?"

"Fuck yeah," said Jeeves.

Joey's mind grabbed onto the idea. "Fucking," he said. "I like it."

"Who the fuck doesn't?" said Jeeves.

"Why don't we have another meeting on this project," said Joey. "I want to talk to some people about it."

Jeeves brightened.

Forty

The idea was good.

Hookers in Hollywood had a long tradition. They came in various shapes, sizes, and forms. But their dynamic was always present in some form. Joey knew they could save him.

He wasn't able to perform in his job in its traditional description, but he could do this.

Jeeves knew someone who introduced Joey to Ginger Abrams. Ginger was a party girl. She was also wildly ambitious. She saw no reason she and her girlfriends shouldn't make the same kind of money as the men they knew and dated. So she orchestrated a system of "charges" for being "fixed up." She was very careful, and had gotten a small-time reputation as the "agent" for some very beautiful and some very normal-looking women who wanted to have some fun.

Joey knew what she was. A pimp. Behind the doors of the simple, contemporary home she leased north of Montana, Ginger ran her office out of the guest house she had made from her garage. She seemed just like anyone else in the neighborhood. Only happier.

Jeeves arranged a lunch date for himself, Ginger, and Joey at L.A. Farm, an industry restaurant in a mall of entertainment offices. The food was great, and there were always big stars lunching. Ginger was under the pretense that Joey wanted to get fixed up, but was nervous his wife would find out.

"No, no, no," said Joey. "I don't want to get involved—not that way. I love my wife. I would never do anything like that to her."

Ginger smiled politely and flagged down the waiter for more passion fruit iced tea.

"I want to explore the possibility of arranging a setup."

Ginger listened, and stirred her iced tea.

"A deal," said Joey.

"Oh yeah?" Ginger was interested, but only mildly.

"I can provide you with a steady stream of business," said

Joey. "But I need exclusivity from you. You can't go anywhere else. I have to be your number-one client. Not me, but my . . . people."

"It's a first-look deal," Jeeves said with an anxious laugh. He wanted this to happen more than anyone at that table. If Ginger and Joey got into business together, he knew that he would be assured a studio deal as well. To keep him happy. And quiet. It would be a life beyond his wildest dreams. He could get rich like this. He could make whatever movies he wanted. Without pitching to idiots. Without waiting for someone else to give him the go-ahead.

"I'm not exclusive," said Ginger. She drained her glass in one gulp.

"I can make it worth your while," said Joey, embarrassed at the cliché. "I can make it a very attractive business situation for you. I can guarantee you a certain volume of clients."

Ginger licked her spoon. She knew what he was talking about, and she knew that this business of his—studio clients—would shoot her into hyperspace. She'd been waiting for an opportunity like this. And here it was.

Forty-one

It happened easily. Joey began to sign deals with actors, directors, producers, and writers that no other studio executive had been able to get. He began to specialize in big action movies—the kind that had tough-guy roles in them. He was the wizard behind the curtain in Oz. Nobody knew how he did it, but suddenly he had everyone on his call sheet.

Many of the biggest movie stars, the ones who could open a picture, whose names were household words, had huge appetites—not just for sex, but for control. Joey understood that their wants had nothing to do with family or love for their wives. He understood, like no one else, that these needs were different. These men's needs—to conquer, to score, to feel powerful, invincible, and uncontrolled—were complicated.

In Joey, they saw his understanding. They heard him talk about how delicate and important families were, and what unencumbered sex meant. They trusted him. They also saw that he could be a huge asset to their personal lives as well as their professional worlds.

These famous men couldn't go out and just "book" a hooker, any more than they could walk into McDonald's and order a shake without the tabloids getting a call from some idiot with a "celebrity eating disorder" story or a "celebrity weight gain" story for sale. Most of these men were famous, and married with children. And those who weren't, hoped to be. For all of them, discretion was priceless.

Joey put a price tag on that discretion.

He understood supply and demand, guns and butter. He saw a niche, an untapped market, and he saw how it would work for him.

Famous, artistic, talented people trusted him. He was well established in his job at a major movie studio. Just as importantly, everyone had seen him with Gabrielle and their son. They knew he was a family man—one of them. They knew that he had a lot to lose, and would be extremely careful with them. It was a good dynamic for everyone. A no-lose situation.

Joey got them fucked.

All they had to do in return was commit to his projects. And after a short while, he didn't even have to ask them to commit to his projects. They'd want to be in business with him. They liked him. He got them girls, he got them deals, he got them box office. Joey was a big success.

He became extremely valuable to Allstar Studios. Nobody cared that he sucked at story meetings and hated creative processes. They didn't care if he showed up at the meetings at all. His niche was solely relationships. He delivered stars to the studio on a silver platter. Which made him completely indispensable.

Forty-two

Nancy was truly happy for the first time since she'd married Landon. When her doorbell rang, it echoed off all the marble floors and bare walls. Nancy jumped and ran, beating out the maid and a passing nanny to get to the door first. She hadn't run in anticipation, knowing for sure that she would be pleased, in ages. Up to lately, all her anticipations had been crushed. By Landon. This was different. She knew tonight would be fun.

"I'll get it," Nancy sang, sliding across the glassy white marble foyer in her stocking feet.

Nancy's home was ostentatious. Especially for the Palisades. Most of the homes were spacious and had the feeling of country. Nancy's was oddly regal. She had the only palatial-looking estate in the understated Riviera section of the Palisades. It was high up on a hill, with a twisted driveway that led to the five-car garage under the house. There were big, white columns on the front porch. Lots of ironwork. The white was crisp and clean. The black, shiny. The doors gigantic. Not quite "a Persian palace," as the realtors referred to overly ornate homes with sporatically placed Greek columns and overdone moldings, but not quite "a little corner we call home," either. There was money strewn about everywhere you looked, and it was meant to be noticed. It was almost easy to forget that if you turned your back on the house, the view in the distance on a clear night was sparkly and stunning.

Nancy swung the door open with glee. She was out of breath and giddy.

"Hi!" said Gabrielle, as she walked in. She was dressed like a model. Perfect and elegant, she glowed and presented herself like a page from a maternity magazine. Unphased by her surroundings, Gabrielle handed Nancy a big bouquet of sunflowers wrapped in clear cellophane and ribbon.

"You shouldn't have," said Nancy, sweeping Gabrielle up into a hug. Their bellies touched—Nancy's was so tiny, and Gabrielle's so big. Nancy's warm greeting was not the double air kiss Gabrielle was used to. She felt welcome and at ease.

When Nancy released her, Gabrielle's head swiveled three hundred sixty degrees.

"I love your place," Gabrielle said. The house was amazing to her. She wanted to see everything. "Who did it?"

"Everyone," said Nancy.

Gabrielle laughed.

"I'm serious," Nancy added. "Isn't it grown-up? Sometimes I forget it's mine. And other times, I just wish I could forget it was mine."

"It's fabulous. I wish it was *mine*," Gabrielle admitted.

"Here." Nancy handed Gabrielle a glass of champagne from a tray of two glasses that a maid brought in. Perfectly timed. Nancy gave the maid the flowers to put in water and took the tray of drinks.

"Oh, I can't," said Gabrielle, not taking the champagne. She pointed to her pregnant stomach.

"It's just champagne," said Nancy. "It's not tequila or anything."

"Do you have any mineral water?" Gabrielle asked.

"Sure," said Nancy, and nodded at the maid, silently instructing her. "We're almost ready for dinner, and we'll take some bottles of mineral water, too."

The maid disappeared, silently. Gabrielle noticed how seamlessly Nancy's house operated. She noticed everything.

Nancy led Gabrielle into the living room. Gabrielle flopped down on a big, soft, dark green print armchair. She flung her shoes off. They landed across the beige print rug. Nancy sunk into the crushed velvet sofa.

"I hate being fat," Nancy said, sighing.

"We have so much working out to do afterwards just to get back in shape," said Gabrielle.

"I'm getting it sucked off," said Nancy.

"Lipo?" Gabrielle asked with discomfort. As if it were in bad taste.

"I tried working out," Nancy said. "I had an entire gym built. Every brand of StairMaster that was ever made is upstairs. I have treadmills and rowing machines. And Radu still comes every day for hours."

"Radu? How did you get him? I heard he's impossibly booked."

"Nobody is *impossibly* booked," said Nancy. "Where there's a will . . ."

Gabrielle liked Nancy's attitude.

"But even with all that, I could never get thin fast enough." Nancy sighed. "I guess I have standards. I never thought about it before. I'm just impatient. On some things. Sometimes." Nancy stopped. She didn't want to get deep or philosophical. She was afraid of depressing herself. "It's much better this way. The surgeries. For me, anyway."

Gabrielle saw the logic. She would never have plastic surgery. Not ever. But she couldn't argue against someone else doing it.

The doorbell rang, and Eve walked into the room, escorted by a maid. Eve looked unsteady. This was all so much for her to absorb. She held on to a piece of furniture, and started when the maid left. Eve couldn't believe the house. It was huge, and so fancy. There was nothing that needed fixing or improving on. This house was the kind of house Eve had only read about. Yet, here she was, an invited guest.

"Hi," said Eve, uncomfortably. "Am I late?"

Nancy ran up to hug her hello, and almost knocked her over.

"No! I'm so glad you could come," said Nancy.

"Whoa!" said Eve. "You're squishing me."

"Sorry." Nancy laughed, and let Eve go. Eve caught her breath.

Gabrielle looked Eve over. Eve was wearing a simple black dress that emphasized her new pregnancy, and flat black shoes. She hadn't been sure what to wear—she'd never been to a girls' night out like this. Not with other Hollywood moms.

Rosa, one of the maids, entered with a huge tray of food, and placed it on the coffee table where a buffet for three was set up for the women. Eve thought the buffet could have been photographed for a magazine.

"Don't tell me you're pregnant, too," said Nancy.

"Three months, barely," said Eve, "but I'm showing already!"

"Oooh," said Gabrielle, mentally memorizing the buffet, as well as everything else here that she was enchanted with. "This looks fabulous!" Gabrielle stood to better examine the food from another angle. She kissed Eve lightly on the cheek, welcoming her, as she stood. "Hello, darling," she said.

Eve liked the familiarity. The quick fitting in. The feeling of being in the cool girls' clique—like in junior high school. But it seemed too easy. She wasn't used to that.

"Thank you, Rosa." Nancy smiled at the maid as she walked out.

"I love your dress," Gabrielle said, as she took a plate and loaded it up with food. "Is it a maternity dress or regular?"

"I don't know," said Eve, looking down at her black dress. "My friend gave it to me."

"Amanda Foster?"

"Yes! How did you know?" Eve was shocked.

"I think I've seen her wear it—a long time ago. At a party. Or in a magazine—*Elle*? French *Elle*. That's it."

"Do you know Amanda?" Eve wanted badly to have something in common with these women. She was trying hard not to feel uncomfortable. Nancy and Gabrielle were so nice, but their lives were so different.

"No," said Gabrielle, "I don't, but I'd love to."

"I wonder if I could get the Fosters in on my Homeless Children's charity," said Nancy. She wasn't eating. Just drinking more champagne. "It's such an amazing cause. We're hosting a garage sale. I got Tom Cruise to donate a bag of used clothes, and Diane Keaton is chipping in some picture frames to sell."

"I'd like to help," piped up Gabrielle, as she sat back down in the big easy chair she had appropriated for herself, balancing her heaping plate on her knees.

"Great," said Nancy. "I'd love to get something from a rock star. Do you know anyone?"

"My husband's making a movie with LL Cool J," Gabrielle volunteered. "Would he do?"

"Perfect," said Nancy. "I'll call you about the schedule of meetings. There's one next month. We're planning a fundraiser for Thanksgiving and we could use help. Eve, are you interested?"

"Sure," said Eve. "I love garage sales."

"Great," said Nancy. "Maybe Amanda would want to get involved. Would you ask her?"

"Sure," said Eve. This sounded easy. Eve took a plate and served herself. Eve wondered if this was how Nancy ate every night. She couldn't wait to get home and tell Fuller about all of this.

"Where's your husband?" Gabrielle asked Nancy. "Is he home?"

"Oh, he's working late." Nancy took a crab cake and dissected it before putting the tiniest little bit in her mouth. She wasn't hungry. She didn't want to eat, but she needed something to do with her mouth, so she wouldn't blab.

Nancy chewed and looked down at her plate. It felt as if a silent line had been drawn. No one was to cross it.

"How about yours?" asked Nancy. She was testing Gabrielle. To see if she would abide by the tacit laws being founded as they spoke. Social laws. "Joey, right?"

"Working," said Gabrielle, curtly. She got it.

They all ate, quietly. Nobody said a word. An order was being established. Eve didn't understand, but she was busy eating. The food tasted amazing.

"Mine's home with Stella," Eve volunteered, her mouth full.

Nancy and Gabrielle looked at her, doubtfully. Eve felt a twinge of discomfort again.

"Landon got caught eating pussy on top of his desk last week," Nancy blurted out. She couldn't help it. She needed to trust someone. She had to break the ice.

Eve's eyes widened. She wasn't used to this language, let alone this kind of story.

"Who caught them?" Gabrielle asked, swallowing hard. She hated to gossip, but she wanted to know.

"Some secretary," said Nancy. "The bitch has a mouth the size of Cleveland. She blabbed everywhere. Now it's all blown out of proportion. Everyone says they're having an affair."

"Who was he with?"

"His assistant."

"Are you okay?" Gabrielle asked.

Nancy felt better than okay. Somehow, when she considered Landon a philanderer instead of a soon-to-be ex-husband, it gave her hope. Adultery was something that could be worked out. Adultery was simple. That alone would be an improvement on her marriage.

"I know it's a lie," said Nancy, taking a glass of champagne. She was buoyed by the conversation. Nobody passing judgment. These were her friends. They were there for her. "He wasn't fucking her—he was just eating her out. It's not like they were having a real affair."

"God, your language," said Gabrielle, catching Eve's eye. Eve was so glad that someone else found offense in all the cursing. "Do you always talk like this?"

"No," said Nancy, starting to laugh at the realization she was making. "In fact, I don't think I ever have. But it's kind of fun."

Eve and Gabrielle found this endearing.

"How do you know?" Gabrielle asked, gently, quietly, when the giggling had stopped. "How do you know that he's *not* having an affair? I mean, to me, it sounds like an affair. That kind of thing."

"Because he's not like that," said Nancy. "I know my husband. He fucks around like a stupid idiot, but never with any one person for very long. He gets bored."

Eve was in shock.

"Is the secretary still with him?" Gabrielle asked.

"I don't know," said Nancy, and she put her fork down, as if that had never occurred to her. "My father used to do this exact same thing, and it was, like, no biggie. My mother used to laugh about it over martinis. His stupid affairs. Men will be boys."

Eve shrugged. That last sentence, she understood. But still.

"Aren't you upset?" asked Eve. "I mean, I would be."

"I'm kind of beyond that," said Nancy. "Anyway, I don't like being upset. I've been upset. I'm sick of it. I want to have some fun for a change."

"You should make sure that secretary gets fired," said Gabrielle. "Really. I mean, what an insult, every time you call him, you have to talk to her."

Eve stopped eating. Her appetite was gone.

"I suppose you're right," said Nancy, hesitating. "It's just . . . she's a really good secretary."

"She slept with your husband!" said Gabrielle.

"She didn't *sleep* with him," said Nancy. "There was no bed involved. There were no sheets. And there was zero sleeping. I told you. It was just oral sex."

"Fine. Then keep her," said Gabrielle, getting frustrated. Then she sputtered, "But . . . give her a lot of personal errands. Make her pick up your dry cleaning, and buy your lipstick refills. Make her buy your Tampax—and your birth control!"

Eve started to giggle. This was all too much.

"What's so funny?" asked Nancy, but she started laughing with Eve. It was infectious. "What the hell are you laughing at?"

"Nothing," said Eve. She was afraid to say, afraid to offend her friends. But this was a ridiculous conversation. "Nothing. Just . . ." Eve was laughing harder and harder. "This is the best cobb salad I've ever eaten in my entire life."

"She's right," said Gabrielle. "Will you give me the recipe?"

"How the hell would I know the recipe?" Nancy laughed. "I don't know how to make eggs. I have a cook to boil water. My cook cooks. And I . . ."

They looked at her, waiting for her to finish.

"I . . . do other things."

Gabrielle, Nancy, and Eve all broke out in big laughs, laughing at themselves.

"Seriously, though," said Nancy. "I hope I can trust you. This is just between us. So, can I? Can I trust you?"

"Of course you can trust us," said Eve.

"Definitely," said Gabrielle. This was going great. "No secrets will leave this room."

"Right," said Eve. She put her plate down, and went to sit next to Gabrielle in a show of solidarity.

"I don't know about you two, but I've been craving someone to talk to. Someone who understands. Someone who I can trust."

"I trust Fuller," said Eve. When the others didn't answer, she added, sheepishly, "I guess I'm lucky."

"We're all lucky," said Gabrielle.

Nancy took another glass of champagne.

"In our own way," she said a little more quietly. Eve patted Gabrielle's leg, but Gabrielle had something to say. She wasn't finished.

"Joey doesn't really have . . . relations . . . with anyone else," she phrased her words carefully, and kept her head down. "I mean, he's not a philanderer." Realizing she'd just made a big faux pas, as Nancy's husband was, in fact, a big philanderer, she quickly added, "Not that there's anything wrong with philandering—I mean, at least it's not a crime."

"A crime?" Eve asked. What was going on?

Nancy just looked at Eve under a steely gaze. Nonjudgmental, and knowing. She wanted Gabrielle to continue.

"He just gets other guys . . . hooked up," said Gabrielle.

She finally looked up at her friends. Eve didn't understand. Nancy not only understood, it seemed like she'd known.

"Now, *that*"—Nancy giggled—"that *is* a crime."

"What is?" asked Eve.

Nancy and Gabrielle looked at Eve with disbelief. They didn't think she was mocking them, but they also couldn't believe she didn't already know or understand what Gabrielle was trying to confess.

"What?" said Eve. "Her husband fixes people up on dates, right? I mean, what's wrong with that? Blind dates?"

Nancy looked at Gabrielle and they couldn't contain themselves. They both burst out laughing, so hard that crab cake and mineral water and champagne spit out of their mouths.

"Blind dates?!"

Eve was so embarrassed that they were laughing at her. "What?" she said. "What's so funny?" She was caught in their happiness and silliness, but she wanted explanations.

"Where are you from?" Nancy demanded of Eve, still cracking up like crazy. So was Gabrielle. They couldn't stop.

"Las Vegas," said Eve, hands on her hips.

"Eeeww," said Nancy, laughing harder.

"Well, where are you from?" Eve demanded, playfully.

"Connecticut," said Nancy.

"Ugh," Eve chided her back.

They calmed down.

"Eve, darling," said Nancy. "Gabrielle's husband has a little side business."

"It's just business," Gabrielle said, defensively. "Sometimes you have to do certain things just to get movies made in this town. Anyway, it's not like we ever talk about it—I don't understand business at all."

Eve didn't understand any of it. "So, it's like a dating service?" she asked, squinching up her face in disgust at the idea of matchmaking. "On the side?"

Gabrielle and Nancy just burst into more hysterical laughter again. This was too much. They rocked back and forth on their chairs, holding on for support.

Gabrielle was relieved to have this outlet. She kept so much to herself. Too much. Sometimes she thought she would just burst. So she cleaned. Or signed up for another class, or worked out. Or threw a dinner party. Idle hands do the devil's work. Busy hands, clear mind. She recited aphorisms to herself when it was all too overwhelming.

"Is she on anything?" Nancy asked Gabrielle, who just shrugged, all this through their delirious laughfest.

"What?!" said Eve, amazed. She stood, and accidentally dropped her plate onto the floor. Food went everywhere.

Gabrielle started dabbing with a damp napkin at the spots Eve's food had made on the arm of the chair and the rug.

"Oh, I'm sorry," said Eve.

Nancy came over to help clean, but they all fell together into a side-splitting heap.

"Call someone!" yelled Nancy as she tried to get up. "Call 911!"

This sent them further into madness. They toppled onto each other and became a twisted mass of pregnant bodies and skinny arms and legs.

"Get off of me!" said Eve, trying to get herself up. She'd quickly given up trying to help the others, and was just trying to get herself untangled, but the more they each tried to get up, the more they fell.

Pretty soon, Eve was hysterically laughing, too.

"Stop making me laugh!" said Nancy, laughing. "I'm going to pee in my pants!"

They were all a laughing mess on the floor, when the maid came in.

"Is everything all right?" Rosa asked, worried.

"Help!" said Nancy, but when Rosa rushed over to help, she got pulled down, too. This made them giddier.

"I'm sorry, Rosa," said Nancy, as Rosa disentangled herself and headed for the doorway.

"I'll get the cleaning things," she said over her shoulder.

"Oh, shit," said Nancy. "Now I'll have to give her a raise. If I don't, she'll go all over town telling everyone I'm very messy."

"And don't forget the part about how her drunken friends collapsed in the living room, and she had to pick them all up," added Eve.

More laughter.

Rosa came back in with a dustpan and a damp sponge. The women all got quiet quickly, as Rosa cleaned.

"Well," sighed Nancy. "Party's over."

Eve pulled herself together. This was the most fun she'd ever had.

Forty-three

Gabrielle phoned Eve the next day for a play date. For their children.

"Sure," said Eve. "Why don't we meet at the park?"

Gabrielle's mind clicked. Only civilians went there. The park was not appropriate for these children. Not unless you were a "somebody" who was really heavy-duty. Like a Schwarzenegger or a Cruise, who knew that their children needed the reality check of normal civilian life the same way they needed vitamins and a well-balanced diet. To round them out.

Maria Shriver took her children, by herself, with no nanny, to the public parks in Santa Monica. For a dose of reality. Gabrielle, who'd grown up with just about enough reality, thank you very much, preferred a more sheltered play date. She'd heard that the Schwarzeneggers had built a separate house. A playhouse. Just for play dates. The little guests never saw where the hosts actually lived. The idea appealed to her.

"How about my house?" Gabrielle asked. "I can make sandwiches."

"Okay," said Eve, picturing peanut butter and jelly on paper plates. "That sounds great."

When Eve arrived at Gabrielle's Brentwood home, a housekeeper quietly showed her and Stella through the spotless English-style house to the backyard, where high tea was set out for the children. The tea set, real china, was on a crocheted white tablecloth. There were cucumber and cream cheese finger sandwiches, little fruit cookies sprinkled with powdered sugar, and tiny carrot sticks cut with fluted edges. In the little teapot was fresh-squeezed lemonade.

Eve was amazed.

There was not a peanut butter and jelly sandwich in sight. Not for miles around, she suspected. Everything was picture book perfect. Eve felt the huge gap between the way she and Fuller lived, in their cramped apartment in the Valley, and all this. Her friends' lives.

Stella ran to Zachary, who emerged from a child-size Victorian playhouse with shutters and real hooked rugs and slipcovered furniture inside. There was even electricity in the little house. Eve saw this when Zachary turned on a mock chandelier in the playhouse. Stella was enchanted.

"Look, Mom! Look at this!" she shrieked over and over. Eve wished she could be carefree about the differences in their lifestyles like her daughter was.

Gabrielle emerged from her own house. She wore a floral sundress and sandals. Her nails were French tip manicured.

"We just built the playhouse," said Gabrielle, as she hugged Eve, and admired the children playing together. "I found out we're having a girl next!"

"Gabrielle!" Eve exclaimed. "This is all so beautiful!"

"Look how well they play together," said Gabrielle.

"Look at these sandwiches!" Eve picked one up. It was cut out in the shape of a star. The cookies were shaped like tulips.

"They were so easy to make," said Gabrielle.

"You made these?" said Eve, biting into one. It tasted divine. "I thought you bought them."

"Oh, no," said Gabrielle. "It's just a play date. Would you like some mango tea in the parlor?"

Eve marveled at how she made the sentence sound so unpretentious.

"It's herbal," Gabrielle added when Eve hesitated.

"Do you think the kids'll be okay out there?" Eve asked.

"Consuela will watch them," Gabrielle said, and, as if she'd been wearing a wire, Consuela appeared with a big smile and waved at the mothers.

Eve followed Gabrielle inside the big house while the children played in the little house. The parlor had big windows from which the children could be seen playing. On the upholstered ottoman was a wooden tray with tea for the mothers. Mango tea, a fruit plate, and warm, homemade scones with lemon curd.

"I did buy the lemon curd," Gabrielle confessed with guilt.

"I've never had lemon curd before," Eve admitted. "I wouldn't know bought from homemade."

"Oh, but you would," said Gabrielle. "I'll make it next time you come. Try this, though."

Gabrielle served Eve, who settled down into a large, loosely upholstered, floral print chair. She sighed. Luxury was wonderful, she decided.

"You know, I guess I am going to have to hire a nanny after all," said Eve, throwing the idea out there. "I never thought I would—I didn't want one, but I guess . . . this is delicious," she said, nibbling the lemon curd on a scone.

"You mean you don't have help?" Gabrielle almost dropped her teacup.

"No," said Eve. She imagined Gabrielle would probably just die if she knew how Eve actually lived. Compared to Gabrielle and Nancy, Eve's life seemed so primitive. "How do you do it, exactly? An ad in the newspaper?"

"No!" Gabrielle admonished. "Never!"

Eve listened hard. Gabrielle obviously knew what she was talking about.

"You must call an agent," said Gabrielle. This was fun, she thought. She considered Eve a pupil in a way. A willing pupil. She could tell from the way Eve was listening and reacting that she would do exactly what Gabrielle said to do.

"You mean, like CAA or William Morris?" Eve asked. She felt smart just knowing the names of the talent agencies at all.

"No!" Gabrielle laughed. "A nanny agent."

Suddenly Eve didn't feel so bright. "They have agents?" Eve was shocked. "Nannies? Have agents?"

"There's Ruth at Heavenly Care. I like her, but she's expensive," said Gabrielle, jotting down the name and number on a piece of paper for Eve.

"How much?" Eve asked.

"Ten percent of a year's salary," said Gabrielle. She couldn't believe that Eve didn't know any of this. "You know, like twenty-five hundred dollars."

"Twenty-five hundred dollars?!" said Eve. She was completely shocked.

"Here," said Gabrielle, handing Eve the slip of paper with the numbers on it. "There's also Nicole. Lots of people use her, but no one's ever seen her. She operates all her business over the phone. She even interviews the girls over the phone. She doesn't really meet them face to face. If you ask me, it's creepy. Try Ruth first."

She looked out and saw Consuela playing happily with Stella and Zachary in the yard. Eve felt grateful to have Gabrielle to show her the way.

"I'll use who you use," said Eve. "Your nanny seems wonderful."

"She was Michael Eisner's," said Gabrielle, self-satisfied. Eve had no idea who Michael Eisner was, but she didn't say so.

"Just don't pay your help more than I do," said Gabrielle. "When they find out each other's salaries, it starts a war, and we all end up giving raises, just to keep them happy."

"What is the going salary?" Eve asked.

"Well, eight hundred a week for an American nanny."

Eve almost fell over. Eight hundred dollars a week? To babysit?

"You can get someone ethnic for four hundred, though," said Gabrielle, sensing Eve's surprise. "But you have to give a lot of paid holidays, and you'll probably have to spring for a car. But it is nice for the children to learn a second language."

"I don't know if we'll do that." Eve laughed. "It just seems kind of excessive. For a babysitter. Don't you think?" she asked Gabrielle.

"You have to be careful," said Gabrielle. "All you need to do is pick up a paper or turn on the news to see what could happen. That Louise Woodward thing just gives me goose bumps. And all those working women who videotape their nannies and find them hitting the children with spoons." Gabrielle visibly shuddered.

"I never thought about any of this," said Eve. She felt very overwhelmed.

"You have to," said Gabrielle. "It's unpleasant, but it's necessary."

Gabrielle sipped her tea. Those words meant more to her than Eve could ever fathom.

To Eve, Gabrielle seemed like she'd grown up rich and privileged. She knew how to make mango tea, buy lemon curd, set up a house, and run a staff. Eve liked and admired her.

"So, how did you meet Fuller?"

The question didn't as much take her off guard, as it shook her back to reality. This was a normal question. To Eve. It was the kind of thing someone in Vegas would ask. But Eve wasn't sure she wanted to get into so much so soon. She hadn't led a rags-to-riches life, but she certainly didn't come from any kind of background she could imagine Gabrielle encountering. She was a little afraid of the reaction she might receive.

"At a restaurant," Eve said, half lying. She omitted the part where she was the waitress and he was a customer.

Gabrielle didn't question this, and Eve didn't offer any more.

"I met Joey at a party," Gabrielle said. "But it seems like a million years ago. How did you meet Amanda?"

Another normal question. "At my wedding," said Eve.

"You didn't mind having your husband's ex at your wedding?" Gabrielle asked. Eve didn't know how Gabrielle already knew that Amanda was Fuller's ex-girlfriend. But she didn't question her. It seemed Gabrielle knew lots.

"No," said Eve, even though she did. She felt bad that she wasn't being completely honest with Gabrielle.

"I'm not nearly as secure as you are," said Gabrielle, admiringly, letting her guard down. Eve felt unworthy of the admiration. She decided then and there she would tell Gabrielle the truth about her past. "I could never have Joey's ex-girlfriends at my wedding."

"It's not like she was his ex-wife," said Eve. "Everyone has old girlfriends and boyfriends. Anyway, she's really nice. We're friends."

"Her husband's ex-wife is married to my father," said Gabrielle. Without a shred of happiness.

Eve had to think for a minute to make all the connections. "Oh," she said.

"Which makes Amanda and I relatives by divorce, I suppose."

"Oh." Eve didn't know what else to say. She hadn't thought that people were ever made relatives by divorce; usually it was the other way around.

Gabrielle smiled.

At that moment, a loud train whistle blew, and the mothers looked out into the yard, where Zachary was riding a nearly life-sized train around an oval track. He pulled the whistle, and made the loud noise again. Smoke even puffed out of the smokestack on the train. In the yard, little Stella's mouth dropped open. Almost as far as her mother's in the house.

Eve enjoyed seeing her daughter's surprise. Gabrielle thought Eve was naïve and wonderful. Flawless. She was sure Eve had no problems. None like hers, anyway.

Forty-four

That night, Eve made cheeseburgers, frozen french fries, and salad with Catalina dressing for dinner. Bottled water was something she'd had to get used to, but Fuller and everyone else assured her it was much better than drinking water from the tap, and when she did taste the tapwater and compared it with the bottled water, she figured they were right. So bottled water it was.

When Eve finally got everything set for dinner, she came to the table. Stella was dipping french fries in ketchup, and Fuller was slicing tomatoes and onions for his burger. Eve collapsed in her chair. The chipped, hard wood of the chair felt wonderful. Just to relax.

"Are you okay?"

"I'm exhausted," said Eve. "I was thinking, maybe we could go away for Thanksgiving—if it's all right. I heard that some people go to Twentynine Palms in the desert. Maybe—"

"Tomato?" Fuller offered.

"No. Bed," she said. "I'm beyond exhausted."

"Twentynine Palms is fine. But will you make me a big, traditional Thanksgiving one year? When you're not so tired."

"Sure." She smiled. "Definitely. When I'm not pregnant, okay?"

"Sure," he said. "Hey, how was your play date?"

"Great!" chimed Stella.

"Oh yeah?" Fuller was amused at Stella's enthusiasm.

"Zachary has every toy in the world. He has a playhouse and a jungle gym with flags on it, and every doll I've ever seen on television—for their new baby! She isn't born yet, and already she has more toys than me."

Fuller looked at Eve for input.

"Stella's right," said Eve, agreeing with her daughter. "Zachary does have everything. Fuller, I've never—I don't know how I'm going to get used to all this."

"Used to all what?"

"The lives here! It's like right off Robin Leach's show about famous people. Everything is . . . different. It's perfect. It's never— Like, when I grew up, there was this chair—a recliner. Right in front of the television. Orange and yellow and black print. With a big rip in the side arm—and you know what? No one ever fixed the rip. For years it stayed that way. No one even mended it. And it's still there. Same chair, same rip. That would never happen here. The chair or the rip."

Fuller fixed his cheeseburger, layering the vegetables carefully in order. Tomato, onion, lettuce. He was quiet. Building and listening.

"Everyone gets things to be perfect here!" Eve was amazed. "I mean, you should have seen the spread for tea. It could have been photographed for a magazine. Everything looked too good to bite into. Oh, and guess what I ate? Lemon curd."

"How was it?" he asked.

"It was fabulous," said Eve, excited. "We had scones, this tea made from papayas or something. Fuller—there wasn't a Lipton's teabag in sight, for miles."

Fuller remembered taking Eve on their first date. He had felt a tad like Henry Higgins in *Pygmalion*. Eve was so untouched. There was so much she hadn't seen before him. He liked that he was the one teaching her about the world. Now, with Stella, his job, and the new baby, he couldn't be the one to teach Eve everything. She was on her own. He wasn't sure he liked other people having the opportunity with Eve that he had so enjoyed. But he knew that there was nothing to do about it. Still, he couldn't help feeling a little jealous. She was his, after all.

"This cheeseburger is great," he said, taking a huge bite. "You're a wonderful cook. You make better burgers than anyone. Doesn't she, Stelly?"

"The scones were very special," said Stella, remembering the play date. Eve noticed her daughter's observation. She'd never heard her daughter speak that way. Calling something "special." Fuller noticed, too.

"I think Gabrielle's husband is having some kind of trouble at his studio, but I can't quite put my finger on it. It's all so mysterious—the way they talk around things. I don't know," said Eve, dismissively. "I just don't understand some things."

"Who's Gabrielle?" Fuller had stopped chewing.

"Gabrielle Gardener."

"Joey Gardener's wife?"

"Yeah," said Eve. "And Gabrielle's father is married to—let me see if I can remember this right—Amanda's husband's ex-wife. Isn't that weird?"

"You were at Joey Gardener's house?" Fuller put down his burger. He was upset.

"Yeah," said Eve. "What's wrong?"

"Nothing," said Fuller, but he didn't eat again. Just pushed his food around and looked down at his plate. He usually had that look when he was thinking of what to say next, but Eve didn't want to wait.

"You're not eating," she prompted him.

"Amanda was right," said Fuller.

"What was Amanda right about?"

"Nothing."

Eve felt criticized. And she didn't like that Fuller was discussing her with Amanda. She thought Amanda was *her* friend.

"You told me to get out and make friends," said Eve, defensively. "Gabrielle is a friend."

"I didn't say that kind of friend," Fuller hissed.

Now, Eve stopped eating. Stella looked back and forth between her parents, trying to make sense of the conversation.

"Why did you talk to Amanda? About me?"

"She called me to see if I knew anyone to fix up with her friend Jocelyn."

Eve didn't like this. Amanda talking to Fuller. Fuller fixing up Jocelyn. Now, Eve put down her food.

"I didn't know you two were such pals," said Eve. She pushed her food around on the plate.

"We're not."

"Pass the ketchup," said Stella. Eve reached across the table for ketchup and poured some on Stella's plate.

"Did you sleep with Jocelyn?" Eve asked.

"Daddy sleeps with you, silly," said Stella.

"Will you please be more careful?" asked Fuller, nodding at Stella.

"Silly Mommy," Eve said to Stella, recovering. "Want dessert? In the living room?"

"Yeah!" Stella roared. Eve stood to get a Popsicle. Her napkin fluttered to the floor as she rose. Eve silently peeled the sticky paper off the blue ice pop, and sent Stella off to watch television with her treat. When she was out of the room, Eve turned on Fuller.

"Fuller, I was just a waitress when you met me, but these women—Gabrielle, Nancy, Amanda—they don't know that. They look at me, and they see something else. They see me as this Hollywood mom. And I like it. I like who I am when I'm with them. I belong to a group. I didn't know I needed that, but I do."

Fuller picked at his food.

"Nothing wrong with being a waitress," he said.

"I know that," said Eve, a little more softly. "It's just that this is a chance for me to have a little adventure. These women, they're nice, and they're different. They're almost foreign—and I've never even been anywhere but here. They're right in my own backyard."

"I have a feeling they wouldn't be caught dead in any backyard east of Bundy," he said.

Eve felt the bitterness in his voice. It was unusual. She also didn't understand what that meant. She was getting a headache trying to understand everything. To learn it all.

"Fuller," she said, laughing, "one minute you tell me not to be ashamed of being a waitress, and the next minute you're telling me to be ashamed of where I live! That my friends won't be caught dead in certain neighborhoods?!"

He banged the table with his fist, but didn't say anything. He was frustrated because she'd articulated his dilemma so succinctly. And he hated having it spelled out so clearly.

"Just be careful," he said.

"Of what?" Eve laughed. She couldn't imagine anything dangerous about Nancy or Gabrielle.

"I don't know," said Fuller. But he did. He was just afraid to say more, as though if he said it, by some wish-fulfilling prophecy the spoken would become life.

They sat there, silently, and Eve felt a rift between them. A separation was happening.

"So, did you sleep with Jocelyn?" she asked, calmly.

"No," said Fuller.

"I didn't think so," said Eve. She snuggled into her chair.

"I asked her out," said Fuller.

"You didn't!" said Eve. She hadn't expected this. "You asked her out?" Eve hated this. "You're supposed to be all mine!"

"I didn't even know you then," said Fuller. "And," he added, "she said no."

"She did?" Eve's curiosity was entirely piqued.

"She wouldn't even remember me, I'm positive."

"Did you ask everyone out?" Eve asked, accusingly.

"Eve!" he said. "Come on! What do you expect? I'm older than you. I've dated some."

Eve scowled, her arms crossed.

"I never asked anyone to marry me but you," he said, as if to end the conversation. It didn't work.

"What about hookers?" Eve asked.

"What?!" said Fuller. "What hookers?"

His outrage seemed to calm her a little.

"Gabrielle said—"

"What did Gabrielle say?" Fuller asked, sternly. He waited for an answer. Ready to pounce.

"I wasn't exactly sure," said Eve, contemplatively. "It's just that between my dinner at Nancy's and tea at Gabrielle's . . . I don't know—it seems so ridiculous. I don't know what they're talking about half the time, and the other half the time, I understand, and I can't believe it all!"

Fuller didn't like this crowd she was falling in with. That was for sure, but Eve didn't care.

"I need you to help me," she said. "To translate."

"Easy," said Fuller. He was practically yelling at her. "Gabrielle's husband is in very deep shit. I'm not involved in anything like that."

The tension was thick.

"Okay, okay," she said. "But it doesn't look that way to me. I mean, their home is so lovely and she's always happy—"

"And you know what else? I'm deeply insulted you think I'd have to pay for sex," said Fuller, releasing some of the pressure with a joke. "You've been to bed with me. You should know I wouldn't have to pay for sex."

He smirked. Eve cracked up. She was glad to be married to her husband. So glad. Finally, they were laughing again.

"What *is* the deal with Gabrielle's husband? Really?" Eve asked now that the tension was dissipated.

"I don't know for sure—I mean, it's all secondhand, but I hear he gets his deals by getting his actors and directors hookers. It's this high-class operation. Very inside."

Eve was speechless.

"It's a mess. I don't know. Ask her. She'll tell you if she's such a good friend," said Fuller. "I just never thought I'd have a wife on the inner circle."

"I don't believe it," said Eve, defensive of her friend. "It doesn't seem possible."

"Good," said Fuller. "But for the record, I don't like Stella having play dates there."

"Oh, honey. It's so innocent."

He glared at her.

"It is!" she insisted. "They play tea party and freeze tag. They're just kids. They don't know what we know. Besides," said Eve, wistfully, "I love being there."

"You do?"

"It's like being on a vacation when I'm with those two. The kind of vacation I've only dreamed about. They tell me these stories, about spas and trainers and fabulous clothes," she said, ending with a sigh.

"You're not going to run off with some rich guy, are you?" said Fuller. "Now that you've seen that kind of life?"

"Looking like this?" said Eve, pointing to her pregnant stomach. "I'll at least wait until I lose the weight."

She smiled at him.

"Just watch your step," he said. Seriously.

"Sure," said Eve, wondering what he meant.

Forty-five

The rainy season was short, but aggravating. El Niño whipped through Los Angeles and made its mark. Roofs needed replacing. Gardens flooded and had to be relandscaped. Streets filled with giant puddles, and traffic had to be detoured. Two Rolls-Royces were left abandoned on the watery Olympic Boulevard in West L.A., as their drivers called for help from tiny cell phones that looked like they were made for dolls. Cable television went down. Phone lines crossed and party lines happened where they shouldn't have. People stayed home rather than drive in the "weather."

Malibu moved one step further toward becoming an island like Catalina. Mudslides crippled neighborhoods and closed the Pacific Coast Highway, the lifeline to the rest of Los Angeles for

Malibu residents. Without PCH, drivers were forced to take Malibu Canyon, hours out of their way, just to circle round and get back to Santa Monica. It was a mess. Sandbags were sold like milk—everybody bought them. And when they couldn't buy them because they were all sold out, Range Rovers and Jeep Cherokees pulled up to the stormy coastline, and entire families and helpful friends emerged, and ran down to the beach to bag their own sand.

A few crazy independent filmmakers took the opportunity to shoot stormy scenes on the gray beach the same day there was actually a tornado watch in effect. The warning came across the emergency broadcast system, interrupting Dr. Laura's radio talk show and all the music programs that played during the lunch hour. The tornado eventually set down in Long Beach and took the roof off of a supermarket. It made the news.

Eve hardly noticed. She was in labor.

She didn't tell Fuller that the pains had arrived. He was sleeping in the bed next to her. She flipped the remote control, not watching, just flipping, trying to distract herself from what was happening to her body, but by midnight, there were no distractions. The baby's birth had become the main event.

"Fuller," Eve roused him.

"Hmmm?" He didn't open his eyes.

"It's time."

"It's . . ." He turned to look at the clock next to his side of the bed. "It's midnight," he said, turning back to her.

"No," she said. "It's *time*."

Fuller didn't understand. Musty with sleep. He blinked. Her face was tense.

"Oh." He was awake.

Eve got herself dressed, as Fuller did the same. When a strong contraction came and Eve had to grab the side of the closet for support, she let out a groan that scared the shit out of Fuller.

"What?" he said, running to her. He was all dressed in sweats, except for one sneaker, still off. "Are you all right?" He was frightened.

Eve couldn't speak.

"Is this one of the contractions?"

The contraction passed.

"We'd better go," she said.

Fuller drove her to the hospital through torrential rain. He let his old Porsche really open up. It was late, and there was very little traffic on the 405 or the 10 freeway. In what seemed like minutes, but was actually just under twenty-five, they pulled up to the emergency exit to Cedar Sinai Hospital.

The whole way Eve was thinking about Stella. She'd hired Gabrielle's live-in babysitter as a temporary measure. Gabrielle had insisted, when she found out Eve still didn't have anyone, that Eve take her person.

"Why?!" said Gabrielle. "I can accept this as a martyr thing. I've seen that. You're going to do it all yourself, so everyone else can watch you suffer."

"It's not that." Eve laughed.

"Is it a political statement?" asked Gabrielle. "A slight on all the rest of us who do have help?"

Eve just burst out in laughter and almost peed in her lacy maternity underpants. To think that she'd done anything political in her entire life was a big hoot.

"It's just that me, Fuller, Stella—we're this little group. I don't know if I want someone else joining."

Gabrielle studied her friend, as if she had just spoken in a foreign tongue.

"Okay," she said. "So you just don't want to hire any help." Gabrielle was trying to understand. "But how are you going to drive Stella to play dates when the baby is napping? Or what if the baby is sick—you're up all night and Stella has something special she has to go to. And the laundry needs to be done. And there's no food in the house. It is physically impossible to have no help!"

Eve thought of her mother, who did everything *and* pumped gas.

"All right!" said Eve. Eve's happiness was giddy and infectious. Gabrielle had had her second baby, Roxy, and now, Eve was about to. "I will get someone. Maybe I just haven't done it."

"Eve, you're going to have a baby. Who is going to stay with Stella when you go to the hospital?"

Eve bit her lip. She didn't know. Hadn't planned that far along. Her mother had always had her father to watch the kids. But Eve wanted Fuller with her.

"What if you go into labor in the middle of the night, and Fuller has to drive you? What happens to Stella?"

Eve was now nodding. Gabrielle was right.

"You need to start acclimating a live-in now!" said Gabrielle, as if she were running for office. "I'll loan you Consuela—at least Stelly knows her from play dates here."

"I couldn't," said Eve.

"Just until you get around to hiring your own. I'm loaded with backups."

And so that was how Eve got "help." Who was sleeping in the bedroom with Stella, as they didn't have a maid's room, like all her friends did. It didn't matter. Gabrielle had been right. Stella was safe with Consuela at home. Eve was lucky to have Gabrielle as a friend.

Fuller pulled the Porsche into an empty parking spot and helped Eve inside. People made way for them, ran to open doors. Sympathetic faces met Fuller's and Eve's as they made their way into Triage. Two nurses took one look at Eve and whisked her away, leaving Fuller behind to fill out paperwork, which had him emptying his wallet of insurance cards, driver's license, papers from the little pockets in the back he hadn't used in ages.

"Can't I go with her?" he asked. It hadn't been like Eve to not say goodbye to him. To not ask him to accompany her somewhere. Fuller was worried.

His wife.

His second child.

He was about to have a family. Not just a baby, like with Stella. This baby would mean they were almost two-point-whatever. They were census bureau numbers. This second baby somehow made Fuller head of a family—with a capital F.

When a nurse in glasses finally called for him, her hand extended offering him a pair of green cotton scrubs, Fuller was relieved and, at the same time, filled with excitement. He quickly dressed in the sterile, fluorescent-lit bathroom. The smell was of disinfectant. He caught a glimpse of himself in the mirror. Husband, father, studio head. He wondered what other people saw when they looked at him.

A knock on the door broke his reverie.

"Coming," said Fuller as he opened the door.

"You all right?" asked the nurse, examining his face.

"Yup," he said. "Where's Eve?"

The nurse led him into a birthing room, where Eve, dressed in a white cotton hospital gown and hooked up to machines, was sitting up, her feet in the stirrups of the table. A team of doctors were assembled by her feet.

"Fuller!" she said. She was sweating, red, half crying.

"I'm here."

Eve did her Lamaze breathing, and occasionally her mind wandered to the people in her Lamaze class—the ones who smiled like they couldn't stop, as they told their outlandish "birth plans." They wanted to give birth underwater with dolphins nearby, hopefully to act as midwives.

Eve and Fuller had just looked at each other, sharing the same thought: These people are nuts. They excused themselves from their cross-legged, pillow-propped circle of new parents, and never came back. That was enough. They both agreed. They had accepted the ripe mothers-to-be who wanted to skip the epidurals and any other drugs, but fish as midwives was pushing the envelope.

They never went back to Lamaze. Eve had laughed it off as loopy, but as her labor came on full force, all fears surfaced. Her mother had had babies as though it was nothing. Eve didn't completely remember all her sisters and brothers being born, but she didn't remember her mother complaining about childbirth. It was just something one did. Eve relaxed into that thought, but as the contractions came closer and stronger, she began to lose it.

She should have taken Gabrielle's advice. She should have hired the private Lamaze coach to come to her home, like Gabrielle did. Gabrielle had pushed her second baby out last month, as though there'd been nothing to it. Or so she said. Eve hadn't seen her much since. She'd been recovering, peacefully. Now it was Eve's turn.

"Hi," said the doctor. Eve didn't answer. Fuller shook his hand.

The doctor was quiet, but alert. Fuller assessed the room. Eve was naked from the waist down. No one acted like anything was abnormal. He hated this part.

Eve grabbed his hand and dug her nails into his flesh, as she followed the doctor's commands to push, wait, hold, breathe . . . and then, the baby started to crown.

"You want a front-row seat?" asked the doctor.

"Oh," Fuller stalled. He wasn't sure he wanted to see his wife that way. He had said no the first time, even though he knew it was politically correct to look. To see the miracle of life happen. But if he saw a human being come out of his wife—down there, through what up until now was his private domain—how would he feel? Would it cause him any permanent . . . trauma? Forget the baby, how about him? He felt forgotten.

He didn't like all these people seeing his wife naked like this—how many were there, anyway? Five? Six? Doctors, strange men. Who knew if they were even doctors, anyway. For all he knew, they could be interns or male nurses. Perverts. Sickos.

"Fuller," Eve called to him. He saw the pain in her face. She was intent and full of anguish.

There was nothing he could do about any of it. It was happening. Without him. He felt impotent and anxious, and wished he weren't there. But he would never leave her. He took her hand and held it.

"One more push," said the doctor.

Fuller stayed where he was. Up by Eve's head. She needed him there.

"Congratulations," said the doctor, as the others swarmed around the new baby, sticking suction tubes everywhere. "You have a girl!"

Forty-six

"Eloise Fay," said Eve. She was on the telephone in her hospital maternity room. The phone was ringing when she was wheeled in, and it hadn't stopped ringing since.

"Seven pounds, one ounce. Twenty inches long."

Over and over, the same information. Eve's room was filled with flowers. Nancy and Gabrielle had sent a huge arrangement of pink and purple flowers that were so lush, they looked like thick velvet. Amanda had sent, with George, of course, a bouquet of two dozen pink balloons that completely took over a large corner of the room. Jocelyn had sent roses from her and all the teachers at Butterflies and Puppydog Tails. And of course, there were the Eloise in Paris books, which everyone sent.

Fuller was elated. He lay in Eve's bed with her, staring at Eloise in her arms, staring at Eve, and staring at the eight-by-ten photograph of Stella they'd taped up on the wall, facing the bed. They finally took the phone off the hook, and just whispered and kissed and caressed the new baby. All of them, squished together in the single bed.

"Everything is perfect," Eve whispered.

"Just us," said Fuller, stroking Eve's hair. "You, me, the kids." He rolled the word around in his mouth, pleased. "Kidssssss."

"That's not all that's perfect," said Eve, quietly. She looked at the flowers and thought of Gabrielle and Nancy, Amanda and Jocelyn. "I have friends. It's like I have roots here."

"That's wonderful," Fuller purred, admiring his wife, and himself for choosing her.

"This is where I live," she said, firmly. Her voice was quiet, but the sentiment echoed for a long, long time.

Forty-seven

Amanda threw a small surprise "après-birth" baby shower at her home for Eve. She invited Nancy and Gabrielle along with Jocelyn for lunch. Nancy and Gabrielle were thrilled to receive the printed invitations scented with gardenia oil. They were curious and excited about meeting Amanda. She was married to a very famous and wealthy producer—they wanted to be in her company. As if her good fortune would somehow rub off on them. This was a perfect way.

They logged about four hours on the telephone just discussing their luck in attending a luncheon at Amanda Foster's home. This clearly elevated them into hyperspace on the social scale. Eve was high in their graces for being the catalyst of their luck.

Jocelyn was less than thrilled. She was swamped. She didn't have a lot of free time on her hands. She had parent conferences, a fundraising meeting with a local business, and a pile of reading to do. There were also phone calls to be returned. She had a phone log as long as any studio head. Plus, she hadn't been to the beach in two weeks. She was having withdrawal symptoms. She needed to be near the ocean.

Jocelyn also wasn't keen on bumping into George Foster. One of the few guys who couldn't get it up in bed with her. They'd dated about three or four times and, on the last date, she'd slept with him. They both expected greatness, but when George couldn't deliver, he was embarrassed beyond belief. Mortified, humiliated, and fearful that Jocelyn would tell. Anyone.

She never did. But he never gave up fear that she would.

So he took preventative measures.

Just in case.

George spread the word all over town that Jocelyn was awful in bed. A complete dud. No sensuality. No idea of what to do. Wouldn't go down on him. Lay there like a board. The list went on and on. George did what he had learned to do in Hollywood. Screw the other guy before he screws you. In that spirit, he set out to ruin Jocelyn's social reputation—with lies—before she could ruin his with the truth.

It didn't completely work, but it did do damage.

Nobody doubted George's stories. Even as he embellished them, depending on the company or the alcohol or the adrenaline in the air.

When Jocelyn first met Amanda, she was prepared to dislike her immediately. Because of George. But Amanda was different— not at all what Jocelyn had expected. She was down-to-earth and very real. Jocelyn liked her immediately. She figured that if this was who George had finally "chosen," then he must have changed since she had dated him. Nobody could be with Amanda and be a total dick.

Amanda didn't know exactly what George had done to Jocelyn. She just knew that she liked Jocelyn, and George didn't really enter into the equation. Amanda's girlfriends were off-limits to George. He had no say in what she did with the girls. Only with him.

That was the essence of what Jocelyn liked about Amanda. She had a grip on her world. So, in honor of her friendship with Amanda, Jocelyn decided to make her peace with George. But George avoided her like the plague. He was petrified that Jocelyn would refer to that ill-fated night.

Jocelyn accepted the invitation to Eve's baby shower at the Fosters' home. Maybe George would stumble in and Jocelyn would finally get to have a few words with him. She dressed for it.

"You look unusually stunning," said Amanda, welcoming Jocelyn to her home. Amanda was barefoot, in white linen clam diggers and a baby pink sweater that was loose and soft. She took the present Jocelyn carried. It was a basket of baby things wrapped up with a giant bow and clear cellophane.

"Hi," said Jocelyn. She wore open-toed sandals and a sleeveless dress that was slit up the side. The dress was chocolate. Her lipstick was the same color.

They kissed lightly then went through the ritual of wiping each other's lipstick off of each other's cheeks.

"The troops aren't here yet," said Amanda with trepidation in her voice. "Come on in."

"Thanks," said Jocelyn, and followed Amanda through the airy hallway of the Mediterranean-style house and into a library. They passed beautiful art, uniquely framed, on the way through the hall.

"Is that a Chagall?" asked Jocelyn, as they passed the art.

"I don't know," said Amanda.

It was. Jocelyn tried to stop and look, but Amanda had something on her mind.

"I'm not quite sure if I should thank you or shoot you," she said, taking Jocelyn's arm to hurry her along.

"What for?" asked Jocelyn.

"You introduced my friend to the deep end of the pool," said Amanda as she brought Jocelyn into the room where the baby shower was to be held.

"What deep end?" asked Jocelyn.

She hung back in the doorway and surveyed the room. It was full of books—in the bookshelves, on the tables, in stacks on the floor. The decor was old Mexican. There was nothing new.

"How could you have introduced her to Greene and Gardener?"

"They gravitated toward each other," Jocelyn said. But she sounded defensive.

"Jocelyn," said Amanda. "You are the only one who orchestrates any 'gravitational pulls' in that entire preschool. If you didn't want them to be friends, they wouldn't be."

"Oh, bullshit," said Jocelyn. "Eve is a grown woman. And you're giving me too much credit."

"I am not," said Amanda. "George says—"

She stopped. Jocelyn wanted to hear the rest.

"What?"

"George says you're the strongest person in Hollywood. If you want something, it happens."

"Really?" Jocelyn wanted to see George. She was glad to be the first one there. "Is he around?"

"I don't know," said Amanda. "Who knows where he is. He could be around. He could be in Cannes. He could be on the Jersey Turnpike for all I know."

"Maybe I could say hello," said Jocelyn.

"I'm just worried about her," said Amanda. "She's not equipped for frontline Hollywood life."

"I think you may underestimate your friend," said Jocelyn, sampling some salmon spread on a rye cracker from a table of treats.

"I think you're stirring up the pot for fundraising support," said Amanda. "I think you're trying to get Eve, Gardener, and Greene to be your donkeys and pull your fundraising cart."

"Donkeys?" said Jocelyn. She was mildly insulted. "What is it you think I do, anyway? Coal mines?"

"Look. Just ask me—I'll get George to donate more money. I don't want Eve hurt."

"You've done more than enough," said Jocelyn, sincerely.

The mood changed. They were both thinking of something other than Eve.

"I can never do enough," said Amanda, quietly. "After all you've done for me. . . ."

Jocelyn knew what Amanda was talking about. It was their secret—the baby Amanda had with the famous actor. Who was married. At a time when she was beginning to see George. It was a mess, but not one that was undoable. And Jocelyn had played a key part.

Amanda had a valuable acting career at the time, and the famous actor who got her pregnant was married, with children. He didn't want a baby with Amanda, and he wasn't about to leave his wife for her. So, Amanda disappeared, and had the baby, then put it up for adoption. Because she was who she was, she couldn't go through normal adoption routes. She couldn't risk being found out. Not just for her, and not just for the father of her baby, who would lose his own family if his wife found out, but for the baby itself.

Kidnapping and extortion or other blackmail were familiar turf for celebrities with adopted babies. If a virtuous family with the adopted baby of a celebrity was ever found out, that baby would be plagued. With sickos, with paparazzi—it was unfortunate, but it was real.

Amanda had to protect her baby. She wanted her child to have the best. And she knew that the best would be with other parents.

Amanda's street sense brought her to Jocelyn's office. Her instincts told her that Jocelyn would be her angel. Jocelyn would find perfect parents.

Informally, but effectively, Jocelyn arranged for a closed adoption. She knew every family on the Westside, and easily found one who would make good parents. Infertility was the herpes of the nineties. Three out of four couples had it. Many couples who couldn't have children, and desperately wanted them, lived here. Placing Amanda's baby was easy. Money wasn't an issue. Everyone involved wanted a closed adoption. Jocelyn's lawyer took care of everything.

Nobody would ever know the true biological parents of the baby boy. Until the baby was twenty-one. Then Amanda's name would be given to the family. The baby, then an adult, would finally be introduced to his biological mother. If he wanted.

Until then, only Jocelyn knew.

That's how Amanda and Jocelyn became the kind of solid friends they were. This secret cemented them.

"I'll never be able to repay you. You paid for scholarships for ten of my students this year," said Jocelyn. "You covered raises for three of my teachers. Do you know how happy and motivated they felt when I gave them raises for doing such a good job? They were ecstatic. They plunged into work. It was just . . . there are no words."

"Well, I'm glad," said Amanda, softly. "And I'm happy to do it. You know I believe in you—but you're dipping my friend in this pond of sharks."

"You gotta let a child go sometime. See if they'll walk or fall."

"Eve's not a child," said Amanda, quietly. She saw the maid letting in Gabrielle and Nancy. They were carrying beautifully wrapped gifts.

"Exactly," smiled Jocelyn. "She's not a child. And I am not her mother. I'm her friend."

"Hello!!" Gabrielle and Nancy sang out, as they walked into the sitting room and gazed out on the patio, where a table was set for five by the pool.

"Hello," said Amanda, not sure whether or not she should introduce herself. She'd run into Gabrielle and Nancy at hundreds of premieres, screenings, parties, and school functions. They weren't strangers, but they weren't friends. They'd never said anything more than a sentence or two about the weather to each other. And the weather never changed. The chatter was merely an attempt to connect. The kind of attempt that went unrequited.

"So nice to see you," said Nancy, kissing Amanda with familiarity. "What fabulous weather!"

"So clear," said Gabrielle.

"Yes," said Amanda. "It's crisp out."

"Your house is beautiful," said Gabrielle, examining everything. Memorizing details.

"Thank you," said Amanda. "Come have a drink. Lemonade? Champagne? Margarita?"

Amanda played the gracious host, and handed her guests champagne from a tray of glasses already poured.

The doorbell rang again. This time, it was the guest of honor.

Eve walked into the house, unaware that this was her party. She was glad to get out by herself and take a break from the children. She no longer had to pinch herself walking into fabulous homes—even one as superlatively fabulous as Amanda Foster's. The wealth was no longer phasing her the way it once had. These were the homes of her friends.

"Surprise!"

Eve walked into her baby shower. She was shocked.

"I don't know what to say," said Eve, and she wept with joy. All the makeup she had put on ran off, as she looked around. She didn't see a famous wife's home that had been photographed for *In Style* magazine. She only saw the baby shower. The balloons, the flowers, and the pink and white cake with the silver dragets. All for her. She just wept. Amanda ran to her and gave her a warm hug.

"Oh, no!" cried Nancy. "You're going to make me cry. Stop!" But Eve didn't. Nancy kissed Eve. "I love you."

Gabrielle ran over and put her arms around them both. "I love you, too," said Gabrielle.

"Oh, all right, me, too," said Jocelyn, joining the group hug reluctantly, but, once in, realizing it was the right thing to do. What the hell.

Only Amanda hung back and watched. Smiling awkwardly. She had trouble trusting people whose intentions she didn't understand. Eve was crystal clear to her. Simple, good, and in love with Fuller. Period. End of story. Jocelyn was practical-woman. She had a passion and a purpose in her school. She was hopeful and at the same time disappointed in her social life. Which made her an American woman defined. Beautiful, strong, still young, but thinking about what she would do when she was no longer thirtysomething.

But Nancy's and Gabrielle's discomfort and fanlike fervor around her made Amanda feel misunderstood and undeserving. She didn't think they really saw her. Just her things. Her house, her car, her husband. They objectified her and her life—that was her fear.

"Come on," said Jocelyn, inviting Amanda into the group hug. "Come!" she commanded. "It's required."

Amanda obeyed, playing the obedient puppy.

"Amanda, thank you," said Eve, meaningfully, as the others peeled away and they were left by themselves. "This is so great."

"Oh, this was nothing. I just called and ordered food," said Amanda, snapping her fingers in the air. "Instant party."

"No, not just for this party," said Eve. "For everything. For getting Stella into the preschool. It's such a great place. Jocelyn is amazing."

"Do you know anyone to fix her up with?" Amanda asked.

"Everyone I know is in this room," said Eve. "I can ask Fuller if he knows anyone."

"I already asked George. He says everyone's afraid of her. Of course, he slept with her once . . . or more than once. I don't know."

Eve was shocked at this news.

"You're kidding!" said Eve. "He did?"

"Before me, of course," said Amanda.

"I guess that makes it okay," said Eve. But she felt unsteady with the idea.

"She's a whirlwind," said Amanda. "She played volleyball in college. Bikini and a visor with dark glasses and zinc on her nose. Come on. Everyone wanted her. She could've gone pro, y'know."

"Really," said Eve.

"She's very athletic. Anyway, George was just one of her many rejects. We don't talk about it—George and I."

"Did you ever ask her?"

"No," said Amanda. "I don't care, really."

"So, it doesn't bother you at all?" Eve asked.

"Nah," said Amanda. "I've got my husband's dick wrapped around my little pinky so tight, I'm the only one he can look at."

Eve laughed at Amanda. It was impossible not to love her. Here she was in this sprawling hacienda, and she talked like a truck driver.

"You want to know a little secret?" Amanda whispered to Eve. "I like that George hates her, actually."

"He hates her?"

"Whenever he hates someone, it shows me he's vulnerable. Human."

"Is that something you worry about?" Eve asked.

"Well, you spend a few decades in this town, it does become a question," said Amanda. "Humanity. I suppose anywhere. Y'think? You're from somewhere."

"Not like this," said Eve.

"That's why Jocelyn is a cold splash of water on a hot day. She has her values. And they're not seasonal."

"She's so in control of everything," said Eve. "I mean, you almost forget how nice she is."

"I know," said Amanda. "That's the thing I admire. Her discipline and drive." Amanda took a long pull on her drink. "It's also why she can't get a date."

Eve looked at Amanda, wondering. "Why?"

"The men want to feel superior," said Amanda. "You know that, honey. You just accept it. If you're smart."

"Fuller is superior to me," said Eve. "I like that. I don't have to compromise."

Amanda smiled beatifically on Eve. "And you will have a long, happy marriage because of it," said Amanda. "Built-in success— that's what you have with that."

"I don't like to analyze everything so much," said Eve.

"And that's what I like about you the most," said Amanda, giving Eve a big kiss on her forehead. "That is why we will have a long and wonderful, fabulous friendship. The kind they write about. With violin music in the end."

Eve couldn't imagine ever being as comfortable with herself as Amanda was. She wondered if Amanda had always been like that. She imagined that a certain amount of comfort came from being married to someone like George. Amanda could afford to live in her own little world. Nonetheless, Eve was glad to be a part of it.

"I can't believe you did this all on your own," said Eve, admiringly.

"I told you, I had it catered."

"Not just the party. All of this." Eve didn't know how to

explain it. "You made it here. You came out here alone, and you just did it. And the thing is, you were just like me."

Amanda felt sad. She looked it.

"What?" said Eve, sensing her friend's changing mood. "What's wrong? You look like you're going to cry."

"You know," said Amanda. "The thing is . . . the biggest secret I can tell you: You're always alone. Even when you feel like you have friends. You're on your own. Even when you feel like you're not."

Eve was silent, trying to absorb Amanda's message. She loved Amanda, but it didn't make sense. And she didn't like it.

"You're not alone," said Eve, and took Amanda's hand. "And neither am I." She stood back and looked at Nancy and Gabrielle, who were noisily devouring a bottle of champagne and picking at the food. They warmed their hands on the fire in the gas-fueled fireplace. Jocelyn walked alone, out by the pool. She looked like she was looking for something.

"I was a little surprised at the crowd you picked." Amanda nodded discreetly at Nancy and Gabrielle. There was judgment in her voice.

"The crowd?" asked Eve. "My friends? What's wrong with my friends?"

Amanda tried to think of words to express herself without upsetting Eve. How could she say that she thought Eve's friends had shallow lives and hollow values? She decided not to even try.

"Jocelyn likes them," said Eve, defensively. She knew that Amanda respected Jocelyn.

"Hey, forget it," said Amanda, trying to break the tension that was building. "Are you drinking champagne?"

"Can't," said Eve. "I'm nursing."

"Lemonade?" Amanda offered.

"Sure," said Eve, and watched as Amanda got her a drink. Amanda's disapproval of her choice of friends irked her, but, ironically, she felt indebted to Amanda for getting her into the preschool where she met Gabrielle and Nancy in the first place. She was torn. She didn't want to do something Amanda thought wrong, but she was not going to drop her friends. After all, they were part of her everyday world, and Amanda was only around now and then. She had her own life.

"Open your gifts," said Jocelyn, checking her Timex, which

looked like a Rolex. "I've got a teachers' meeting, and I want to see your loot before I leave."

Eve laughed and broke her quiet reverie.

"Okay," said Eve. She regained her party joy, and settled into the sofa to open her most beautiful presents: tiny handknit sweaters with buttons shaped like animals, from Fred Segal, and an exquisite country French diaper bag from Neiman's. Those were from guests who couldn't make it—Stella's teachers at school. Nancy had bought baby Eloise an entire set of little antique rattan chairs with a coffee table. The chairs had beautiful seat cushions that Nancy had had made to order. They were floral prints. Eve just gushed. She couldn't imagine a more beautiful gift. Gabrielle gave Eloise an English tea set and a gift certificate for Eve for a postnatal massage at Burke Williams along with a facial and a manicure/pedicure.

"I've never had a facial," said Eve. The others couldn't believe it, and were so glad that Eve was finally going to do it. They're wonderful, everyone said, at different times. A funny chorus.

Amanda gave Eve a baby-sized six-month black leather zip-front jacket and a baby black beret for Eloise.

"She's gotta have style," Amanda said as the others oohed and ahhed.

"Where did you get this?!" said Gabrielle, admiring the jacket.

"It's actually vintage," said Amanda. "I bought it at a flea market. In Paris."

Nancy and Gabrielle just loved Amanda's style.

Jocelyn mentally checked the party off as Eve's official initiation into Hollywood mom-dom. There was nowhere else in the world where this exact shower, or anything like it, would take place. She wondered where George was.

"Excuse me," said Jocelyn. "I'm going to find the powder room."

Jocelyn left the room, but she wasn't looking for a powder room. She was looking for George. She hadn't had her legs waxed for nothing. She wanted to talk to him.

Forty-eight

Jocelyn wandered through the Fosters' house, and finally found George on the second floor in his office that adjoined the master bedroom. He was walking on a treadmill and writing notes on a pad that was affixed to the exercise machine. His handwriting was nearly illegible, but he didn't care. A television was on behind him. The videotape of *War of the Worlds* was playing. Nobody watched.

Jocelyn stood there, watching him. What a life, she thought. Luxury and fear all rolled up in one. George looked up. When he saw her, he stopped walking and almost fell.

"Have trouble staying in a room with so many women?" he asked, as he stepped off the treadmill, and caught his breath. He'd been on it for a long time.

"Why'd you do it?" Jocelyn was shaking.

"Do what?"

"Why'd you talk about me the way you did? All over town? Why did you make it so any man who talks to me is nervous as hell?"

George didn't answer. He knew exactly what he'd done. He knew he'd hurt her.

"It's not like we were going to get married," she said. "It was just one night. . . . You didn't have to set out to destroy my social life."

"What do you want," he asked, amused, "that you'd bring up something that happened so long ago?" He laughed. Bitterly. Defensively.

"You can't ruin me," she said. This is why she'd come. This was what she'd wanted to say to him. For a long, long time. "Because I don't care about the same things you do."

George got a towel, and dried off his neck and face. Considered what to do next. He took off his clothes. Piece by piece, staring at Jocelyn the entire time. In defiance. She was shocked. George finally stood there, in front of her, stark naked. An erection in place.

Jocelyn was startled. But she remained as cool as she could. She was aware that the door was cracked open. She wondered what anyone passing by would think. Maybe nothing. Maybe George was like this all the time.

"You're a pig," she said.

George laughed. "Would you mind shutting the door? I like privacy."

She shut the door, and turned the lock.

"Should I shower first?" he asked. "Or are you in the mood for a little true virility? Maybe that's what you like."

"I wouldn't fuck you even if your dick worked," she spat out at him. It felt good to curse like that. She knew she'd stung him. She wanted to.

George hesitated. His erection began to die.

"Does yours?" he asked.

"What the hell is your problem?" Jocelyn asked. "You have a great wife, a great career. Why are you such a bastard?"

"Why'd you come up here?" he asked, walking toward her. He was inches from her. She could smell him, and in a second she'd feel him. "To finish what never happened?"

"You know," she said, turning and opening the door, wide, so anyone passing could see George in the buff. "I have no fucking idea—but I'm sure glad I did. Because you are . . ." She couldn't finish. She didn't really know what he was. A contradiction if anything. She left, and slammed the door, so it made a loud noise. She thought she heard him laugh.

Forty-nine

As Eve opened the presents, she felt bathed in approval and love. It wasn't the presents, but the circle of friends around her. It was the first time she felt like she really belonged somewhere. Somewhere fabulous. Falling in love with Fuller was one thing, but having girlfriends was a whole other story. She had a wonderful time that afternoon, as the guest of honor at her party, and as part of a group, despite Amanda's disapproval.

At the end of the party everyone hugged and kissed goodbye, then penciled in lunch dates with each other and play dates with each other's children over the next month, while Amanda's maids piled the presents into Eve's car.

Jocelyn reappeared way after any normal person seeking a powder room would have.

"You okay?" Amanda asked her.

"Sorry. I just love looking at your art," said Jocelyn. "I forgot myself."

Amanda checked Jocelyn for disheveled clothing, smeared lipstick, any sign of trouble.

"Would you donate a piece for the fundraiser?" Jocelyn asked. "Something good—I really like that Picasso."

Amanda knew immediately that something was up. The Picasso was worth over a million. And Jocelyn knew it, too. Jocelyn never asked without reason.

"I'll have to talk to George—"

"I already did," said Jocelyn, quickly. Amanda noticed how Jocelyn's mood had changed. Something was definitely up. What the hell did George do to her, Amanda wondered. "He said it'd be fine."

"Okay," said Amanda, and walked down the hall. She unhooked the small Picasso from its place on the wall, and handed it to Jocelyn. "Here. I'll call the insurance company and have the coverage transferred."

"Great," said Jocelyn, feeling a little better. "This will help a lot."

"Good," said Amanda. "I'm glad you came."

"Me, too," said Jocelyn.

Eve joined them. "Thank you," she said to Amanda. "For everything."

"Tell Fuller I said hello," said Amanda. "And forget what I said before."

"I can't forget anything you say."

"I was wrong," Amanda insisted. "You do have friends. Everybody needs people around them. I'm just not like everyone else."

"See you at school," said Jocelyn.

They hugged and cooed their thank-yous, did a little air kissing for sport, and left, bubbly and sated. Eve couldn't help but notice a rift developing between herself and Amanda.

Fifty

Eve drove home with a wayback full of presents. She was drunk with happiness. She found Fuller and Stella cooking dinner. The sink was piled full of dirty dishes. Tomato sauce was splattered on the floor, walls, and table. Eve missed having the live-in help she had enjoyed when Eloise was first born. If she were still there, this all would have been cleaned up. But Consuela was only a loaner, and Gabrielle had needed her back, but now that Eve had taken a taste of "help," she missed it. She was tired.

"Hey!" said Fuller. "Look what we made."

"I can see," Eve said with a laugh, collapsing into a chair with the presents she was able to carry in. "A mess!"

"This isn't a mess," said Stella. "It's dinner."

"Thank you for cooking," Eve said.

"Presents!" said Stella, and started exploring the gifts.

"We need a new house," said Fuller.

"What's wrong with where we live now?" Eve asked, although she'd been coveting the beautiful homes her friends all had. She instinctively found a sponge, and started to mop up the mess.

"I want more babies," said Fuller.

"Not another one!" said Stella. "We just got the girl!"

"She's not 'the girl,' young lady," Fuller said, wrestling Stella to the floor. Stella squealed with delight. "She's your sister, and don't you forget it, miss!"

Eve looked down at Eloise, who sat strapped in her car seat on the floor. She was sucking on her fingers, watching everything with great interest.

"Watch the baby!" Eve warned.

Fuller pulled Stella up to her feet, and started to set the table. "How was your party?"

"It was just great."

"Really?" Fuller took a good look at Eve. She was beaming. He was glad.

"The car is full of presents—wait'll you see them. They're amazing things. Nancy bought a whole set of miniature furniture for Eloise. And Gabrielle gave her this tea set. Really, you were all wrong about these people. They're just the nicest—"

"That's great," Fuller interrupted. "How was Amanda?"

"Amanda was fine. I have to call and thank her again. I can't believe you kept it a surprise from me."

"While you were out, one of those brokers called about a house."

Eve sighed and rolled her eyes. She was instantly superexhausted just thinking about househunting.

"They're always calling," she said, and noticed a big pile of faxes by the fax machine Fuller had bought. She flipped through the faxes. They were from Ruth at Heavenly Care Nanny Agency. Résumés and recommendations for nannies with photo I.D.'s, thumbprints, and driving records.

"I went to see it," said Fuller.

"Huh?" said Eve. She read a recommendation from Roseanne, for a nanny who had worked for her. Another was from Michael Jackson's wife. Her head whirled at all the work ahead of her. Just interviewing these nannies was overwhelming. She had to try to forget how organized her friends were, because catching up to them seemed a gargantuan task. Just picking a nanny made her feel anxious.

"I went to see the house," said Fuller.

Eve looked up. "You did?" She was incredulous. She could never get Fuller to go with her. He was always busy.

"Yeah, I took the kids."

"Liked it," said Stella, and Eve forgot that Stella was hearing and processing everything they said.

"I think you should look at it."

"You do?"

"Yeah," said Fuller. "It's in Brentwood. And it's big."

"That's near Gabrielle and Nancy," said Eve, happily. She put down the nanny résumés. Joy!

"And Amanda," Fuller reminded her.

Fifty-one

Eve drove to see the house the next day, and called Fuller from the car phone, as she circled the block.

"Are you crazy?" she asked into the speaker of her car phone. "It's not a house. It's a mansion."

"I told you it was big," he said.

"Fuller," said Eve, picking the phone up off its base. "It's five bedrooms and a million bathrooms."

"I like the waterfall that goes into the swimming pool. Do you like that?"

"We can't do this," said Eve.

"What do you mean?" asked Fuller. "Of course we can do it."

"It's two million dollars, Fuller," she said, pulling the car over to catch her breath.

"I think it's a good investment," he said coolly.

"Are things that good at work?" she asked. "I mean, I should ask you more. I just never have a chance. This nanny hiring business and Eloise and Stella . . ."

"Don't worry about that stuff," said Fuller. "By the way, did you hire a nanny?"

"No," she said. "I wouldn't hire one without your approval."

"You don't need my okay," he said. "I trust you. Besides, it's your domain."

"I just don't know how to do it." She sighed, overwhelmed. "All these women have worked for Meryl Streep and Demi Moore and Val Kilmer—what are they possibly going to do for me?"

"Same thing they do for Val Kilmer and Meryl Streep and any other mother or father."

Eve took a deep breath to calm herself.

"If it's okay with you, I'll call the broker and make an offer on the house," he said. "Let me handle it from here on in. I just want to get your okay."

"My okay. . . ." Eve's voice was lost. She took the key out of the ignition and turned around to see the kids in the back seat. Stella was asleep, and Eloise was asleep in the baby seat next to her. The sight grounded her.

"Fuller," she said quietly. "You have my okay. On everything."

"Great," he said, energized. "I'll call you when we have it."

"Love you," she said quietly, then put her hand over her mouth and fought back tears, but they came anyway. She was glad the kids were asleep so they didn't see her weep. This was so overwhelming—all this success.

"Me, too," he said and hung up.

Eve drove back to the Brentwood house and parked across the street. She stared at the house that was going to be her new home.

It looked like a fairy tale. The house was a sprawling contemporary ranch house shaped like a U. In the middle of the yard was a beautiful swimming pool. There were fish ponds and fountains. A stone wall surrounded the property. The wall had grass growing out from between the rocks. Rosebushes lined the walkway. Purple and white flowers sprouted along the sides of the house. It was lush and an oasis.

Eve couldn't believe that this was where she was going to live and raise her family. This was nothing like the run-down house she'd grown up in on Prairie Star Street with dust for a lawn. It wasn't even anything like the apartment she and Fuller lived in now. Things had already changed so much and so quickly since she'd come to California. Somehow, now, Eve had a feeling the ride had only just begun.

Fifty-two

"Peter Shelton, please."

Shelton had three secretaries. Two sat outside his office, one had her own office. Of the hundred fifty calls that came in to his office each day, only about ten actually got through. The others went on the daily phone log. Shelton had the secretary in the office handle most of them.

"I'm sorry, Mr. Shelton is in a meeting. Can I take your number and have him call you back?"

"Tell him it's Cheryl Brown," said the voice on the telephone.

"Oh. Just a moment, Ms. Brown."

Inside Peter Shelton's office, the atmosphere was that of a lair. Dark, large, cozy. A suite furnished with velvet Shabby Chic couches and floral print chairs. Peter puffed a cigar and listened to a pitch by two of Hollywood's top writers, Bingham and Cross. The two forty-year-old guys had six smash hit comedies, one of which was nominated for an Oscar eight years ago, and Peter wanted to be in business with them. The Amtel machine on his oversized antique desk chimed. Peter saw Cheryl's name typed across the machine, which only he could see.

"Excuse me," Peter said to Bingham and Cross. He quickly picked up the phone.

"What's the news?" Peter said to Cheryl. It was never good with Cheryl's calls, but he liked her. She always gave him an opportunity to know what her tabloid was about to print.

Bingham and Cross looked at each other. If Shelton interrupted their pitch, it must be big. They watched his face, and noticed the color drain. He didn't speak, just puffed on his cigar.

"Okay," said Peter. He put the cigar down. "Let me call you back. I've got some people in my office. Don't move."

"Yepper," said Cheryl. She could tell from Peter's reaction that the whole story was true.

"Fellas," Peter got up from behind his desk, and walked across the room while he was talking, "I have a little unexpected fire to put out." He held the door open for them.

The writers rose, taking their cue. They hadn't finished their pitch or drank their complementary beverages.

"I'm very interested," Peter lied. "Don't pitch this anywhere else. I'll have Helga call your agent and set up something for tomorrow." But Peter could see the confusion and annoyance in the writers' eyes as they walked out of his office. "Helga, call Marty and set up a dinner meeting with Bingham and Cross for my first available," said Peter so the writers could hear him. "Make it the Grill or the Ivy." He thought that plying them with expensive food would help.

The writers left, but had barely walked down the hall when Peter barked at Helga, "Get me Gardener."

Joey Gardener's office phone rang and rang, but nobody picked up. Not the answering machine in his office. And not his home phone.

Peter got Cheryl's boss, Bob, at *Believe It,* on the phone.

"What can I do to kill this story?" Peter pleaded.

"The checks for Ginger Abrams are Allstar checks," said Bob, seriously. He tried to hide his glee at this story. The truth was, he loved these conversations with the studios. Bob, like everyone in America, liked having some connection with anything Hollywood, and the higher up, the more inner the circle, the better. "And we all know what Ginger Abrams does."

"Bullshit," said Peter. "It's bullshit."

"The police just arrested Ginger Abrams. She's going to talk."

Peter put down his cigar. This was bad. "Ginger Abrams will never talk," he said. Peter knew that Ginger, like Bob, like the writers, all wanted to be in business with him—in some way. None of them would jeopardize that opportunity.

"She will if she doesn't want to go to jail," said Bob.

Peter weighed the situation. Would Ginger put a Hollywood career—of sorts—ahead of going to jail? Peter strategized. Only if jail was a truly real threat.

"She won't go to jail," said Peter. His mind raced, trying to remember the name of the officer whose sister-in-law wanted to be an actress. He would have to get her a role, quickly. Maybe a big one. "This is a nothing story," he bluffed. He wished he could get ahold of Gardener and find out exactly what had happened.

Bob was silent. He knew this was a huge story and he knew that Peter knew it, too.

"Okay," said Bob. "I guess we'll both find out. Nice talking to you—"

"Look," said Peter, checking his watch. He was pissed as hell that he was spending time on this. "I don't give a good goddamn about the facts. I just want the story killed. Now what do I have to do, and what is it going to cost me?"

"I talked to Gardener," said Bob, ominously. Now he was lying.

Peter knew he was in deep shit. "A mil? Cash?"

"I'm a journalist," said Bob. "I can't kill a story for money."

Peter started to laugh, although it was hard. "You're a journalist? You know what you are? You're a cocksucking-motherfucking-goddamn-sonofabitching whore, a douchebag with

Twinkies for balls, hiding behind the first fucking amendment. I swear that if this story runs, you are fucking finished. Not just your silly-assed career, but your life. Your family. You're dead.''

Peter slammed the phone down. And sat there.

The Amtel chimed. Peter looked down. His wife was on the line. Peter picked up Helga's phone—''Tell her I'm busy—and get me Vicky.''

Fifty-three

Joey sat at the wheel of his shiny black BMW 750 with the black leather interior. A rich, bad-boy car. All the studio execs had them. Even the women. Joey was sweating huge rings under the arms of his white button-down shirt. The back was already sweated through. Joey popped a couple of prescription sleeping pills he kept in the glove compartment, and swallowed them down with a beer.

The car was parked on the dusty shoulder of the road, up on Mulholland Drive. Joey sat and looked out on the valley. He could see the brown smog line that cut across the horizon. He thought about suicide. Pills, razor blades, driving the car off the side of the cliff only inches in front of him. The thoughts went away. But the idea that he was trapped didn't.

He had written checks to Ginger on the studio's accounts. The paper trail led straight to his office. He hadn't bothered to cover his tracks. He had felt impervious at the time. It had never occurred to him that this could happen. Or had it? On some deep level. Shit, he couldn't psychoanalyze himself now. If ever.

He closed his eyes and tried to pray, but he'd never been big on God. It felt phony and unnatural. He wished he was just an average guy with a construction job and a drawer full of sleeveless undershirts. He'd trade in his fancy car in a second for a flatbed pickup truck if he thought it would take away the pressure he was feeling. He tried to picture Gabrielle's face if he ever drove up in a flatbed pickup truck. That's when, all of a sudden, it came to him. In a flash. The answer.

He was saved. Joey threw back his head and laughed, alone, in his car. Maybe it was the pills, maybe it was the beer, maybe it was the thought of Gabrielle! Whatever, he knew what he had to do.

Fifty-four

Gabrielle hung up the telephone, feeling breathless. Peter Shelton was coming over to the house! She slowly looked around and made a mental note of everything she would do to make Peter comfortable when he came.

"I'm home!"

Gabrielle leapt. It was Joey. Only, he sounded drunk.

"Consuela, make some coffee," she said before she ran to greet her husband at the door. "Honey, guess who's coming over? Peter Shelton!"

Joey just laughed. He wasn't just drunk, he was completely out of it. He swept Gabrielle into a big kiss, and stuck his tongue down her throat.

"Let's do it," he said, pushing her toward the bedroom. "We'll make a baby."

"We already did," said Gabrielle, removing his hand from under her dress, where he was groping. "Ugh, you smell like scotch."

"How's my son?" asked Joey, kissing Gabrielle's pregnant belly.

"You should shower," she said. "Peter Shelton is coming over."

"He's probably coming to fire me," said Joey, walking to the refrigerator. "Where's the beer?"

Gabrielle thought Joey was joking. "It's in the refrigerator in the garage," she said, then listened as Joey walked out into the back toward the garage. His footsteps faded away, and, just as quickly, she let the idea of Joey being fired disappear from her mind. She had other things to concentrate on. More important things. Like appetizers that Peter would like.

"Consuela," she said, loudly, as if the volume would make

the housekeeper understand. "I want you to go to the store and get me a bottle of wine." Gabrielle wrote the name of the wine on a piece of paper, and shoved it at Consuela. Consuela stared at the paper. The wine was written in French, *"Vino,"* said Gabrielle, louder.

"I know, I know," said Consuela. "Wine. *Sí, sí.*"

"Quickly," said Gabrielle, handing Consuela her car keys. *"Rapido!"*

Fifty-five

"Anybody home?"

"Peter, we're all out back," said Gabrielle. She had quickly showered and changed, and put a blanket on the grass for Zachary, who was wearing a three-hundred-dollar outfit and playing with toys. Baby Roxy was wearing a white lace gown, and sleeping peacefully in a bassinet on the patio. Gabrielle had tried to get Joey to shower and change, too, but he refused.

He was, however, cooperating, by grilling shrimp and vegetables on shish kebab skewers over a huge gas grill, and Consuela was setting a beautiful picnic table with bread, steaming corn on the cob, and salad.

"I hope you'll change your mind and stay for dinner," said Gabrielle, trying to impress her husband's boss. Joey kept his back to Peter, and flipped shrimp. He was completely toasted.

"Beer, Peter?" said Joey, his back still to him.

"Joey thinks you're here to fire him." Gabrielle laughed. Peter tensed. Gabrielle saw him tense and panicked. "Is something wrong?" she asked, knowing in that split second, that something was, in fact, very wrong.

"Joey, let's go in the other room," said Peter, as he kissed Gabrielle on the cheek, smiled at Zachary, and admired Roxy. Gabrielle felt awful. It was true. It was happening. This was how bad things went down—in the other room.

"You and the kids look great, Gabrielle," said Peter, ignoring her words, and nodding to Joey for him to move it. "Come on, Joe. Let's go."

Joey obeyed. He left the grill, beer in hand, as Peter led him into the house. Gabrielle stood there and watched them go. She was confused, and suddenly scared.

When Joey came back out a few minutes later, he was smiling. Gabrielle was relieved. "Is Peter staying for dinner?"

"No, he had to get home," said Joey.

"What did he want?" Gabrielle asked.

"He fired me." Joey still couldn't look at Gabrielle.

"What?"

"I was a bad boy."

"What happened?" She got between Joey and the grill. Joey was practically ready to pass out. "Joey, put down the beer and talk to me."

"Joey was a very, very bad boy, and needed to get some time out."

"You got fired for what?! What did you do?"

"I talked," said Joey and started to giggle.

"Who did you talk to?"

"You don't want to know, babe," he said.

"Come on, Joey," said Gabrielle, getting impatient. "I know about the hookers."

Joey looked at her, stunned. Maybe she did want everything out in the open.

Fifty-six

Gabrielle was furious. Livid. Ever since Joey had gotten fired he was around the house—a lot. There were no meetings for him to go to if he didn't make them. And he didn't make them. He was depressed, embarrassed, and high. He knew he'd let down the woman he loved. He wasn't sure what to do next. But for now, he was just in Gabrielle's way. Underfoot. Like dogshit. Which is what he felt like.

Gabrielle thought about moving out, and leaving Joey, but they couldn't afford separate homes. Not even separate apartments. They could barely afford the big home in Brentwood, the help, the decorator, the parties. Now that Joey was fired from the studio, and demoted to independent producer, he would be making no salary and no real money unless he got a greenlit movie, and that was hard work. Joey was not up to it.

The worst part was that when Gabrielle was working around the house, she kept bumping into Joey. Literally.

"You need to get out of the house," she said to him, tensely.

"And do what?" said Joey.

Gabrielle took a deep breath, and tried not to lose her temper. "Anything."

"I have a problem," said Joey.

Gabrielle rolled her eyes. "We are all too aware of that," she said. Her testiness was coming through loud and clear. There was no use trying to hide it.

"My therapist says that I have a drug problem," said Joey.

"You know what your problem is?" she asked. "It's that Jeeves person. He's the one who introduced you to Ginger Abrams in the first place. I don't know why you don't just dump this whole thing on him. Frankly."

Joey was amazed. Gabrielle had every angle figured out. He started to laugh because she was so right. It would have been a beautiful move. To dump the whole thing on Jeeves.

"What?" she said. He was acting crazy. "What's so funny?"

"You're brilliant," he said.

She was still uncomfortable that he was laughing. "So, then do it," she said.

"I can't," Joey said, sobering.

"Why the hell not?"

"Because," said Joey. "It's not ethical."

"What?!" Gabrielle nearly screamed. "Now you've got ethics? *Now?!*"

"I always had them," said Joey, gravely. "I just didn't use them."

"Why not?"

"Because," he said, not finishing what he was thinking. His ethics got clouded by love, he thought but kept to himself. And he wanted them back. He wanted himself back, but he didn't want to lose his family in the process.

The only way was to be down and out. It was the only way out of this loop he had gotten into. Only he couldn't tell Gabrielle. He had to do this alone.

"Right now, I have a drug problem," he said.

"How easily you confess," she said. She was livid. How dare

he create a problem in the world she had worked so hard to perfect? And one as self-indulgent as drugs.

He thought she sounded like an actress—and a good one at that. "What do you mean?"

"I may be the only person in Los Angeles who's never seen a therapist," she said. "I believe in good old-fashioned values. Hard work. Taking responsibility for your life." She paced back and forth. If she didn't move, she'd explode. "Drugs!" she sputtered. "Spare me the details. Drugs are the least of your problems. If your therapist wants to know about your problems, show him *Daily Variety,* or *Vanity Fair*—did you know they're doing a story about you in *Vanity Fair?* Probably too late to kill it. If we're lucky, that is. It's a very positive piece."

"He wants me to check myself into a drug rehabilitation clinic," said Joey.

Gabrielle studied him, mercilessly. He hadn't shaved or showered in at least a day. His clothes were dirty and he smelled bad.

"Well, then do it," she said, reaching over to fluff a pillow. "If you're lucky, you'll meet some interesting people there, and come out of the whole thing with some kind of deal. Maybe one of those kids who keeps getting arrested for battery and drug abuse. I bet if you try, you could stage a comeback for one of them. They're very talented—just like you."

"They want you to go with me," said Joey. "For therapy." He felt awful that he was taking such a hard line, but he knew he had to. It was the only chance he had at getting Gabrielle to fall back in love with him—if he could take care of himself. Really take care of himself. And then her. But through all of this, he was still so turned on by her. Not just her beauty. Not just her appearance—but her courage and determination. In the face of anything—even this. She was one of a kind. He wished he didn't respect it so much, but he did.

"To a drug rehab?" She laughed. "Me?! At Betty Ford?" Joey hadn't seen her laugh so hard in ages. She had to sit down or lose her balance. "Please, that's the funniest thing. . . ."

"My shrink says you're part of the problem."

She stopped laughing and turned on him.

"I do not have a problem," she said. "I am raising our children, which takes all of my energies. I keep a perfect home with a full social schedule, and I am a supportive wife—"

"You're a wonderful wife and mother," he cut her off. "Amazing. I'm not criticizing you."

"I'm not going with you to Betty Ford or any other rehab," she said, scared and angry. Gabrielle composed herself. "Not even to visit."

"Okay," said Joey. "Okay."

"If you need to go," she said calmly and evenly, "then, you go. You take care of whatever things you feel you need to take care of. But I am staying here. I have responsibilities. This is my home."

Fifty-seven

Eve got the kids to bed and collapsed on the sofa. Her sweatpants were stained with Eloise's spit-up, and her T-shirt smelled like pee. She had baby food on one elbow, Stella's creamed spinach on the other, and meat loaf gravy she had made for Fuller on the front. She was dirty and exhausted.

Flipping through the mail, she found a dozen solicitations from realtors. When Fuller made their offer on the house, he and Eve drew attention from realtors. They had a preapproval for a mortgage and a third baby in Eve's belly. Eve and Fuller Evanston weren't just lookyloos. They were players.

Eve tossed the solicitations in the trashcan, but not before glancing at each one. The phone rang, and she let the machine pick up. She flipped through the rest of the mail. There were a few catalogs. Victoria's Secret, Hanna Andersson and the Pottery Barn. There was also an invitation to Ellie Bing's fourth birthday. Eve rolled the name over in her mind.

Ellie Bing, Ellie Bing.

She couldn't remember at first, and then she did. Ellie was a little girl in Stella's preschool class. She was quiet, and loved to play dress-up. Eve was sure Ellie had never said two words to Stella.

Eve opened the invitation. It was engraved. She held the paper up to the light. Crane stationery watermark. Eve read the inside, carefully. Come to a circus for Ellie's fourth birthday. Sunday at noon. RSVP to a phone number with an extension. Eve dialed the number.

"Mrs. Bing's office." The voice was male, crisp, and clear.

"Hi," said Eve. "I'm calling to RSVP to the party for Ellie."

"You're the first!"

"Oh." Eve wasn't sure she liked that. "Well, Stella will be there."

"Great!" said the man.

"Are you Ellie's father?" Eve asked.

"Me?" The man laughed. "No, I'm Nate. Mrs. Bing's secretary."

"Oh," said Eve.

"Ellie is registered at Imagine on Montana Avenue. For your convenience," said Nate. "And we're thrilled you're coming."

"Registered?" Eve didn't understand.

"At Imagine. It's a toy store in Santa Monica."

"Registered—like a wedding?" asked Eve.

"It's really for your convenience," said Nate. "We'll see you there."

"Great," said Eve. They hung up.

Eve didn't put the receiver down. She dialed Amanda.

"Hey!" said Amanda.

"Hey, babe," said Eve. "You won't believe what I just got."

"What, *babe?*" said Amanda. "Since when do you use the word 'babe' in your conversations?" It was so phony, and yet Eve was so glib with it. Amanda was taken aback.

"I got an invitation to Ellie Bing's birthday, and get this— she's registered. For toys!"

"Oh yeah," said Amanda. "I got the same invite. She must have gone through her agent's Rolodex to get to me. I don't even have a kid."

"Is her father that big director?"

"Yeah," said Amanda. "Holden Bing. Her mother is a composer. She did the score for George's last movie."

"Wow," said Eve. "Are you going?"

"Nah," said Amanda. "Are you?"

"Yeah, definitely. Why aren't you going?"

"I don't know them," said Amanda. "Why should I go?"

"It might be fun."

"It's going to be full of industry people."

"So?" Eve did not understand Amanda's point. "It's just cake and whatever. Pin the tail on the donkey."

"Look," said Amanda. "I'll come to Stella's party for cake

and pin the tail on the donkey. But not Ellie Bing's. I wouldn't know the girl if I tripped over her."

"Well," said Eve. "I'll miss you."

"You'll probably have Nancy and Gabrielle to keep you company."

"That's right!" said Eve. She couldn't help notice the pejorative way Amanda talked about her friends.

"Well, I should get going. George wants attention, and far be it from me to deny him the sexual position of the week."

"Goodbye, pervert," said Eve.

"See ya, *babe*," said Amanda.

They hung up. Eve fingered the invitation. It was the most beautiful invitation she'd ever seen, with raised lettering and a picture etched on the front of the card. A clown with a handful of balloons in front of a Ferris wheel. She really liked it. She couldn't wait to go to Imagine to see what a four-year-old registered for.

Fifty-eight

"There it is!" yelled Eve. She spotted the big balloon banner that arched over and across the street. It was a spectacle. Fuller pulled the car into the line of guests' cars, waiting their turn to valet park for the birthday party.

"I want cake!" Stella shrieked. She sat strapped in her car seat in the back of the Cherokee, scrubbed and dressed for the party. Next to her, in her baby car seat, Eloise was wearing the sweetest pink dress and matching hat with her little, chubby legs and bare toes sticking out.

"Valet parking?" Fuller asked. "For a four-year-old's birthday party?"

Eve didn't answer. She couldn't. She was staring at the elephant in the driveway.

"Is that a real elephant?"

The elephant swaggered slowly up and down the driveway with children on its back. A ride for the guests.

"An elephant!" screamed Stella, craning her neck to see the festivities. "Mom, Dad, look!"

Fuller pulled the car up to the curb, and four valet parkers rushed to each of the four doors. One helped Eve, one helped Stella, unbuckling her from her car seat, and lifting her to the sidewalk. One took the baby car seat and the stroller and transferred baby Eloise from one to the other. The fourth valet parker took the festively wrapped birthday present from the trunk, and handed it to Fuller. Then one of them drove off with their car, up Benedict Canyon, to park it with the other guests' cars.

"Welcome to Ellie's birthday!" the valet parkers greeted Eve and Fuller, cheerfully.

Eve and Fuller exchanged glances.

"Thanks," said Eve. Fuller handed the waiting valet parker a five-dollar tip. They exchanged nods.

"I want to ride the elephant!" Stella screamed.

Fuller took Eve by the elbow and they walked up the driveway past rented fairground rides—a spinning Dumbo the Elephant ride, a small Ferris wheel, and two Moon bounces on the tennis court. Cartoon characters strolled the property, singing and painting children's faces. The kids were delighted. The characters were dressed as Hercules, Madeleine from the book and the movie, Woody from *Toy Story*, and Luke Skywalker and Darth Vader from *Star Wars*.

Eve thought she'd mistakenly gone to Disneyland instead of someone's home, or a party for a four-year-old.

Stella was in heaven. She pointed, screeched, laughed, and giggled, then ran to her friends, who were having their faces painted by Snow White. Eve had never seen her so excited. Even Eloise was mesmerized.

"Please tell me we don't have to do this for our kids," Fuller whispered to Eve.

"Eve!" Nancy shrieked, and ran to greet the Evanstons. Fuller quickly ran after Stella, who'd spotted a live monkey and was about to pick it up.

"Excuse me," Fuller said, over his shoulder, but he was already gone.

Nancy didn't mind that Fuller took off as soon as he saw her. She knew he didn't like her much, and she knew that Eve did. She also knew that Fuller loved Eve, and would never make her drop Nancy or Gabrielle. Their bond was strong.

"Where's March?" asked Eve.

"With Digby somewhere . . . thank God for Digby. None of the nannies can handle her. Why does my daughter need a companion with a degree from Princeton, who's being paid close to a six-figure salary to be *my* personal assistant, to talk to *her* about coloring and dress-up?"

"She's precocious," said Eve.

Nancy looked into the party and sighed. It seemed like a Hollywood movie premiere party. There were celebrities with their children everywhere. They were all in their best casual clothes. "I think Zachary and Roxy are with Consuela, who went to find March and Digby. I wish that March could be more like them. Gabrielle's done such a good job with her children."

"What do you think of Ellie being registered for gifts?" said Eve. "I can't get over it."

"Actually, I thought that it was a good idea," Nancy said. "She has so many toys already. If she gets doubles, you just end up donating everything to Goodwill as soon as the party's over."

"Huh," said Eve, mulling the concept. Doubles.

"I bought Play Dough," Nancy shrugged. "It was one of the toys she registered for."

"We bought a house," Eve said.

"Really?" said Nancy, caught off guard.

Eve could hardly contain her excitement. "We just found out they accepted our offer—wait till you see it. It's amazing. It's like a mansion."

"Is the deed in both of your names?"

Eve had been about to go on and tell about the house, but Nancy's question stopped her cold.

"I don't know," said Eve, thinking it a strange question.

"I guess it doesn't matter," said Nancy. "You guys don't have a prenup, right?"

"A prenuptial agreement?" Eve was shocked. "No! Do you?"

"Sure," said Nancy, "and it looks like it's going to be put to use."

Nancy had tears in her eyes.

"Nancy," said Eve. "No!"

"It's okay." Nancy rested one hand on her pregnant stomach. "Maybe I can still get him back. Everyone at the agency says he still loves me. And not just the assistants. The agents all say it." She knew she sounded desperate, but it was all that came out of her mouth lately. Desperations.

"You will," said Eve, trying to comfort her friend. "I know you will."

"The food is fabulous!" exclaimed Gabrielle, running over with a plateful.

Eve put her arm around Nancy's waist and held her close. Nancy put her head on Eve's shoulder. And they hugged, sideways, while they listened to Gabrielle chirp, obliviously, about caterers.

"You okay?" Eve asked Nancy, softly.

"No. I wish she'd get that food away from me," said Nancy. "I'm fat enough as it is."

"Oh, stop. I'm fatter than you," said Gabrielle, sticking out her big, pregnant belly to compare with Nancy's. "Even at three months. I just popped. Joey is desperate for another boy."

"Well, I'm not going to be thin for long," said Eve.

Nancy and Gabrielle looked into her eyes to see if it was true. "Eve!!"

"You're not."

"Again?" whispered Nancy. "What is it with the three of us?"

"I didn't think you could get pregnant while you were nursing," said Eve.

"You're still nursing?!" said Gabrielle. "Isn't Eloise one?"

"Eight months," said Eve. "I think it's good for the babies to nurse for a while."

"I don't know how you do it," said Gabrielle, shaking her head.

"Me?" Eve laughed. To her, she didn't know how Gabrielle and Nancy "did it all." She felt like an amateur around them.

"You have to just try this food. I'll throw up if I eat all of this," said Gabrielle, trying to balance her plate with all the different foods on it. "Try some, you guys. Please."

"Everybody has to throw up once in a while," said Nancy.

"Some of us, nightly," said Gabrielle, with a smirk.

"You don't still do that, do you?" Nancy asked.

"No," Gabrielle said emphatically. "Never when I'm pregnant."

Eve stared curiously. "You throw up? On purpose?"

"I love to eat," said Gabrielle. "What am I supposed to do? Get fat?"

"You could diet," said Eve. "Or exercise."

"You're adorable," said Gabrielle. "I love that retro side of you."

Eve had no idea what that meant.

"Lipo is much more pleasant," said Nancy. "And they give you great drugs to recover."

"You've had lipo?" Eve asked, looking Nancy over. Nancy looked perfect. She couldn't imagine making any improvements.

"Yeah," said Nancy. "A lot of good it did me. I'll be back in the plastic surgeon's office as soon as I have this baby. Like the very next day."

"Where's Amanda?" Gabrielle asked, scoping out the crowd.

"She isn't coming," said Eve. "She doesn't like groups."

"Do you think she liked us?" asked Gabrielle.

"Of course," said Eve, then quickly changed the subject because she hated lying. It made her sick. She was aware that she garnered special status as a friend of Amanda's.

"Hey, where's Joey?" Eve asked Gabrielle. "I never see him around."

Nancy looked at Gabrielle, wondering what she would say. She knew through the grapevine that Joey had been fired from his job and was at a drug rehab. She also knew Gabrielle was pretending he was away on some business.

"He's out of town," said Gabrielle breezily. Nancy looked over at Eve to see if she would buy that. She didn't, but it didn't matter to her. She could see that the subject was uncomfortable. There was an awkward beat, and then Eve broke it.

"Hey, we bought a house!"

"You're kidding!" Gabrielle hugged Eve. "When can we see it?"

"We're moving next week," said Eve. "I'll call you as soon as the phones get hooked up. I'll throw Stella's birthday party there. You'll all see it at the same time."

"I hope you have room for the elephant," laughed Nancy, and they all scurried out of the way as the real elephant clumped down the driveway toward them.

Fifty-nine

Eve sat at the antique wood kitchen table in her grand new home. The kitchen was the size of most living rooms. Mexican terra-cotta tiles offset the rustic woodwork. There was a huge island in the middle of the kitchen. Pots and pans hung over the island. Eve had bought a large double stove, thinking she'd throw lavish dinner parties at some point, and with the stove, she'd have the firepower for caterers to cook. She didn't like flat-out caterers, who brought in cooked food. But if they prepared the food for, say, thirty guests, right in her kitchen, so it would be completely fresh, well, then, so be it.

There was a living room area in the kitchen, with a built-in sofa and a free-standing sofa, both facing toward a media center that she intended for the children. They liked to watch videos while she was making dinner, or else just hang out, comfortably, and talk to her while she cooked. The wall that faced the backyard was ceiling-to-floor windows. French doors opened onto the patio that was part of the backyard.

But the place in the kitchen that Eve spent the most time was the built-in desk area. She paid bills, made dates for the children and herself and Fuller, talked on the phone, and wrote letters there, while all around her, food boiled, bubbled, cooked, grilled, and was finally eaten.

Life was good, Eve thought. When she had a free second and a clear mind to just appreciate everything that had happened to her, and everything that was hers.

Eve sat at the desk, inert, frowning. She held a pen poised to write, but the paper in front of her was blank. Fuller wandered in. She turned when she heard his bare feet shuffling across the tiles.

"Hi," she said, glumly.

"What's wrong?" he asked.

"I don't know," she said.

Fuller sat down next to her, and started massaging her shoulders. "You're tense."

"I know." Eve sighed.

"Is it the pregnancy?"

"No."

"You upset about your friend getting divorced?"

"She has a name," said Eve.

"Nancy," said Fuller. "Is that it? Nancy's divorce got you down?"

"No," said Eve. "She'll be okay. She's remarkably strong in her own way."

"So, what is it?"

"It's Stella's birthday," Eve spat out. "I don't know what to do."

"Buy a cake and invite some friends over."

"That's not enough," she said, sighing dismissively, and killed an ant that was crawling across the large pine breakfast table. "I can't believe I have an entire staff of maids, and we still have ants. Can't someone buy a goddamn can of Raid?" She slapped another one which was crawling on the floor, with her bare foot.

"Then hire someone," said Fuller. Eve was now standing, and tracking the ants to a tiny hole in the baseboard where they were coming into the house. "One of those clowns. Then blow up some balloons, get some of those party favor gifts, I don't know. It sounds like a party to me."

"I have to do something no one has done before," she said, as she stomped the ants with a tissue.

"Why?" Fuller asked.

"Because, I want to."

"It's a birthday party for a four-year-old," said Fuller.

"I can't believe we have ants," she said, examining all the crevices where the ants were coming and going. Dealing with the ants kept her from dealing with her life. "Where the hell are they coming from?" Eve went to the sink to wash her feet with a sponge.

"Everybody has ants," said Fuller, watching her.

"Not after I've had all these Mexican pavers installed," said Eve. "I'm going to do something about this."

Eve stalked the ants, one by one, until she'd killed them all. Then she looked for more. Fuller silently chalked her mood off to hormones, and went back to bed.

The next morning Eve woke up and looked at the clock. Ten a.m. Esperanza, the nanny Eve had hired, was taking care of the children in the kitchen when she staggered downstairs, and reached, not for the coffee, but for the phone. She dialed Gabrielle.

"I have it!" she chirped groggily into the phone. Her voice was still a few notes below where it would be postcoffee and a shower.

"That stomach virus that's going around?" Gabrielle asked.

"No! I got an idea! For Stella's party. I was up all night brainstorming, and then at four-thirty I thought of how we had ants, and that's when I got it—I almost called you."

"Did you check your answering machine?"

Eve looked. There was one message. The light was blinking.

"No," said Eve. "I just got up."

"Nancy had her babies."

"What do you mean—babies?"

"She had twins!"

"No!!!"

"Yes!!!"

"You're kidding! Oh my God! Oh my God! That's great! Is she okay?"

"Six pounds, nineteen and a half inches long. C-section. They named her Leonora. And six pounds, six ounces was Max."

"Why didn't she tell us?"

"I don't know. She said she didn't know."

"Come on—didn't she have an ultrasound?"

"Eve, she probably got knocked out for the ultrasound. This hasn't been her happiest time. She's a little out of it—to say the least."

"No kidding," said Eve. She started biting her nails. The cuticle stuff from her manicure tasted terrible.

"I think she just blanked out a lot."

"Twins is a lot to blank out."

"Nancy is a maestro at blanking a lot out. Anyway, they're here."

"Oh my God. Did Landon show up?"

"No," said Gabrielle gravely. "Her mother flew in to help."

"That Landon is such a jerk," said Eve. "I mean, I knew he was a jerk, but this is beyond being a jerk. This is professional jerkiness. I can't believe Landon didn't come to the hospital for the birth of his children."

"Not everybody has a perfect husband like you," said Gabrielle. "Meanwhile, I'm as big as a house. I can't believe I've got a whole 'nother month before I have my baby."

Eve wondered how Gabrielle could simplify things and move on so easily.

"Have you seen Nancy?"

"Yeah, I was at the hospital this morning," said Gabrielle.

"Already?" Eve asked, surprised. Gabrielle must have been up at the crack of dawn.

"She's doing great. I think she's coming home tomorrow. The babies are beautiful. I sent flowers from both of us. You owe me a hundred bucks."

"I'm hanging up and calling her," said Eve.

"Wait," said Gabrielle. "What did you get? What were you going to tell me about?"

"Oh! Stella's party. I got the idea from all the ants. Listen to this: I'm doing bugs and reptiles!"

"Eww, gross," said Gabrielle. "I don't think that's a good idea for a girl."

"Miss Spider, silly!" said Eve, referencing the name of Stella's favorite book series. "It's a Miss Spider party."

"Oh, that is good, Eve," said Gabrielle. "You're very good."

"Thank you." Eve loved Gabrielle's admiration. She was proud of herself.

"I have to go and book a tarantula and the Reptile Lady. After I call Nancy. I'll talk to you later."

She hung up the phone and turned to the kitchen. Stella was sitting and eating cereal and toast. Esperanza was feeding Eloise oatmeal and raisins.

"Fuller! Nancy had twins!!" Eve yelled into the house. Her voice echoed. Fuller didn't answer. He was somewhere her voice didn't reach. A different wing.

"Oh, well." Eve turned to her girls. "Good morning, sunshine kids!" Eve swooped over and kissed them. She was feeling especially triumphant over the party theme she had come up with. "Stella," she said, kissing her happily, "you are going to have the best birthday party in the whole world, honey."

Sixty

Stella's Miss Spider party immediately elevated Eve's status to a leading Hollywood mom. The professionally printed invitations were sent out to fifty of Stella's closest friends and their families. Eve had also gone through the Rolodex in Fuller's office, and invited the people with whom he was cultivating movie deals. Especially the ones with names that she recognized from *People* magazine. When she'd finished as best she could on her own, she called Jocelyn.

"I'm calling about Stella's birthday," said Eve. "She's such a big girl already! I want to have a nice party for her, and I thought maybe you could help."

"I always say, invite as many guests as two times your child's age," said Jocelyn. "Stella's going to be four, so I'd invite eight children."

"Too late." Eve giggled. "Did you get the invitation?"

"I did, but I won't be able to make it."

"Oh, I want you to come," said Eve, disappointed. She knew that Jocelyn at her party would be the icing on the cake, so to speak. It would be like having the Godfather attend. Getting her blessings by her mere presence. If Jocelyn would just come to Stella's party, Eve would feel invincible. And she was feeling pretty close to it.

"I can't," said Jocelyn.

"Oh, no!" wailed Eve. "You have to!"

"You know what it would do to my life if I accepted one of these invitations? I'd have to go to every kid's party every weekend for the entire year. You have a handful of friends. I have several hundred who think I'm their best buddy because I take care of their child. I just can't do it all, hon."

"I thought that since you came to my baby shower——"

"If you tell a soul I came to your baby shower, I'll be in big trouble," said Jocelyn. "And I'll hold it against you."

"What if I fixed you up with the most fabulous guy—I'm inviting him to the party."

"I've met every fabulous guy in town already," Jocelyn replied, laughing. "But what's he like anyway?"

"Fuller says he is absolutely a perfect match for you. He's coming to Stella's party, and he's dying to meet you."

Well, well, well, thought Jocelyn. She hadn't pegged Eve for this kind of thinly veiled technique.

"He's so cute," said Eve, trying to tantalize Jocelyn.

Jocelyn wondered how long it would be before Eve started writing checks for charitable donations to the school in exchange for social favors, like this.

"Look," said Jocelyn. "Even if you offered me a sizable donation to the school, I wouldn't come. I can't. I'd have to hire a personal assistant and a publicist if I accepted birthday invitations for the children."

"Oh," said Eve, dumbfounded. She hadn't thought of this as an option, but suddenly, numbers raced through her mind. She wanted Jocelyn at Stella's party, and the idea of a donation didn't seem like a bad one. She wondered how much she could offer without upsetting Fuller.

"Because if you do, I'd still say no," said Jocelyn. "I have a policy, and I stick to it. Even for a fabulous date. Even if there were such a thing anymore."

"I was really hoping you'd come," said Eve, surrendering. It was clear that she wasn't going to get Jocelyn. "It'd be a real feather in my cap. To get you."

Jocelyn laughed at Eve's honesty. She could really see why Amanda liked Eve so much.

"I just want my daughter's party to be great," said Eve.

"Stella would rather have a family visit to Disneyland with lunch at McDonald's, than a huge party with me as the status guest."

"I know," said Eve. "You're right. I guess I got carried away."

"So then why do this extravaganza? I know it's going to be amazing. You're a fabulous woman. But why show it this way?"

"This party is going to be incredible," said Eve. "Did I tell you the theme? Miss Spider's Party. We're having reptiles and insects and spiders!"

Jocelyn knew this conversation was over. For her, anyway. She was not coming to Eve's party, and Eve was clearly firmly involved in a group that had . . . standards, of a sort.

"I'm sorry I'll have to miss it."

"I can't believe my guest of honor isn't coming," Eve pouted.

"The guest of honor will be there," said Jocelyn, pointedly. "The guest of honor is Stella."

"I know, I know," said Eve, needing to get to the next item on her agenda. "Listen. Before you hang up. Could you point me in the right direction? On the guest list?"

Jocelyn knew what Eve wanted. The list. She had been right about Eve from the minute she met her. Eve was going to be a powerful force, as mothers in this town went. That was for sure.

"So, what? You want industry parents?" Jocelyn asked casually.

"Anyone you think would be compatible," said Eve. "I completely trust your instincts."

Compatible. Jocelyn spotted that code word instantly. It meant that Eve was asking for help. For her husband. Not that he needed it. The help was really for Eve. To elevate her husband's status was to elevate her own. The list was one of Jocelyn's treasures in the locked metal drawer of her standard-issue Staples desk. She saved it for her heavy hitters.

"I'll fax over the list," said Jocelyn. "But, Eve. Next year— twice the number of guests as your child's age. It's really better for Stella. And the others. Maybe you can start a trend. I have a feeling people will follow your lead."

"You got it," said Eve. "And thanks for the list, Jocelyn."

"You're welcome."

Jocelyn hung up and sighed. She reached into her bottom drawer. The one with the lock on it. She had the list Eve wanted, already made up. It was the class roster. Names, addresses, and phone numbers, plus the same information on other children's families from different groups in the school. They were the ones that made up Hollywood's movers and shakers. The ones who made deals over lunch, and never stopped working. Even at their children's birthday parties. They pretended to be there for the kids, but really, they were there for themselves. There was no crime in it. There was even a strong puritanical work ethic at play. But there was something odd about deals that used to get made over games of golf, now getting made over cake and juice boxes.

If the tabloids ever got their hands on any of her class rosters, her lists, they would make a mint. She had the home address, phone number, beeper number, emergency number, for each parent of her students. Past and present. Jocelyn faxed it to Eve's home.

Eve went to work on her laptop computer. Fuller had brought it home for her, shown her how to use it, and she'd taken to it immediately. The laptop was where Eve kept her lists. Jocelyn had the coveted lists, but if anyone knew just how many and how detailed Eve's lists were, they would be after her, too. Even Eve knew that that day was going to come.

She worked hard on her lists and had more categories and resources on them than anyone. There were personal lists, home improvement lists, shopping lists, domestic help lists, phone number lists, play date lists, family vacation lists. The lists helped her sort out the huge amount of information she was having to absorb. Moving from Vegas to Los Angeles was one thing, but marrying, raising a family, and being a Hollywood mom required tools for survival. For Eve, those tools were her lists. They helped her measure exactly how much she had accomplished, what she had yet to accomplish, and what the choices "out there" were. They kept her from being overwhelmed. They kept her sane. She lived by and for them. In a way, Eve was only as good as her lists— and, luckily, her lists were outstanding.

For Stella's birthday party alone, Eve had a computer file full of lists that included: guests (civilians, noncivilians—and subcategories for those guests who had children, those who didn't, those who wanted them, and more), possible caterers, possible entertainers, possible rental companies for tables, chairs, and tent.

She scrolled down her "to do today" list. Landscaper. She telephoned Alejandro, and in the "household" Spanish she'd quickly learned to talk to the help who didn't speak English, she asked him to plant some special navy and purple flowers. Those were the colors she'd picked for the party. They discussed what was in season.

Eve went down the list day after day, night after night, until, finally, it was the big party.

Sixty-one

The Party Guys showed up right on time. Eve had hired them to "do" Stella's party. The Party Guys were on time, and in costume. They wore spider, assorted bug, and reptile outfits. Eve was delighted. She instructed them to stroll the grounds, greet the guests, and just act casual.

"Hi."

Eve was in the kitchen catching a sip of cappuccino in a rare free moment. She turned and screamed.

A giant tarantula was standing next to her.

"I'm sorry," said the spider. "Are you okay?"

Eve had spilled her cappuccino on her white T-shirt.

"It's okay," said Eve. She wanted to go upstairs and change right away.

"I just wanted to introduce myself," said the tarantula.

Eve tried to pretend she was interested. All she wanted was to get the cappuccino-stained T-shirt off.

"Is it hot in there?" she said, trying her best at small talk.

"It's all right," said the tarantula. He took off his spider head. He was blond, but his hair was pasted to his red face. He looked familiar.

"Do I know you?" Eve asked.

"I'm an actor," said the tarantula, as if that alone explained everything.

"Oh . . . that's great," said Eve, waiting for some cue as to what she was supposed to do with that information. "Maybe I've seen you in something."

"I understand your husband's in the movie business."

"Well, yes—"

"I also heard the Fosters are coming here today," said the actor-tarantula.

Eve was surprised. She didn't expect her hired insect to know her guest list.

"We did a sibling party over at Meg Ryan's," said the actor-tarantula. "One of the guests there had been invited here. That's how I know. They were talking about who was coming—don't worry, I'm a very good tarantula."

"I'm sure you are," said Eve. She saw guests arriving in the backyard, and she really wanted to change her clothes.

"Meg Ryan really liked my work. I get requested constantly," said the tarantula. "Sean Penn's wife wants me for their kid's next birthday—I heard he reserved me three months in advance."

He waited for Eve to comment. She did, but a beat later than was necessary to show genuineness. The actor-tarantula didn't care.

"Anyway, I keep my ears open. Word gets out about who's going to which party. I'm a huge fan, and if I could meet George, that would just be too, too fab."

Eve stared as if she hadn't heard right. But she knew she had.

"I don't know if this is an appropriate time," she said, quietly.

"This is a chance of a lifetime for me," said the tarantula. "I don't know when I'll get to meet a producer like George Foster again—and I'm good. This party circuit thing—it's just until I get an agent. I'm really a serious actor."

Eve didn't know what to say.

"Please," the tarantula begged.

"I don't know," said Eve. "This is a family party."

"Look, lady," said the tarantula. "I'm the best bug at the Party Guys, and I turned down a party today on Rivas Canyon—Warren Beatty and Annette Bening are going to be with their kids—but I heard you had George Foster. So I came there."

Eve was so taken aback. By his brashness, his focus and purpose, and his face—there was something about his face. . . .

"You think I love being in here, sweating ten pounds off at each party, getting dehydrated, and method acting insects for a bunch of bratty freaks? The bottom line here is, I get a job off this job, or I don't."

Eve was floored.

"These are children," she said emphatically. "They're not—"

"I know, I know, I'm sorry." He touched her arm. There was something so familiar. "You just don't know what it's like to be me."

They both laughed, and the tension broke. This guy's passion to get a job impressed her. Eve knew the feeling of wanting something; she'd just never seen it expressed so succinctly, and without shame. By an insect.

"I'll ask him," she said, as if in a trance.

"Thank you." The tarantula beamed at her. "My name is Corey Alexander." He offered his hand to her.

"Corey . . ." she said, as she shook hands. "I know you! You were a waiter!"

"I've waited a lot of tables," he said.

"Gladstone's—years ago!"

"I worked Gladstone's," he said. "I'm sure I must have cleared your dirty dishes at some point. Seems like I've cleared everyone's dirty dishes in all of Los Angeles."

"Don't you remember me?" she said. "It was my first day in Los Angeles. It was seven years ago—almost to the day! I'd just driven here and you brought me a drink. I cried."

"You know," he said, "you might look familiar, but I really can't place you. Have you had work done?"

Eve was shocked. That he didn't remember her, from such a landmark day in her life—her first day in Los Angeles! And that he thought she had had work done—plastic surgery!—*and* that he'd had the nerve, the gall, to ask her, it was all unreal.

"No . . ." she said. How could he not remember her? "Are you sure you don't remember? I mean, I cried, and you held me."

"Huh," he said. "Sorry. Now, what exactly does *your* husband do? I can remember the actors by their faces, but the studio people, the agents—they keep changing jobs. It's harder to keep up."

Eve wondered who had changed more that he didn't remember her. Her? Or him?

"Eve!" It was Gabrielle with Zachary and Roxy. She looked even exponentially more pregnant than at Ellie Bing's party. Consuela helped the children into the party. Joey was not with them.

"Excuse me," said Eve, as she left the tarantula to hug her friend.

"You will introduce me, right?" he yelled after her.

"Sure," she said. She owed him that. It was karmic payback. She didn't know what she'd tell Geoge Foster about the tarantula, but as she worried about that, she realized, she probably wouldn't have to say a thing. The tarantula was perfectly capable of taking care of himself. Just like she had been.

Sixty-two

The party took on a life of its own. Eve had done so much solid groundwork ahead of time, that there was nothing left to do the day of the big event. But enjoy herself.

The children and their parents arrived, and milled about the house until the parents systematically found the entertainment, where they could leave their children. This was where the party started. The "bug brigade" organized games and songs. The parents saw that their kids were entertained, then they went off to find phones within the house that weren't occupied. Especially the fathers. They loved to call their offices. Just to check in. Being out of touch was personal and career suicide.

After twenty minutes of insect entertainment, March Greene got up and slugged an iguana. The actor inside the iguana suit was thirty-five years old, 180 pounds, and in good shape. That a four-year-old girl caught him bent over and off guard, and got in a good shot to the eye, was a testament to her cunning. None of the parents noticed, and the bugs didn't tell. They didn't want to risk any confrontation, which could get them a bad name. They were like the spin doctors in Washington. They needed the parents to believe that they could handle any party. Besides, they'd been at parties with March before. They knew she was hard to handle and that her mother wasn't interested in hearing any grief or handling these situations.

Next thing everyone knew, March had felled the iguana and was heading for the centipede guy. Zachary adored March, and was quickly her second-in-command. In less than a minute, the two children had a group of kids behind them. The centipede guy was backing up, in fear of March and her gang, when Arnold Schwarzenegger, one of the parents, came over and intervened. Good-naturedly, of course. Nobody wanted trouble.

Nancy was holed up in Eve and Fuller's bedroom, with Gabrielle for company. Nancy was embarrassed to be seen in her state. She hadn't lost nearly as much weight from her pregnancy as she had wanted, even though the twins' birth was just weeks ago. That she was out at all was a miracle. But she was ashamed of the way she looked, that her marriage had failed—she wanted to be here for Eve, but she really didn't want anyone to see her.

From Eve and Fuller's master bedroom, she had a perfect view of all the action. She saw her nannies with the twins—one nanny for each baby—and March terrorizing the party. Nancy sighed. There was nothing she could do about it—not yet.

Fuller had a great time. He videotaped the party, but every now and then he put the camera down to compose himself. Even he was amazed at the turns his life had taken so quickly of late. Prepared to shoot some simple family movies, he looked around at the "professional party" going on. He was amazed. It all looked like the fabulous entertainment party of one of his more successful friends. Not something in his own life. Not his. But it was.

"Nice gig."

Fuller turned around. Amanda was standing next to him, eating a birthday taco. Taco meat dripped down her chin.

"Hi," he said. "You look great."

Amanda wiped her chin. "You always liked me with food on my face," she said.

They both privately remembered sex. It was hard not to when Amanda was around. Fuller felt uncomfortable. He didn't want to be thinking these thoughts.

"Eve really pulled this thing together," said Amanda, but there was an edge in her voice. And it wasn't kind. "I didn't know she had it in her."

"Neither did I," said Fuller, looking around. "I don't know half of these people. How did she get James Cameron here? Does he even have kids?"

"No," said Amanda. "But he's got Oscars. I imagine that Eve wants you to meet him."

"Oh, come on," said Fuller. "You think?"

"I don't know. It looks to me like she's got half the agents in town and a couple of very hot comedy writers here. And that's just who I recognize."

"She's amazing," said Fuller. "My wife."

"Mmmm-hmmmm," said Amanda, wiping more taco off her face with the back of her hand. "I didn't know you liked this kind of amazing."

Fuller turned to look at her straight on. "I do."

Amanda took a huge bite of taco, and with her mouth full, said, "You've changed."

"It's all a process," he said. "Maybe I have, maybe I haven't."

"Since when did you get so wise?" Amanda asked.

"I don't know," said Fuller. "Since when did you get smart enough to realize how wise I am?"

"That, I always knew," she said.

Eve came over, and kissed her husband and then hugged and kissed Amanda.

"Hey!" she said. "How are the duck tacos? Can you taste the duck?"

"They're amazing," said Amanda. "This whole thing is amazing. It's like the World's Fair."

"Oh, come on," said Eve, enjoying the praise. "I just wanted to give Stella a party she'd remember."

"I don't know about Stella, but Fuller is pretty impressed." Amanda laughed. "And so am I."

"Don't we have any pin-the-tail-on-the-donkey stuff?" Fuller asked, half joking.

"No, honey." Eve laughed. "I booked the Reptile Lady."

"*The* Reptile Lady?" Fuller asked facetiously.

"She's very hard to get," Amanda clued Fuller in. "Usually she's booked up a year in advance. I hear Stallone flies her and her entire squadron of reptiles down to Miami for his kid's party. On a private plane."

"I'm afraid to ask what the Reptile Lady does," said Fuller.

"It's pretty tame stuff," said Kurt Russell.

They all turned to see Kurt extend his hand to Fuller. "Hi," he said. "I'm Kurt. Glad to meet you."

"Same here," said Fuller. "I'm a big fan."

"Thanks," said Kurt. "And I'm a fan of yours, too."

"Thank you," said Fuller, pleased. "Have you met my wife, Eve?"

"Hello," said Kurt. "Great party. The kids are having a blast."

"Thank you for coming," said Eve. "I hope you're having a nice time, too."

"I am," said Russell. "I think I even cast that tarantula in my next movie. He'd be perfect for this part. I'm directing—did you hear?"

"No. Congratulations," said Fuller. "I'd love to see your film. Oh—this is Amanda Foster."

"We've met before," said Kurt, shaking Amanda's hand.

Amanda excused herself. Eve stayed. This was going so well. She was just extremely pleased with the way everything had worked out. Even for her long-lost tarantula pal.

"So what, exactly, *does* a reptile lady do?" Fuller asked. Kurt and he shared a dirty laugh. "I mean, at kids' parties."

"Just live bugs and creepy things," Eve explained.

"Is that it?" Fuller asked, nervously. "I don't think an ant farm is going to work with this crowd." Fuller eyed the children. March had now incited a toddler riot that even Schwarzenegger was having trouble quieting. He yelled to Jim Carrey for help. Jim assessed the situation and said no. He wasn't going into the morass of kids. His daughter was not part of that mess. He hung back and watched. Proud of his daughter's instincts.

"Is one of you Eve?"

Eve, Fuller, and Kurt turned to see none other than the Reptile Lady. She was in her late twenties, and dressed in khakis with an explorer-type khaki vest, and had a ponytail hanging down her back from underneath her pith helmet.

"I am," said Eve. "You must be the Reptile Lady."

"Yes," she said. "I'm Beth, from the Party Guys."

"Hey!" said Kurt, sweeping the Reptile Lady into an embrace. They said their hellos. Eve introduced Fuller. Some of the other celebrity parents recognized Beth and came over to say their hellos. Then Beth ran off and opened up the back of her van and started pulling out cages, boxes, tubs, and laundry baskets full of creatures. Most of them writhing around in pillowcases and under blankets that covered them.

"What's wrong with Amanda?" Eve asked Fuller. "She's not friendly to me like she used to be."

"She's just overwhelmed," said Fuller.

"Huh," said Eve. "I wonder if that's really it."

She felt Amanda's constant disapproval lately, and it bothered her. Ever since she'd sent out Stella's invitations, Amanda had made excuses for not getting together. Every time Eve called to invite Amanda for lunch, Amanda was busy.

"How much is all this costing me?" Fuller asked.

"You don't want to know," Eve said lightly, and kissed him on the cheek. "Anyway, it's a business expense. It's tax-deductible, yadayadayada."

"Since when do you know about taxes?" Fuller asked.

"Everybody knows about taxes, silly," said Eve. "Don't they?"

"Do you have any live rabbits?" Beth asked as she pushed a wheelbarrow inside, past Eve and Fuller. They saw that the wheelbarrow was filled with turtles and cages of insects. Eve stared, horrified. She had imagined pristine spiders like in the Miss Spider books. Not creepy crawlers. But the kids who caught sight of Beth and the wheelbarrow whooped for joy. They were excited at the show they knew was to come next. Eve sighed with relief. It would be a hit.

"No," said Eve. "No rabbits."

"Cool," said Beth, and started to set up in the backyard.

The Reptile Lady did her show, pulling out frogs and turtles, then graduating to giant centipedes, slugs, and snakes. The children were enthralled, and Eve took the opportunity to preside over the grown-up buffet. She had authorized the caterer, Along Came Mary, to hire extra kitchen staff to set out and serve the food they prepared. There was cold pasta salad with sun-dried tomatoes and goat cheese, mixed baby leaf salads, duck tacos, lamb quesadillas, fruit salads, and an assortment of mineral waters and fruit-flavored sparkling waters.

The parents ate from the buffet, and remarked on the Reptile Lady's grand finale: pulling out from a large sack a twelve-foot, pale yellow, albino python. Everybody screeched, oohed and ahhed. The Reptile Lady laid the python across the laps of all thirty children. It was an enormous snake. Eve was glad for this finale that would leave everyone buzzing. She wanted them all to remember this party. The albino python did the trick.

Finally, the party was nearly over. The birthday cake was wheeled out on a cart. It was a triple-layer, full sheet cake with a giant candle shaped like a number four. It had white chocolate icing with a chocolate-chocolate-chip cake and big cake-sculpted bugs on top for decoration. Fuller ran the video camera like a proud dad, and carried Eloise around while Eve cut the cake for the kids and helped hand out juice boxes. Fuller started to shoot some home video when Eve came over and told him to put the camera away.

"I hired a professional," she said and pointed to a cameraman, who was videotaping at the same time.

"Oh," said Fuller. "I didn't know." He put the camera away.

"So you could just enjoy," said Eve.

"Oh," he said, and put the camera down, reluctantly.

He wanted to video, but he didn't want to upset Eve. She'd gone to great lengths, and this was her domain. And she'd been a huge success.

When the cake was eaten, the whole thing was over. Each child had taken home a specially wrapped bottle of bug bubble bath. Eve collapsed into Fuller's arms. She was elated. The party went exactly the way she had seen it in her mind.

They watched their children open presents from an enormous pile of lavishly wrapped boxes. Stella ripped the wrapping paper off, and handed the trash to Eloise, who was thrilled. Then she examined the gift for about ten seconds, and went on to something else. Fuller and Eve both smiled.

"I should be taking videos of this," Fuller said. "But I'm too exhausted. Where's that camera guy when you really need him?"

"Next year I'll make sure he stays," said Eve.

"I was just kidding," said Fuller.

"It's a good idea," she said, seriously.

"I knew you were extraordinary, but I had no idea you could do all this," said Fuller.

Eve felt proud. This was the best compliment.

"Is everyone gone?" Nancy whispered from the staircase. She was leaning on it for support. Her balance and strength were waning. Her nannies carried Leonora and Max, and passed her on their way to the car. The babies were dressed impeccably. They looked like miniature clothing ads for French *Vogue*.

"Yes," said Eve, running to kiss Nancy goodbye.

"Well, it was a great party—one for the books."

Gabrielle came down the stairs behind Nancy. "You are amazing," said Gabrielle, kissing Eve on both cheeks.

"Are you all right?" Eve asked Nancy. "Is there something I can do?"

"Can I help you to the car?" Fuller asked.

"Thanks," said Nancy, "but I've got more hired help than I know what to do with. I think Landon feels guilty. Which he should. He's given me more cash than I can spend. How often can you say that?" She laughed sadly, but the laugh fizzled into something that sounded like choking.

"Come on, hon," said Gabrielle, gently. "Let's get this limo on the road."

"You know, I'd love to throw you a baby shower," said Eve. "Kind of 'post,' like mine was."

"You're great," said Nancy, "but I'm not really in the mood, and there's nothing the kids need. You just carry on. I'll be back in rare form in no time.''

Nannies and drivers came in to help Nancy to the car. She waved, air kissed, and was gone. Fuller and Eve watched from the doorway.

"Do you worry that that's going to happen to us?" Eve asked, quietly.

"You can't not," said Fuller.

"I'll be so good you won't want to divorce me," said Eve.

"You already are," he said. "You don't have to try."

"You can't not," she said back to him.

"Eve!"

They both turned toward the voice that broke their quiet conversation. It was the Reptile Lady, coming toward them with a grave look on her face.

"Did you tip her?" Eve whispered to Fuller.

"Twenty-five bucks," Fuller whispered back.

"We have a little problem," the Reptile Lady said.

"You should have given her fifty," said Eve. "She looks upset."

"Don't worry," said Fuller, reaching for his wallet as Eve turned to go back in the house. "I must have forgotten to take care of a couple of the bugs."

"It's the albino python," the Reptile Lady said to Fuller.

"What about it?" said Fuller.

"It's missing," said the Reptile Lady.

"Eve!" Fuller called. Eve stopped and turned. "I don't think she wants a bigger tip."

Eve waddled her pregnant body back over. "What do you mean?" she asked.

"The python's missing," the Reptile Lady repeated.

"It's twelve feet long and eight inches around," said Fuller. "How could it be lost?"

"I'm aware of its dimensions," said the Reptile Lady to Fuller. "It's still gone."

"But that's impossible!" said Fuller. "How can you lose a twelve-foot python at a party?"

"I didn't lose it," said the Reptile Lady. "It was in its cage and I was getting ready to load it into the van. I don't know. One of the kids must have opened the latch on the cage, and it took off. You're sure you don't have any live rabbits around here? It smells the flesh and it just takes off."

Fuller and Eve looked at each other with the same thought. "The kids!"

They both ran and grabbed the children in the other room, and held them while they walked back to the Reptile Lady. The children cried for their toys, back on the floor.

"I've got to go," said the Reptile Lady, fingering her car keys. "I have another party in an hour, and it's all the way up at Point Dume."

"Wait a minute!" said Eve, juggling Eloise, who was wriggling around, trying to get away back to the gifts.

"What are we supposed to do?" asked Eve.

"I'd hold on to those two until you find it," she said, nodding at the children. "Especially the little one." The Reptile Lady got into her van.

"What?!" Fuller exploded. "Wait a minute! You can't just leave!"

"Is it dangerous?" asked Eve, her eyes widening. "The snake?"

"Well . . . not usually . . . but when it's hungry, I can't be so sure."

The Reptile Lady started her engine.

"Wish I could stay to help you," said the Reptile Lady. "But I've got this gig tonight—it's Charlie Sheen. He's out on probation, and he booked me at triple my usual rate."

"Charlie Sheen doesn't have kids," said Eve.

"I know," said the Reptile Lady.

"Who cares about Charlie Sheen?!" Fuller yelled.

"My pager number's on the receipt. I'll come back when that party's done," said the Reptile Lady. She drove off. Eve and Fuller just stood there, in front of their estate, holding their children.

"Now what?" they both said at the same time.

Sixty-three

Eve and Fuller searched the property for four hours, looking in nooks and crannies and crawl spaces that they didn't even know their house had. But the snake was still missing. The sun was starting to go down, and it would be dark in less than an hour, so Fuller got out flashlights, and they poured over the backyard for the fifth time.

"I think we'd better notify the neighbors," Fuller said to Eve.

"Oh, God, you can't."

"Why not?"

"I didn't even invite them to the party," she said.

"So what?" said Fuller. "I think they need to know there's a snake loose."

"They'll be so insulted I didn't invite them."

Fuller looked at Eve like she was nuts.

"I couldn't invite everyone!"

"You're exhausted," said Fuller.

Eve hadn't put Eloise down since she had learned the python was missing. And she hadn't let go of Stella's little hand except to wipe the sweat off, and then quickly reach down and clutch it again.

"Lemme take her," said Fuller. He reached for Eloise and took her from Eve. Eve heaved a sigh of relief. She didn't even realize how heavy Eloise was, until she was out of her arms.

"Fuller, I'm so embarrassed," whispered Eve. "I don't want the neighbors to think we're irresponsible."

"We're not irresponsible," he said.

"We let a giant albino python get loose! What do you call that?"

He could tell she was on the verge of losing it.

"We don't have a choice," he said. "We can't not tell them. What if it turns up and eats their dog? Or those people across the street with the newborn baby—that thing probably does eat babies."

"Only if it's hungry enough," said Eve.

Fuller didn't want to argue with her.

They glared at each other. Eve hated him looking at her that way. She tried not to cry.

"I'm sorry."

"I'm not saying anything," he said. "But if we'd had a simple pin-the-tail-on-the-donkey game, and cake and ice cream, none of this ever would have happened."

"You met Bruce Willis because of this party," Eve said. "Do you think Bruce Willis would come to a party that had pin the tail on the donkey and ice cream?!"

"Yes!" Fuller yelled. "They're not coming for the entertainment. They're coming to be with us! To meet friends."

"Fuller! Don't be naïve!"

"What?" He started to laugh. The absurdity of how things had turned around got to him.

"I mean it," she said.

"Look, who cares about the party," he said, trying to hold it together. "I've got a twelve-foot python loose on my property! So, fuck Bruce Willis."

"What's 'fuck' mean, Daddy?"

They both turned and saw Stella, staring up at them with scared eyes. Tired eyes. They'd completely forgotten her. They thought she wasn't listening. She was normally so quiet, they just forgot.

"Oh, no," said Eve, bending down to Stella's height. "Daddy is just tired and grouchy, hon. We both are."

"I know that," said Stella, rolling her eyes. "Duh."

"I'm sorry, Stella," said Fuller. "I shouldn't lose my temper that way."

"I know," said Stella. "But what *does* 'fuck' mean?"

"Oh, shit," said Eve, covering her mouth as soon as she did. It was too late. Stella repeated her.

Sixty-four

Police, animal control, and a reporter from the *Los Angeles Times*, who must have been tipped off, showed up within the hour. Eve packed the children into their car seats, and sat with them as they started to doze off. After all the professionals had searched the house and the yard, and the neighbors' yards, and had come up empty-handed, they circled around Fuller and Eve.

"You can go back in the house," said Officer Pinnavaia of the Brentwood Police unit.

"But what about the snake?" asked Eve.

"We searched the entire property, ma'am," said Pinnavaia.

"Thoroughly," said the animal control guy, who was wearing big, thick, industrial-looking gloves that reached up to his elbows. He carried a net and a long metal rod with a hook on the end.

"So, that's it?" Fuller said.

"We searched everywhere," said Pinnavaia. "What else do you suggest we do?"

"Just keep a close eye on the kids," Animal Control piped up. "Those pythons can squeeze the life out of you in a second. A little kid, in about a half a second."

"Is it really safe to go back in the house?" Eve asked.

Pinnavaia and the animal control guy exchanged glances. "We can't advise you," said Pinnavaia.

"I wouldn't," said Animal Control. "But that's just my personal opinion."

"Thanks," said Fuller. He felt sick.

They all got in their vehicles and drove away. Fuller, Eve, Stella, and Eloise looked at each other and their house.

"The kids need to sleep," said Eve. "We all do."

"Then let's go check into a hotel."

"We can stay at Gabrielle's. Or Nancy's. I could call them from the car. We can borrow their kids' clothes. . . ."

"I'm not staying at Nancy's house," said Fuller. "She gives me the creeps. And I'm not staying at Gabrielle Gardener's."

"I didn't know that Nancy gave you the creeps," said Eve, surprised. Fuller was too tired to explain. "Well, there's Amanda's."

"I don't want to stay at my old girlfriend's house."

Eve had never heard her husband call Amanda that. His old girlfriend.

"Okay," she said. "Well, there's always the Bel Air Hotel."

"Let's go," said Fuller, hopping in the car.

"What about packing some stuff?" Eve asked.

"Are you kidding?" Fuller said, looking at the house. "I'm

not going in there. Not without a gun. You think I want to meet up with a twelve-foot python—who hasn't eaten in at least eight hours? I have a family."

"Okay," said Eve. "Then, I'll wash our underwear in the sink. We can buy toothbrushes in the gift shop."

Sixty-five

Nestled in Stone Canyon, the Bel Air Hotel never looked so inviting as when Fuller and Eve carried their sleeping children across the bridge, over the fish, past the swans sleeping on the lawn, and into the lobby. They made quite a picture, no luggage, checking in for an indefinite amount of time. The atmosphere was cozy and safe, and Eve and Fuller allowed themselves the giggles.

Later, snug in their lush floral suite, with the children sleeping in the living room in a crib and a rollaway bed, and their room service dinner consumed, Fuller held his naked, pregnant wife under the clean, crisp sheets.

"Promise me something," Fuller said.

"What?" Eve asked. She looked out the open doorway that led to their private patio with a bubbling fountain.

"No more Hollywood birthday parties."

Eve frowned. "Why?" she pouted. "This one was so good."

Fuller looked at her, incredulously.

"Everyone had fun, I threw a great party, and we end up here, at the Bel Air. What's so terrible about that?" she asked as she kissed him.

"You're amazing. Unbelievable. I always knew that—even when you were waiting tables in Studio City."

"I ran into someone from my past today," she said. "Another waiter. From Gladstone's. He was the tarantula."

"The one hitting on Amanda?"

"I think he was more interested in hitting on her husband. He's an actor. Wants a job."

"What am I? Invisible? How come he didn't hit on me?"

"Because you didn't win an Oscar yet."

Fuller was silent.

"*Yet*," she emphasized. She hadn't meant to make him feel bad about it.

"You ever think of getting away from all this? Moving to the middle of nowhere?" he asked her.

"And doing what?" she asked.

"I don't know. We could wait tables. It's an honest life," said Fuller. "How many people here can say that about themselves?"

"What's wrong?" she asked. "I thought everything was going great."

"I just don't like it," he said, seriously. "Something about all this—I don't know, 'success'—makes me feel like I'm losing you."

She thought for a second, but only a second.

"Losing me?" she said. "Or losing yourself?"

He looked at her, as if struck, then smiled.

"How do you do that?" he asked. "I'm the goddamn genius in the family—remember that, will you? You're the sex goddess, and I'm the genius."

She laughed, and he did, too. "It's true," she said. "I'm fine. It's you who can't handle it."

"Okay, okay," he said. "So, I'm the weak one. But just don't pull me into the deep water, okay? Not just yet."

"Okay," she said.

"Oh, by the way," he said. "Happy birthday to you."

"Thanks," said Eve. She was a little disappointed that she had been forgotten in the extravaganza that was Stella's party. This was, after all, not just her birthday, but the day that Fuller had proposed marriage to her.

"I almost forgot," he said, and pulled a box out from under the pillow. It was black velvet: a ring box. Eve's heart leapt. He hadn't forgotten. This wasn't the kind of box that you picked up in the gift shop at the last minute.

She opened the box. It was a huge, pear-shaped diamond ring.

"For my Hollywood wife," he said.

"Fuller!" She took the ring out. It was amazing. "I don't believe it."

"I thought you'd like it," he said.

"I do, I love it. It's so . . . extravagant."

"Happy birthday, blue eyes," he said, and held her hand up to admire. "I like it on you."

"Me, too," she said.

Sixty-six

Twenty Butterflies and Puppydog Tails mothers were gathered in Gabrielle's living room. Consuela had her hands full serving them cappuccinos and the homemade muffins that Gabrielle had whipped up at five in the morning.

"Welcome, everyone," Gabrielle said modestly. "I'm hosting this meeting for the annual fundraiser, so please help yourself to muffins. They're fat free. And let's all welcome Sarah, the committee chair."

Gabrielle walked to the back of the room, past all the mothers, over half of whom she had never bothered to say so much as a hello to when she ran into them at preschool. Sarah, a civilian mother, started the meeting by discussing bake sales and decorations.

"What a waste of time," whispered Nancy, sipping a cappuccino. She had lost a lot of weight since Stella's party, and she looked amazing. Gabrielle and she sat next to each other in the back. "I could be shopping at Savannah. I need all new clothes."

"How do you have time to shop?" asked Gabrielle. "I have a crate of private school applications to fill out."

"How many schools are you applying to?" asked Nancy, anxiously.

"All of them," said Gabrielle.

Eve walked in late and made her way back to her friends.

"Hi," Eve whispered.

Sarah talked about the silent auction. The civilian moms took notes.

"Did they find the snake?"

"No," said Eve. "Not yet. Who's that?" she asked, as she settled in next to Gabrielle.

"Sarah Roberts," said Gabrielle. "She's insane. She has no help at home."

"Nice ring," said Nancy, grabbing Eve's hand.

"No help?" Eve said and snatched a pumpkin muffin with her free hand. "Why not?"

"Because she's crazy. She has four girls, she's still nursing two of them—" Gabrielle suddenly noticed Eve's ring as Nancy shoved it in her face. "Wow."

"Birthday present," Eve said, nonchalantly. She was thinking of her own mother, with five kids, no help, and her daily ten-hour shifts at the gas station. "From Fuller," said Eve, her mouth full of muffin.

"I hope everyone"—Sarah paused for emphasis, and glared at Eve, Nancy, and Gabrielle, who'd been talking throughout her speech—"will volunteer for a committee."

"Do we have to?" whispered Eve. "I'm so busy."

"Just get on the silent auction committee," said Gabrielle.

"What's a silent auction?" asked Eve.

"Do we have to teach you everything?" Nancy laughed. "I can't believe you don't know what a silent auction is."

"I'm sorry," said Eve. "Maybe one day I'll teach you something you don't know."

"Doubt it," said Nancy, teasing.

"You're in a good mood," said Eve, putting her arm around her friend.

"It's an auction," said Gabrielle. "We get people to donate things—trips, plane tickets, gift certificates to restaurants and stores—hit up the ones you use the most. And then we lay all the donations out on tables, and the parents bid on them by writing their name and a dollar amount. The money goes to the school since everything was free, and the parents get whatever they buy."

"I heard that Amanda Foster donated a Picasso for the silent auction."

"A Picasso?" said Gabrielle. She was shocked. They both turned to Eve for validation.

"I don't know." Eve shrugged. "I didn't hear anything about it."

"That's amazing," said Nancy. "Do you have any idea what it's worth?"

"Close to a million," said Gabrielle. "With this crowd."

Sarah glared at Gabrielle for talking. Gabrielle stopped, but when Sarah looked away, she continued.

"So, where are you applying for private school for Stella?"

"Private school?" She had barely learned about silent auctions, and now there was something else. Sometimes she felt like she was only keeping up by the skin of her teeth.

"I'm going to really zero in on Crossroads," said Gabrielle. "Pull every string I can. It's very competitive. I'll use John Thomas Dye as a backup. We go to Maui with the director's brother-in-law."

"Does anyone go to public school?" Eve asked.

"No," said Nancy, bluntly. "They don't."

"You don't know who they'll meet in public school," Gabrielle admonished.

"Did you go to private school?" Eve asked her friends.

"When I wasn't cutting classes, I did," said Nancy. "But I wasn't big on school. Besides, I didn't learn anything there that I needed to live here."

"I didn't," said Gabrielle. "Which is why my children are. And if Zachary doesn't get in to Crossroads, Joey is going to make heads roll."

"I went to public school," said Eve.

"And we're having to teach you things you should have learned long ago," said Nancy. "Which is why you want your kids to go to private school. You don't want Stella growing up not knowing what a silent auction is, do you?" she joked.

Eve reached for another muffin.

Sarah stopped speaking and glared dramatically at Eve, Nancy, and Gabrielle. Everyone in the room turned toward the back to see what the problem was.

Gabrielle suddenly banged Eve on the back, pretending she was choking, to divert Sarah's blaming glare.

"She can't help it," Gabrielle said to the group. "There are nuts in the muffins." As if that would explain Eve's behavior. "She's allergic to macadamias."

Eve tried not to laugh, but it was impossible. She started choking for real.

Sarah continued.

"I better make some calls to private schools, I guess," said Eve, when the attention was off of them.

"I'd say so," said Gabrielle. "I'll give you my list, but you'd better hurry. Or else you'll wind up in public school."

Sixty-seven

Nancy and Landon sat side by side in the barren white interviewing office at Crossroads, one of the most popular Westside private elementary schools. They were waiting for their interviewer, who sat across the desk from them, to finish her phone call.

"Do you have a gun?" Nancy asked Landon quietly.

"Sure," he whispered back. "Several."

She didn't flinch. "Ever use it?"

"Why? You scared?"

"Not of the gun," said Nancy.

Landon smiled at her.

Nancy was aware she could still make him smile. She clung to that shred. Any shred that let her hope they might still make it.

The interviewer, still on the phone, looked over and gave them the one-minute sign with her finger.

"Fuller Evanston got one," Nancy said. "They think there's a snake in their house."

Landon squinted. "Why didn't they just get an exterminator?"

"It's a big snake."

"I'll tell you," said Landon, putting his hand over his mouth to make sure the interviewer didn't hear. "I think there's a lot of snakes in a lot of houses."

Nancy ignored the metaphor. "I just don't know whether I can send March there for play dates—I mean, first there's a snake in the house, now there's a gun."

"Do you think the Evanstons worry about sending their kids to your house? I mean, you're not exactly Donna Reed."

"Fuck you," Nancy mouthed the words.

"Well, here we go," said the interviewer, hanging up the phone. She shuffled through her files. "March's parents." She smiled up at Nancy and Landon, waiting for them to say something. They didn't.

Landon smiled back and reached over and took Nancy's fingers in his and caressed them. Nancy took his fingers to her silicone lips, and kissed them.

"Well," said Mrs. Schuyler. "You two seem to be a perfect Crossroads family."

"We really want this school," said Nancy.

"March has a lot of friends who go here," said Landon.

Nancy looked over at Landon, surprised that he was being assertive. She was glad he had agreed to fly into town to go to this admissions interview with her, but she hadn't expected him to be so agreeable. She thought he'd be a pill, show up unshaven and grunt a lot. But here he was, an ace. He even wore a suit.

"I'm very active at Butterflies and Puppydog Tails," said Nancy. "I love volunteering."

"She's always at the school," said Landon.

"I can't wait to dig in and get involved at Crossroads," said Nancy. "I'm on this big committee for the fundraiser at Butterflies. I do everything, and I just love it. It's my life."

Mrs. Schuyler looked across her desk at the Greenes and smiled. She'd been doing this for seven years—interviewing parents who were desperate to get their children into Crossroads. She looked down at the preschool teachers' evaluation sheet for March. The handwritten comments were kind, but there were some negative checkmarks in the grid that measured social skills and maturity. The form said that Nancy always paid her bills on time, and was a generous financial contributor. Very generous.

"Have you toured the school?" Mrs. Schuyler asked.

"Last week," said Nancy. Landon hadn't shown up for the tour. "It was very impressive."

"Of course, we are building a new facility. Our groundbreaking is in November."

"We'd love to make a donation," said Nancy, not skipping a beat. She knew that groundbreakings meant fundraising. "If it's appropriate," she added quickly. "I mean, once we get in."

Mrs. Schuyler smiled shrewdly. Yes, Nancy Greene was a player, and Mrs. Schuyler appreciated that.

"Donations of all kinds are appreciated," said Mrs. Schuyler. "Spending volunteer time in the classroom is just as valuable as contributing financially."

"Anything for the children," said Nancy.

"Exactly," said Mrs. Schuyler.

Sixty-eight

"You played her pretty well," said Landon, with admiration.

"Thanks, babe," said Nancy. They walked down Fourth Street to the parking lot. She felt good. They had been a team for the first time in ages. "You did your part, too."

Landon just snorted.

"Hey, you did!" Nancy reassured him. "I appreciate your coming and doing this for March. If she gets into this school, it'll be great. It'll mean a lot for her future. And the twins."

"How about I take March for the weekend?" Landon offered. "Give you a break. Get to know her a little better. I know you've still got the twins, but . . ."

Nancy just about fell over. She had never expected this paternal donation.

"That would be great," said Nancy. "Should I send a nanny along?"

"No," said Landon. "I'll pick her up after school."

"Alone?" Nancy asked. She didn't want March with Landon and any of his bimbette girlfriends.

"Just the two of us," said Landon. "Maybe I'll just check us in to Shutters on the beach for fun. I'll take her to the pier. Does she like rides?"

"Yes," said Nancy, feeling glad that Landon was doing the dad thing so graciously. "It'll be nice for her to spend time with you. She needs a father."

"How about you?" Landon asked.

Nancy's heart fluttered for a second. She was still attracted to her husband. She still loved him. If he asked her back, she'd jump.

"Is that a proposal—of some kind?" Nancy asked, stunned.

"No, not really. Just a friendly question."

"Oh," she said, feeling sad. How could he do this to her? She was doing fine without him, and bam! He could upset her so easily. Taunt her with the idea of being back with him.

"You seeing anyone?"

"No," said Nancy. "I hardly have time with the twins. . . .
Why—should I be?"

"Yeah." Landon sighed. "You should."

"So the divorce . . . ?"

"The papers are all drawn up," he said.

"You sonofabitch," she muttered. "You fucking sonofabitch."

"Hon," said Landon, condescendingly, "what did you expect?
The fairy tale?"

"No!" Nancy couldn't believe the question. "I didn't expect
a fairy tale. I expected you to stick around. I expected a marriage.
I expected a partner. I expected a husband to grow old with. I
expected children and a house with a white picket fence and a
dog." She stopped. He was smiling at her. Fuck, she thought. He
thinks I'm cute. "I'd love to know," she said, crying, "what did
you expect? Out of the marriage?"

Landon laughed. "Me?"

"Yeah," said Nancy, toughly wiping her tears with the back
of her hand. She felt like a little girl. A tomboy. Challenging her
brother to a fight. "You." She wanted to push him. Poke him.
Just like she did her brother.

"I got what I expected," he said.

"You know," said Nancy. "I can't stop wondering . . . if I had
been a Jewish wife . . . if I had fit in . . ."

Landon laughed. It made her feel worse, but Nancy kept talking.

"Would you have treated me this badly?" she asked.

"If you had been a Jewish wife," said Landon, "I never would
have married you."

Nancy was confused and enlightened, both at the same time.
Everybody she knew—all her friends—were non-Jewish women
married to Jewish men.

"Why?" she asked.

He didn't answer.

So she pushed him. Pushed his chest with both her hands. He
stumbled backward. *"Why?!"* she hollered, pushing him again.
He didn't answer, and she realized she was making a spectacle
out on the street. She pulled herself together, then looked up to
the window where they'd just had the Crossroads interview. She
didn't want any bad behavior seen by the interviewers. "You
trashed me," she said bluntly. "And I let you! I allowed it! So,

now, you owe me! You owe me an answer to my question. At the very least.''

"You're a goddess, Nance," Landon said, shrewdly, raising one eyebrow. "Always were, always will be."

"All I tried to do was be better," she said. "I didn't try to be a goddess."

"I don't deserve you," said Landon. "Never did. I don't deserve most of what I get. But I get it, and I love it."

"You just love the getting part," she said, understanding. "You love the chase. You don't love whatever it is you're chasing."

She felt calmer now. Understanding was a bitter pill, but it brought relief.

"Losing me is the best thing that could happen to you," said Landon. "You don't deserve me. You never did."

"I don't want a divorce," she said.

"You should," said Landon. "You should've trashed me long ago."

"I know," she said, crying now.

"I would've liked it," he said. "I would've stayed if you had."

She stared at him, shocked, because it was the missing piece to what she knew about who she had married.

"You would've stayed if I treated you like shit," she said, quietly. Getting it. Getting him. Who he was.

"Probably," he said. "But it was a lose-lose situation. I knew you'd never do things like that. I knew you couldn't."

"You're sick," said Nancy.

"You gotta love me," said Landon, and smiled evilly.

"Do I?" asked Nancy.

"Yeah," said Landon. "I'm poison, baby."

Nancy looked around. Cars. The mall. The parking structures. Stores she'd never been in. Normal people's stores. Michael's. The art supply store that Gabrielle frequented for her art projects. For the five thousand tissue paper flowers she would carefully craft for Jocelyn's fundraiser.

She felt the air. They were only four blocks from the ocean. The air was cooler than where she lived. Inland. Where her home was. She felt alone. Naked. Exposed. Nothing to separate her from the civilian moms around her, dragging children in polyester mall clothes with Disney characters on their fronts across the street. Quickly, before the light turned red.

For a split second, it felt like nothing mattered. Not Landon, not Gabrielle or Eve or Jocelyn, not her house or her clothes, not her cars or her parties, not befriending Amanda Foster or getting into Crossroads. Nothing mattered. Except March and the twins. The children connected her to the earth. In a primal way that didn't include Landon. He was fleeting. It was time for him to go.

"So, I'll pick up March, then," said Landon.

Nancy snapped to. She looked at Landon. He was just a man. He'd never know what it was to be connected to the earth by a child. Connected to more than just the earth.

"Sure," she said. She felt refreshed and renewed. "Have a good time with her. She's pretty amazing. I hope you can appreciate her."

"I'll try," said Landon, and he walked away, leaving her alone. Again.

Sixty-nine

Eve sat amidst a pile of colored tissue paper squares, wood rods, and wire, on the floor in their suite at the Bel Air Hotel. She had volunteered for the decorating committee for the preschool fundraiser, and was assembling child-sized paper birds and birdhouses. She had been at work for four hours, since the children had gone to bed in one of the two bedrooms of their suite. Room service had been delivered and devoured. Eve's fingers were now numb from twisting wire to make decorations.

She picked up the phone and dialed.

"Yes, it's Eve again. Is Amanda back yet?"

"Hold, please," said the sweet, overpaid secretary who answered the Fosters' phones even late at night. Eve knew that Amanda was avoiding her. If she was out, the secretary would've known. That she had to check was a giveaway.

"I'm sorry, but Amanda is out for the evening," the secretary said.

Eve sighed. This was the fourth call in a row that Amanda didn't take from her.

"Tell her somebody died," said Eve, crisply. "I need to talk to her urgently."

"Oh," said the sweet secretary, pity in her voice. "One second."

More hold. And then came the Queen.

"Eve, what happened?" It was Amanda; she sounded concerned.

"Nothing," said Eve, half embarrassed. "I just wanted to talk to you."

"Minnie said that someone died," said Amanda.

"I just said that to get you on the phone," said Eve.

Silence followed.

"Well, it worked."

"Please don't be angry."

"Don't do it again."

"I won't," said Eve. "I'm sorry."

"Good."

"So, how are you?"

"Fine," said Amanda, calming down. "I'm fine."

"I need your help," said Eve.

"From the looks of the party you threw Stella, you don't need any help at all."

Eve refused to be insulted. "It's kindergarten," said Eve. "I'm desperate."

Amanda started to snicker.

"I know, it's insane," said Eve. "Please put me on the right track."

"Don't know if I can do that," said Amanda. "You're a mighty big train these days. I heard you're chairing the Sparkle and Shine luncheon."

"Will you come?" Eve asked.

"Send me an invitation," said Amanda, not committing.

"I will. Maybe I can give it to you myself. Are you ever free for lunch anymore?"

"I'll check the books."

Eve remembered how not so long ago, Amanda used to always have time for her.

"I guess you heard about the python loose in my house," said Eve.

"No," said Amanda. "I'm not part of the inner circle."

Eve did her best to not get into a fight.

"The python from Stella's party got loose, and they can't find it. We're all a wreck, thinking it's going to turn up in the toilet or under a bed one day. So we moved into the Bel Air Hotel."

"How can you lose a python?" Amanda asked.

"I don't know," said Eve. "I really have no idea how it happened."

"Well, good luck snake hunting," said Amanda, wrapping up the call.

Eve panicked. She wasn't done.

"So, what do I do?" she asked. "About private school?"

Amanda sighed audibly. It was a brush-off sigh. This part of the call was obligatory niceness for Fuller's sake. Eve could tell. Amanda did not want to be on the phone.

"You look at *all* the schools," said Amanda. "Including the public school—what district are you in? What's your public school? Kenter Canyon? Charter?"

"I don't even know," said Eve. "But everyone says public schools are terrible here."

"Make your own decision," said Amanda. "And then when you decide what's best, you campaign like crazy to get in."

"That's it?" said Eve. "That's your help?"

"What did you want me to say?" asked Amanda.

Eve held her breath.

"You're in the big leagues now. Swim with the sharks. I'm sure you can run across a few of them at the pool at the Bel Air. Do they still have camp counselors who serve fruit and Evian there?"

"What did I do?" Eve asked. "Why are you being like this?"

There was a pause that spoke volumes. She had obviously done something.

"Listen, I really have to go. George is calling me. Why don't you call Hazel during the day, see if she can put you on the books?"

"Okay," said Eve, sadly. She was now relegated to calling Hazel. She took the rejection like a bullet. They both hung up.

Eve sat there, wondering exactly what she had done to make Amanda shun her. She took off her clothes, and plunked her naked body into the hot tub on the patio of the hotel suite. She couldn't wait until Fuller got home from work to ask him what the fuck—yes, that's right, she was now going to curse like never before—what the *fuck* was wrong with Amanda Foster.

Seventy

Nancy drove with March in her big, shiny black Toyota LandCruiser. She cried silently as she pulled onto the 405 North freeway, wiping the tears away so March wouldn't see. What had happened? And, more importantly, what was she going to do about it? Nobody was on her side. Nobody was helping her. Her friends had their own lives. Her family had abandoned her long ago. Her party girl facade had been eaten away by a bad marriage and the work of raising three children.

She glanced at her eyes in the rearview mirror. They weren't innocent eyes. They'd seen more than she prayed her children would ever see in their lives. There were even wrinkles beginning to form, way too early. She thought about having them done, but a car honked at her. She had swerved into the wrong lane, looking at her eyes in the rearview mirror.

Nancy pulled off at the Mulholland Drive exit and drove up past the private schools.

"Honey, you okay?" she asked March, who was silently sulking in the back seat. March mostly frowned these days. It was almost as if her mouth naturally turned down at the corners.

"I like it when the driver takes me places, better," she said.

Nancy thought about the driver, the help, the staff, the house, the life she'd been living. She had signed her prenup agreement long ago, but if she recalled correctly, it didn't leave her with much. Not this much, anyway. She'd come to their marriage penniless, and was going to leave it taken care of, but not rich. Not by a long shot. Life was going to change drastically for her and her children.

"You want some music?" she asked March, who didn't respond.

Nancy turned on the radio anyway. She found some old Fleetwood Mac. March put her hands over her ears so she wouldn't hear. She turned the radio off, and concentrated on her driving.

"I want strings," said March.

Nancy looked back at her daughter. Strings?

"I want violin music," she said. "My teacher played music at school, and it had violins. 'Peter and the Wolf.' I want that."

Nancy rolled the radio knob until she found the classical music station. "How about that?" she asked.

"That's the cello," March yelled, on the verge of a tantrum. "I want violins!"

She rolled the knob around some more.

"Just turn it off!" March yelled. "It's hurting my ears."

Nancy turned the radio off. In the quiet of the car rolling quickly down Mulholland Drive, she wondered how long before she'd have to give back this car. The house. . . .

"Here we are," she sang out as they pulled into the parking lot.

March gave her mother the finger. It was the wrong finger, but the bravado with which she stuck it out at her made it even more offensive than had it been the correct finger.

"Just shoot me now," said March.

She looked back at her daughter. That a five-year-old would say such a thing was just bizarre. But March said a lot of bizarre things, lately.

"I'm a good driver, honey," she said. "Look, I didn't hit anything."

"Luck."

Nancy wondered how on earth March had gotten so precocious and so negative in one fell swoop. She only thought it for a fraction of a second. She knew the answer. Landon.

Nancy pulled into the parking lot of the Mirman School for the Gifted. Children in uniforms were playing in the schoolyard and at a table four mothers, who didn't look a thing like her, were dishing out lunch.

"Come on," she said, and yanked March inside.

"Hello," said Dr. Griffin, almost as soon as Nancy and March were inside the school's front lobby. Dr. Griffin was sixty. He had gray hair and blue eyes behind large rimless eyeglasses. He paid zero attention to Nancy. His eyes were focused on March.

"Hi," said Nancy, taken aback. "I'm Nancy Greene."

Nancy stuck out her hand to shake, but Dr. Griffin just gave her a short, weak, obligatory shake.

"And you must be March," he said, turning all his attention toward her. This wasn't like the other private school interviews, Nancy thought, where the parents were scrutinized and the children were just faceless names and ages on paper.

This was all about the child.

March scowled at Dr. Griffin. Nancy prayed that March wouldn't give Dr. Griffin the finger. She made silent deals with God.

"Would you like to come into my office?" Dr. Griffin asked March.

No answer. Dr. Griffin was unphased. He just led the way. Nancy thanked God for March not flipping the bird so far.

"Would you like your mother to come into my office, or wait outside?"

"Wait," said March. "In the parking lot. Or out on the highway. On the median strip."

Nancy blushed. She was very embarrassed, and thought of making some joke to cover her daughter's bad manners, but she didn't get a chance. She didn't notice that Dr. Griffin was impressed with March's correct use of the word *median*.

The door to Dr. Griffin's office slammed shut. A sign that read TESTING IN PROGRESS—DO NOT DISTURB swung back and forth on the doorknob.

Nancy stood in the middle of the lobby. She looked around. Children's art decorated the walls of the 1970s architecture.

"Magazine?" the receptionist asked Nancy.

"Thanks," said Nancy, expecting *Vogue* or *Elle*. The receptionist handed her the school's *Parent Newsletter,* and pointed her into one of two chairs outside Dr. Griffin's office. Nancy sat. She put her hand on the empty chair next to her. The one intended for the father of the child being tested. The seat was cold.

She glanced at the newsletter. Boring. She looked around, and spotted a stack of magazines on a table. She got up and walked across the lobby to the table. The magazines were *Intermediate Physics, Scientific American,* and *Neurolinguistics*. Nancy walked back to her seat empty-handed. She saw the receptionist watch her go back, without a magazine, and Nancy was sure the receptionist had smirked.

Nancy sank down into the chair, and tried to sit still. That forty-five minutes she was alone was the first time Nancy had been by herself with nothing to do in five years. There were no women's magazines to pick up and read. There was no cappuccino joint or juice bar nearby. There was no one to talk to.

Nancy took her cell phone from her purse and dialed. Gabrielle's housekeeper said Gabrielle was out. Eve's housekeeper said Eve was at a doctor's appointment. Nancy put the phone

away, but without it she was antsy. She made herself sit still and
do nothing. At first it was impossible, but after a while, she was
in a trance. Then she heard church bells. They were far away.

"Is there a church around here?" she asked the receptionist.

"I don't know," said the receptionist. "There must be. I hear
the bells."

Dr. Griffin opened the door, and March charged out with a war
hoop. Nancy jumped.

"Come inside," said Dr. Griffin. "March, we'll be right back.
I'm going to talk to your mother privately. You can wait here."

Nancy never left March unattended. At home, a nanny followed
her around twenty-four hours a day, seven days a week. At
March's beck and call. She eyed her daughter nervously, wondering what mischief she would stir up unattended. The door shut.

"Sit down," said Dr. Griffin. Nancy sat. The office was bare
bones. White walls. Many educational diplomas of Dr. Griffin's,
as well as those of the husband and wife who'd founded the
school.

"March is exceedingly gifted," said Dr. Griffin.

Nancy was confused. Dr. Griffin's face was so focused that she
was under the impression he was telling her bad news.

"She scored between one hundred seventy and one hundred
eighty on the I.Q. test I gave her," he said. "Of course, there is
a five-point margin on either side of that number."

"Is that good?" Nancy asked.

Dr. Griffin looked over his glasses at Nancy. He didn't see
Nancy's plastic surgery. He didn't see her fabulous clothes. He
didn't see the five-hundred-dollar haircut or the perfectly applied
makeup. He just saw the mother of a gifted child.

"I don't like to think of intelligence tests as rendering 'good'
or 'bad' scores," said Dr. Griffin, calmly.

Nancy bit her nails. She'd never bitten her nails before in her
life. "She's not . . . slow, is she?" Nancy asked.

Dr. Griffin looked at Nancy again. "Slow?"

"Retarded?" Nancy whispered, her eyebrows raising. "We've
had some behavior problems at school."

"Frankly, I'm not surprised," said Dr. Griffin.

Nancy's heart sunk.

"With an I.Q. of one eighty, your daughter isn't going to find
much stimulation at a quote unquote *normal* school," said Dr.
Griffin. "She's probably frustrated. Imagine if you couldn't do
what you wanted to do—for years," said Dr. Griffin, trying to

explain March's predicament. "Imagine if you were born to do something, and you weren't able to."

"If you only knew," said Nancy quietly, thinking about herself. There was sweet relief that someone finally noticed that she and March hadn't been in the right place.

"Good," said Dr. Griffin.

"So, is a one-hundred-eighty I.Q. normal?" asked Nancy, hoping to God that it was.

"No," said Dr. Griffin. "It's not normal. Mrs. Greene, your daughter is gifted. Way above the intelligence level of most people, let alone children her age."

Nancy squinted, trying to get a grip and put this all in perspective.

"Haven't you noticed?" Dr. Griffin asked, critically.

"Well." Nancy thought. "I've noticed that she acts out. Gets in trouble a lot."

"She counts by nines," said Dr. Griffin.

"I know," said Nancy. "And twos, fours, fives, sevens. She likes numbers."

"Do you know that that is not normal for her age?"

Again, hearing "not normal," Nancy had the feeling something was wrong.

"She's not just more intelligent than most other children," said Dr Griffin, calmly. "She's more intelligent than other adults. March is more intelligent than ninety-nine point nine seven percent of all people. At least according to my tests."

Nancy sat back. "So, basically, she's not retarded at all," said Nancy.

Dr. Griffin bit his lip. He had had many surprises in talking with the parents of highly intelligent children. Nancy was the biggest surprise Dr. Griffin had ever seen. "No, dear," said Dr. Griffin. "She is not retarded at all. Let's go over her test."

Dr. Griffin showed Nancy some shapes March had drawn in crayon on paper.

"If you look closely at this circle, you can see that the east quadrant is slightly concave," said Dr. Griffin, seriously. "Her motor skills could use some attention. I would pay strong attention to her circles."

"Her circles?" Nancy squinted, trying to concentrate. "I thought you just said she was a genius or something. What does she need to work on her circles for?"

Nancy wanted a cigarette. She wanted drugs. She wanted something. She tried to pay attention to Dr. Griffin as he went on about March's use of metaphors and listening comprehension skills, but she kept zoning out.

"We want March in our school," said Dr. Griffin, finishing up. He slammed the desk drawer, and woke Nancy from her trance. "I have a space for her in kindergarten, and if money is a problem, we have a scholarship program."

"Huh?"

No one had ever assumed money was a problem for Nancy. If anything, everyone was always passing her their bills to pay. This was a first.

"We have all kinds of children from all kinds of families," said Dr. Griffin. "Financial assistance is nothing to be ashamed of. We take our children based on their I.Q.'s, not how much money their parents have or make."

Nancy started to giggle. She couldn't help it. Everything in her life was turning out to be the opposite of what she had expected. Her giggles turned into laughter. Inappropriate laughter.

"You're laughing," said Dr. Griffin. Which made Nancy laugh harder. "Is anything wrong?"

"No," said Nancy, her face flushed. She was laughing hard. "Nothing." She pulled herself together, and stopped. "For the first time . . . something's right. You'll have to excuse me."

"Here's an application," said Dr. Griffin, handing Nancy a packet of papers, ignoring her outburst, the same way he had ignored March's rude behavior. "But it's just a formality. March is in—we want her. This is the only place a child like March really belongs."

"She starts fights," said Nancy. It was the first time she'd been up-front about what a problem March had been for her. For some reason, she wasn't embarrassed about it here.

"We'll take good care of her," said Dr. Griffin. "She'll straighten out once she's challenged. I'm sure of it. I've seen this a thousand times."

Dr. Griffin led Nancy back out into the lobby. March was talking to some children who looked like they were nine and ten years old. Nancy saw her daughter differently than she'd ever seen her before. The older children were listening to March. And March was listening to them.

"Just like her father," Nancy said to herself. "But not completely."

"Goodbye, March," said Dr. Griffin. March looked over. "It's time for you to go."

March said goodbye to the children. For the first time, she looked like part of a group. Nancy felt tears come to her eyes. She didn't realize how much it had meant to her to see her daughter fit in. Somewhere.

"Would you like to go to this school?" Dr. Griffin asked March.

"Whatever," she said, and swaggered a five-year-old's swagger toward the car.

"I hope to see you in the fall," Dr. Griffin said to them both and walked away.

"Dr. Griffin," said Nancy.

He stopped and turned.

"I have twins at home."

"We have a sibling policy," said Dr. Griffin. "Bring them in when they're four. We'll have another chat."

"Great," said Nancy. "Thank you!"

Seventy-one

Eve crouched in the corner of the kitchen of her house. She whispered into the phone. Her eyes moved constantly, looking for the snake, as she talked. She was always looking for it.

"It's been six weeks, and the house still isn't sold!" Eve was frustrated. "We've camped out at the Bel Air Hotel so long the bellboys and waiters know us all by name!"

"It must be costing a fortune," Gabrielle yelled back into her car phone. She was driving to Butterflies and Puppydog Tails. There was static on the line. "With the suite and everything. Room service . . ."

"Fuller's charging it to the studio, but you're right. It is. I just want to sell this house. I don't think anyone's going to buy once the holidays come around. We have to do it now!"

Several strangers walked into the kitchen and started opening cabinets and drawers. They saw Eve, and smiled apologetically, but kept right on going, opening her refrigerator and scrutinizing the inside.

"Someone will buy it," said Gabrielle. "Don't panic."

"I don't know," Eve whispered, trying to make sure nobody in the house heard her. "We marked it down twice already. Nobody's made a single offer. Not one."

"It's because of the python," said Gabrielle.

"Does everybody know about it?" Eve cringed, waiting for the answer. She already knew what it would be.

"Everybody knows," said Gabrielle ominously. "Speaking of which, rumor has it you bought a gun."

"Fuller did," said Eve. "Just in case the snake shows up."

"I hope you have a safety lock on it," said Gabrielle. "Nancy and I are very concerned that you have a gun in the house. I mean, I don't have to tell you about all the tragedies that happen—"

"I have a safety lock," said Eve.

A new group of strangers traipsed through the kitchen, cracking gum.

"You don't have to snip at me," said Gabrielle. "I'm just telling you because I don't want an accident."

"I'm sorry," said Eve. She was on the verge. "I'm just really edgy. I was up till three in the morning last night, making papier-mâché birds for the fundraiser. My fingers are all stiff, and that stuff is stuck under my nails. This isn't a life," said Eve. "Snakes and strangers and room service and giant papier-mâché birds—"

There was static and then the line went dead. Eve just hung up, and didn't redial. She hugged her knees and got fetal in the corner of the kitchen.

Seventy-two

On the other end of the line, now dead, Gabrielle hung up. She didn't call back either. She was in her car, in front of the preschool. No parking spots, so she parked in the red zone, not caring if she got a ticket. She got out, beeped her alarm, and went inside.

Jocelyn and Gabrielle hugged their hellos, then gave each other the requisite quick once-over. Jocelyn wore clothes from Banana Republic. On sale. Gabrielle, from Dolce and Gabbana and Pamela Dennis. Ordered at a trunk show and purchased off the rack at Neiman's. Respectively.

Gabrielle had quickly become one of Jocelyn's unofficial ladies-in-waiting. She was one of the few mothers who could get Jocelyn's personal attention during school hours. Without an appointment.

"How are you?" Jocelyn asked.

"Jocelyn," said Gabrielle, seriously. "I need to get Zach into Crossroads. Only it's everyone's first choice. I'm a wreck."

Jocelyn shut her office door so none of the passing teachers or parents or children could hear the conversation. Jocelyn had a good idea where this conversation was going.

"What do I have to do to get in?" Gabrielle asked.

"It's very competitive."

Gabrielle wanted to tell Jocelyn to cut the crap and get to the chase part. But she kept her manners.

"I know you know everything," Gabrielle said, trying to laugh, but it was hard. She was determined to get in to Crossroads. She would do anything. This was no laughing matter. But she did. Because she thought it would help.

"Look," said Jocelyn, softly. "You're an active charity mom. You volunteer. You can make a contribution to the schools upfront if you want, but you may lose it. You still may not get in with all that—and all that puts you at the front of the pack."

"I want this," said Gabrielle. "I'll do anything."

Jocelyn sighed. She wished she could tell Gabrielle what she wanted to hear. She loved Gabrielle's drive, but there were some obstacles that were insurmountable. Even for someone like Gabrielle.

"It's very tough," said Jocelyn, shaking her head. "And going in as a single parent is especially tough."

"I'm not a single parent," Gabrielle said, indignantly.

"Let me rephrase that," said Jocelyn, backtracking. "Going in without Joey is going to make it tougher. How is he, by the way?"

Gabrielle bit her lip. She hadn't talked to her husband since he left for the rehab clinic. He'd called a couple of times; once, she'd even been in the kitchen, right by the answering machine, when he left a message. But she didn't want to talk to him. Not until he was fixed. She just didn't know when that would be.

"He's out of town," said Gabrielle, heatedly. "Don't other fathers go out of town?"

Jocelyn didn't want a confrontation with Gabrielle, who was clearly in denial about how badly off her husband was.

"Did you tell Crossroads about Joey?" said Gabrielle, suddenly, realizing that Jocelyn not only knew everything, but that she was in on this admissions process way more than she was letting on.

"No."

But Jocelyn reddened.

"You told them!"

"I didn't tell them."

"You had no right—you don't know what's going on! You don't know the whole story!"

Gabrielle was furious. How could Jocelyn have betrayed her by telling the admissions committees that Joey was in drug rehab. She was so mad she could have hit Jocelyn.

"I didn't tell them, Gabrielle," said Jocelyn, feeling sorry for her. "They already knew. Everybody knows."

Gabrielle considered this possibility.

"They told me, if you want to know the truth," said Jocelyn.

"You already talked to them," she said quickly.

"They called about your application. They call me about all the applications from my school."

"You could have denied it," said Gabrielle.

"The admissions counselor said, 'Isn't Mr. Gardener in the hospital?' Just like that. She knew, Gabrielle. I don't know how she knew, but she did."

"God, this can be such a small town!" Gabrielle stamped her foot on the floor. "Everybody knows everyone's business."

"You know," said Jocelyn, "it's not such a crime to have an addiction problem. Half the town has one."

"Joey doesn't have an addiction problem," said Gabrielle. "He just hit a rough patch."

"Look, I'm not going to argue. Frankly, I don't know the truth, and the truth doesn't matter."

Gabrielle laughed a snorty laugh.

"The bottom line is that without Joey, it is going to be more difficult for you to get in. Period."

Gabrielle's heart sunk. The idea of not getting in to Crossroads was devastating. Her mind raced. Bad situations always sent her into restrategizing mode.

"I can't believe you and the schools all talk about this," said Gabrielle.

"Why?" Jocelyn asked. "They call for a reference. The same way you do when you hire help."

"Is that how you think of us? The families? As hired help?" Gabrielle asked, immediately sorry she had.

"You know that's not true."

"I bet you all decide who's going to get in where."

Jocelyn didn't say anything.

Gabrielle knew she was right.

"It makes complete sense! If I got in to four schools, and everyone else got in to four schools, the schools would be completely screwed up trying to complete their rosters—they'd be at the families' mercy, waiting to see which acceptance the parents made. They'd be at the parents' mercy."

Jocelyn reddened.

"It's illegal—and if it's not, it should be!"

"It's the admissions process," said Jocelyn. "There has to be some order. The schools have to have some control."

"Control?!" Gabrielle was on a roll. She was the first person to ever get Jocelyn up against a proverbial wall. "Control??! I think it's pretty simple. It's manipulating a marketplace. You're forcing the parents into a seller's market. That's what you're doing!"

Jocelyn marveled at Gabrielle's mind. Nobody up until now had figured it out.

"It's old-fashioned antitrust fodder," said Gabrielle. She was pleased with herself.

"You're exaggerating," said Jocelyn. "Coordinating and sharing information saves all the schools time, money, and, most importantly, reputation."

"You know," said Gabrielle, "I had a feeling last year, when everybody got into only one of their private school choices, that you all coordinated. What do you do? Have a barbecue and decide who's going to get in where? Boy, would I love to be invited for a burger to that one. I bet tickets are harder to come by than for the Oscars."

"That's not true," said Jocelyn. There was a momentary stand-off.

"Jocelyn, I don't know any person who got into two schools—and everyone applied to at least six or seven. That's not statistically possible—I'm not a mathematician, but it isn't logical."

"Gabrielle—"

"If the admissions process were on the up-and-up, then there would be multiple acceptances," Gabrielle was thinking as she spoke. Her mind whirred. "Families would get in to several schools that they applied to—not just one! The way it is, the private schools have a better chance of *their* first-choice family accepting—because if each family has only one choice—"

"Gabrielle! Stop it!"

Gabrielle shut up. She and Jocelyn stared at each other.

Jocelyn didn't mind being found out, so much. She just didn't like being punished for it. Or threatened—and she wasn't sure if that was what Gabrielle was doing. Or planning on doing.

Jocelyn's telephone rang. She didn't pick up. She focused on Gabrielle. The answering machine clicked on, and the call was recorded.

"Just tell me what to do to get Zachary in."

Jocelyn was tired. Of all of this.

"I'll tell you what . . ." Jocelyn tapped her pen on the desk. "I'll see what I can do."

Gabrielle smiled. She knew she had done it. She would be in. Jocelyn would see to it—she could just tell. She felt triumphant and proud.

"Thank you," said Gabrielle. "I appreciate it."

Gabrielle left. She walked through the children playing inside, then out into the schoolyard. She barely saw their individual faces. She was inwardly focused on her win.

Suddenly, she had a flash. She realized what Joey must have felt like when he was so desperate to keep his job that he would resort to anything—even hookers. This was the same thing.

Gabrielle took her cell phone from her purse and found the number for the rehab center. She dialed and asked for Joey. It took a few minutes for him to get on, but she used that time to find a private corner between two stores on Montana, where nobody would overhear her.

"Joe?"

"Gabrielle," he said. He sounded rested. "Hi."

"I miss you."

"You do?"

"I was just thinking of you, and I wanted to tell you that I love you."

"Really?" He was pleased and surprised, and not sure whether to trust her words. They were too good.

"I just understand, that's all. I understand why you did what you did."

"You do? What happened?"

"I just found myself wanting something really badly, and I would have done anything to get it. I understand how badly you wanted to do well at the studio," she said. "I know how much you wanted to make movies and keep your job."

"Gab," he said, "I don't want to make movies. I don't give a shit about my job. I just didn't want to lose you."

"What will you do?" she asked. "When you get out."

"I don't know," said Joey. "I figure something will come to me."

She hated this laissez-faire attitude. It wasn't what she wanted. She wanted him to be gangbusters. She wanted him to be a rocket. A missile. She wanted him to be different.

"I hope so," she said, fear coming back into her voice.

He heard it, even in its most subtle nuance. He was losing her. He could tell.

"I love you," he said. "I really do. How are the kids?"

"The kids . . ." She started to cry. "I'm having a helluva time, Joe."

"What's wrong?" He was worried and suddenly anxious.

"Getting Zachy into Crossroads is turning into a slim-to-nil chance. I don't know what I'll do if he doesn't get in. They don't like that you're in rehab."

"But the kids are okay, right?"

"The kids? Well, sure. But if Zach doesn't get into Crossroads—"

"They're not sick or hurt?"

"No!" said Gabrielle. "But, you know, this is a big deal."

"I'm coming home soon," he said.

"Good. I need you," she said, thinking of what suit would be appropriate for interviews at Crossroads, and maybe Brentwood as a second choice. And then Carl Thorpe as a backup. Or Curtis.

"You do?"

"I hope your Armani still fits—I think it'll be perfect for interviews," she said. "We're going to have to try to get in to see them all, even though the interviewing process is closed."

"Interview for jobs?"

"No!" said Gabrielle, frustrated. Why couldn't he understand? "For kindergarten, Joey! Kindergarten!"

Seventy-three

Eve crept out of the kitchen, and up the back staircase. She could hear the realtors greeting new potential buyers and their real estate agents. She didn't listen to their words. Just the tones. Jovial and hopeful. Those emotions sounded like a foreign language to her.

Eve made her way down the second-floor hall to the master bedroom. Her master bedroom. Her old master bedroom. She didn't want any of the open house people to see her. She was too exhausted and worried to produce another phony smile in hopes that someone would like her enough to buy her house. It was all a ruse, fading fast. Now, she scowled as she went into her bedroom and shut the door. She looked around at the bright airy room with the view from the windows of the Santa Monica Mountains in the distance. Palm trees and bougainvillea climbing Spanish-tiled roofs of neighbors' homes in the nearer distance. Tired, she went straight to her big, fluffy bed and jumped up on it. The mounds of pillows were inviting.

She remembered when this room used to be a haven. A treat. A luxury. Now, it was a scary place. You could never relax too much here. There was always the possibility that the big snake would show up.

She picked up the phone by the bedside and dialed a number she hadn't dialed in ages. The long-distance number rang differently on the wire. The sound was brittle and far away. A voice picked up.

" 'Lo?"

Eve listened hard. It was hard for her to imagine that her mother's voice was just one state over. It felt like a lifetime away.

"Hello? Anybody there? I'm hangin' up!"

"Mom," said Eve. "It's me. Eve."

"Eve!" Her mother was surprised to hear from her. "Did you hear the news? Tracey's pregnant. Six months along. Doesn't know the name of the father."

"You're kidding!" said Eve. It was like no time had passed between them. Her mother just launched right in. In a way, it was comforting. "Doesn't she have a boyfriend?"

"She did," said Betty. She sounded harassed. Eve could picture her standing in the kitchen talking on the old, yellow telephone. Placing her hand on one hip, changing positions with her feet, looking for a comfortable way to stand after standing all day. "They broke up, and she tried to make him jealous. Dated her brains out, and then they got back together, only she finds out she's pregnant, so Evan splits again."

"Is that her boyfriend's name? Evan?"

"Was," said Betty. "I'm out of my head about all this. I mean, the baby is good news, but I sure would like it if she was married. Hell, I don't have the energy to take care of another one, myself. Not even help out. I'm just tired."

"Why wasn't she using birth control, Mom?"

"You know I don't like talking about that kind of thing with you girls," said Betty. Eve could hear her mother take a sip of some drink. "Wooo, I burned myself on this coffee. You need coffee? You want me to pick some up and send it to you?"

"No, Mom." Eve smiled. "I have coffee here, but thanks."

"Anyways, it's just something you learn," said Betty, jumping topics. "I did."

"Were you a virgin when you married Dad?" Eve asked.

"Sure," said Betty. "Isn't everyone a virgin when they get married?"

Eve had to laugh. Her mother laughed with her. Eve couldn't remember her mother ever laughing with her. Not once.

"Anyway, forget about me. How are you? Is everything okay? How's that Jewish fella, Fuller?"

"Fuller's fine," Eve said, smiling. It was funny to her that Fuller had so many different facets, but all her parents could remember about him was that he was Jewish. "The kids are great, too. Did you get the pictures I sent?"

"They're up on the refrigerator," said Betty. "I'd love to come see them, but the trip is so hard. I've been having trouble with my hip lately. And your father's been having trouble remembering things. Driving me crazy. And now with Tracey's baby coming in only three months, she's gonna need me."

"I'll send you plane tickets, Ma," said Eve. "Would you come if I sent you tickets?"

"Well, sure," laughed Betty, not expecting that. "That'd be swell." She hesitated. "You sure your husband won't mind? I wouldn't want to come on any of his holidays—they have special holidays, y'know."

"He'd be happy if you came to visit," said Eve.

"I don't know," said Betty. "I don't know how Tracey'd make out without me. And your father."

"I miss you."

Silence. Betty didn't comprehend.

"How can you have time to miss me? Don't those kids o' yours keep you busy?"

"They're good kids," said Eve. "Ma . . . I'm tired, too."

"Shoot," said Betty. "You're too young t' be tired."

"I just . . . I don't know," said Eve. "Everything just gets— got—so complicated so fast. Like I didn't even see it coming." She didn't know how to tell her mother about the python and private school and the preschool, and her friends with their lives at rehab and fundraising, and the nannies—her mother wouldn't understand. Or wouldn't believe her.

Betty chuckled again, a sound Eve wasn't used to hearing.

"I know what you're talking about," said Betty quietly. Eve knew that Betty didn't know. Even if she said she did. Eve couldn't imagine Betty understanding a fraction of what her life had become.

"Everything's so different."

Eve heard a noise in the master bathroom. It was a shaking noise. Like pills in a bottle. Her heart leaped to her throat. The python.

"Ma, I gotta go," said Eve.

"All right, honey," said Betty. "You take care, alright?"

"Love you, Ma."

"Love you, too, sugar."

They hung up, and Eve tiptoed, quietly, slowly, to the bathroom door, expecting to see the giant snake. She looked in—and saw a man, well-dressed and -groomed, standing in front of her medicine cabinet, taking prescription medications from the shelves and pocketing them.

Eve must have gasped, because he suddenly turned and saw her there. His hands were full of pills, his pockets bulging with bottles. He spilled some as he turned to face Eve. The pills fell to the floor, and rolled around on the tiles. He didn't pick them up.

"What are you doing?" she gasped.

"Get out of here," said the man. He finished loading his back-pack from her medicine cabinet, cleaning up what was fallen on the floor. Scooping it up, randomly, and dumping it in his back-pack. "Scram."

Eve realized that he thought she was a broker.

"I'm calling the police," said Eve, and went to the phone by the bed.

"Wait," said the man. "Wait, don't."

She turned. At a little more distance, she saw that he didn't look like a junkie or a burglar. He looked like someone she'd meet at a party or a premiere. In fact, he looked vaguely familiar.

"I'm sorry," he said, trying to recover. He stuck out his hand to shake hers. "I'm Eric Jeeves. I work at Allstar Studios. I'm a producer."

Eve looked at his hand, and didn't shake it.

"This isn't what it looks like," he said, trying to recover.

But Eve didn't buy it. Not for a second. She was scared. Es-pecially when he started to laugh. He looked crazy. Sick. She backed up toward the bed.

"Look," he said, coming toward her, thinking he could just calm her down a little—he didn't need this getting all over town. "I don't blame you for being mad. I must have scared the shit out of you."

"Why are you taking my medicine?" she asked, backing up.

"I wasn't taking it—I was just looking."

"You had it in your pockets. You were filling your bag with it. Do you go around to open houses and raid medicine cabinets?"

"Look, this *is* an open house," he said with real bravado and implied violence. This was no longer a conversation. It was a struggle. They both felt it. "I want to buy this place. So don't give me a hard time, lady."

She went for the door, but he blocked her way out of the room. She slowly changed her direction to get the phone. But he reached around her for it. She felt him touch her as he went for the phone. She could smell his cologne. He reached past her and grabbed the phone off the nightstand, and yanked it away so she couldn't dial. The phone fell onto the floor between them. Eve panicked.

"No problem," she said, reaching behind her for the nightstand. She knew the gun was in the top drawer in the lock box. "I'll just be out of your way—I need my address book."

He went around the bed to get the other telephone, while Eve quickly fumbled with the combination on the lock box, trying to make sure he didn't see what she was doing. The box opened smoothly. The gun was inside. She didn't pick it up. Not yet. If she picked it up, she would cross some line. She would have picked it up, with intent to use it. She'd never used a gun in her life.

"I was just checking the medicine cabinets," he said, still trying to extricate himself from the situation, even after he'd violently yanked the phone from the wall. "My wife likes well-made fixtures. Built-ins, especially."

Eve turned to face him. She needed to see him, to make sure he wasn't going to attack her. She felt the gun in her hands behind her. She removed the childproof lock on the trigger without him seeing. Keeping her face to him, the gun behind her back. Her hands were shaking. She'd only done this once or twice, when Fuller had taught her after he'd bought the gun. Jeeves saw she was doing something behind her back at the nightstand. Something she didn't want him to see.

"Hey, what are you doing?"

She didn't answer.

Now he panicked.

"I said, what the fuck are you doing??"

He moved toward her, and, shaking, she raised the gun with one hand, then used her other hand to steady herself. She aimed the gun at Jeeves. He froze.

"Don't touch me," she said, her voice wavering, but also gaining strength. She didn't have an opportunity here to worry, analyze, or second-guess. This was immediate danger.

Jeeves instinctively backed up when he saw the gun. He had never had anyone pull a gun on him in his life. The gun looked like a toy, but he could tell it wasn't. Not from the weapon itself, but from the way Eve was focused. She was intent. He knew that he had to do something fast.

"Look," he said, faking calm. "I know you don't know me, but it would be really awful for me if you called the police," he said. "It would kill my career."

"Stay back!" she yelled, wondering why none of the realtors who were constantly in her face and denying her privacy here didn't show up now.

"Maybe there's something I can do to make this work out for both of us," Jeeves suggested.

"Put my pills down," she said. He took what he had from his pockets, and dumped them on the bed between them.

"Done." He smiled.

Eve couldn't believe that he didn't even act nervous. She crouched down and picked the phone up off the floor with one hand, keeping the gun aimed at him. She hit nine-one-one on the dial pad. Jeeves recognized the three numbers. Emergency. Police.

He panicked and lunged for her.

Eve reacted. She pulled the trigger.

"Hello? Hello? This is the emergency operator. Is anybody there?" The voice from the phone on the floor was small, but it was the only voice that Eve heard.

"Is anybody there? Is this an emergency? Hello?"

Seventy-four

Jeeves fell to the floor. He was half sitting up, leaning on his good arm, looking intently at his bloody arm and then back to Eve, who clutched the gun and recovered the phone receiver. Jeeves got back up, and lunged again. He grabbed the phone from Eve.

Frightened, she scuffled backward to get away from him. She still held the gun, but he scared her.

Jeeves sat on the floor, wincing in pain. He took the telephone in his good hand and smashed it against the floor, as hard as he could, until it broke. The plastic cracked.

Eve watched him, horrified. She held the gun aimed at him. He lay on the floor with the phone, breathing hard. Not sure what to do next. He was angry.

"Help!" Eve screamed out to anyone in the house who could hear. She didn't recognize the sound of her own voice. She smelled the gunpowder, smoking, but she didn't put the gun down, even with Jeeves, shot, on the floor.

"I'm not going to hurt you!" he said.

"Help! Somebody!!" she yelled again, louder.

"Stop it! Don't call anyone," he said, still trying to get to her. To shut her up. Even though he was shot, he could still move toward her. Eve got up and started to run out of the room, but a realtor ran up the stairs and into the bedroom at the same time.

"What happened?" the realtor asked, as Eve ran out, past her.

"Call the police," said Eve, and went for the phone in the upstairs den.

The realtor looked in the master bedroom, took one glance at Jeeves on the floor, bleeding, and shook her head.

"Oh, shit," she said, pulling back and shutting the door so any prospective buyers who were inspecting during the open house wouldn't see. "Everything's fine, just a little domestic quarrel."

"Call the police!" Eve spat at the realtor from halfway down the hall.

"Will you put that goddamn gun away," the realtor whispered, furious.

Eve realized she was still holding the gun.

"You're going to scare the customers," the realtor hissed.

"That man is shot in there," said Eve.

"I've got a very interested couple in the kitchen right this second," said the realtor. "Do you realize how much work that was for me?"

Eve stared in disbelief.

"She's right," said Jeeves, nodding at the realtor. He had gotten to the door and pushed it wide open with his foot.

Eve gasped, and raised the gun at him again.

"This kind of thing could kill a sale," said Jeeves. The realtor and Eve stared at him in disbelief. "I noticed you've already made a couple of reductions."

The realtor extended her hand to Jeeves, who was still on the floor. "Betty Burger," she said. "I'm with John Douglas."

"Eric Jeeves," he said, shaking her hand.

Eve couldn't believe this. She had just shot a man, and he was trying to help close a deal on her house—as he lay, bleeding, on the floor in her bedroom.

"I think I know your wife," Betty lied. It was a line she always used on men she met in business. It kept them from hitting on her, and it kept the family theme going, which was important because, in the end, it was families that gave her the most business.

"Really?" asked Jeeves. "Which one?"

"The first wife," said Betty. She knew from experience that that was a safe line. There was always a first wife.

"Are you both out of your minds?!" screamed Eve.

They looked at her, like she was the one who didn't get it.

"Will you please put the gun away," said the realtor. "And stop playing Peggy Lipton or Charlie's Angels, or whatever the latest girl with guns show is."

She and Jeeves shared a laugh. Eve put the gun down. This was insane, but it didn't look dangerous.

"I could use a couple of Tylenols, myself," said Jeeves, nodding at the gunshot wound. "Got any?"

"I'll look in the bathroom," said Betty and left. "Do you own or rent?" she asked Jeeves, as she disappeared into the bathroom.

"I'm calling the police!" screamed Eve, and, still carrying the gun, she walked straight downstairs, into the kitchen. The sight of Eve with the gun sent prospective buyers fleeing. With shrieks. Eve didn't care.

"That's a gun! She has a gun!"

"Yeah, and it's not included in the sale," said Eve. She'd had it.

Disheveled, and sweaty, she picked up the telephone in the kitchen and slammed the gun down on the counter. She dialed nine-one-one; after that, she dialed Fuller.

"You better get home," she said into the phone, spinning the gun around on the kitchen island and wiping the damp hair on her forehead. She smelled her hair. It smelled of burnt gunpowder. "I'm having a really bad day."

"Do you want me to get you an acupuncture session for tonight?" Fuller asked, concerned. "Or an adjustment?"

"No," said Eve. "A lawyer."

Seventy-five

Fuller drove home fast. He found Eve sitting in the back seat of a police squad car in front of the house. She had already cried. Her face was pale, her makeup smeared and mostly washed away; she was a wreck. The police officer greeted Fuller.

"She's fine, just a little shaken."

Fuller smiled noncommittally and got into the back seat with Eve.

"What happened?" he asked her.

"Oh, Fuller, I shot an independent producer."

"What?!"

"He was stealing drugs from our bathroom, and I walked in on him. I thought he was a robber or something, and he tried to get the phone away from me, and I was scared, and so I got the gun and shot at him. I think he has a first-look deal at Allstar."

"Did you kill him?" Fuller asked, amazed.

Eve stared at him. She hadn't thought of this. Her heart started beating fast, and her breathing shallowed.

"Oh my God, I don't think so. I don't know."

Fuller started to visibly sweat. His mind reeled through the lawyers he knew. Criminal defense lawyers. He started thinking about bail money.

"I mean, we were talking after he was shot. He said he needed some Tylenol. They took him to the hospital. Do you think I killed him? Do you think he died after he left? Oh, my God. Fuller, do you think I'm a murderer?"

"No, no! Calm down, honey. It was self-defense." He hoped.

Eve burst into tears. This was all too much.

"I'll take care of everything," said Fuller, as he held her and tried to stop her crying. "It *was* self-defense, wasn't it?"

"Yes!" said Eve, looking at him like he was nuts that he could think it was anything but. Fuller grabbed her shoulders and looked hard into her eyes. "It'll all work out," he said, and then he kissed her. "Don't worry. Not for one second."

"Thank you," she said.

"I'll take care of everything. Don't worry. You've had too much . . . just too much. I'm sorry."

"Thank you," she said.

"I'll be back. Will you be all right?"

She nodded, so he left her in the car, and went out into the fray. To take care of things.

The night turned into a flurry of publicists, lawyers, and law enforcement agents. When the press showed up, everyone who was integral to the case convened inside the house. Eve had to answer some questions, then Fuller sent her up to bathe and go to sleep.

"Do you feel safe in the house?" he asked before she ascended the stairs.

Eve just stared at him, blankly.

"We haven't slept in this house since Stella's party. Since the snake escaped. Do you want to go back to the hotel?"

Eve shook her head.

"I'm tired of running away from that stupid snake," she said. "Where are the kids?"

"At the hotel. With Esperanza."

Eve nodded. She knew that they would be fine. She was grateful for her help.

"Where're all the people?"

"The news media set up camp at the curb, outside," said Fuller. "Keep the blinds shut."

"I'll wait for you," she said. "I'll just rest up there."

He kissed her on the forehead, and she went up.

After she showered, Eve got into bed, under crisp white sheets. She was clean, scrubbed from head to foot. No makeup. No perfume. No clothes. Just naked under the sheets. She stared at the bloody stain on the carpet where Jeeves had lain, shot.

She must have dozed off, because when Fuller came into the room, it was close to three in the morning.

"So here's the deal," said Fuller. He paced.

"I'll recarpet tomorrow," she said, turning on a light.

"What?" Fuller wasn't following.

"We can't sell the house with that," she said, pointing at the stain. "I bet Gabrielle knows someone who can recarpet on no notice."

"Eve," said Fuller, sitting on the bed next to her. "Listen to me. This is important."

"Oh, Fuller," she said, suddenly realizing. "I bet this is going to be on the news tomorrow! We'll never sell the house if this is on the news! We'll never sell the house now. This place is cursed!"

"Maybe it is," said Fuller. "But we're not."

He took her hand, and held her face so she had to listen.

"This guy you shot was an accident waiting to happen," Fuller said. "He doesn't want any publicity—at all. He's embarrassed. He's in enough hot water with other things you don't even need to know about."

"Like what?"

Fuller hesitated.

"*What?*"

"Hookers, phony studio deals, drug use, stealing—"

"And now I've shot this guy. Shit, Fuller, we're freaks."

"Only by association."

He had made a joke. She didn't find it funny. She didn't even get it.

"Am I in trouble?" she asked.

"No," he said. "You didn't really do anything wrong. Except that I didn't have a proper permit for the gun. But everyone knows about the python, and none of those police officers could blame us for having one. They're going to help me around that."

"I want the gun out of the house. Nancy was right. She told me to get rid of it."

"Already done," said Fuller. "I donated it to the police department."

"We'll never sell the house now," said Eve, biting her nails. "First the python, now a shooting in the bedroom." She reached for a bottle of Evian by the bed.

"The house is sold," said Fuller.

Eve was shocked. "What?!"

"We're going to sign a legal agreement not to talk about what happened tonight—to anyone." He glared at her, intently. "That includes your friends."

"My friends?"

"It includes the press. That includes any million-dollar offers from *Hard Copy* or anywhere else."

Eve didn't say anything. She just swallowed.

"And I am going to give Jeeves a deal at my studio."

"What?!" said Eve. She was wide awake now. "He tried to rob us! He made me shoot him!"

"And he is going to buy our house," said Fuller.

"What?!?!?" Eve couldn't believe it. The air went out of her body.

"We made a deal. We worked out a fair price." Fuller was speaking slowly, and emphasizing every word. He was giving her a lot of information, and he needed her to understand it. Even under all the circumstances of the past twenty-four hours. "This guy—he doesn't care about the python—we're lucky to unload the house at all."

"But he's a drug addict, Fuller—he was stealing drugs."

"He has agreed to undergo massive counseling. He'll do rehab. He'll do parole—"

"Fuller!"

"Eve, what do you want? This is a messy situation, and I did the best I could. I think that under the circumstances, I did a pretty goddamn good job."

She felt badly. She saw how tired he was.

"I've hired special publicists to work out some story about the shooting, everything," Fuller said. "It will be on the news."

"But you sold the house?!" said Eve. She couldn't believe it.

"Yes. It's part of the deal—but you have to keep your part of the bargain," said Fuller. "You can't talk about this to your friends. It has to be our secret. You, me, Jeeves, and the lawyers."

"Okay," said Eve, but she was speechless. Fuller tried to see behind her eyes. He needed her to comprehend and cooperate. He was worried that she would tell her friends. He knew how close she was with Gabrielle and Nancy, and those women scared him. He didn't trust them, but he knew that she did, and he knew that, after all that had just happened, she was going to need to talk. If she did, the deal would be broken.

"This is a very important deal, Eve."

She nodded.

"Now what?" she asked.

"Now, we are going to take a nice long vacation," said Fuller. "To Hawaii. Until this all blows over."

Eve tried to process everything. She was close to overload.

"But what about the fundraiser for the school?"

Fuller was silent. He just stared at her. Hard.

"Hello? Are you there?" she asked. "Fuller, I can't abandon the school."

He didn't answer. Just looked her straight in the eye. His silence was frustrating.

"Yup," he said, finally. "I am definitely here."

"I don't like this deal," she said.

"That's the thing about deals," he said. "You don't get everything. You never do."

"Okay," said Eve. She took a deep breath, and then another one. "I understand, but I wasn't in on the negotiations—I wasn't represented."

Fuller started to laugh. They were both glad for the opportunity.

"I planned to chair the charity luncheon, honey."

"I know," he said.

"I'll go to Hawaii . . . but can we come back in time for me to throw the lunch? It's not for me. It's the charity. And I won't talk to anyone—I won't breathe a word of this. I promise.''

Fuller looked at her. She squirmed a little.

''I promise,'' she repeated.

Seventy-six

The weather was unbearably warm in Beverly Hills. The air was dry. Drier and hotter than normal. Record highs, said the weatherman. The news showed ways people were keeping cool, and warned of dehydration. This was not a typical winter. The rain just wasn't coming.

But, despite the heat, every person who emerged from their expensive cars at the Peninsula Hotel looked cool. They were all beautifully dressed and made up behind their requisite sunglasses. The circular driveway at the hotel was so jammed with cars, and the women in them were so eager to get into the hotel, they were just leaving their cars with the keys in the ignition. Not bothering to wait for a claim ticket. Not bothering to turn their motors off. They left their cars, doors open, letting huge blasts of icy air conditioning hit the valet parkers who ran from car to car to car.

The parkers wore wool vested uniforms and sweated, with gritted teeth, trying not to burn tire rubber as they moved the cars out of the driveway as quickly as they could. They knew that, later, these ladies would tip fives, tens, and twenties if they had a good time, and more than one glass of wine with lunch.

Inside the hotel, the sunlight was gone. The lobby was dim and the entrance felt cavelike—but exclusively so.

The Sparkle and Shine luncheon to benefit Los Angeles children born drug-addicted and with special learning challenges, was held in the Garden Ballroom. As the luncheon-goers got close, the din of a thousand ladies, and a few devoted men, was near deafening. Sparkle and Shine volunteers distributed name tags with table seating assignments, and encouraged the women to purchase raffle tickets or other items for sale in the lobby. All to benefit the charity.

The sound of air kissing was matched only by the noise

of checks being ripped from checkbooks, as raffle tickets were bought.

The dining room had fifty tables set for lunch, with twelve seats at each table. Each table was festive and bright. Colorful center-pieces were wrapped raffle ticket prizes. The enormous crystal chandelier, designed like a tree with thousands of crystal leaves, twinkled magically. The room looked like a fairy tale.

Nancy had had a glass of wine in the limo on the way over, and another in the lobby just minutes before. She weaved as she made her way to her table.

"Eve!"

Eve turned in her seat at the head table, where she was re-hearsing the welcome speech she was going to give as chair-woman of the charity lunch. She had dressed more Melrose than usual. She wore an Azzadine Alaia dress that accentuated her pregnant-with-her-third-baby belly. She also defied motherhood with very sexy black shoes. Her clothes lent a capricious air to her fundraiser mom spirit. She'd also chosen Fuller's Tom Ford Gucci clothes herself, forcing him to shed his Armani serious-movie-guy look for this lunch. She'd wanted something different, and she got it. In her clothes, anyway.

She waved at her friend. Nancy was busting out of a too-small Jill Sanders number, and Gabrielle, coming up behind her, was wearing something similar. They made their way across the room to Eve.

Nancy was out of breath and pale. She tried to remember when she used to meet Landon here for sex. It seemed like a lifetime ago. She remembered being naked beneath a coat, tripping through the lobby, feeling like any minute hotel security was go-ing to arrest her, knowing she was just meeting her husband in their usual room. This was where March was conceived.

"I'm so glad you're here," said Eve. "I've missed you both."

Eve kissed Nancy on the cheek. "You're sweating!"

"I'm feeling a little . . . you know," said Nancy, fanning her face with the Sparkle and Shine luncheon program. "But I would never miss your first fundraiser."

"Eve!" Fuller called her from across the room. Eve looked over. Fuller was talking to a group of men in suits. The only group of men in the whole place.

"Excuse me," said Eve to her girlfriends.

"What's that?" Gabrielle said, grabbing Nancy's arm and turning it over, exposing the Rug Rats Band-Aid on the inside of her elbow.

"Nothing," said Nancy. She pulled her arm away. "Which is our table? I forgot to get a place card on the way in."

"Here," said Gabrielle, leading her to their table. "I know you're too old for a polio vaccine," she continued, "and heroin addicts don't go in for Rug Rats brand Band-Aids."

"Just some blood work," said Nancy, distractedly.

"You're pregnant again, aren't you?" asked Gabrielle, wide-eyed. Nancy was thin as a rail, but Gabrielle had seen her friend pregnant and this thin before. "I don't believe it."

"I'm not," said Nancy.

"You had a pregnancy test," said Gabrielle, grabbing Nancy's arm for proof.

Nancy yanked her arm away, and didn't argue. She was too tired to argue. It was easier to let Gabrielle believe whatever she wanted. "Where's my seat?"

"Here we are," said Gabrielle. They sat at the table Nancy had purchased as a gift to Eve. She had paid twelve hundred dollars for the twelve seats, and gave the hundred-dollar tickets to all the preschool teachers. The teachers now sat excitedly, but uncomfortably, watching the mothers who did this kind of luncheon fluently and knew the drill.

"Will you look at that?" Gabrielle was staring intently across the room. Nancy followed her gaze.

Nancy saw Eve at a back table greeting some guests, all dressed in non-Armani, off-the-rack suits.

"Our little Evie is working this room," Nancy said with a hint of pride in her voice.

They watched. Eve was definitely shmoozing. "Who are they?"

"The entire board of directors and some of the admissions committee from Brentwood School," said Gabrielle, quietly. "I can't believe she invited them here. I never knew she had it in her."

"Well, she's had to be doing something," said Nancy. "I mean, she's pretty much written us out of her book. Has she called you?"

"Called me? No," said Gabrielle. "She doesn't even return my calls."

In fact, Eve had flaked out on all the fundraiser committees she'd volunteered for. She'd left brief messages that she wouldn't be able to "fulfill her committee obligations." A bright and breezy "Sorry" was all the explanation she gave. Sometimes, she mumbled some excuse about having her plate too full already. Whatever it was, it wasn't like her. Everyone said so.

"Did you know she's not at the Bel Air anymore?" said Gabrielle. "She checked out, and didn't tell us. I had to find out from the front desk."

"She has an answering service," said Nancy. "But she doesn't return my calls, either."

"If I didn't see the nanny driving the children around, I'd think she'd dropped off the face of the planet."

"Except for all this," said Nancy.

"Which she did entirely without us," said Gabrielle. She didn't like it. Not a bit. "I heard they want her at Cedars-Sinai to do their Myofacial Pain fundraiser."

"Really," said Nancy. "And now she's shmoozing the admissions committee to Brentwood like a professional politician. I never knew Eve had it in her."

"Come on, Gabrielle," said Nancy. "We all have it in us."

"Look!" said Gabrielle, suddenly, and pointed Nancy carefully in a different direction, to a woman making out with a tall, handsome man in a suit. They were standing in the corner, out of the fray, but still, the only ones in the room who were necking.

"Who is that?" Nancy asked, trying to focus on the couple. But as soon as she asked, the woman turned around. It was Jocelyn.

"Oh my God," Nancy and Gabrielle said at the same time, and grabbed each other.

As the waiters served grilled salmon lunches, Jocelyn disengaged from the man, and they said their goodbyes. Jocelyn made her way toward the table, where she sat next to Nancy. Everyone at the table was eating. Nancy ordered another glass of wine.

"How are you?" Jocelyn asked Nancy discreetly and meaningfully. The others didn't notice. They were focusing on the envelope that was passed around the table. The mothers laughed and plucked twenty-dollar bills from their purses, stuffing them into the envelope, and at the same time, taking numbered slips from the same envelope to see who would win the centerpiece raffle prizes later.

"How are you?" Nancy asked back.

"I have a boyfriend!" said Jocelyn. She looked like a different person. She was happy and relaxed.

"We saw," said Gabrielle. "Who is he?"

"Oh, you saw him?" Jocelyn giggled. "Isn't he adorable?"

"He's very handsome," said Gabrielle. "Who is he and how did you meet him? And why haven't we seen him before?"

"He's an ear, nose, throat guy," said Jocelyn. "George introduced me, and he doesn't hang in Hollywood circles."

"George introduced you?"

"Foster," said Jocelyn.

"How did George know him?" Nancy asked.

"George had a sore throat." Jocelyn laughed. "And as you know, no Hollywood producer worth his salt would take vitamin C or suck on a Sucrets and just get some rest. They call—"

"A specialist!" Gabrielle, Nancy, and Jocelyn all said at the same time.

"How long has this been going on?" Gabrielle asked, as they calmed down.

"Couple months," said Jocelyn. "Maybe more. George and Amanda set me up. It was a blind date."

Gabrielle's head swiveled around as she tried to get a better look at him. "What's his name?"

"His name is Glenn. Dr. Glenn Heiser."

"And you kept this from us?"

"Not intentionally," said Jocelyn. "I've just been busy." She giggled. "Anyway, I'm telling you now."

"Is he sitting at our table?" Gabrielle asked, immediately looking for a free chair.

"No," said Jocelyn. "He had a colleague in from out of town here today, so he stopped by to see his friend, and me. He's got patients. He can't stay."

The envelope came their way. Jocelyn had her twenty-dollar bill ready. So did Gabrielle. Nancy had two twenties.

"I think I'm in love—I can't believe it. I mean, I was so skeptical. I've dated so much. Why would Glenn be any different from anyone else I've been with? You know?"

"Maybe it wasn't Glenn who was different," said Nancy.

Gabrielle looked at Nancy with different eyes. It wasn't like Nancy to have an insight like this. Then she looked at Jocelyn. It wasn't like Jocelyn to be happy like this. Gabrielle felt jealous.

The envelope came to her, and she became busy putting in her money, taking out her raffle tickets and getting the attention of the woman on her other side to pass it along to.

"Did they schedule your surgery?" Jocelyn leaned over and asked Nancy.

"Tomorrow," said Nancy quietly.

"Tomorrow?" Jocelyn was surprised.

"Why not tomorrow?" Nancy smiled.

"Right," said Jocelyn, and squeezed her hand. Nancy fought back a tear. "Did you tell anyone?" Jocelyn asked.

"Uh-uh," said Nancy, shaking her head no. "Landon'll stay with the kids."

"How about . . . ?" Jocelyn nodded toward Gabrielle.

Nancy shook her head no. "I don't want to worry her," she said. "Or Eve. They have enough going on in their own lives."

"Yeah, but this is important," said Jocelyn.

"I'll be fine," said Nancy.

All of a sudden, everything started to move. It was a jolt and a loud noise that came from everywhere—above, below, in the kitchen, in the lobby. Stuff falling, the huge, practically room-sized chandelier tinkling dangerously. Then the voices. Murmurs grew louder. Some voices raised. A few screams.

Everyone grabbed on to something—a chair, a purse, each other—as the eerie rolling motion got violent and then slower. Some people ran, but then stopped, when they realized there was nowhere to run. This was an earthquake, and for those who'd lived in Los Angeles for more than a decade, they knew it was less than a seven but more than a five on the Richter scale.

Nancy loved it. She was the only one smiling in delight. A ride! Unpredictable, and she had a front-row seat. She even gave a little war whoop.

"What do you think?" She turned to Gabrielle. "A five?"

Gabrielle just sighed. She hoped she would be able to get a ride home with someone, because everyone was going to jam the valet parking guys at once now.

Jocelyn hoped the foundation bolting at the preschool held. She tried to remember where she had filed the insurance company forms just in case.

"I better go," said Jocelyn and left them both. "I need to check the school."

Eve grabbed hold of Fuller and burst into tears. She'd never been through anything like this before. She immediately thought of her children.

"It's just an earthquake," said Fuller, watching the chandelier above. It was swinging now. He knew that the bolt that held it in place was strong, but he wasn't sure how much swinging it could endure before it gave way. If the chandelier fell, there would be many injuries.

"This is awful." Eve wept, frightened.

"It's just your first time, that's all," he said, kissing her hair, but still watching the light fixture above.

"The chandelier!" someone yelled.

Everyone looked up and watched the ceiling. New fright swept the room. People rushed the doorway to try and get out.

"What should we do?" Eve asked Fuller. She was pale. "What are we supposed to do?"

"I don't know," said Fuller, gripping Eve, watching the chandelier. "I hope that doesn't . . . oh, shit. I think it's going to . . . let's get out of here."

Fuller pushed Eve ahead of him, and into the furthest corner to get out of the way of the chandelier, should it fall.

"The chandelier!" someone else yelled. It was a man. "Get away!"

The major jolts and rolling stopped considerably, but the room still moved back and forth, slowly, as if it were a small ball in someone's palm, sliding back and forth. Every table was covered with spilled drinks. People were helping each other up.

The panic subsided, as everyone realized the worst was over. Now was just the weirdness. The rolling. A few smaller jolts. Cell phones were zipped out. Everyone dialed someone.

"Can you get a signal?"

"Can anyone get an outside line?"

"Can I borrow your phone?"

The cell phone calls went through and everyone was safe. Property was broken and lost. There were some cuts, scrapes, and bruises. A few twisted ankles, necks, and wrists. Car alarms got stuck in alarm mode all over the city.

Outside of the Sparkle and Shine luncheon, one by one everyone turned on television news. The anchormen were all in their element, cutting back and forth between the butch-looking earthquake expert at Cal State Northridge, insert shots of the Richter scale needle shooting wildly up and down every time an aftershock occurred, and then, one by one, reaction shots of real people and real lives. Store shelves where groceries had fallen. Personal accounts of where individuals had been, what they felt, when this earthquake had hit.

Nature democratized Los Angeles. It brought everyone together. Without warning. Earthquakes were the city's curse and its gift. Everyone's stories were listened to equally. From neighborhood to neighborhood, people recounted past earthquakes.

On the freeway, Landon had been out in his Rolls-Royce when the earthquake hit. He didn't take the Rolls out often. It had been nothing but trouble since he'd bought it. The engine had been replaced already. The brakes were no good. When the car started rocking back and forth, Landon cursed the car, and made the driver pull over to the shoulder of the road and check under the hood. Then he called Rolls-Royce on the car phone and threatened to sue them because now the car was shifting to the left *and* to the right.

That's when call waiting interrupted.

"Did you feel it? Wasn't it great?"

Landon recognized his soon-to-be-ex-wife's voice. They were waiting for the paperwork to make the divorce legal, but they already lived their lives separately. It was as good as done. "Nancy?"

"Where are you?"

"In the fucking Rolls. The sonofabitch car is acting up again. It's got this rocking action going. I think it needs a new carburetor or something."

Nancy started to laugh. "Landon, your car isn't acting up. We just had an earthquake."

"What earthquake?" he said, looking outside. Some cars had pulled over, and everyone was on their cell phones.

"You'll find out," she said. "I just called to see if you were still alive. I was hoping that maybe a chimney had fallen on you or something."

"Nice sentiment," he said. He liked it when she was like this. Slightly mean. "Thanks for the call."

"Not that it matters. I suppose I'm out of the will—but I could take the kids on some extraordinary shopping sprees if you got killed. They're still in."

"You'd like that, wouldn't you?" he said. He got aroused when she was like this. It had been a long time.

"No," she admitted. "But you would. I bet you have a big erection, just thinking about it."

"You want to do something about it?"

"Yeah," she said, and hung up the phone on him, laughing to herself.

"Bitch," he murmured, wondering if she'd consider dating him again.

Back in the ballroom, Fuller had maneuvered Eve along the periphery of the room, and out the door into the lobby, where there were no large light fixtures. A few crystal leaves had fallen off the chandelier, and everyone had screamed, but no one was really hurt.

"I'll call home," he said.

"Let's get out of here," said Eve.

"You're the hostess," said Fuller. "You can't just leave."

A thought hit Eve and she realized something for the first time. "Fuller, I don't want to be the hostess anymore. I just want a simple life."

"You sure?" he asked.

"I've had a taste of all this," she said.

"You're very good at it."

"Yeah." She sighed. "But it's getting the best of me."

"You mean, there's even more of you—even better than this?" She hugged him hard. She was shaken, but also centered.

"I love you," she said to him. "I loved you when I thought you were unemployed."

"What?" He didn't understand.

"When we first met—at the restaurant—I didn't know if you had a job. I didn't know our life would be like this."

"I loved you when you were a waitress," he said.

"Is it cruel of me to want to put all of this behind me? Even the charity?" she wondered.

"You'll do charity," said Fuller. "In your own way. In your own time."

"Right." She nodded. Everything seemed clearer than it did before the earthquake. "Let's go."

"You sure you're ready?"

"Fuller, I'm so ready, you wouldn't believe it," she said, starting to walk. "You coming?"

"Yeah," he said without a second's hesitation. "Right behind you."

Seventy-seven

$\mathcal{M}$arch twenty-first was a red-letter day.

Jocelyn took her phone off the hook and went out of town. She did not want to be reachable on this particular day. She drove to the Four Seasons Hotel in Carlsbad, where Glenn had booked a room for them for the weekend. She waited for him to finish seeing patients and drive out to join her. She swam laps in the pool while she waited. She missed volleyball, and planned to take him to the beach when summer came. She wanted to play again. Get her body moving without thinking of anything except the ball. Without thinking of anything that had to do with her work. Her school. She knew that her name would be repeated millions of times today—in praise, in blame, in wonder. Today was the day that Hollywood moms would find out their children's fates for the next seven years.

The mailmen knew it. It was hard not to. All over town mothers waited on corners, sipping Starbucks, wearing workout clothes, flagging down their mailmen, trying to get their mail first. There was adrenaline in the air. Desperation coupled with excitement. Sometimes the mothers sent their housekeepers to meet the mailmen, with strict instructions to *run* right back home, as soon as they had the mail in hand. Others met their mailmen personally. Their eyes were bright, their hair wild, their hands outstretched while the mailmen sorted through the mail, looking for that particular mother's mail.

Once they had their little stash in hand, their focus was solely on the admissions letters. They snatched, rifled through, and pounced until they found what they wanted. Some waited to get home to tear the envelopes open. Others did it right there, on the street corner, ready to show the world (or whomever was walking or driving by), where their children had gotten in to school.

Gabrielle got one fat letter and five thin ones. Everyone knew that the fat letters contained admissions applications and schedules. The thin ones, rejection letters. Polite but meaningless wait lists.

"We got Crossroads!" Gabrielle screamed. Nobody answered. Consuela was out with the children. Joey wasn't there. Gabrielle dialed Nancy. Landon answered the telephone.

"Landon?"

"Yeah. You looking for Nancy?"

"I'm just surprised that you're there," said Gabrielle. She couldn't imagine a reconciliation, but stranger things had happened.

"Nancy's out of town," said Landon.

"She is?" Gabrielle was shocked twice in one call, now. "Where?"

"Didn't she tell you?" But Landon immediately knew she hadn't.

"She might have," Gabrielle bluffed. "But it's been so busy—did she hear about March? About schools?"

"Oh, that—yeah. March is going to Mirman."

"Mirman? What's Mirman?" Gabrielle panicked. She had missed a school, but that was impossible.

"She'll tell you all about it," said Landon, "when she gets back."

Gabrielle hung up the phone, unsettled. What the hell was Mirman? And where was Nancy? She picked up the phone and dialed Eve. Nothing. She left a message on the machine. Then dialed Jocelyn at home. Nothing again. She left another message. Damn it, thought Gabrielle. What the hell is the use of getting something good when there's no one to share it with? She thought of Joey, but did nothing. She sat there, alone, with her success in an envelope on her lap, and wondered what had happened.

"Oh my God! We got Crossroads!" screamed Eve. She was immediately embarrassed for buying into the excitement, but she couldn't help it. She liked being part of the group. Even if the group was, well, warped. It was still like a family. She knew that she wouldn't be sending Stella there. She wanted to tell her friends everything she'd been going through, but she couldn't. Only with Fuller could she share. They were bound together by everything that had happened. But when she beeped into her answering service, and heard Gabrielle's call, she quickly dialed her back. She missed Gabrielle. She missed their friendship—or what she remembered it used to be.

"We both got Crossroads—Eve, that's so great!" said Gabrielle, thrilled with the call. It couldn't have been better news.

Eve didn't share the fact that she would not be sending Stella. She just wanted to be in the moment of acceptance. Just for now.

"You can't believe the anxiety I've been through," said Gabrielle. "I am just so relieved. I really didn't think I could do this all by myself."

"By yourself?" Eve asked.

"Joey wasn't much of a help," said Gabrielle. "Between you and me. I mean, if anything, at this point, he was more of a liability."

"Does he know? Is he excited?" asked Eve.

"No," said Gabrielle. "I haven't told him."

Eve didn't even consider this strange behavior from Gabrielle. That everyone knew Joey was in rehab, and nobody talked about it—least of all Gabrielle, who didn't even admit it—was just the way things worked.

"How about Nancy?" Eve asked.

"Nancy's out of town," said Gabrielle. "And Landon's with the kids. He said March is going to Mirman."

"Mirman? What's Mirman?" asked Eve.

"I didn't know either—it's for gifted kids," said Gabrielle. "I did a little research."

"Gifted?" Eve was confused. "March is gifted? At what?"

"Apparently everything," said Gabrielle. "She had to take an I.Q. test to get in."

"Can Stella take the I.Q. test?" Eve asked. Her heart was racing. She'd never felt so competitive. "I mean, do you think she should?" Eve was immediately aware and ashamed of the question.

"I don't know," said Gabrielle. "I don't see why not. But—"

"I don't get it," Eve interrupted. "March Greene is a genius?"

"Don't ask me," said Gabrielle. "According to Mirman she is. But—"

"That kid's going to end up in jail one day," Eve interrupted again. "She's got that look."

"Eve!" Gabrielle scolded her, but laughed at the same time. "Do you really want your children at that school? Hold on. I've got call waiting. Hold on."

Eve sat on hold. She knew Gabrielle was right. She had to stop coveting what other people had—especially before she even knew what it was that they actually did have. But still, she fondled the acceptance letter from Crossroads, and riffled through the forms and documents that went with acceptance. She knew it was all a game, but still, she couldn't help wanting to play. Right or wrong. There was something so appealing about winning.

Gabrielle clicked back on Eve's line. "That's Nancy—she's calling long distance, I think. She talked to everyone and Emily got into Brentwood, too."

"Emily? Oh my God," said Eve. "Emily got in?! She's not even one of us. She's a civilian!"

"Eve—" said Gabrielle, but she couldn't finish a sentence. Eve was all worked up.

"We didn't get into Brentwood! I did all that charity. I donated, I made hundreds of birdfeeders for the fundraiser. You don't think the earthquake ruined the effect, do you?"

"Eve!" Gabrielle said. But Eve was on a roll.

"I just don't understand why Jocelyn didn't tell me about Mirman. I mean, Stella's just as smart as March! I bet Nancy made a donation to Mirman."

"She still had to take an I.Q. test," said Gabrielle.

"I bet she paid for extra points," Eve said.

"Eve, get a grip!!!" Gabrielle ordered, then clicked the phone to get Nancy back on the line, but she was gone. And Gabrielle couldn't get her back.

Seventy-eight

The April issue of *Playboy* magazine was all everyone talked about. In whispers, of course. And they hid it, as if they were teenagers. Only it wasn't teenagers taking peeks—it was mothers sneaking the issue, and they just couldn't shut up about it. The pictorial article was titled "Luscious Wives."

Nancy was the featured luscious wife.

While the four inside pictures were provocative at most, her limbs and carefully draped clothing covering her most private parts, the full-page photographs on four pages were not. They were simply soft-core pornography. Nancy gazed out at the reader with bedroom eyes, as if urging lurid actions. She was naked with arched back in one, within an inch of touching herself in another, and on all fours in a third. The fourth was under the waterfall of a swimming pool. Her body was partly wet, partly dry. The whole thing was outrageous.

Jocelyn found an issue hidden in her office. The teachers had passed it around, heaping disapproval on the earmarked pages, stashing it where they could retrieve it immediately to show anyone who hadn't seen. In the short text of the article, Jocelyn's preschool, Butterflies and Puppydog Tails, was mentioned as the place where this playmate's children attended. The preschool phone hadn't stopped ringing. The content and tone of the calls ran the gamut.

That Nancy had done this was a shock to everyone who knew her. That she had kept it a secret from them was beyond her friends' comprehension.

Gabrielle got Nancy on the phone.

"What were you thinking?" asked Gabrielle.

"That it would be fun," said Nancy. "I'm not going to look like this forever, you know."

Gabrielle sighed. This was going to be more work than she had anticipated. "Listen, I'm taking you to dinner. I want to talk to you."

"I can't eat dinner," said Nancy. "I'm not hungry."

"Then drinks," said Gabrielle. "Tea! Iced blended mochas?"

"No, thanks," said Nancy. She didn't want to get lectured, and she knew that however well meaning, Gabrielle was going to lecture.

"Then I'm coming over," said Gabrielle.

"I'm too tired," said Nancy. "I can't."

"It's the middle of the afternoon," chided Gabrielle. "Your nanny has your children, all the good soap operas are over, get out of bed—you are in bed, aren't you?"

Gabrielle left a message on Eve's answering machine and at Fuller's office that there was an emergency, and Eve was needed at Nancy's house immediately. It was the best she could do, and she knew that if Eve would come, she'd have a better chance of getting Nancy to deal with whatever problems she had that were making her behave this way.

"Now, tell me," said Gabrielle, once she had barged into Nancy's house and barricaded herself in the kitchen with Nancy. "Why did you pose for that magazine—and *why didn't you tell us you were going to do it? We would have protected you.*"

Nancy rolled her eyes. Gabrielle didn't budge. Nancy drummed her fingers on the counter.

"Where's Eve?" Nancy asked. She slurred her words. Gabrielle noticed but didn't say anything about it.

"She'll be here," said Gabrielle.

"She's probably throwing a dinner party for lots of fabulous people, and not inviting us," said Nancy, changing the subject. It just happened. She wasn't interested in talking about herself. "Why doesn't she like us anymore? Why has she cut us out?"

"You know, you look like hell," said Gabrielle. "You really need some new vitamins or something. They must've airbrushed a lot in the magazine."

"Mind if I sleep through this?" Nancy asked, putting her head down on the table.

"Fine, but I'm cooking you a meal. You look like you haven't eaten anything nutritious in months."

Nancy just closed her eyes and tried to rest. Gabrielle opened the refrigerator and pulled out things to cook, slamming the food down on the island. Unable to doze, Nancy got up and helped herself to a bottle of wine from the wine refrigerator next to the back door. Gabrielle heard the cork pop and whirled on Nancy.

"Put that wine down," said Gabrielle.

"Go to hell," said Nancy. She poured a glass and drank.

"I know you don't mean that," said Gabrielle, dicing tomatoes, peeling garlic, and chopping onions at an amazing pace.

Nancy just drank and watched Gabrielle. She was a whirling dervish with the food.

"Hi." Eve walked in. She had Stella and Eloise with her. She looked at Gabrielle's cooking. There was water boiling, garlic and onions sautéing in a pan, and Gabrielle was chopping a salad. She sniffed the air. "Smells great in here. Where's the emergency?"

Gabrielle took the *Playboy* from her bag and tossed it to Eve, who caught the magazine.

"I just drove down the Pacific Coast Highway, and I'm going to have to go back during rush hour. Do you know what that's like?" Eve asked.

"Page sixty-four," Gabrielle said.

"Do you live in Malibu now?" Nancy asked. "Not that you'd actually give us the address if you did. . . ."

"Yeah," Eve said, as she turned the pages. "We're renting this place—" Eve stopped talking, as she'd found page sixty-four. Her face revealed what she was thinking. Shock, horror, disbelief.

"Want a bookmark?" Nancy asked, smugly.

"Girls, go on upstairs and find March and the twins." Stella and Eloise obeyed. They knew their way. Eve flipped through the pages, and her mouth just dropped open. "Nancy!"

"This is about Landon, isn't it?" said Gabrielle, softly. Nancy didn't answer. "Is this your way of trying to get him back? Appeal to his finer sense of sleaze?"

"Give me some more wine," Nancy said. "You're just so goddamn direct, Gabrielle. A person needs to be drunk just to be around you."

"Get it yourself," said Gabrielle, stung by Nancy's words.

"I worked hard at my body," said Nancy. "I'm proud of it. Why shouldn't I have it photographed, goddamnit?"

"Then buy a bikini and go to the beach," said Gabrielle. "Don't pose naked like a tramp for a zillion strangers.

"You posed for the cameras in your perfect body without an ounce of fat on it, acting like you were just—better than everyone else," Gabrielle spat out. "You never mentioned that, for a hundred thousand dollars and change, anyone could get that body. You gave the impression that you were perfect, when we know— and you know—that couldn't be further from the truth."

"Gabrielle!" hissed Eve. "Easy."

"You're jealous," said Nancy.

"I'm your friend, goddamnit," said Gabrielle. "I'm trying to save you because you don't seem to understand the rules."

"What rules?" said Nancy.

Both she and Eve were now focused, worriedly, on Gabrielle.

"People don't like pride," said Gabrielle. "It's like envy and lust and greed. If you have it, then you keep it to yourself. Talk about your problems like everybody else, for God's sake. Nobody wants to hear how well you're doing, and they certainly don't want to see it."

"Gabby," said Eve, gently. "Just back off a little."

"You didn't have to mention our preschool, either," said Gabrielle. "I mean, do you realize what that can do to Jocelyn, let alone all of us? There is a certain reputation that needs to be maintained."

Nancy started to laugh. Gabrielle looked to Eve for help. Eve just shrugged, helplessly.

"You're lucky you're going to that freakazoid school, Mirman.

Because any normal school would have expelled your child for this kind of behavior.''

"There are laws in this country," said Nancy, gently. "You can't expel a student because a parent poses nude in a magazine."

"Wanna bet?" asked Gabrielle. "This isn't just 'this country.' It's the Westside."

Gabrielle went back to cooking furiously.

"Why did you do it?" Eve asked Nancy.

"I don't know," said Nancy. "How often do you get to do that kind of thing? I mean . . . bodies change. Lives end. I don't know. It seemed fun."

"Was it?" Eve asked. "I mean, would you recommend it?"

Nancy smiled. Sadly. "Maybe . . ." said Nancy, seriously, "maybe I did think that if Landon saw how great I looked . . ."

"You do look great," said Eve. "I wish I looked half this good."

Nancy smiled gratefully.

"If he saw I was still the party girl I used to be . . . the way I was when we married. When he loved me. . . ."

She didn't finish. She just poured herself another glass.

"Nancy," said Eve, gently. "He's not worth it. You don't need him. You're terrific. On your own or with someone who's appreciative."

Nancy gulped her wine.

"This is getting a little too honest for me," said Nancy. "I like it better when we lie to each other and pretend we don't."

They all squirmed uncomfortably.

"I don't know what you're talking about," said Gabrielle. "You're drunk, you're on drugs."

"Why are you beating me up?" asked Nancy. "What about Eve? How come she gets off scot-free?"

"Eve's a chronic social climber," said Gabrielle.

Eve tensed. Nancy stifled a laugh.

"Well, she is," Gabrielle told Nancy, then turned to Eve. "You are. With your charity, and your kissing up to the admissions committees all over town, and Jocelyn, and Amanda—I bet you lost that python on purpose, just for the publicity."

"You're sick," said Eve, sadly.

"Eve's harmless," Gabrielle continued. "But you"—she pointed her finger at Nancy—"you went outside our circle with this stupid escapade."

Gabrielle threw a pound of pasta into boiling water. The hot water splattered. Gabrielle burst out crying. Nancy and Eve were shocked. They'd never seen her cry. Ever.

"Oh, Gabrielle . . ." said Eve. She hadn't seen this coming, and she chided herself because she should have. "Are you okay?" But Gabrielle couldn't answer.

Nancy and Eve hugged her. And she let them. They all huddled together, holding on to each other, until Gabrielle stopped crying. It took a while because she started to sob hysterically first. And then, when there was nothing else to come out, Gabrielle quieted.

"Are you better?" Eve asked.

"Give her some wine," said Nancy.

"No," said Eve.

"I have some muscle relaxers," Nancy volunteered.

"She just needs to eat," said Eve.

Gabrielle stopped crying suddenly. As if a switch had been flipped off.

"I'm fine," she said. "I have to go home. I have to get ready. Joey is coming home. He's been at Betty Ford. For a long time. He says he's ready. Supposedly, he's fixed."

There was silence in the room. They had all known, but Gabrielle had never said it aloud.

"Fixed?" Eve said it to keep Gabrielle talking, but Gabrielle whirled defensively, ready to pounce, but her mouth didn't work. No words would come out. She studied their faces. There was not a mean stitch among them. No judgment. Just question. And concern.

"Why else would you go there?" Gabrielle asked Eve. "Really, Eve."

"How long has he been gone?" asked Eve, doing the math in her head, trying to figure out the last time she saw Joey.

"Couple months," said Gabrielle, wiping her face. She got up and started putting glasses on the table. "Consuela has been working extra hours, helping me with the kids, and, as you can both see, I'm completely fine."

She got up and poured the pasta into a strainer in the sink, and put it in a serving dish, then poured the homemade sauce over it. "This is real food, Nancy," said Gabrielle, tossing the salad and placing it on the table with bread and butter. "Eat it. Or I'll fucking kill you. Okay?"

"Okay," said Nancy, sipping her third glass of wine.

Seventy-nine

Gabrielle's third baby arrived with little fanfare. She delivered quietly with no family or friends around. Joey was still in rehab. She didn't call him when she went into labor. Had he known, he would have raced back to the city, but Gabrielle didn't want him around. He depressed her monumentally. Even at a time like this. She preferred to not have his presence to distract her. She had work to do. A baby to deliver. She had no fears about childbirth. Like other things in her life, it was something she knew she could do, and she would. And she did, practically directing the doctors and nurses all the while. She was calm through her pain, and the delivery was uneventful. The baby was a girl. Gabrielle named her Regan Williams Gardener.

She called Joey after the birth, from her room at Cedars-Sinai Hospital. He wished he could have been there, but lately he wished a lot of things had been different. He checked himself, and realized that truthfully, he was mostly glad she was okay. The baby was okay. He knew that things would never be the same again. He had to take one day at a time. He used the birth of his third baby to end his tenure at rehab. It seemed right. He packed and got a ride home.

Nancy was thrilled about Gabrielle's new daughter, and sent a motorized Barbie vehicle big enough for two children to drive, filled with gifts. But she was too exhausted to come to the hospital herself. She visited after, but not much. She had a lot going on, she said. Gabrielle could only guess. They didn't speak about the *Playboy* spread anymore. It was over.

Eve sent several beautiful outfits from Tattle Tales on Montana, a sweet, exclusive boutique with children's and baby clothes. Gabrielle was happy for the gesture, but skeptical about Eve. She felt Eve pulling away. She felt Nancy pulling away. Jocelyn was never around school anymore. Gabrielle was alone at sea. That's how it felt. She threw herself into her work. Even with three children and her husband returned from ''out of town,'' she immediately became intensely involved in running the preschool fundraiser.

"I'm doing it for Jocelyn and for the school," became her mantra. Even Sarah, the chairperson, who had never been a fan of Gabrielle's, was converted. Gabrielle was amazing. She worked round the clock, and never let anyone down. Not a single Hollywood or civilian mom.

When Joey arrived home, she kissed him on the cheek, looked him over, and told him there was a lot to be done around the house. She couldn't deal with confronting him. She didn't want to know what he planned to do next. She didn't want to know how he was. She was afraid of the answers. Afraid that the wrong one would split her open into pieces on the floor. She had to work to stay sane.

Joey accepted her greeting. He knew that he had completely taken her life off track. He was prepared for some variation on this. While she was working, he spent the time being with his kids. For now, he thought, this was good.

The day of the preschool fundraiser, the mood was extremely festive. The Valentine family had volunteered their ranch in To-panga Canyon for the day-long event. The student body's parents were all grumbling about the distance from their West Side homes, but the police and the insurance companies were thrilled. The silent auction was filled with costly items, and the prospect of theft from the peaceful and hard-to-reach Topanga Canyon was something they could relax about.

The theme was Western, and the Valentines' ranch was transformed by the preschool fundraiser committee headed by Sarah. The Valentines were tacitly guaranteed a spot at their first-choice private school by making this gesture. Jocelyn would see to it. Everybody knew it. To volunteer a property for a school fundraiser rated big returns.

Rental companies had been coming and going for several days prior, setting up tables, chairs, umbrellas, tents, a dance floor for the square dance. There were rides, too. A Ferris wheel, a merry-go-round, and a teacup ride. There were also ponies for a pony ride, a petting zoo, and arts and crafts tables, cookie decorating tables, and a good old-fashioned baked goods sale.

Then there was the barbecue to end all barbecues. Ribs, chicken, steaks, and chopped salad, Caesar salad, Chinese chicken salad (because it was Jocelyn's favorite), hot dogs and burgers for the kids—there was nothing missing.

On one lawn of the big house on the ranch, a puppet stage with a black velvet curtain was set up. A puppeteer performed for a group of thirty children and their parents. Dustin Hoffman sat with his kids, and George Lucas with his. Bruce Springsteen got up to leave, bored. The puppeteer was sweating. This was the most important audience he had ever performed for.

An ensemble of professional square dancers in costume were beginning to perform on the stage built under the tent. Music was in the air everywhere. It was a typical Butterflies and Puppydog Tails fundraiser.

This year, however, one thing was different. There were over a dozen security guards. Half of them armed. They flanked the table in the row of items for the silent auction, at which the Picasso that Amanda had donated was set up for display. The Picasso drew a crowd. Jocelyn knew that this year, the silent auction booty would cover her costs for a good decade. She stood by and watched.

"Another fabulous party."

Jocelyn turned to see Amanda with George. They were decked out in Western theme wear. Kerchiefs around their necks and cowboy hats—distributed at the door to all who bought raffle tickets for drawings during the day. She reached for Glenn's hand. He was wearing a Stetson and eating an apple.

"Thank you for the Picasso," said Jocelyn. She aimed the comment at George.

"I want that Picasso back," he growled. He was pissed. He saw Glenn. "Hey, doc," he said.

Amanda greeted Glenn and Jocelyn.

"I bet you're the only one here who can afford it," said Jocelyn. "Why don't you go bid on it?"

George scowled at her. "Bid on my own painting. Right."

"Honey, would you get me a water ice?" Jocelyn asked Glenn.

"Sure, sugar," said Glenn, and left, but not before kissing Jocelyn and tipping his hat at Amanda and George.

"God, he is so adorable," said Amanda. "And you two are a great couple."

"I know," said Jocelyn. "Thank you for introducing us. Your blind date has kind of taken on a life of its own. I'm in love."

"Just wait," said George. "He'll get to know you, and it'll be all over."

"I can't believe you said that" said Jocelyn. "After all this time, you still hate me."

"You're just bitter about the painting," said Amanda to her husband. "You can afford to give it away, for God's sake. Besides, it's just money."

George scowled.

"George, sincerely," said Jocelyn. "Thank you. It is going to help the school. A lot."

"I bet," said George.

"I wish you two would shake hands and make up," said Amanda.

Jocelyn was uncomfortable. She knew that Amanda was aware of the friction between her and George. She didn't know how many details Amanda was aware of.

"I hate your husband," said Jocelyn, folding her arms across her chest. "And he hates me. I don't think it's ever going to be any different."

"Hate is not a strong enough word," George responded, looking around to make sure no one else was overhearing.

"The only people you can hate are lovers," said Amanda, crossly. "Or people you wish were lovers."

Jocelyn was amazed. Amanda truly had balls. And insight. And personal security.

"What the hell's the matter with you?" George snarled at his wife.

"You are," she said. Then she turned to Jocelyn. "And you are, too."

Jocelyn felt shamed.

"The two of you work like animals. And not the impressive kind. Not lions or tigers. You work like ants."

"Oh, please," said Jocelyn. She was getting annoyed at being taken to task. She could only stay in that position for so long. "This is not about work."

"Look at that." Amanda nodded at the Picasso. "It's a painting. So the hell what? You two are way more important to me than that painting. I could give a shit about that painting. But I care about you."

"It's a goddamn Picasso," George said.

"Which would you rather have: a Picasso or your favorite night of sex with me?"

George hesitated. Then didn't answer. Amanda smiled. She knew he'd chosen her.

"So have your fantasies about Jocelyn when you're jerking off in the bathroom—I don't really care."

George was pissed. "I'd rather have the plague."

"I'm not asking you to take out a full-page ad apologizing in *Variety*. I'm asking you both to take the high road—she's a person, for God's sake. Get over each other and move the hell on!"

George sighed. He looked a little relieved.

"And you"—she turned on Jocelyn—"are going to have to treat my husband like one of those very gifted, very difficult children. Because he's a man. And we all know what that means."

She and Jocelyn laughed together, and then hugged. Nothing could get between them. Not even husbands or boyfriends or former lovers who were both.

Eighty

Gabrielle couldn't stop working. Even when exhaustion crept in. She still felt naked without her "old" husband—the Joey she had married—and without her friends. Despite the huge ordeal of the fundraiser, all she felt was that people were staring at her.

Joey going off to drug rehab had made life extremely tough for her. And now that he was back, she thought everyone whispered, pointed, and looked her way. She was just sure of it, and it was awful for her. She felt postpartum fat, conspicuous, and like she was the wife of the biggest deadbeat dolt in Hollywood. A complete loser.

People said they wanted to help. They wanted to have coffee. The proverbial coffee, which meant nothing about beverages and everything about gossip. Even civilian moms had the audacity to approach her, but Gabrielle didn't trust any of them. Not one. The "how are you?"'s sounded empty, hollow, and salacious. Gabrielle was positive that the phone wires were burning up—people she knew saying how sorry they felt about "poor Gabrielle," and she hated it. She hated being "poor Gabrielle."

She couldn't figure out how things had gone so wrong all at once. But she was damned if she wouldn't do something about it. She wasn't sure what, but something. She was not a sponge for pity.

The one place she knew she could turn—the only place she found that she could ever turn—was to her real friends. The other Hollywood moms.

She found Nancy stumbling around, looking for a corner to sneak a cigarette. She swooped Nancy into a hug. Nancy's body felt tiny and as if Gabrielle could knock her over with a sneeze.

"You look terrible," said Gabrielle. "You should get some new makeup. A different shade of foundation."

Nancy and Gabrielle hugged, both relieved to find each other. Nancy leaned on Gabrielle for support. She was weak. "I need a latte," Nancy said with a sigh, as she lit up a cigarette. "Isn't this great?"

"Yes!" said Gabrielle joyously, huddling into the corner with her friend. They linked arms and stared out at the barrage of festivities from their foxhole.

"Where are the kids?"

"Nannies. How about yours?"

"Nannies. And Joey."

"How's that going?"

"You shouldn't smoke."

"I know." Nancy put the cigarette out. Stared at it, then lit up another. "I have to go home. I'm exhausted."

Gabrielle turned to assess her friend. She looked different. Thinner, at the very least. Paler.

"Did you have any more work done?"

"My kitchen," said Nancy. "I'm putting in a skylight. I spent a fortune on wallpaper, and now that it's up, the colors don't work with my lights."

"Not your house—your body."

"Oh," said Nancy, unoffended. "No. Nothing." Then she remembered. "Oh—except I had my butt lifted."

Gabrielle laughed.

"I did," said Nancy, turning to show her friend. Gabrielle inspected Nancy's rear. It did look higher. "And I had a little work done on my cheekbones. You like? Nothing major." She turned back around so Gabrielle could look at her face.

"Sure," said Gabrielle. "I don't care what your face looks like, Nancy. I just—"

"Did you see *Vogue* magazine—that woman—the one in the afternoon group?"

"No!" said Gabrielle.

"She's in *Vogue* this month."

"A mother in the afternoon group!?" Gabrielle was shocked. "For what? Why?"

"Hollywood Mother."

"What?" Gabrielle was appalled. This was her milieu, and she considered herself arbiter of Hollywood mom-dom.

"Apparently we missed one," Nancy snickered. "Her husband is some big TV producer. They're from Canada. She's posing in Richard Tyler and talking about her glamorous life."

"Let's call her," said Gabrielle. "What's her name?"

"I don't remember. Get the magazine. I'm zonked." Nancy slowly got her things together. "Besides, *Vogue* is tired."

"So are you," said Gabrielle, then grabbed her arm.

"Look. It's Eve."

"Hi!" Eve waved at them. Her pregnancy was flattering. She looked like an earth mother. Happy and unflappable. Fuller, Stella, and Eloise danced around her, looking at everything, all talking and laughing at once.

Fuller waved at Nancy and Gabrielle, and took his daughters to get lunch, after kissing Eve on the mouth. She came over to her friends.

"Where's your nanny?" asked Nancy.

"I gave her the day off," said Eve, kissing them all hello. She noticed Nancy's appearance, but didn't ask.

"You came without any help?" Nancy was amazed.

"It's not that bad," said Eve. She saw Amanda and Jocelyn with George over by the Picasso, and waved. They all waved back, but didn't move toward each other.

"I heard you sold your house," said Gabrielle.

Eve smiled, but didn't elaborate.

"You did?!" said Nancy. "To who?!" Then she turned back to Gabrielle. "Why didn't you tell me?"

"I wasn't sure," said Gabrielle, grinning. "I was just bluffing."

"Well, we did sell it," said Eve. "And I can't talk about it."

They looked at her, curiously.

"What do you mean, you can't talk about it?" asked Nancy. "Who bought it? What about the snake?"

"I don't want to talk about it," said Eve. "We've been in Hawaii, and now we're in this huge, run-down rental in Malibu, and we're just staying still for a while. Until this baby comes."

"You'd better hire another housekeeper," said Gabrielle. "It's the only way."

"I'm not hiring any more help," said Eve. "I want to raise my own kids. I mean, isn't there something wrong with all this?"

"All what?" asked Nancy, innocently. She held herself tight. She was starting to shiver.

"All *this*," said Eve, waving her arms about at the fundraiser. "Didn't we all come here just to raise a family?"

"No," said Gabrielle.

They all sized each other up, quietly.

"I came for the parties." Nancy shrugged. "A long, long time ago, I came here to find the best parties. Period."

"I came to give the best parties," said Gabrielle. "To have a great life."

"I came to have a new life," said Eve, solemnly. "Did you two know I used to be a waitress?"

They didn't.

"My family lives in Vegas. They run a gas station."

Eve had always hidden this from them, afraid that they'd think she wasn't worthy. Now that she didn't care, she saw that they didn't either. She was pleasantly surprised. And relieved.

"Maybe we all got what we wanted," said Nancy, coughing.

They looked at each other again. Uncertainly.

"Ladies!" A man in a cowboy suit came over and kissed them all on the cheeks.

"How are you? It's nice to see you all," said the cowboy.

None of them recognized him. Nancy, Gabrielle, and Eve exchanged looks—who *is* this guy?

"Oh, God! The tarantula! Corey!" said Eve, remembering him finally. "Corey was the tarantula at Stella's party!" she said to her friends. They just gaped. "How are you?"

"Well," he said. "Eve, you look fit. Hey, I heard some news."

Gabrielle and Nancy just exchanged looks with Eve, that said: Who the heck *is* this guy?

"Jocelyn? Well, she's wearing a ring. If you know what I mean."

The women all swiveled their necks to look for Jocelyn so fast they got whiplash all at the same time.

"Well, I've gotta run," said Corey. He knew he had their attention. "I'm in this square dance number, but I'm sure I'll see you all again. Give my best to your husbands! And maybe we can have lunch one day. I'm free on Fridays.''

Corey left, stopping to press the flesh on his way through the crowd to the square dance floor.

Eve, Nancy, and Gabrielle broke up, laughing.

''Looks like we've got a new best friend,'' Eve said through giggles. They had a good laugh. And when they saw Jocelyn in the crowd, holding hands with Doctor Glenn, they saw she was indeed wearing a diamond ring.

''Well, I'll be damned,'' said Eve.

''Good for her,'' said Nancy.

''Congratulations!'' Eve yelled through the throngs to Jocelyn and Glenn. They both waved and mouthed the word: ''Thanks.''

''Guess we're throwing a little wedding shower, girls,'' said Gabrielle.

Eighty-one

Gabrielle hand-delivered fifty invitations for Zachary's fifth birthday party, zipping around in her newly leased Navigator. She drove all over Brentwood, Santa Monica, and Beverly Hills. She'd designed the invitations herself and found a printer who did excellent work. Each black-and-white engraved invite had a picture of a race car on the front, and Gabrielle had tied a miniature black-and-white-checkered racing flag to each card. They had to be hand-delivered so the flag wouldn't get crushed by the postal service.

The race car birthday party was impeccable. Gabrielle held the bash at the Petersen Auto Museum in Los Angeles. She had their party planners do the whole thing. Which was a huge step, not doing it herself.

''Amazing party,'' said Joey, as he hustled around with the video camera.

''Did you talk to Peter?'' Gabrielle asked, not looking at him. She was afraid to.

''Yeah,'' said Joey, his mouth full of food. ''I did.''

''And? Did he offer you a deal?''

"Yeah," said Joey. "Housekeeping deal on the lot. I said no."

"Why?!" Gabrielle turned to face her husband in shock. This was exactly what she was afraid of.

"I don't want to do movies," said Joey. "I'm starting a band."

Gabrielle said nothing. She set her drink down on a table.

"I used to be scared of you," said Joey.

Gabrielle took a deep breath. She felt as though she was getting air before diving under a deep wave. She hated when Joey talked like this—open and honest and sharing. It had been like this ever since he came back from rehab.

"You're so good at everything," said Joey. "No. Not good. You're amazing. You could do my job, Peter Shelton's job—any job in town, and you could do it better than the person who's got it now. You could probably run the country." He laughed. Because it was true.

"I don't know about that," said Gabrielle. She was very uncomfortable with this kind of overt flattery.

"I think I stopped being scared of you when I started looking to you as an inspiration instead of someone I was jealous of," he said.

Gabrielle took another deep breath. She would just concentrate on breathing, and get through this. She hated when he talked this way. Why couldn't he just go to the office, come home, and act normal?

"That's why I'm not taking the producing deal."

Gabrielle tried not to lose control. Not at her son's birthday party. Not with fifty of the most important people in Hollywood as her guests. Never mind that fifty others had said they couldn't make it. No doubt because Joey was not as important as he used to be. Tom Cruise's children were here. At her soiree. So, they came with a nanny instead of Tom and Nicole, big deal. They were here.

"It takes years and years to form a successful band," said Gabrielle. "It's long and slow."

"I know." Joey nodded. "But I have some shortcuts. I know a lot of people. I even told Peter Shelton about it, and he was jazzed."

Gabrielle snorted.

"What will we do? Where will we go? I hope you don't expect me to sell the house. I've done a tremendous amount of work laying down roots here. I've gone through a lot, and I'm not going to give it up now."

"We can talk about it later," said Joey. "Everything will be fine. As long as we have each other."

"I am not pulling my children out of the preschool," said Gabrielle. "And Zachary is going to Crossroads. So you'd better come up with a way to support your children's education."

"Piñata's ready," said the party planner.

"Come on," said Joey, pulling Gabrielle over to the area where the piñata was hanging. "I still love you," he said. "A lot."

Gabrielle felt like she was walking through someone else's life. She fought to maintain consciousness.

The party planners had lined the children up and they had each taken a turn whacking at a life-size piñata of a Mexican girl with pigtails wearing a big sombrero, but the piñata was nowhere near cracking, and the kids were starting to whine and cry for the candy inside.

"And now, ladies and gentlemen," said the party planner, turning to the guests. "Our host for today, Gabrielle Gardener!"

She handed the bat to Gabrielle, who refused to take a whack at the piñata.

"Go on!" said Joey. Gabrielle turned to see Joey aiming the video camera at her, filming her.

For the camera, she took some whacks, but she was weak, and the piñata remained intact. The children wanted candy.

"Pretend it's Joey!" goaded Nancy, who was leaning on Eve for support. That got a big laugh from the crowd.

"We need candy," said Roxy, pulling on Gabrielle's sundress. "Mom, *we need candy!!*"

"*Break it, Mom!*" yelled Zach.

In a daze, Gabrielle took the bat and started to swing at the piñata. The first thwack, she remembered. The bat hitting the papier-mâché figure.

"More!"

"Go, Gabrielle!"

Everyone was yelling at her. She hadn't slept much. She hadn't eaten enough. Goddamn the video camera in her face. This was probably the last party like this she'd ever get to throw. If Joey went on the road with some sleazy band—ha!—they'd be broke for years supporting his pipe dream.

"Hey!"

"Get back!"

The mothers ran to grab their children and pull them away. Gabrielle was hitting the piñata with the bat, and she was going wild. She was hitting hard, and throwing her entire body into it. The piñata cracked, and the candy started to trickle out, but Gabrielle didn't stop. She slammed the thing until it was completely disemboweled. And then she whacked the hell out of the shreds of piñata on the floor.

"Gabby!"

"Gabrielle, stop!!"

Gabrielle stuck the bat into the body of the piñata and plunged it, stabbing, until all the candy fell onto the lawn, and she felt someone—a man—Joey—and he was pulling her away from the piñata, and whispering in her ear, so no one could hear:

"It's okay. . . . Calm down. . . . It's okay."

She looked around to see if anyone else had seen her lose it, but the children swarmed the candy on the ground, and the mothers were all helping their kids. Some kids knocked heads and were crying. The big ones had pockets full, and the little ones were crying because they had none. It was all normal. All back to normal.

"Okay," Gabrielle whispered to Joey, and handed him the bat. "I'm okay. . . . I'm okay. . . . I'm okay."

She looked up and found Eve and Nancy in the crowd. Their eyes were glued to her. She found their gaze comforting. Eve nodded at Gabrielle, even though they were at a distance.

"You're okay," Eve said. Gabrielle couldn't hear her, but she knew.

Eighty-two

Nancy's funeral was beautiful. The guests wore Dolce and Gabbana, Versace, and Richard Tyler. Most of them had to grab something from their closets on last-minute notice. Nancy's death took most by surprise, although, in hindsight, everyone said she hadn't been looking or acting right for, well, for a long, long time. They just never knew that something was really wrong.

Gabrielle actually owned an unworn funeral dress she'd bought especially for such an occasion, should one arise. In the end, that summed up who Gabrielle was, or who she wanted to be. In control. Capable and able. Even when people were dying. Even her best friend.

Gabrielle had organized her closet, alphabetically, by occasion, while Joey was in rehab. The little black dress was a toss-up. It could have easily landed under *C* for cocktail party. But at the last minute, she decided it was not quite sexy enough for a festivity, and hung it, still in its red, white, and blue Fred Segal plastic wrapping, under *F* for funeral attire. She never dreamed she'd wear it for Nancy.

Eve stood on the beach to get ready. She was dressed to go, except for her shoes and socks. Barefoot, she stared out to sea. How could this have happened? How could one of her dearest friends have died? How could Nancy's life have ended, and her children's hadn't? Wasn't everybody supposed to go down together? So that nobody would be left to grieve—least of all the children. Who would take care of them? And what of Landon?

Eve kept thinking, what if she were the one who had died, and Fuller were left with the children. Or if Fuller died, and she were left alone. She felt hollow and profoundly sad. The tide came in higher, getting her trouser legs wet. Eve didn't notice.

"Eve!"

Fuller was calling her from the deck of their rented home.

"We have to go."

She broke her reverie and looked down at her wet feet and pants legs. She'd have to change. Quickly. She started to leave, but something caught her eye. Something in the sand was glistening. She bent down to get it. It was gold. Buried in the sand. She dug, ruining her manicure. It was a chain. Gold, slippery. Someone must have lost it. She pulled it out of the sand, rinsed it off. There was a charm on the end. She held it up to get a good look—and her heart all but stopped.

"Eve!"

She didn't answer. She couldn't. She stared at the necklace. It was impossible.

"Eve!"

The necklace in her hand was the one she'd lost on the beach, years ago, the first day she'd come to Los Angeles after driving through the desert. It was the Saint Christopher's medal her mother had given her for the trip. For her birthday. To mark her new life. Only the necklace she'd been given was cheap metal.

Tarnished and worthless. This one was gold. She looked at the marking on the back of the charm. Fourteen karat. But it was exactly the same. . . .

She turned to Fuller. He was waving her in.

Eighty-three

The flowers that decorated the tent at the graveyard were from An Empty Vase. The florist had delivered especially for Nancy. The gravesite was way outside their delivery zone, but Nancy had been a good customer. The florist took special care with the arrangement on the casket. Dozens of pink roses intertwined. It was breathtaking.

Everybody was there. A reporter from *Variety* came to pay his respects, and get a column. All her friends, including her plastic surgeon, huddled together, stunned, mourning, and looking fabulous. Even some civilian mothers had snuck in.

The preschool closed for the day. Jocelyn didn't want to shut down, but all the teachers wanted to go to the funeral. It was a Wednesday. Jocelyn put a note on the gate. The group of teachers from Butterflies and Puppydog Tails huddled together, sharing tissues and introducing each other to the other group of teachers who came from March's new school, Mirman.

The eulogy began. "Nancy Greene was a caring and devoted mother and wife with a rich life. Rich in the true sense of the word. Layered with experience. This was a woman who would brighten up a room. She had her own special light."

There were some hundred guests in two-hundred-dollar sunglasses and three-hundred-dollar shoes at Forest Lawn Cemetery. The children were all at home. The nannies all wept. Whether they liked her or not, Nancy had been a mother, and that was something that drew them all together.

"She put her family first and foremost," the eulogy continued. "She oversaw all the details of her children's lives. Their school, karate, ballet, swimming lessons. Play dates, parties. That she kept her fatal illness from many was only a small example of who Nancy Greene was. She didn't want to worry anyone. She didn't want to burden any lives. She was selfless in this ordinary and elegant way."

Eve and Gabrielle stood close to each other. Joey put his arm around Gabrielle, but his fingers touched Eve's shoulder. She looked across Gabrielle and smiled at Joey. She and he had never had a conversation that lasted more than five whole minutes. But they both loved and respected Gabrielle.

"Nice necklace," Gabrielle whispered to Eve, nodding at the Saint Christopher's necklace around her neck.

"Thanks," Eve whispered.

"Is it new?"

Eve hesitated just for a second, then smiled. "Not really. No."

Gabrielle turned to her husband.

"Do you have to wear that thing?" she asked Joey.

"Yes," said Joey, touching the yarmulke he wore on his head. "It's a Jewish funeral."

"It's half Jewish," said Gabrielle. "And that hat looks ridiculous."

"Tough," said Joey.

"I liked you better on drugs," she said quietly so nobody else would hear her.

"You know," said Joey. "I'd like you better if you were on drugs, too."

Gabrielle suppressed her laughter.

"Did they teach you that at rehab?" she asked.

"Nah." He smiled. "Picked it up myself."

Eve felt a tap on her shoulder. She turned around and didn't recognize Amanda. At first. The giant sunglasses. The hair pulled back in a bun. No makeup. Requisite black dress.

"Amanda," said Eve. Amanda hugged her.

"I'm so sorry," said Amanda. "I know she was your friend."

"Amanda!" said Gabrielle. She was shocked and pleased to see Amanda Foster at her friend's funeral. "Is George here?"

"No," said Amanda. "He didn't really know Nancy."

"Nancy would be so glad you were here," said Gabrielle.

Amanda smiled. "I'm glad."

Eve knew Amanda had disliked Nancy and Gabrielle. She looked at her old friend and wondered what she was doing here.

"Are you coming to the shiva thing?" Gabrielle asked. She was uncomfortable with Jewish traditions, but she wanted Amanda's company for as long as she could have it.

"No," said Amanda. "I have to get back."

"To the set?" asked Gabrielle. "Are you shooting something? I heard George is shooting something."

"I just came to pay my respects," said Amanda.

Eve took Amanda's arm and pulled her away. "I'll catch up with you at the shiva," Eve said to Gabrielle, then steered Amanda away so they could talk.

"Thank you for coming," said Eve, as they walked among the gravesites. Jocelyn waved from the back where she stood with the teachers. She was crying.

"I hope I didn't bring any paparazzi with me," said Amanda, glancing over her dark glasses. "They're like flies around me."

"How are you?"

"I'm fine," said Amanda. "Pregnant."

"No!" said Eve, delighted. She looked Amanda over.

"Two months, that's all. Nobody knows. Except George. Don't—"

"I won't," said Eve.

"How are you?"

"Me?" asked Eve.

"Firmly ensconced in Hollywood?" Amanda chided. "Finger-nails gripping the studio eaves?"

"Huh?" Eve didn't understand.

"Nothing," said Amanda. "Forget it."

"No, Amanda—listen. You were right," said Eve. "About everything. All of it. But I couldn't just take your word. It wouldn't have worked. I had to try it. You know, just a taste. The life. Everything. I had to figure it out myself."

"You're not in the thick of it?" Amanda asked. She was surprised and pleased, but didn't entirely believe what she was hearing.

"Extricating myself," said Eve.

Amanda was surprised and impressed. "Really?"

"I had a tough year. I had to shoot someone. Did you know that?"

"You're shooting? I didn't know you wanted to direct."

"No!" said Eve. "I shot a gun. I *shot* shot someone, Amanda."

"No, you didn't."

"I'm serious. I shot a producer in my bedroom."

Amanda stopped laughing. "What?"

Eve tried to memorize Amanda's face. She remembered the time not so long ago, when Amanda used to make her face look like that. Surprised like just when you thought you'd heard everything, you realized you hadn't.

"He was stealing drugs during an open house—we had to sell the house because that python got loose during Stella's party, and we were afraid to live there."

Amanda stared into Eve's pupils to see if she was on drugs. She wasn't.

"I thought he was a burglar, and when I tried to dial the police, he ripped the phone out of my hands and I shot him. It was self-defense. I thought he was going to attack me."

"Eve!"

"Lucky I didn't kill him. I mean, it would have been okay, legally, I think. But I couldn't have lived with myself. Anyway, he bought the house from us."

"Eve!!" Amanda took her sunglasses off to get a clear look at Eve. "You're not joking, are you?"

"No."

"And now your friend died."

"Nancy. I didn't even know she was sick. I thought everything—she was depressed, she was sick from her implants, she was drug addicted—I mean, I never dreamed she had leukemia."

"Eve, there's no way you could have known—not with everything you've just told me going on."

"You know, Landon told me she didn't want chemo—she didn't want her hair to fall out. Isn't that so Nancy?"

Eve started to cry. Amanda held her.

"She was just one of a kind. I liked her. She was my friend."

"So, now what?" asked Amanda.

"We're living in Malibu." Eve sighed. Just thinking of the place brought relief. "Did you know Indians used to live in Malibu?"

"Yeah," said Amanda.

"I walk in the ocean every day," said Eve. "And Stella's going to public school."

"No!" said Amanda, her eyes widening. "Do your friends know?"

"I can't remember if I told them or not," she said, trying to remember. "We're not really close friends anymore," said Eve.

Amanda nodded. "So, you are okay."

"Yeah," said Eve, thinking about it. "I was always okay. It was a long path through the garden to get to know that."

"Glad you found your way," said Amanda. "I knew you would."

"Really?" Eve asked.

"The moment I saw you."

"You know, a long time ago, when I came to Los Angeles by myself, I wanted things to be different than where I came from."

Amanda just listened.

"But the thing of it is, it's all the same. Hard work, marriage, and making babies. Whether you're working in a gas station or throwing a charity event. I don't know. Do you think it's the same?"

"I don't know," said Amanda. "I really don't."

"I wonder what it would be like to go back," said Eve.

"Try it," said Amanda. "Go visit."

"Not for a visit," said Eve. "To live. Go back home."

"I don't know," said Amanda, shaking her head skeptically. "I don't think it works that way."

"No," said Eve, biting her lip as she considered the possibility. "I guess it doesn't. I guess you can't really go back."

"Forward," said Amanda.

"Forward," said Eve. And for the first time, she felt that she really knew which way was straight ahead.

Eighty-four

Landon held shiva in a Wilshire corridor condominium that he owned. The children ran around and ate bagels with their nannies while the adults gathered around over the food and spoke softly. All around were pictures of Nancy with her children and Landon. Her family flew in from Connecticut. Her brother and his lover, from New York. There were no conflicts, no fights, no cares that Landon held a Jewish mourning ceremony when Nancy wasn't Jewish. None of it mattered to her family—nuclear and extended. That she was gone, and that they were together to mark her death, was all that mattered to them. It was peaceful.

"How could we not have known," said Eve. "I mean she looked terrible. We should have known."

"I told her to stop eating cookies and buy better makeup!" said Gabrielle, guiltily. "Can you believe I said that?!"

"You didn't know," said Eve. "None of us knew she had leukemia."

"But, how could we not have known?" Gabrielle echoed Eve's feelings. "We knew everything. How could she not have told us? I mean, we told each other every detail."

But as soon as she said it, the fallacy of those words echoed loudly.

"No," said Eve. "We didn't, hon."

"Well," said Gabrielle, feeling awful. "We should have, then. I mean, what could we really have said to have shocked each other?"

Eve rolled her eyes. She could only imagine.

"What could we have said that would be so bad?" asked Gabrielle. "Really?"

"I'm the worst," said Eve. "I feel terrible. I thought she was just a drug addict."

"She was," Gabrielle said, starting to laugh. "She was taking all those medicines to control her disease."

They were quiet. Gabrielle held out her hand. Eve took it and squeezed her fingers.

"You don't have any secrets like that," asked Gabrielle, "do you?"

"Well," Eve hesitated, then whispered, "I'm not supposed to tell—I promised Fuller, but if you can keep a secret . . . I shot someone."

"Oh, that. Jeeves, the guy with the producing deal. I already know that. I heard he's got a huge action film that's coming out this summer."

Eve was dumbfounded. That Gabrielle knew, and that she was so glib about it.

"How do you know?!" asked Eve.

"Small town, babe." Gabrielle winked at Eve. "Anyway, the action film should put Fuller deep in the black. The box office on those movies is untouchable."

"You should run a studio." Eve laughed. "Really. You'd be amazing."

"I already do," said Gabrielle, smiling mysteriously. "In a

way. We just haven't greenlit anything yet. But when we do . . .
watch out.''

Landon walked over and put his arms around Eve and Gabrielle. They hugged him back. It was the first time.

"Hey . . .'' Gabrielle couldn't talk.

"Landon,'' said Eve. She didn't know what to say. He looked
old. Tired. Eve wondered if he felt guilty at all for the way he'd
treated his ex-wife. She'd loved him all the way. All the way to
the end.

"She loved you,'' he said to them, as if he'd read Eve's mind.
"I don't know what she would've done without you.''

"How are you doing?'' Gabrielle asked. Landon nodded, but
he'd been crying a lot.

"I wish we could've been there in the end,'' said Eve.

"You are,'' he said, and reached into his jacket pocket for
something. "She left this for you.''

He took out an envelope. It was addressed to Gabrielle and
Eve. He handed it to them.

"I didn't read it,'' he said. "The day she died, she asked me
to give it to you. That's how I knew she was going. She wouldn't
leave without talking to you. You were her best friends.''

Landon started to cry. Eve put her arm around him. So did
Gabrielle.

"Pizza!'' Fuller yelled. He was at the door, paying the Dom-
ino's guy. The children came running. Fuller slammed the door
with his foot, and stood with a tower of pizza boxes in his arms,
when he saw the children coming for him. He tried to step out
of the way, but there was nowhere to go. Joey saw what was
happening, and ran to help Fuller. But it was too late. The kids
attacked Fuller with the pizzas, gleefully grabbing for the food.
He couldn't hold out. Not even with Joey helping. Laughing, and
yelling at them, both at the same time, Fuller and Joey lost their
footing. Everything came tumbling down, and the children all
pounced.

Joey and Fuller just looked at each other, and laughed.

"Thanks anyway,'' said Fuller.

"Hey,'' said Joey. "No prob.''

They looked up and saw Landon, Gabrielle, and Eve just staring at them on the floor. Nobody spoke. Everyone grinned. There
was nothing left to say.

Eighty-five

Dear Gabrielle and Eve,

I can't believe I'm writing to you for the last time. I hope you're not mad at me for keeping this a secret. Leukemia was boring and I hated it and I hated the drugs, and when I was with you two, I didn't want to talk about it or think about it. I just wanted to be with you. So that's what I did.

Thank you for forgiving me for that.

I always felt kind of badly that I was never up to speed or as good as any of you. I was never as smart or as funny or as clever—I didn't have ideas like you. I wasn't ever as capable or talented as Gabrielle or as vulnerable and genuine as Eve. I always felt badly that I wasn't as good as you all, but in the end, I guess I was smarter than both of you because I had both of your company, and you only had mine.

I know you're all going to be around for a very long time, and you won't have to think about saying goodbye to anyone yourself, so here's what you think about when it's time:

Lucky, lucky me.

I had everything. I had a great husband—I know, I know, all those bad times we talked about, but somehow, now, with the credits rolling at the end of the show, they don't matter. All I think about are the good times. The exciting part of the ride. The falling in love and getting married. My wedding. Making babies and parties and birthdays. The vacations we took. The love we had when we had it.

And my gorgeous little angels—the most difficult part. I'm counting on you to watch over them and help Landon. I hate it that I'm not going to be around, and how disappointed they'll be. Lucky me, they love me so much. But maybe it'll be okay. That's what I'm going out believing. And I know they'll be in good hands. So watch out for March, Leo, and Max, okay?

Last thing is this. My best times in life were never landmarks. They were all little moments in the kitchen, moments at birthday parties, talking on the phone together. They were the three of us. My best friends. When I think back about what I loved most about being with you, it's one big, fuzzy blur. I loved that you were my friends, and I'll miss you desperately, wherever I'm going, and I want you to always be friends.

Love each other. Don't fight and don't say bad things about each other (I know you will, anyway, but I hope you at least feel guilty when you do). Take care of each other, and see that our children are always friends. I'd like that.

I will miss you. And if I do come back, I'll look you up. For sure.

Love forever,
your best friend,
Nancy

P.S. Enclosed, please find two gift certificates to Fred Segal for you. I love saying goodbye knowing that you guys are going shopping on me. Wish I could be there with you, but it seems my calendar is booked. Who knows. If a shirt drops off a rack, or a dressing room curtain blows open when there's no wind, maybe it'll be me. I hope. I know I'd love to be there with you. So, get good stuff.

Circle Time

Eighty-six

Eve stood in the crowd of parents at preschool graduation. Stella's class sang "Uno, Dos, Tres Amigos." She watched Stella and wondered, Was she happy? Was she confident? Did she feel safe? Would she have a good life? She hoped the answer to all those questions was yes.

It was the only thing that mattered. Sometimes she had forgotten that along the way. Now, she remembered it. She was grateful for the reminder.

This preschool graduation marked her realization that goodbyes were in order. Not just her children's goodbyes, but her own. Things needed to change. She had already decided that. Just knowing that that decision was in place, accepting it, made her feel peaceful. Calm. Content.

Eve looked around. She saw the proud fathers. Mothers. Grandparents. Some loyal housekeepers standing in the background, behind the families. They beamed at their charges as if they were their own children. They loved that the kids spoke Spanish in this song. Eve saw the parents and grandparents smile and nudge each other, proudly. They sat in white, padded, wooden rental chairs in a larger circle around the kids. A videographer stalked the periphery, making a professional video of the graduation ceremony.

And Corey. Jocelyn's newest addition to her staff. He didn't have the academic educational background that her other teachers did, but as for practical experience, three years as Hollywood family party entertainment, he was ahead of the pack. He was a preschool teacher, now. Somehow, Eve knew he would be moving on and up.

"And now, it's time to present diplomas to our Butterflies and Puppydog Tails graduates," announced Jocelyn. Her boyfriend beamed at her from the back row. Jocelyn's modest diamond engagement ring sparkled. It was fresh and bright. Jocelyn looked younger than ever. She looked thin and athletic, tall and capable, and with her long, blonde hair hanging loose, she personified the Southern California of myths.

She called each child to receive a diploma and a trophy. The children gripped their goods, trying not to drop them. There were flashbulbs and tears among the parents. Fuller choked up a little when Stella was called. When it was March's turn, Gabrielle and Eve cried.

"How's Joey?" Eve whispered to Gabrielle.

"Who?" Gabrielle said, sarcastically. She was so angry at her husband, she couldn't even acknowledge him. She was miffed at Eve for bringing up his name, and spoiling this perfect morning.

"Never mind," said Eve. "Forget it."

"He formed a band. Can you believe it? Landon set him up with some musicians he knew from his music biz days. That kid, Digby, is, like, managing them."

"Nancy's personal assistant?"

"Yeah," said Gabrielle. "Landon is putting up the money. It's all too bizarre. Landon actually admires my husband. I mean . . . what do you make of that? Good news or bad news?"

Eve started to laugh.

"He says he likes Joey's spirit."

"No kidding?" said Eve. "He's been talking to Fuller a lot on the phone, you know. I think they even had lunch. Did you know that? Fuller likes him. They're going to go surfing together."

"Surfing . . ." Gabrielle smiled, reminiscing. "I remember when I first met Joey. He used to surf all the time."

"I think they're friends," said Eve.

"I don't know what's going on, and he's making me insane," said Gabrielle. "Can you picture me and the kids, on the road?! In one of those buses with beds and televisions nailed to the walls?"

Eve had to laugh.

"He said he wrote a song for me." Gabrielle rolled her eyes. "I'm scared to hear it."

"Y'know," said Eve. "I think you're going to like being a rock star's wife."

"I don't know, Eve," said Gabrielle. "You think he's really going to be a star?"

"With you behind him?" asked Eve. "Absolutely."

Gabrielle shared a laugh with Eve. She knew Eve was right. They watched a little longer until Eve found the courage to reveal a secret she'd been keeping.

"I'm sending Stella to public school."

Gabrielle gasped, and grabbed Eve for support. She was going to faint. "What?!"

"In Malibu," said Eve. "We're going to stay for a while. In the rental."

"You're kidding?"

Eve nudged Gabrielle. "Look."

Zachary stood in the circle of children and gave a little speech about how he wanted to be a teenager when he grew up. Everyone laughed. Gabrielle saw, but her mind was elsewhere. Joey was taking video like a madman.

"Mom, Mommy!"

They all turned to see which child was calling. It was March.

"Oh, God," said Eve.

"Mom!" March cried. She had fallen, and skinned her knee. Landon ran to her, and scooped her up.

"Daddy's here," he said. She stopped crying.

Eve and Gabrielle watched, quietly. Fuller came over and put his arm around Eve and Gabrielle. None of them took their eyes off March and Landon. March stopped crying and, suddenly, wiggled out of her father's arms and ran over to Eve.

"Hey, Eve," said March.

"What is it, honey?" Eve bent down to March's height. She admired March's shoes. Pom D'Api. Nancy would've been so pleased to see her purchases worn so well.

"Will you guys all take me shopping after graduation?"

Eve and Gabrielle held back tears. It was so—so Nancy to ask that. "But not him," said March, pointing at Fuller. "Just the girls. The moms."

"Good idea," said Fuller, and he backed away and went over to Landon to explain the change in plans. Joey joined the fathers.

"My mother always said when I graduated she'd take me shopping and buy me new shoes and a dress. I'd like a watch, though."

"Well," said Gabrielle, looking at her own watch. "I'd say it's after graduation." She looked at Eve for confirmation.

"Take the car," Landon yelled over to the women. "Just tell the driver where you want to go."

"Thanks," said Eve, and she blew Landon a kiss.

The fathers rounded up their babies, and the diaper bags, and the nannies. Eve watched Fuller, who caught her looking. She loved the way he looked, the way he moved, the things he did.

She loved that he was hers. She tried to hold that feeling—the feeling of being lucky to have so much, and in one person.

"Okay, I have my purse," said Gabrielle.

"My mom would've loved to have come with," said March. "She loved to get new shit." And with that, March turned and ran, happily, to the car. "Can we stop for mochaccinos on the way?" she yelled back to Eve and Gabrielle.

"Sure," Eve yelled back. "But no caffeine for kids."

Eve felt something and looked down. It was Gabrielle's hand. Eve smiled at her best friend.

"I want to call my mom," said Eve. "I just do."

"Call from the car," said Gabrielle.

Eve hesitated. "In front of March? Do you think she would mind?"

"Not at all," said Gabrielle. "I don't think she'll notice. And if she does . . . it's not a bad thing."

Gabrielle and Eve walked, hand in hand, toward the car, where March was waiting. Their own children saw them, and started running toward the car. They were all screaming gleefully.

"Come on!" the kids all called.

"Seat belts and car seats!" Gabrielle told them, as she buckled everyone in.

"One last Frappuccino," said Eve. "Before we all go off to different elementary schools and never see each other again."

"We'll see each other," said Gabrielle.

"No, we won't," Eve said, smiling. "You know we won't. This is it. We're off in different directions. We'll bump into each other at the Barney's airport sale. And at premieres, but we'll be seated at different tables, and it'll never be like this again. I'll see you on *Entertainment Tonight* when Joey's band plays Madison Square Garden, and I'll send you dorky Christmas cards with family photos. But this is the end of this. It just is. Nothing we can do to stop it, but get out of the way, and let it happen. Let it end, gracefully."

"I love you," said Gabrielle, hugging Eve.

"I know," said Eve. "Me too, you."

"Let's go," said Gabrielle to the driver.

"Let's go," said Eve.

The children echoed the mothers until their chant became a song. "Let's go, let's go, let's go!"

Eve and Gabrielle watched the Westside as the chauffeur drove them all to the stores. It was already a good day.